gabriel Veiga

YESTERDAY IS NOT YET GONE

GABRIEL VEIGA

ISBN: 978-1-7771919-0-0

Imprint: Independently published

Cover design by: Ebook Launch www.ebooklaunch.com
Library of Congress Control Number: 8742968631

Printed in the United States of America

For all the incredible women in my life who have helped me become the man I am today, including my mother Nathalie and my late beloved grandmother, Murielle.

YESTERDAY IS NOT YET GONE

PROLOGUE

The American Dream

Before the tragedy happened, young Bulgarian couple Marko and Lilyana Kovachev had one dream: to move to the United States of America. Marko was a well-known painter and shoemaker, living in the small town of Kotel. As for Lilyana, she was a stay-at-home mother. Both were working as hard as they could to provide a decent living for their family, but it wasn't enough. Marko had been left with little money and crushing debt after his parents' deaths, and Lilyana was doing everything she could with what they had to provide enough bread, and sometimes some meat and vegetables, for the dinner table.

Like many, they had had enough of a hard living and wanted a better life for themselves and their children. Well, one child. They had only one, and his name was Viktor Kovachev. Viktor was a young boy with many talents, and like his father before him, he had a passion for the arts. He loved to perform magic tricks for his family and friends, not unlike the grand Houdini whom he admired in the far-off United States. He was learning to juggle, and his father was showing him how to paint. Viktor was also a gifted runner and loved to take part in races with his friends and neighbors.

When Viktor was fifteen—about to turn sixteen—his parents finally decided that they wanted to try their luck by immigrating to the United States. But it wasn't as easy as one hoped. This was the 1980s, it was the communist era, and immigration was restricted. But Marko needed to go.

He had somehow managed to make travel plans and be transported to the United States for a visit as a tourist a year before. His first stop had been the Big Apple. He had heard there were lots of immigrants there, but quickly had found it too busy and loud, dirty and, frankly, too expensive for a decent life—the kind of life he was envisaging. So he continued to drive around New York State until he came upon Rockland and immediately fell in love with it. It was a small town by the river, and it was so lovely and welcoming. It reminded him a little of his village in Bulgaria.

He managed to persuade the owner of some land to sell for a very cheap price, on the condition that Marko come and work for him at a metal factory. Marko accepted and shook hands on it. He was so happy. It would be a great place to live.

When he came back to Bulgaria, he immediately tried to get the proper visas and papers, but it took forever. Marko kept hassling the U.S. Embassy for nearly two years. Finally, some guy at the embassy offered to expedite their visa if Marko could compensate him. Marko felt shame, but he was desperate. He had already spent too much time investing in this dream, so he found a way. He took all the money he had left and requested two or three advances in wages from the American factory owner. After some more pain and struggling, he finally got the proper visas and papers.

Marko ran home to his family and quickly stuffed everything they would need into bags. He told them not to bring much. They were finally on their way.

They arrived in Rockland, New York in 1986. School would start in September for Viktor, a day or two after their move. It had been a chaotic trip, but they made it.

They settled themselves in the farmhouse, which, to their surprise, had a fireplace. Only rich people in Bulgaria had fireplaces. Wow, this was another life!

Viktor started school and seemed to be enjoying himself. He had looked forward to American life. He had spent his time watching TV as much as he could. It was mostly American television, and because of that he spoke the best English in his family. He made some friends right away, and two weeks later asked Marko and Lilyana if he could join the football team. Marko was ecstatic and agreed right away. He thought football was awesome. He didn't know it wasn't the same football as in

Europe—this version wasn't played so much with the feet! That took some getting used to. Viktor appeared to be doing well. His friends seemed nice and thoughtful. Viktor even talked about girls and one in particular that he had his eye on. He smiled, his eyes bright with happiness, whenever he mentioned her. "America is wonderful!" he kept shouting all over the house.

Marko and Lilyana were enjoying their new lives as well. Lilyana was staying at home most of the time, taking care of the house and tending to a small garden. Marko had made some friends at the factory and the money was good enough—better than anything he had seen in Bulgaria. It was sufficient to ensure the health and safety of his family. They were very content with their lives now.

Then, one day, something happened. At the start of June, less than a month before their son Viktor was set to finish his first year of American high school, the Kovachevs' lives took a dramatic turn: Viktor did not come home from school.

They waited for him for hours and hours on end, but there was nothing—no phone call, no sign of him coming back, nothing. After wandering around the house and swearing for hours, Marko finally decided to call the police, and the force started a full search for the boy. The cops told them not to worry until 48 to 72 hours had passed. "These situations usually resolve themselves," they said.

But Viktor did not come back. Out of thin air, he had disappeared. They kept searching and searching for the teenager, but in vain. They asked friends the boy had made, and teachers, but none of them had answers. Viktor had left school as he had normally done and had been said to be on his way to his parents' house, but not a soul appeared to have followed him, or seen him, or even heard from him after that. No one had any clues.

The search continued... for a while. Days, and weeks. Then it stretched to months without an answer or any comprehension of what had happened to the Kovachevs' boy.

A year went by. Then two.

And slowly, everyone in town began to forget about him. "He must be dead," they said. "Maybe he had been taken," they said. Who knew what had really gone on and where Viktor was now....

Thirty years had passed since then, and there was still no trace.

The Kovachev family and their dreams had been destroyed. Their hearts remained forever broken....

PART ONE

CHAPTER ONE:

THE RETIRING DETECTIVE

"Detective, I think your bagel is burning," said the officer.

He was right. It was burnt, and so was she. At least, Judy Hunter thought so. She had spent the last thirty years building a successful career as a police detective, and now her retirement plans were about to come to fruition. One more day! One more day in this chaotic, most often vile and suffering-filled environment. She was about to become a normal person, with normal hobbies, and normal pastimes. She would be able to have normal conversations with people. Conversations that did not involve gory details about a little girl found in a ditch with her throat slit by a creepy pedophile, or discussions about a man who had been killed with seven different knives, which have yet to be found.

The words "to be determined," "under investigation," and "classified" would no longer be part of her vocabulary. The victims would no longer be depending on her; the department would not be pressuring her to abandon a case because they thought it was hopeless. She was free. No more tears, no more chasing, no more running, no more arguing, no more headaches—it all felt amazing, surprisingly. It would just be Judy in her new home in North Carolina with an open-air garden and a pool where she would spend most days reading a James Patterson or Agatha Christie novel. She would now be looking at the criminal world from the outside, from the fictional and often over-the-top perspective. Would people find her boring now? She would not have anything interesting to say, except that she had enjoyed a manicure or a massage that day, or she would complain about her gray hair. It would be a new life. *I will be happy*, she thought. *Judy, you will be happy.*

Judy picked her burning bagel out of the toaster and united it with a plate. She poured herself a coffee and sat down in the break room of her most fabulous precinct. She looked around the room, staring at the walls for a minute. The paint was fading, the walls were still of a green, almost turquoise color. You could see a couple of holes that had gotten bigger and bigger over time, and some marker stains here and there. Judy could tell stories about all of them. The room used to be yellow, and they had tried a hideous red before that. It did not last long. A psycho, by the name of Alex Grimley, had once fired a gun all around the room and took several of the cops as hostages here. Another time, Judy had to arrest one of her friends, Samson, as he was pouring coffee because he turned out to be a vicious abuser of the opposite sex. So many hours she had spent in this room, more than anyone should be asked to spend in any one place that's not home.

Judy sipped her coffee, turning her spoon around inside her cup as people came in and effortlessly greeted her. She didn't even know if anyone knew she was leaving today, or if they even cared. *That does not matter*, she thought. Just like a turtle, she would withdraw into her shell and not bother any more souls with her ancient mind and ideas.

Today felt anticlimactic to Judy, and a bit unreal. Here she was, in the same place she'd been coming to for so many years, and everybody was going about their business as usual. This was the last day she'd ever be here and she had to put in a typical day's work, as if nothing unusual was happening!

Her partner was late as always, but when he came in, he brought with him a bag of Dunkin' Donuts. How clichéd! Still, it was sweet. Fred Gibbins wore a hat on his brown hair and had a beard that was half gray. He was somewhat overweight but not excessively so. He was a great man. He had stuck with Judy for the greater part of her career. She had welcomed him on his first day with open arms and had trained him over the years, watching him grow to become a brilliant detective. She saw him get married, have kids, and care for them. They had gone through so many things together. She would take a bullet for him, as he would for her, any time, any place.

Fred gave Judy a kiss on the cheek. His breath smelled of garlic. She still hadn't found that dreadful toothpaste anywhere in the grocery store. If it wasn't toothpaste, who knew what he did in the morning. Perhaps before he left for work, he ate a whole garlic clove or two. It is good for the body, they say. Fred looked at Judy for a second and smiled. It was genuine and sweet. Then he looked down at her bagel and noticed the file folder under her plate. He lifted the plate and took away the file, tucking it under his arm.

The case was bothering her. For months now they had been hunting a killer who called himself the Bride Killer. Just like his name implied, he took pleasure in taking the lives of newly married women. The killer usually did it right after the marriage ceremony. How cruel and demented was that? He would steal them away from the party and kill them, usually with a knife to the heart, and then leave them on a street close to the wedding area for the husband and family to eventually find. Truly horrible, and nobody had any clues right now.

"Don't worry," Fred said. "Nobody will let him get away."

That was a bit comforting, Judy thought. There were more than a hundred cases in this precinct alone that had not been solved over the past twenty years. Hopefully, this one would not join that list.

"How are you feelin'?" he went on to ask. "Nervous?"

"What do I have to be nervous about?" Judy asked. "I feel relieved, actually."

He gave her a smile. A smile that was both understanding of her joke and sad at the same time.

"You're not gonna miss it?"

"Sure, I will." She grabbed his shoulder. "It's okay, I'm sure you're going to be busy. Apparently that new guy is a handful."

"Looking forward to it," he replied sarcastically.

Tomorrow, Fred would have a new partner, coming straight from Louisiana. The detective's reputation preceded him, but not in a good way. He had been kicked out of the Baton Rouge police force after allegedly reassuring a white woman that cops only kill black people. It was all over the papers the next day. *Racist douchebag*. Now he was coming here to replace Judy. What was Captain Murphy thinking? Clearly, he wasn't thinking at all. Maybe he agreed with the guy, maybe not. This had made a splash in the New York papers too, obviously. And it was already tarnishing the reputation of the NYPD. But even if this made her sick to her stomach, Judy didn't need to care.

"I'll be back," she said cheerfully. Hopefully she wouldn't have to visit often, but he needed to know that he could call her anytime with a case.

"You'll see—those books will keep you rolling for a week, and then you'll be searching for something to do. I'll keep my phone close."

"I'm sure the donuts will be waiting," Judy replied.

He bowed his head. It was hard for both of them after all these years. They had been to hell and back together.

Suddenly, the white doors opened. Captain Howard Murphy came in—tall, slightly bald, and composed. *Slightly* bald because he still had black hair at the back of his head, in the shape of the letter U. His wide brown eyes looked more content than usual. Maybe he was filled with joy at the thought that the next day he would once again find his department filled with only men. It certainly wouldn't be surprising if he was regarding that prospect with pleasure. But for the moment, Murphy needed to restrain himself. He was about to tell the valiant detectives that they were needed. Nobody should display a cheerful expression when a corpse has been found.

"Didn't you get the call?" he shouted.

There was indeed a crime scene for them to go to. A poor soul had died on 57th and Park. Hard to miss. It was apparently all over the news. Nobody had let Judy and Fred know they were needed. No call had been received. As soon as they heard the name of the victim, Fred went pale, jumped out of his chair, and looked over at Murphy, stunned. A bunch of officers in the room did too. Judy didn't recognize the name, but apparently she was the only one to whom it meant nothing.

"Another conflicted Hollywood prick," Murphy murmured.

Fred stared at Judy for a long second. His eyes looked dead.

"A fan?" Judy asked.

His subtle nod seemed to confirm that he was.

CHAPTER TWO:

THE NOTE

Her retirement could not come soon enough! Judy knew she would have a long day ahead of her, with a lot of press to handle and a lot of excessive "fandom."

Maybe I could just take out my good old Taser and shock them if they get out of hand, Judy thought. A fun and noteworthy end to a career.

Ethan Gregory was the name. The one who was murdered. He was apparently a very well-known artist of our modern age. Judy was never into celebrity-mania. She would go to the movies once or twice a year and she could never remember the movies she saw, good or bad. She knew that her ex-girlfriend, Alina, had taken her to the new Star Wars film last year, that she remembered. She was not totally oblivious to what was going on. She just didn't care that much.

That probably annoyed Alina out of her mind and she couldn't stand me anymore.

The breakup was all her fault, Judy thought. She just felt as though they were telling the same stories over and over again, and she was getting bored with them. She tended to fall asleep in the theater, and it had probably been disrespectful to Alina. She would give her that.

Movies were also a bit too passive for Judy. The retiring detective was more into sports and outdoorsy activities than anything else. She didn't watch much TV and didn't like to stay inside. On her days off in retirement, she would surely go for bike rides or go for runs with her dog, Rush.

She had grown up in North Carolina with gorgeous fields of green (the place she intended to retire to, having inherited the family home after her father's passing) where her dad had made her fall in love with the great outdoors. During her childhood, the two of them would spend most weekends going on bike trips for hours and hours on end. He had taught her a lifestyle that didn't allow for any laziness. "If you got a body and you can run or walk, then go out and stay healthy. You'll get plenty of days on the couch when you're eighty." Judy had faithfully applied that philosophy. Alina had been annoyed by that, too.

Well, she's not in the décor anymore, let's forget about her.

So when it came to remembering actors' names and what they'd appeared in or what their next big movie would be, Judy Hunter was completely out of the loop.

And now here they were, about to enter this Hollywood craziness. The two detectives arrived at the Four Seasons Hotel, dropped off by an NYPD police car, and peered out at the white brick building that looked almost church-like. As she got out of the car, Judy became aware of screams all around her. There were two lines of people on each side of the building's entrance, being pushed back by police officers and reporters like animals in a zoo, yelling questions at them. Judy knew that as soon as she pulled out her badge, they would come after her. Fred did it before her, showing it to the officers at the door. Judy immediately felt the screams entering the depths of her ears. She pulled out her badge as well. The officer looked at it for a few seconds, a few seconds too long, then he nodded and Judy was finally able to hustle her way through the revolving doors.

It suddenly went quiet. They were alone in the lobby, but for a few police officers here and there. There was probably another circus upstairs for the main event.

The hotel manager greeted them with a frustrated face. He was overweight and short, his large pants falling off his hips. He had thick brown eyebrows and a big forehead, and his hair was short and fixed in place with copious amounts of gel.

He kept frowning as he approached them. He clearly did not like to see his hotel invaded by police like this. No business wanted to have to deal with the after-effects of a murder that had happened behind its doors, especially a hotel as luxurious and highly rated as the Four Seasons.

He showed them to the elevators. The manager pressed a key against a pad to unlock the fifty-first floor.

"Presidential Suite," he stated.

Wow, that Ethan Gregory was really a big shot. Hollywood royalty. Judy wondered what he did with all that space. Was it necessary to live in such a large room to play a character on Broadway?

Really? You are not that important, brother!

The hotel manager had probably offered it to him. A huge movie star in his building only meant more attention for his hotel, and ultimately more guests. Though Judy was pretty sure he wasn't enjoying the kind of attention he had to deal with today.

Judy asked, "How did the killer or killers even get up there without a key? Can just anyone be on that floor?"

"Absolutely not," the manager replied.

"Did you see anyone go up there?"

"No. My employees say that he was alone last night when he arrived."

"But a killer did get up there," Judy replied.

The manager stayed quiet. He had no answer for her.

"Might have taken a key from the maid?" Judy then turned to Fred.

Her partner nodded. Fred looked ghostly pale, sweat dripping from his forehead. He played with his tie, loosening it. She had never seen him like this for any other murder in all the years they'd worked together. He must have been a huge fan. Why hadn't he mentioned Gregory before?

"I don't think any of my employees are that careless!" the manager quickly said, insulted.

"Is there any other way they could have gotten up there?" Judy continued.

"We don't have cameras in the shafts and ventilations, if that's what you're asking," the manager replied innocently.

"I was thinking of an emergency stairwell. Surely you have those. Complying with the law," Judy retorted.

The manager gave her a look. He hated her and wanted her gone from his hotel.

"Sure," he said. "But we don't have cameras in there."

"Of course you don't," Judy replied, annoyed. "So, whoever did this could have moved in and out without you noticing... Still, prepare those tapes while we check out the crime scene, please."

The elevator came to the fifty-first floor and the detective exited. The scent from the perfumed elevator quickly changed to a heavy, disgusting smell—a smell very similar to rotten meat or eggs. The smell of violent death.

As the detective started walking towards the crime scene, the hotel manager mumbled, "You think you'll be here long?"

Fred looked at him curiously, and so did Judy. They turned back.

"This is a mess," the manager said. "Blood everywhere. I hope they clean it up... It's everywhere! Ugh..." Then he coughed. His voice took on some assurance. He started speaking louder. "A bunch of people left... They're scared. The guests... Listen, I've got a business to run. I knew that this jackass was gonna bring trouble. I knew it."

"How did you know?" Judy asked, now going into detective mode.

"He was an irritating little bitch. That's what he was."

"Guess our case is solved, then," Judy said.

"Really?" the hotel manager exclaimed. He brightened right up.

"Yeah. I guess you killed him," Judy said coldly.

Both Fred and the hotel manager turned to her at the same time.

"What?" The manager started scratching his head nervously. "I don't understand."

"You have motive," Judy continued. "'An irritating little bitch.

"Oh, no, no. That's not what I meant. Really. I swear."

Judy grinned at him. She liked messing with people. He didn't look like a murderer. Hell, he hardly looked like someone who'd ever had a speeding ticket.

"Are you sure? I mean, we could spend time checking out the crime scene and stuff. But you don't seem to want to give us any."

The hotel manager shook his head. "No, no. Take all the time in the world. You have all the time you need. I—Yes. Please. No rush."

Judy nodded at him with mock gratefulness.

"We'll find out and let you know," Judy muttered.

The manager went back to the elevator, nodded nervously, the doors closing quickly behind him.

They were already in the room—the suite must take up the entire floor—and it was enormous. It felt like a large condominium. An officer standing not far from the elevator pointed them to the left, where they could see a great number of their friends waiting for them, all gloved up.

Fred saluted the forensic, a new guy whom Judy had never seen before. His transparent glasses gave him a nerdy look, even without the lab coat. He was Chinese and had deep-black hair. He was very smiley and friendly. He turned to Judy and looked at her for a second, analyzing her. Then, his mouth opened wide, showcasing his straight white teeth. He looked stunned.

"I'm Vincent Price. Very nice to meet you, Mrs. Hunter," he exclaimed.

Judy looked at him quizzically.

"I know, like the movie star," Price said. "Quite funny. I'm forensic, he was in horror movies, dead bodies... you know."

Judy didn't care about films, but she politely faked enthusiasm.

"Nice to meet you too, Vincent Price," Judy replied. "Where's Brandy?" she then asked Fred.

"Brandy? Like the liquor?" questioned Price, looking towards Fred. "Oh, right! The gal who's usually here. She's dead, I'm afraid. Yellow fever. Really sad."

"What?!" Judy turned back to Price.

"She's fine. She had her baby last night," reassured Fred.

"Did she now? Wonderful." Then she quickly added: "Are all the women in this department leaving? I feel like I should stay now."

"Don't worry, I won't stay long, just the time she's gone," replied Price. "I wanna work for the FBI anyway," he added, without shame.

"Wow, big dreams!"

"Yes." Price advanced towards her and grabbed her shoulder. "Hey, it's you, it's really you!" he said, half yelling. "Fred told me he was working with you, but I couldn't believe it. You're really here. Oh, my lord. I read all your cases, watched all your interviews. You really are the modern Sherlock Holmes, aren't you?"

He kept going as Judy answered, embarrassed, "Well, I don't know about that..."

Judy knew she was no Sherlock Holmes. She was only going by facts and evidence, and a little of bit experience, not mad genius or out-of-this-world intuition. She was good at reading people and she had fine powers of observation, like any decent detective out there, but she could not tell if a person had eaten eggs with avocado toast and marmalade that morning or if they had changed the laces of their shoes four times—no, scratch that—five times, just by looking at them for a second and a half. Judy would need more time than that.

"He said it was your last day, too," Price went on. "How can you leave? You're so brilliant. New York City will fail without you. Hell, I will—"

"All right, Price, where's the... that body, huh?" Fred cut off, clearly irritated.

"Right, sorry, sorry. I just can't believe it," he mumbled. "It's right over there, by the window. You guys come with me."

"What the hell happened? The hotel manager told us it was messy."

"Well, yes. Yes. But I've seen worse." A look of sadness came over his face, so he looked a little like Fred now. "This guy was awesome!"

They moved into the living room. It was indeed messy. The white carpet was stained red with blood in a dense, thick line. There was more of it than usual. Then Judy began to understand why that was. A little farther away, she could see two legs lying on the floor. A body hidden behind a couch. She went to it. Slowly.

As she approached, she began to see shapes. Athletic shapes. The man lying on the floor was fit. This guy was supposed to be a movie star. He was in incredible shape, but he was also fifty years old. It was impressive.

Judy reached the couch and peered over it. The movie star had no head. It had been ripped away from his body. Ethan Gregory's head had been severed.

"Jesus!" Fred shouted.

It was the first time he had talked in a while and his tone was beyond agitated.

"Yeah. I know," said Price.

"Any idea what did it? An ax?"

"No. An ax is way too unclean. I'm thinking more of a... Bruce Lee–type thing. Someone with art and passion!" exclaimed Price.

"A sword, you mean?" asked Fred.

"Katana." Price looked delighted. He seemed to be enjoying this. "A Samurai sword like they used in old times for taking care of their prisoners. You didn't expect him to die from a little gun, did you? No, no. That would have been way too dull for Gregory. Wouldn't have made great news."

"John Lennon was killed with a gun," Judy said. "It was pretty big news."

"Sure, but this is Gregory—he... Anyway."

Judy ignored Price, and slowly bent down, careful not to touch the floor.

"What time was the body found?" she asked.

"Around eleven this morning, by the cleaning staff," Price informed her.

"And what time do you think he died?"

"I am only guessing here, but by the skin tone I'd say a little before midnight."

"Did anyone hear anything?"

"It's the only room on this floor."

"Right. We'll look into that afterwards with the officers." Judy looked around. "Where's the head?"

Price pointed his gloved finger to the bookshelf in front of them. Judy carefully walked over, hopscotching over the blood. Fred followed her. They looked around the library until Fred stopped. He let out a startling sound. Judy looked at him with her soft green eyes. He was holding a black basket. A trash can. Fred looked petrified.

Judy went to him and looked inside. There it was. Gregory's eyes were open. He was blond, with beautiful long hair. He looked as scared as Fred was in this instant. Judy turned her head swiftly away. The smell was truly horrendous. It was as if thousands of people had vomited in the same basket. She pinched her nose and looked at Fred.

"What the fuck?" Judy cried.

"You wanna look inside it?" Price said.

"Excuse me?"

"Inside. There is something you gotta see."

Nobody knew what Price meant. Inside the head? They had to open him up?

What the... ?

"The mouth," he clarified.

Judy still wasn't getting it. Nonetheless, she picked up the gloves that Price handed her and put them on. Her hands then went to the head inside the basket. She didn't want to do this. Who would? Judy touched Gregory's tight lips, trying to open them up. She could see something in there, stuck between his perfect teeth. It was white and small. A piece of paper. Her fingers carefully reached for it, trying to free it without ripping it apart. Slowly but surely, she succeeded. She left the head inside the basket, on the floor, and focused her eyes on the piece of paper. She unfolded it.

The note was all in bold capital letters:

A RECKONING IS COMING

No signature, nothing.

Judy looked at Fred. He stayed frozen in place, still looking at the head, clearly disturbed. Judy stared at the note again. She felt a big question mark drawing itself on her forehead.

CHAPTER THREE:

THE GIRL WITH THE RED HAIR

Charlotte Gibbins had just been punched straight in the jaw. Brian Haze offered her a hand so she could get back up. She sighed at him, almost spitting in his hand. She didn't need help. She was fine. That was a soft and weak punch. She got her beaming red hair out of her softly freckled face and quickly jumped up. Brian looked at her, admiringly.

"Are you gonna just let me win now? Just because you feel bad for me?" Charlotte asked.

Brian shook his head.

"Please don't cry," Charlotte added.

"Cry?" Brian responded, confused.

"I know that punch hurt you more than it hurt me. You're still shaking." She smirked.

Brian shook his head. He was in his late twenties and extremely tall, with brown eyes and dark hair. He looked like a fashion model, beautiful and stylish. He didn't look like the average American, there was something foreign about him, in his looks but also in his mannerisms and attitude. He had Old World manners and was romantic and delicate. He had passion, and he wasn't scared of being in a serious relationship. He was like no man Charlotte had ever met. This one treated women right, with respect. She secretly loved him as much as he loved her. Maybe more.

Amazingly, she was equally tall, maybe even a bit taller than Brian. Her height was intimidating to most men, but not to Brian. He had told her that tall women were his type.

Charlotte put her fists up to fight again.

"We should probably end it here. You're gonna be too tired for tonight," Brian said.

"It's fine. I don't think I'll be going anyways," Charlotte replied.

"He wants you there."

"What? Do I have to? It's not like it's his party. He's not the one retiring, she is."

"There'll be a bunch of cops there. Maybe you can learn a thing or two… and get some support, before you talk to him," suggested Brian.

"Hell no. It's hard enough to talk to him as it is. He thinks I'm studying at the library all day today. I can't imagine him finding out where I am right now. It would be even worse if I told him that I rejected my acceptance to med school."

"You'll have to tell him eventually."

"Yeah, but not today, home boy."

Not only was she going to have to tell her father that she had decided not to go to medical school, but also that she wanted to become a cop just like him. Charlotte knew for a fact that he would never accept it, let alone allow it. Every time she had asked him to give her some fighting lessons—so she could defend herself in school—she was shut down dramatically. "Girls don't need to fight," he had said. "Just go to the principal and tell him those kids are annoying you. He'll take care of it." Charlotte didn't want that, she didn't want to be a snitch. She would have been bullied even more. "It's the right thing to do," he had explained.

But Charlotte didn't want to hear that. Her father was fighting all the time, defending the world from bullies and criminals. Why couldn't she do the same? "I have a badge, it's my job. Plus, I'm a man," he probably would have responded.

Says the man who has a woman as a partner, she invariably thought.

So, no, Charlotte did not have the support of her father. He would never allow her to join the police force. Then she met Brian, who accepted her for who she was. He also knew kickboxing. He was a trainer and offered to give her lessons. That's how they'd connected at first, before falling in love. She had been training with him for the past six months and loving it. She was getting good. Really good. She was almost ready for the police academy. Hell, the people at the police academy barely knew how to fight, as her dad was always saying. She was more than ready.

Charlotte didn't even have to tell her father she would be enrolling. She was twenty-two, more than an adult at this point. She could make her own decisions. Charlotte feared his reaction, though, and what he would do to her.

The redhead raised her fists again, attempting to jab-punch Brian. He stopped her fist and made a sudden and quick move, putting her arm on his shoulder and throwing her off to the ground.

Brian looked at her to see if she was hurt. Charlotte took that opportunity to kick his leg and he fell onto the ground, ending up beside her. He mumbled a few curses.

"Or you could just do that to your dad!" Brian exclaimed.

They both laughed. She took him by the face and kissed him. Then, when she saw he was enjoying it, she punched him in the stomach.

"Distraction is weakness!" she exclaimed.

Brian squealed, as if he was hurt. "Just grab a beer. Stay for like a half-hour and then say you have to go, that you have to wake up early in the morning or something. He will be pleased," he added.

She hesitated, then sighed. "I'll go home and hit the shower, then I'll see."

Brian nodded, looking satisfied. He tugged her hair away from her gorgeous face, looked into her deep-blue eyes and kissed her again—

this time holding her arms in place so she couldn't punch him. She giggled.

CHAPTER FOUR:

FISH AND CHIP

"I can't leave you now!" exclaimed Judy, looking at Fred. "Not after this."

What they had found at the Four Seasons that morning was not something Judy saw herself forgetting anytime soon. A man's head had been chopped off and the killer had put it in a garbage can. Plus, it was not an ordinary victim—it was a Hollywood and now Broadway star. The public would go crazy when they learned that information. It was enough that a celebrity was presumed dead, but what riot would this cause when they learned that he had been murdered by some psychopath in the most horrible way imaginable? Captain Murphy was to go on air any minute now to state what had happened to the beloved Ethan Gregory.

They left the crime scene and drove to the Shubert Theatre, on 44th and 8th, where Gregory was supposed to perform for the first time that night. They talked to Jackson, his manager, and a bunch of other actors, including Sofia Marlow, another very famous actress, or so Judy was informed. Beautiful and Italian. She was the lead character in the play. All of them said the same thing: Gregory had left the place near nine, after rehearsals, and they saw him get into his car and his driver was headed straight for the Four Seasons. They were all in shock at Gregory's death. "He was a pretty sweet gent," one said. Another exclaimed, "Oh my God. Who would wanna kill him? Jesus. That doesn't make any sense." And an actress named Penny Strumble claimed, "There was something wrong with him for the last few days..."

Judy and Fred asked her what she meant by that and she replied: "Y'know, he was just starting to be late to rehearsals, he forgot to come out of his dressing room in the middle of the play, we were all wondering where he was, where he had gone. And then Jackson and I found him with a bottle of gin in his hand, sitting in his dressing room. I could have sworn I saw tears in his eyes."

Gregory's driver said that he had left him at the hotel. They had agreed on a pick-up at one o'clock the next day, and he had seen Gregory walk into the hotel and never look back. The driver was in shock as well. He didn't know who could have done it. "Mr. Gregory was always nice to me, gave me super-huge tips and always thanked me for the rides. Not what you would expect coming from someone like him."

As for all their alibis, they would still need to check those out. Again, they all said the same thing: they went back to their hotel rooms to sleep. Opening night was supposed to be tonight, and they needed a good night's sleep before then. As for the driver, he went back to his home in New Jersey to his wife and two daughters.

Judy kept thinking about it all, asking herself what the dreadful note found in Gregory's mouth could mean. What did the killer mean by "reckoning"? Would there be something happening next? "Reckoning" as in punishment? Who was the killer going to punish? And why? Also, she thought about Penny's thoughts on Gregory. It was a little weird. Had Gregory been sensing something? He might have known who his killer was and that he was after him. That could be the reason he was disturbed and started missing parts of rehearsals. They would have to check Gregory's phone, the calls he had made and received. They would also have to find out what his folks in Los Angeles knew, and if they could tell them anything that might help the case.

Or no, *they* wouldn't have to find out—*Fred* would have to find out. Judy was to let all this go. She was to retire at the end of this day and move on with her life. She couldn't assist Fred with solving this case, it was out of her hands. Nor did she want to. She truly wanted peace and calm in her life. Still, she had a bad feeling about it all. The note, the way Gregory was killed—it was all a little too disturbing to just turn around and forget about.

The great detective took a breath. Then Fred smirked a little at her and sputtered a few words: "We'll be fine."

Judy looked at him, clearly not accepting that response. "It all seems fishy. I don't like it. Maybe I can convince the Captain to—"

"We'll be fine!" he said again, more firmly this time.

Judy kept staring at him and then put her straw between her teeth and sipped some of her water. They were sitting in a fish and chip shop a few minutes away from the precinct. Ronnie's, it was called. It was their spot. They would go there at the end of their shifts every day, usually at five p.m. It was now 3:45 p.m., but nobody would care if Judy got off early today. She knew they wanted her gone anyway. The sooner, the better. Most of the work was done, and they had seen enough for one day.

Judy had recently transitioned to veganism and Fred hated it. He felt she had ruined their tradition, as she could only eat one thing on the menu now, one boring thing: the beet salad. Though, God, was it good! She didn't know if she was making herself like it or if she really did. It did taste good. Of course it did. She had always had an affinity for beets, hadn't she?

"You shouldn't go to Punta Cana for your vacation, you should go to LA instead," Fred had said once. "There are plenty of your people out there." *Your people*, meaning the vegans, the great people that they were. It was obviously meant sarcastically. Judy laughed it off; she knew he wasn't ridiculing her. He meant well, just wanted to tease her a bit. After all, it was a difficult subject for someone like him to address.

She kept eating away at her salad. Fred didn't look hungry. He stared at his plate for a long second, then brought his fork towards it almost as though he was forcing himself.

"Are you all right?" Judy finally asked.

He nodded. "Yeah, just feeling a little under the weather, that's all."

"It's my leaving, isn't it? Didn't know you could cry." She mocked.

"Sure," he chuckled.

Judy pursued. "It's not about Gregory, is it?"

He coughed, picked up his water glass, and sipped some of it nervously.

"I mean, you were pretty shaken up at the crime scene, just like you are now. Were you that big of an admirer?"

"Yeah, he was a talented man. A great, great actor," Fred said.

"Didn't know you as a movie fan," Judy replied.

Fred stayed laser focused on his drink for a while and then went back to her, arching his eyebrows.

"Well, there are still lots of things you don't know about me, Hunter."

Judy laughed slightly, but she was surprised. Fred was a pretty open man and not once had he mentioned anything about his Hollywood admiration.

"Do you want another beer?" he quickly went on. "We need to celebrate."

They did have a couple more drinks, and then that was it. Fred walked his partner down the street, heading to her apartment, for what could be the last time. She was about to leave him. He would become partnerless and would have to solve all the next cases by himself. Or at least for a little while, until that loathsome Louisiana detective, Edward White, arrived.

Fred walked as slowly as he could, making sure to enjoy the last moments he had with Judy as a cop. Even though she wanted to match

Fred's pace, Judy reminded him that she had to get home because Rush was waiting for her. She didn't want him to pee everywhere.

Rush was a small dog, a four-year-old male Cavalier King Charles Spaniel—the cutest little thing anyone had ever seen. He had been waiting for her since early morning.

Fred painfully agreed to walk at a somewhat faster pace.

They reached a lovely glass building at 59th and Park, Judy's apartment complex. It was not far away from the Four Seasons Hotel, and in fact Judy could have walked home if they hadn't gone to the Broadway theater afterwards. The building was silver-white and sparklingly clean. The warm spring sunlight shone through the windows. It was not very tall by New York standards, but tall enough that its size felt welcoming. On top was a roof garden where one could see numerous plants and flowers hanging around, which gave the building a very green, natural look. The building was also close to Central Park, which was perfect for her.

It was a little far from the precinct for walking, but it was worth it. Judy had tried living in Hell's Kitchen like Fred, but she couldn't handle it. It was too tough for her, which was ironic considering her job, but that was her job and her personal life was something else. She wanted calm and nature. She could go out on her bike or go for a run or to Central Park anytime she wanted.

Fred opened the front door for Judy.

"You're gonna have to let me go eventually," she said, smiling, as she walked through.

"I know," he replied, saddened. "I'm just gonna say bye to Rush."

"I'm not dying, Fred. You can come visit us whenever you want."

Fred nodded and followed her into the elevator and up to the seventh floor. The elevator door slid open and they stepped out into a hallway. Judy saw something moving near her door at the far end. A small red-and-white spot in the middle of the floor—more white than red, actually. The spot had big, adorable eyes filled with love. Her dog, Rush, was hanging out in the hallway with a tall, almost bald man. It was Captain Murphy! He was holding a leash with Rush at the end of it. Judy looked surprised. What was he doing here? Better question, what was he doing here hanging out with her dog in the hallway?

"Captain? What—" she began asking, before Murphy quivered as he turned around and saw her. He looked shocked.

"Hunter. Hmm... Fuck... Hmm," he nervously replied.

Judy looked to Fred and he looked back at her, shaking his head. She kept walking towards her apartment door, looking at Murphy and Rush. Rush saw her and straight away began dancing around. The dog gave a little bark, pulling on the leash. Judy went to him, taking the leash from Murphy's hands.

"They said to take him out. He... He rang the bell and, huh, I was beside him..." Murphy said.

"They?" Judy asked, confusingly.

Murphy gave Fred a look. She could hear music now, coming from inside her apartment. Judy put her hand on the doorknob and carefully opened it.

In front of her were two or three dozen people, in her kitchen and living room, drinking champagne. They were all talking to each other, not noticing her right away. A huge sign had been put up on the wall: *Happy Retirement.* It was almost too positive, too joyful in here. As though they had been awaiting this day for so long!

Then Vincent Price noticed her and yelled, "She made it! Guys, she made it!" They all turned around and went wild for Judy. The crowd all came together, Fred joining them and grabbing a glass of champagne. The great detective shook her head at him as he shouted, "Surprise!"

CHAPTER FIVE:

THE PARTY

Her whole precinct had thrown her an enormous party. There were way too many people for Judy's apartment to handle.

It was only now that she realized why the people of the 18th precinct had been acting weird all day. She had been thinking that nobody cared that she was leaving. But she had been terribly wrong! They were all there cheering and shaking her hand, thanking her for her thirty-one years of service. She could see everyone from the low end of the precinct to the other detectives, the lieutenant, the sergeant. And of course, though she couldn't see him, Captain Murphy was just outside with Rush.

Fred then came by and handed her a glass of delicious champagne and walked her through the room with an big smile on his face, happy at what he had successfully pulled off.

"You didn't think I'd let you go without a bang, did you?" he said to his retiring partner.

"I had hoped you would, but thank you," laughed Judy.

"Stop it now. They all love you."

"You know I could arrest all of you for breaking into my apartment!" shouted Judy.

A laugh echoed across the room as she said that. Women and men were shaking her hand, some people she had never even seen before. She didn't know if they had ever worked in the precinct or if they had just come for the chips and alcohol. One guy named George said he worked as an administrative assistant for them for six years and had admired Judy for the longest time. Some people also revealed themselves as SWAT team members, and understandably Judy couldn't have recognized them because they were mostly wearing masks when she saw them in action. Judy did, however, recognize most of the people. There was Janet, the secretary, Luke Tennessee, Pauly Jameson, Erica Clay and Sergio Sanporo—officers with whom she had worked on many cases. Then there was Alex Riddick, another detective who was mostly assigned to cold cases and cyber investigations. Judy saluted them all, truly grateful that they were here for her.

The only person missing from the precinct was Brandy Thomas, the precinct's medical examiner, who had given birth to a little girl the night before. Price was going to take over until the new mother returned from maternity leave. Judy and Brandy had hit it off from the medical examiner's first day and had become good friends. They shared a similar sense of humor and often ran half marathons together. They were also the only women, along with Erica Clay, in a very male-dominated precinct.

Brandy would have certainly made the night less boring. They would probably be dancing right now, annoying the neighbors with loud music. She would have loved to come to the party and drink with Judy, but there would be plenty of other occasions for them to go out and laugh together. Brandy was a big trivia-night girl and had invited Judy many times. Judy never had the chance to go because she was either busy working on a case or didn't feel she would be good at a pop culture quiz game. There was also the fact that Judy had a lot of puzzles to solve at work and didn't want to solve any more in her free time. But enough with the excuses! She needed to go now and play with Brandy before she moved back to North Carolina. It would be fun.

Judy had just received a picture on her phone from Brandy's husband, Ian. The new mother was in her hospital gown. Even though she looked a little tired, she had a radiant expression on her face and a bright smile. She was holding the most perfect baby in her arms. Ian sent another text saying they had named her Sara. Judy imagined herself babysitting her. The girl was adorable! Judy had never wanted children, but she loved them. She wanted to be the favorite aunt even though she was an only child.

Judy was staring at the picture when the door of her apartment burst wide open. Captain Murphy walked in with Rush, his bald head and black uniform now dripping wet. He was breathing heavily. "It started raining!" he bawled out, trembling. "He... He wouldn't..."

Judy understood right away what had happened and quickly took Rush from Murphy. She removed his leash and collar and said, "Yeah, he is not a big fan. I'll take him out later. Thank you, Captain."

Rush, like many dogs, dreaded the rain and it was practically impossible to make him pee while it was raining unless you wanted to stay outside for an extra ten minutes—until the dog understood you would not go inside until he peed. But that meant both of you getting soaked, and the Captain didn't seem to enjoy the rain very much either. Murphy looked like a scared little puppy in this situation, which Judy and Fred found hilarious. Fred walked up to him and helped him off with his coat.

Judy put Rush down and he began running around, dancing his way through the crowd. He greeted everyone with his wagging tail. Judy looked at him for a moment, ensuring that everyone was comfortable with having him around, and then she heard Murphy's voice: "Does she like it?"

"Not sure, she still looks shook up," Fred laughed.

"Months of planning, Hunter. Months of planning," Murphy muttered.

"I'm very grateful. To both of you," Judy replied, getting closer to them.

"And we're very honored to have had you in the police force for this long, Mrs. Hunter," called out a voice in the background.

The person owning the voice was Penelope Cloud, the Commissioner's Chief of Staff and long-time underpaid assistant before that. She was an overweight blonde lady with short hair. Tonight, she was wearing a sexy and revealing blue dress.

"Very honored," added another voice next to her, a high-pitched voice that sounded less sincere.

He was a shortish man with a salt-and-pepper tuft of hair. He had tiny lips, long ears, and resembled a goblin. This unprepossessing individual was Commissioner Lester Crowley. He and Penelope had joined Captain Murphy to speak with Judy and Fred.

What the hell is the Commissioner doing here? Judy asked herself.

You might think that the Commissioner of the NYPD would be here because Judy was highly respected as a detective in this city, but in fact the Commissioner wasn't here for that reason. The truth was Lester Crowley didn't like Judy Hunter. Yet he was here.

The Commissioner was an old-fashioned man who had grown up in the sixties. Judy had worked with him as a cop in the past. He was the head of a precinct in Harlem at one point—an utter disaster. Ever since the beginning of his career as a cop, but more so since his appointment from the Mayor, Lester Crowley had shaken up the city, oiling it with his racism, homophobia, and misogynistic views of women.

So why had he come to this party? To embarrass Judy? Because he was so happy to be saying goodbye to her? *Okay, I'm leaving tomorrow, we get it. The woman who terrorized you with her big mind since day one and proved you wrong many times with her detective skills is leaving. We get it—this is a big day in your life. Now go.*

"Quite a case you got today, Captain," Penelope Cloud started.

"Yeah—" Murphy managed to say before the Commissioner immediately interrupted him. That was his way, interrupting people.

"The public is pretty upset, Captain," he said, looking grumpy and red-faced. Sweat was trickling out of the Commissioner's ears.

"Yeah—" Murphy tried again.

"The Mayor's been on me all day, wanting details..." the Commissioner continued. "Listen, he's a liberal prick for sure. But Ethan Gregory was a beloved figure. People from around the world came to this city to see him this weekend. Now they're scared, and apparently many tourists are booking flights home. The Mayor is not at all happy with this situation."

The conversation turned political. It reminded Judy of her conversation with the hotel manager. So many tourists came to New York, and now they were leaving! It was not as if New York was a small town or lacking celebrities, or even needed them in the first place to fill up the city with tourists.

"They're pointing fingers. They're blaming the NYPD!" Lester Crowley almost shouted, irritatingly. "The city feels dangerous to them. If someone got to one of these Hollywood stars, then any killer could get to anyone in this city. It feels like we've lost control, Howard."

Murphy tried again to speak, but in vain.

"The media are hounding us for details. A world-beloved movie star beheaded, that's very bi—" Cloud added before Crowley lifted his finger to silence her. She obeyed.

"On our watch! This isn't small news, Howard..." Crowley added, and then repeated, "The Mayor's on my ass."

That was his thing: the Commissioner liked talking and asking questions, but he didn't like them answered. He enjoyed the sound of his own voice and being right all the time. Cloud and Crowley both did.

"He was beheaded with a sword?" Crowley then asked.

"A Katana, yes," Judy replied for Murphy.

"What's that you said?" The Commissioner looked at Judy with a big frown. He hadn't set his eyes on her since the beginning of the conversation.

"It's Japanese," she responded. "The sword."

"Oh, like a samurai sword?" Penelope then understood and looked at her boss. He shushed her again.

"Wow. Why? Is this the Middle Ages?! Why not use a knife or a gun? Fucking hell," Crowley went on.

"Gibbins and I are still trying to figure that out—" Murphy replied nervously.

"So, a Japanese did it?" Lester Crowley quickly interrupted.

"We don't know, sir," Murphy said. "We—"

"Goddammit... Please, find out and catch him!" the Commissioner said, suddenly bursting into rage. "We need to find this fucker now, Howard!"

The Commissioner's voice raised four octaves. Murphy nodded. Everyone in the room turned. They all saw Lester Crowley shaking, becoming agitated.

He shook his head again, took a breath and said a little more calmly, "I'm sorry... It hasn't been like this since the Towers... I tell you, it needs to be settled soon. We need answers."

"You will get them," Fred said.

The Commissioner was begging for them to get answers, for them to do something. He was like a child begging his mother for candy, but that was all he was doing. He wanted his slaves to do the work, right fucking then, but all he was going to do was sit in his chair and furrow his brows. But then, he'd never really done anything as a police officer or a captain.

The Commissioner continued blabbering to himself, "It's just sick. It makes me nauseous."

Crowley took a tissue that Penelope handed him and put it against his crooked nose to reinforce his state of being. He didn't appear sick, though. He looked like a man who wanted to ensure that his integrity and reputation were salvaged. In short, he didn't want to get fired by the Mayor. People were blaming the NYPD for Gregory's death and Crowley was feeling that pressure. It was more about himself and keeping his business in order than solving a crime.

"Did you look into the black folks, by the way, Howard?" the Commissioner asked without any shame or reservation.

"Black folks?"

"Harlem... It's for sure coming from there," he said.

Murphy hesitated. He was shy.

"I mean, it wouldn't be surprising," added Penelope Cloud in a whisper.

That Crowley allowed.

Murphy peered at Judy and Fred for a second before saying, "No, we didn't. We have no substantial lead yet..."

"Well, you should look into it," the Commissioner said. "I am willing to bet you a hundred bucks one of them did it."

Judy rolled her eyes while looking at Fred as she took another sip of champagne.

"What do you think, Gibbins?" the Commissioner then shouted at Fred.

"I think it's a Japanese high on severe opium, definitely," he nodded.

Fred gave Judy a funny look and frowned. She laughed on the inside.

Penelope Cloud frowned at her, understanding that Judy was making fun of her beloved boss.

"Damn yellow man! I knew it!" Lester Crowley almost screamed in both joy and anger, slapping the wall beside him.

Judy then quietly stepped away into the kitchen.

"Or it's one of those Syrians we let in last month. I told the Mayor we shouldn't have," Judy heard Crowley add, talking to Murphy and Fred. Penelope Cloud was nodding. "They do that in their country, y'know. That's how they execute people they don't like."

Fred stepped away and came to Judy. He sighed. Then, before he could speak, they heard another sound bite coming from the Commissioner.

"Eddie White will be a nice addition to the team. Thank you for taking him on, Captain... Solved a great many cases in Louisiana. It's exciting... Hopefully he'll be able to help you out with this one."

Murphy nodded, not looking overly excited. "No problem," he muttered.

It finally dawned on Judy. Murphy hadn't lost his mind; *he* hadn't hired that racist man by the name of Edward White. The Commissioner had done the deed and had forced White onto their Captain. *Take care of my child. Make him feel welcomed and respected,* Judy imagined the Commissioner was thinking. It was so Lester Crowley–like, she thought. Who could be a more perfect addition to the police force than a man who thought just like Crowley about humanity, color of skin, and probably women?

Captain Murphy, of course, had to say yes if he wanted to keep his job. The request came from the Commissioner, who was appointed by the Mayor, and it was not to be denied. And now Murphy had pushed White into Fred's arms, and it was Fred who would have to work with the guy and tolerate him. White probably wouldn't last a half-hour under Fred's wing. Or maybe Fred would end up liking him. Judy had found Fred a little prejudiced when he first started working with her, fifteen years back, including about her being a woman, but she believed that she'd softened him up over the years.

But as it turned out, she would not have to wait long to see if her partner had really changed. No, not long at all. As Judy poured herself more champagne and grabbed a cracker from a bowl, there was a knock on the door. Captain Murphy was, by default, in charge of opening the door. He swung it open and everybody turned around. Standing in the frame was a tall young woman with red hair accompanied by a beautiful dark-haired man. Charlotte Gibbins and Brian Haze stepped into Judy's apartment.

CHAPTER SIX:

THE ANNOUNCEMENT

"Hi, Dad." Charlotte said, touching her earring shyly.

Fred Gibbins charged forward to give his twenty-two-year-old daughter a hug. He held the hug a bit too long, almost preventing her from breathing ever again. He looked so grateful that she'd come. This was the happiest Fred had looked all day. With that Gregory situation and all, Charlotte was the breath of fresh air he needed. Fred then noticed Brian standing there as well. He smiled.

Charlotte looked radiant and beautiful. She had chosen to wear a sparkling purple dress with red and yellow dots on it. As for Brian, he wore a plain black shirt and black pants. It looked fine, but Judy thought he could have done better.

"Charlotte, you know the Captain," Fred said, and turned. "And this is..." Fred hesitated.

"Is this your daughter, Gibbins? My, how she's grown!" exclaimed the Commissioner.

Lester Crowley's eyes wouldn't back away from the redhead. His tongue was almost hanging out.

Judy saw that Charlotte was somewhat disturbed.

"And this is Brian Haze," Fred awkwardly broke in. "Her... Her... He's her—"

"Nice to meet you. I'm Charlotte's boyfriend," Brian said as he stepped forward.

Fred had told Judy he had only met Brian a couple of weeks ago, and he clearly wasn't yet sure about the state of his daughter's relationship with the man. He had told Judy that he thought Brian and Charlotte were friends the first time he met him, that he hadn't felt any chemistry at all between them. At the same time, Fred thought that Charlotte should consider dating Brian, because he seemed nice and organized. Then one day Fred had arrived at the precinct and started jumping around agitatedly in front of his partner. He had supposedly seen the two of them arrive at his home the night before and make out on his porch for five minutes. That was not a friendly kiss, he had said! When Fred asked, Charlotte had ignored him and moved on to other subjects. She found it weird to discuss these matters with her father, Fred had said. "She shouldn't find it weird. I am her father. She can tell me anything." *It must have been a bit awkward to say the least*, Judy had thought. "She never had a boyfriend before," he then explained. "I was just a bit shocked to see it."

The great detective thought it was all hilarious, but she could relate. Her father was the same towards her, except that Judy mostly liked to bring women home, which had added another layer of confusion for the late Mr. Hunter.

Now, Fred stepped forward to shake Brian's hand. "Happy you could both come," he said.

"Dad, we just heard the news. Have you learned anything about Gregory yet? Do you know who did it? Do you have evidence?" Charlotte quickly asked.

"We don't have much," Fred said, shaking his head.

"It's so sad, Dad," Charlotte replied.

"I know," Fred said. "Brian, this is my partner, Judy Hunter."

"*Old* Partner," Judy added, teasing.

"Not yet," Fred insisted.

"Nice to meet you. Thank you for your service," Brian said kindly.

Judy gave him a look of appreciation, shook his hand, then looked to the young woman at his side. "Hello, Charlotte!" Judy hugged the tall redhead. She had always liked Fred's daughter, who was bubbly, fun, and full of energy. "Thank you for coming."

"I wouldn't miss it, Judy. We love you," Charlotte replied, sweetly.

"Why, that's very kind," Judy said.

"So, where is the alcohol in this place?" Charlotte asked.

Her father threw her a look. Judy and Charlotte both laughed. They loved teasing Fred.

"We brought you a bottle of wine, we just wanted to put it somewhere," Charlotte explained, looking at her father.

"Wow. Thank you," Judy said gratefully. The detective grabbed the bottle and walked to the kitchen with it. She placed it on the counter along with the others. There were quite a few now. Judy was impressed by how kind everyone had been.

Charlotte and Brian sat at a table and Judy gave Brian a beer. Fred sat next to them, by his daughter's side. Judy joined them.

"So, how's life, Charlotte? Is school still going on right now?" Judy asked.

"No, it just ended," Charlotte replied quickly.

Brian looked at his girlfriend. Judy observed that she was getting a little nervous and he could clearly see it. The retired detective then watched as he drank his beer, not saying a word.

"How many years do you have left?" Judy asked.

"I am done now," Charlotte said, again quickly. "I got my bachelor."

"Oh, how wonderful!" exclaimed Judy.

"Yeah, she's going to med school next year," Fred said.

Charlotte looked uncomfortable but widened her smile for her dad.

"Sweet Jesus, Charlotte, that is so exciting. Congrats! You're going to be a doctor? No way!" Judy said.

"Yeah, my baby girl is a brilliant one, I told you, Jude." Fred almost jumped up and down. "You won't believe where she got in, either."

"Where?" Judy asked.

There was silence again. Charlotte hesitated to speak. She gave Judy a smile and then looked at Brian.

"Go on, say it. Don't be shy!" pushed Fred.

"Huh... Harvard," Charlotte muttered.

"What was that?" Judy kindly asked.

"She said *Harvard*," Fred replied. "Isn't that great?... Isn't that 'sick,' as you young people say?"

"Sure is. Wow!" Judy said.

Charlotte sighed, barely smiling. Judy's expression started to shift. There was something not right here. They were probably in need of a change of topics right about now.

Fred stood up and raised his glass. "We should make a toast."

"No, Dad, it's all right," Charlotte said.

"All right? No, Charlotte, it is beyond all right!" Fred turned to the police crowd. "Everyone! I got a big announcement for you guys. Everyone!"

The crowd all at once stopped chattering and moving. They were now frozen statues, staring in the direction of the foursome.

"Judy Hunter is no longer retiring!" he then shouted.

People looked at each other, wondering. Judy also looked at Fred, not knowing what was going on.

"No, that's a joke!" Fred said. "I wish she would stay."

People laughed.

Judy smiled softly at Fred. Then she went back to Charlotte, continuing to study her. The latter was not enjoying this at all. She had her head in her hands.

Brian stared at Fred, looking displeased. Judy stood up before Fred could say another word.

"Fred, I don't think—"

But her partner cut her off. "My own daughter is going to Harvard!"

A wide cheer echoed across the room. The officers as well as Captain Murphy were clapping heartily for Charlotte. This lasted a long moment, until another voice shouted, “She’s not!”

It was Brian who had stood up. Judy noticed that Charlotte still had her head in her hands.

Fred turned around, spilling some of his drink. He saw Brian, staring at him. Fred was now the confused one.

“She’s not,” Brian said again.

“Excuse me?” Fred replied.

“She’s not going to medical school, Fred,” Brian insisted.

“What are you talking about? Of course she is.”

“She doesn’t want to,” Brian replied.

“Brian...” Fred said.

“Ask your daughter!” Brian said. “Ask her!”

Fred stared at Brian for a moment in fury, then finally turned to his daughter and saw her looking at the floor, avoiding his gaze.

Judy stared at Charlotte. The redhead seemed almost paralyzed. She couldn’t look at her father. What did she not want to tell him?

“Charlotte, it’s okay. You can tell us,” Judy said.

“No. No, I can’t,” Charlotte finally sighed.

“Why not?” Judy asked.

“’Cause I know... I know what he will say.”

Fred didn’t reply to this. He had his head down now, too, looking ashamed. Another long beat echoed across the room. Everybody gazed at Charlotte, confused.

Judy didn’t know what to do.

“I talked to Mom and she’s okay with it,” Charlotte said. “She supports me.”

Charlotte took a deep breath before finally saying, “I don’t want to be a doctor, Dad... I never wanted to be... I want to be a detective. Just like you.”

CHAPTER SEVEN:

FATHER AND DAUGHTER

The police force was ecstatic. Charlotte wanted to be just like her dad, and everyone seemed to think this was both sweet and wonderful. Her father's old partner was smiling at her, clearly proud. However, Fred wasn't saying anything. He didn't even appear to react to what she had just expressed. He stood there motionless.

"I gotta get some air," he finally said, in his usual grumpy tone. Charlotte knew that face. She hated it. She knew what would come next.

Fred was now the one avoiding his daughter's eyes. He grabbed his coat from a chair and quickly went to the door.

Charlotte saw Judy try to stop him.

"Fred?" she said.

"I'll... I'll be back." He expressed politely to the retired detective.

Charlotte saw Judy push people out of the way, calling out Fred's name but to no effect. Fred was quickly out the door and his daughter heard him walking at a fast pace down the hallway.

Her worst nightmare had come to life. Her dad had rejected her. He wouldn't even look at her. What was she to do? Go after him? No, she couldn't do that. Her father didn't deserve an explanation. She had said what she needed to say; now it was his problem. She was twenty-two years old, for God's sake! She could do whatever she wanted.

But Brian was running for the door.

"Brian, no!" Charlotte said.

He took a beat, then turned around. He looked angry.

Even her mother approved of her decision. In fact, come to think of it, that might be why her dad was so frustrated. It added another layer to the whole affair. Her mom, formerly Madelaine Gibbins, had filed for divorce a year and a half ago. She was now remarried to a younger man named Patrice Bélanger and was living in Montreal with their newborn baby. Yes, Charlotte had a stepsibling, a stepbrother to be more precise. All of this had troubled Fred profoundly. His ex-wife was now with another man, had a son with him, and was wearing another name. She was no longer Madelaine Gibbins, but Madelaine Bélanger. And he hated it.

Now she approved of Charlotte being a cop, and she hadn't consulted him to get his opinion before giving her daughter her blessing. Charlotte knew her dad didn't like to think of Charlotte as a cop. He wanted her to go into medicine; she was good at science, the top of her class, but she didn't like it and Fred never saw that. What she did like was solving puzzles and the idea of bringing justice to the world. She looked at her dad and admired his will to sacrifice his life to protect the innocent and save lives. She had wanted this for herself for the longest time. Ever since she was seven.

She had tried to comply with his wishes and go to college. He was right about that, after all. College was great for the mind, and it had helped her grow so much as both a citizen of the world and an adult. She understood life better now. However, she also understood that she didn't want to do more chemistry or learn the periodic table. She was done with that. Yes, Charlotte could save many lives by going into medicine, but the idea of toying with organs and hitting the wrong nerves terrified her. Charlotte instead wanted to learn how to fight, but also go into the psychological side of things. She loved trying to understand people's minds. She thought serial killers were fascinating, and she wanted to step into their shoes for a short while to understand why they did what they did and how she could stop them from going after their next victim.

She also knew that medicine meant money, but doing something for money that you didn't even like just felt wrong. Charlotte was going to follow what she believed to be her own path, her own passion. And that was it.

Charlotte had expected exactly this reaction from Fred—her father walking out on her as he learned the news. Though she would have expected him to yell at her and say, "You're a woman!" or "You're my daughter, I won't let you do this." No, he'd just walked out and left. Not even looking at her.

Brian took her hand, caressing it. He kissed her on the temple. Her lips curled to make a smile. "Oh well," she said with a sigh.

Then they heard a noise and turned around. The door of the apartment opened and Judy came in, walking up to them.

"I'm so sorry, Charlotte. I'm sure he didn't mean to be like that. He just loves you... and uh..."

"It's okay," Charlotte replied.

Nobody knew what to say, but Charlotte had made her peace with her decision. She had tried. She had said what she had to say. Now it was up to her father to come to his own conclusions.

"I think you would make a great detective," expressed a short man with a kind and genuine face. He said his name was Price. "I have difficult parents too," he went on, in an attempt to reassure her.

Charlotte replied with a polite grin, just like the one Fred had given Judy before he walked out. It was not what she wanted to hear; she just wanted her father to come back and hug her.

But Fred didn't come back. Judy, Brian, and Charlotte stared at each other for a while until the couple finally decided to head out. Charlotte hugged Judy, thanking her for her kindness and wishing her good luck on her next adventures.

As Brian and Charlotte stepped out onto the sidewalks of Manhattan, looking at the dark sky in front of them, Charlotte peered around at the long buildings. Among the many people walking the dirty streets, and amidst the many garbage bags lying on the ground, Charlotte could find no trace of her father anywhere. Fred was really gone. Brian gave her a sorry look and the two walked into the distance.

CHAPTER EIGHT:

THE NIGHT'S END

It was now time. The guests were leaving one after the other, a tiny bit more drunk than they were before the party had started. Judy hoped they would be in good health to protect and serve the next day. She didn't need to worry about herself, however. She was now free. No more puzzles to solve, no assignments or attachments—no job, period. Judy had just handed her badge and her gun to Captain Murphy, and the police force had cheered her off before stepping out the door. She was no longer a detective, no longer a member of the NYPD—she was, for the first time in a long while, a civilian.

It was going to be a new beginning for everyone. She only wished Fred had been there to see it. She had hoped he would be the last one leaving. Judy felt so sad for Charlotte. She deserved better, to feel supported and loved. Fred would come around, it was not going to take long, Judy knew it. He was a bulky man who appeared tough, but he was in fact a big teddy bear with a good heart and would come to reason eventually. Charlotte would make a fantastic cop. Judy was proud that another woman wanted to join the wild ride that was detective work. It was nonetheless a job where you were surrounded by men who believed they were smarter and stronger than the few representatives of the other gender. It was going to be hard, but Charlotte could do it. She was strong and incredibly intelligent.

Judy wished Charlotte could have seen the reaction of Judy's mother when Judy announced she was going to pursue a career in the police force. It was a lot of "It's a man's job, why would you need to do that?" or "It's dangerous." Or even worse: "You're so smart, Judy, why in the world would you need to become a cop?" Thankfully, Judy's father supported her and found her admirable for wanting to serve. Just like Fred with Charlotte, he was worried, but in the end, he believed in Judy and never regretted believing in her until his death. He had observed Judy's successful career for nearly twenty years before passing away.

The truth was that Judy had fallen into this career. It was not as though she had really wanted to become a detective and enter this hyper-sexist world. Her uncle worked as a sergeant in the Wilmington Police Department and Judy was looking for a summer job after high school. Like most of her friends, she hadn't figured out her life yet. So her uncle took her in and the department gave her a job as a secretary. That's how she got her foot in the door. Then one rainy night a couple of detectives jokingly asked her advice on a case, and she jokingly gave them her two cents' worth. It turned out she was right: they caught the murderer the next day. Quite the story. After that, they kept asking her for more insights and help. Until they finally kicked and pushed her to go to the Police Academy.

After a few years she had moved to New York, wanting to get away after some family drama over her being openly gay—her mother once again the problem. Her move to New York also meant more money for Judy, and that was great. Then, after another few years, she finally became a detective, and the rest was history.

But Charlotte knew what she wanted, that much was clear. It seemed to have been clear to her for a long time. She just didn't how to approach it... how to approach her father. Judy felt for her.

Judy took Rush out one more time so he could do his business before going to sleep. The now-retired woman imagined herself lying in bed forever, so Rush had to do it now, because he would probably have to hold on for a while after that. In truth, though, she was an early riser.

She found that her brain worked better in the morning. But work for what now? Maybe she would start a novel, and gaze at the magnificent sunrise while sitting on her balcony. She would need to start packing her suitcase. *There we go, that's the work I need to do.* She was leaving for Punta Cana tomorrow.

Her mother had asked her to come to Scotland instead, to spend some time with her. But Judy declined the offer. She wanted to experience peace and solitude for at least a week in her life. She wanted tranquility. Her mother would feel like another puzzle she needed to solve, or something she would always feel the need to change, or, even worse, she would be treated like a child again. "What are you going to do with your life now, Judy? You can't just stand around and do nothing," Judy imagined her saying. Or, "Are you done with that lesbian phase now?"

Her mother still played golf and went mall shopping every other day, so she wouldn't get bored. Judy didn't want to do either of those things. Even at eighty-three years old, her mother still treated her like a child. But she was fifty-three! It was kind of sweet, but Judy wanted to wait a while before enduring that great sweetness.

She also didn't want to leave Rush for too long. Judy liked when he was with her. She did not like leaving him at the dog hotel if she could avoid it, but for this vacation she would have to. The resort she was heading to did not accept dogs, even the cute ones like Rush. Brandy had recommended the resort. She used to spend a lot of time there, looking for a husband, before she met Ian. It was apparently a place for singles, or for married couples wanting to mingle away from the real world for a while. Young and old, there were all kinds of people there. Judy wasn't exactly looking to find someone, even though she was always open. No, she just wanted to relax and enjoy the beach. Apparently, this place had the most wonderful water, a crystal-blue sea with a comforting, warm sand with not too many shells and rocks in it.

Judy was excited! She would grab her piña colada and stay under an umbrella reading a book for seven days straight.

She finished cleaning her apartment, even though several officers had volunteered to help before leaving. There was still a mess in the sink and on the table. Then she turned off the lights and went to her bedroom. She got inside the sheets and looked at the ceiling for a moment.

Judy thought of Ethan Gregory and what she had seen today at the Four Seasons. She could not get Gregory's cut-off head out of her mind. It was all just sickening, what had happened to him. Then she thought of the note. The killer had said a reckoning was coming. What reckoning, and when? Sounded very much like a serial killer who had done this. And if so, who was going to be the next victim? Judy stared out the windows for a second. She could see New York City's infinite lights and illuminated buildings, and she heard cars and police sirens scurrying around. Whatever was going on out there, even if a part of her was curious to know, it was not her problem anymore.

CHAPTER NINE:

NOTHING WOULD STOP HER

Charlotte woke up early and made breakfast for herself. She had slept over at Brian's place in Hell's Kitchen, as she had often done in the past few weeks. It was a great refuge when conflict arose with her family, like the previous night. The apartment was not far from Fred and Charlotte's place, just a few streets away.

The redhead wanted to get her own place, but she didn't have the means for it yet, and Brian said he didn't mind her staying over. He liked it, and Charlotte knew that. He was older than her, by seven years, and had a permanent, well-paid job as a martial arts and kickboxing teacher at the gym, so he could afford to live by himself. His apartment was cozy and comfortable. Brian had chosen nice furniture that went with his white-painted walls. Charlotte had made some tiny changes since first visiting it, giving it some feminine touches, yes, but also garnishing the style and making the apartment seem cleaner and tidier.

Brian was still in bed, probably dreaming of electric sheep. He had weird dreams. He would wake up in the middle of the night sometimes in a complete sweat. She usually calmed him down with a few kisses and by caressing his soft black hair. She would then ask what he had dreamed about and he would tell her something like he was being chased by a crocodile or a big dog around a house and was being eaten by it just before he woke up. Or, even funnier, he would say that he had dreamed he was a woman and that he was constantly on his period and didn't know what to do to get out of it, and everybody was laughing at him and found him ridiculous.

The kettle started whistling and Charlotte picked it up before it drove her crazy. She made herself some tea and went to the dining table and sat in front of her computer. She then looked at her phone. There was nothing—no phone calls, no texts. Charlotte thought her dad would eventually say something and apologize, but for the moment he was remaining a silent ghost, as she had predicted. Never mind him. She turned to her computer and opened a page on the internet. At the top, it said: NYPD ACADEMY. Then she pointed her mouse to the right of the screen, a button that said: APPLY HERE TO JOIN. She clicked on it.

She heard a yawn coming from the back. She turned around and Brian was already pouring fresh coffee into a mug. He was in his dressing gown.

"Morning," he whispered, still getting his voice back from the land of dreamers.

"Hi," Charlotte quickly replied before returning to her computer screen.

"Got a good night of sleep?" Brian then asked.

"Sure," Charlotte said.

Charlotte could sense that her response was unconvincing. She was clearly lying, and Brian knew it. She didn't hear moving anymore.

"You're really doing this," he said, almost excitedly.

"I am," Charlotte replied, focused on the website.

"Don't you think you should call him?" Brian then said.

Charlotte didn't reply.

"Charlotte?" She heard him slowly moving towards her. He grabbed her shoulders, massaging them smoothly. He turned her head around, so she was looking at him.

"I'm fine. I've made my peace," she said.

He kissed her. She could taste his bad coffee breath even though his lips worked magic.

"All right then," he said. "But you should still call him."

As far as Charlotte was concerned, Fred was the one who should call her. She heard Brian step away from her and return to the kitchen.

She finished typing up her application and was brought to a schedule grid for her entry exam. Charlotte selected a date. It was next week. She stood up and took bouncing steps, feeling ready to do this. After all, this was all she had ever wanted.

CHAPTER TEN:

THE VACATION

Fred Gibbins called Judy early in the morning, sounding grim. “I’m so sorry, Judy. I should have stayed and said my goodbyes properly. That was such a cowardly move.”

“Don’t worry,” Judy replied.

“I wanted to be there with you. We had so many great memories together, Judy. I love you. You’re my friend, my partner. How could—”

“Fred, it’s all right!” Judy interrupted.

“No, it’s not all right!... I should have been there...” Fred went on. “Charlotte hates me now! She thinks I am some awful father who doesn’t approve of her dreams. I am not. I want the best for her. I just, I just... I don’t know what I thought. I was just scared for her. The thought of her being in the— I don’t want her to get hurt, that’s all.” He sounded genuine. Then he added, “Of course, she’s going to make an amazing cop!”

Judy smiled. It was comforting to hear him say that.

“You should say that to Charlotte,” she suggested.

“It’s not because she’s a woman, I swear,” Fred added.

“I know it’s not. Just tell her that, give her support. That’s all she wants, to know that her daddy loves her.”

A silence came through the phone. Judy heard numerous sighs. Fred then said, exasperated, “And I just left... Wow, what a great father I am.”

She thought she could hear him crying.

"Nothing is broken, Fred. It's not the end of the world. We all make awful mistakes in the moment. Have a chat with her and tell her what you just told me. She'll understand."

There was a short pause. Judy heard him sobbing. Then there was another long pause.

"Okay..." he finally said. "What time are you leaving?"

"At two," Judy replied.

"Damn, all right... We'll have a drink when you come back, then. Gotta... Gotta solve this Gregory case... White is arriving tomorrow."

"Absolutely, when I come back," Judy said.

"Have fun," he said.

The retired detective held her shoulders back as Fred hung up. Judy was happy about what she had just heard. She knew he didn't want to control Charlotte's life; he just had a hard time accepting change.

Judy finished the last bit of packing, put the perishable groceries into the trash and cleaned her apartment some more. She walked Rush to the dog hotel on 56th Street beside her apartment, with all his things, then she kissed him goodbye. She went back home and ordered a taxi for eleven thirty so she could be at the airport two hours in advance.

She got to the airport a little past twelve and checked in. The plane boarded on time and she took her seat in economy class. She sat next to a mother and her four-year-old child. The latter kept staring at her, smiling. The boy was so excited to go to the beach and make sandcastles. He asked Judy if she had ever been. She said no. He made her excited to get there, though.

The plane was soon moving, New York disappearing into thin air. Judy Hunter's vacation had started. Now it really felt like she had retired.

CHAPTER ELEVEN:

FRED

Charlotte finally decided to return home early the next day. She had been at Brian's place for two nights in a row now. She had enrolled at the police academy, she had made her own decisions, and now she was done being angry and scared about what might come next. It was time to talk to him. She did not care what her father might say. Her mind was at peace. He had texted her yesterday afternoon to arrange a dinner with her, but she had not replied because she had needed some more time to decompress. She was now ready to face him.

She walked through the streets of Hell's Kitchen from 38th Avenue and arrived at 45th Street. She headed to her father's apartment building and walked through the door. She took a deep breath. This whole place, her home, seemed unwelcoming now. It felt strange to be back here. It was just the stress, she told herself. She needed to calm down.

Hopefully, he's already at work, she told herself. *It's early, but detectives work hard. Maybe there's a dead body he had to go to. And he has the Gregory case to solve...*

She continued along the hallway and stopped by the mail. She opened a cabinet with a key and a few envelopes spilled out, landing on the ground. She sighed, picking them up one by one. This hadn't been emptied in days. Then, as she was finishing up, she heard steps coming down the stairs. Charlotte saw this short blond man, looking genuinely lost. She thought he was handsome. But then he spoke.

"Sorry, ma'am! Can you help me?" he said with a thick Southern accent.

"What do you need—"

He cut her off after looking at her for a moment. It was like he recognized her.

"Oh! Lord Almighty! You're the man's daughter! You're a gorgeous one, aren't you?... Charline, isn't it?" The man took out a hair comb and drew it through his honey-blond hair.

"Hmm... Do I know you?" she asked, confused.

"Yes, yes. Well, no. We have not met yet, really. I would have remembered you. I sure would have, huh... Name's Edward White, pleasure, ma'am."

"Okay..."

"Gonna work with your pop, well, if he could show up. Ha ha," Eddie White said with a slightly creepy, slightly annoying laugh. "You haven't seen him, have ya?"

"He's not in?" Charlotte asked.

"Well, we were supposed to meet here at nine. I'm a little early, as you can see. As I am always." White kept staring at her. Then he added, "Do you think he's asleep? Does he tend to sleep a lot?"

Charlotte scratched her head. It was not like Fred to not be on time.

"Er..."

"Maybe I got the apartment wrong... I'm his new partner, you see. I'm sure he told you about me. He was probably excited to meet me."

"No, he never did," Charlotte quickly replied. She didn't see the handsome face anymore, it was gone. Only White's vibrant, prick-like personality was shining through now.

She then noticed his outfit. He was wearing a dark-green suit and a brown, almost orange, tie. His shoes were very silver, with tiny red stripes. He looked like a clown.

"I guess I could check—"

"Yes, please. After you," he cut her off again.

Charlotte hid the mail inside her coat and started walking up the stairs, heading to the fourth floor. As she went up, she knew exactly why White wanted her to go first, to get a good look at her from behind, but she didn't care. She just wanted to get this over with and see this jerk go.

White kept speaking. "Have you lived here long? I wasn't expecting much from this place. But this... Are you guys movin' or somethin'? Is this your temporary home? Of course, it must be, it's hmm... How can I say?" He then stopped as she stared at him.

"Excuse me?" she said, threateningly.

"I mean, this place could use a little bit of renovation. It's, hmm... Y'know. Y'know what I mean."

Charlotte sighed. She didn't even want to engage anymore. She couldn't wait for her father to meet him and put him in his place. It was a very nice building, the cleanest brownstone building in Hell's Kitchen, with very nice people living in it. It was true that it was old and hadn't been renovated, but it was safe and comfortable.

They arrived on the fourth floor. Charlotte speeded down the hallway, heading to the last door. She heard White lagging behind. She looked back. White was analyzing every inch of this place.

"I've been here, ma'am," he said. "Ya, that's right. I came here. I had the right door. I couldn't have been in the wrong. I knew it. Impossible. Ha ha."

Charlotte wondered why her father had not answered if this White person had the right door. Maybe Fred had seen through the peephole how clownish White looked and had ran away.

She knocked and waited a few seconds. Nothing happened.

"Like I said, I've tried that," Eddie White confidently exclaimed. "Ain't in there. Do you think he's asleep? Maybe he's gone for a walk with the dog. Or maybe he drank too much last night and he—"

"We don't have a dog," Charlotte cut him off before White made some comments about her dad he would regret.

"So, you got someone in your life, beautiful?" he asked her.

"Yes, very taken," she said firmly.

"Lucky man, isn't he, then!" he responded, still checking her out.

She put her key in the door and walked in. It was totally dark. The curtains and blinds were still drawn.

"Dad?" she shouted.

No answer. The apartment had a strange, rotten smell. It was not how she had left it. She walked to the kitchen and saw a whisky bottle on the table. Dirty plates in the sink. There was untouched food on the counter, food that belonged in the fridge.

She turned to Eddie White, who was looking at her. He was waiting for some answers. Charlotte called again, "Dad?"

"I don't think your old man's here," White said, pinching his long, sharp nose.

Charlotte started to walk to the bedroom. She heard the buzzing of a fly across her ears on the way there. She pushed the door open and screamed.

She couldn't believe her eyes. She had found her father. Fred's feet were not touching the ground. He was hanging on a rope by the neck. His cold and lifeless eyes staring at her.

CHAPTER TWELVE:

QUESTIONING

He was gone. Her father was gone. Charlotte kept staring at the cold and ghostly pale corpse in front of her. Fred was suspended on a rope by his neck, his broken neck. Suicide? Was it possible? Had her father really taken his own life? What the hell?

Charlotte couldn't say a word. She had so many feelings boiling inside her, she couldn't express how she felt. She was frozen in place, not understanding if this was a dream or reality. She felt tears rinsing her cheeks, her eyes hurting. Charlotte could hear a voice beside her, mumbling something. A hand was touching her shoulder, trying to steer her away from the scene. But she wouldn't move. She stood there looking at Fred.

After a beat, she heard shouting and doors slamming. She slowly managed to turn her head. Cops were flying in from the corridor. Charlotte saw a few officers notice her, then they seemed to disappear into the walls, spying around the apartment. She saw a very tall man appear in the crowd, a man she knew as Captain Murphy. He spoke to her, but she could not understand what he was saying. Only his lips were moving. She couldn't hear the sound.

Murphy pushed her away from the door and made Eddie White sit her down in the dining room. Then she saw Murphy speed into the bedroom, looking stunned and shocked when he took in what had happened in there.

White called for an officer to stay with Charlotte. Then White joined Murphy in the bedroom. Charlotte finally heard words. Murphy was asking White how he had discovered the body and why he was here. The investigation lasted for ten minutes or so, before the young woman heard another sound coming from the front door. She saw Brian fumbling in, accompanied by officers. He gave Charlotte a look, then peered inside the bedroom for a moment. His face became pale too. Then an officer showed him to Charlotte. He went to her and took her in his arms right away.

"I'm so sorry, Char, I'm so sorry," he said.

He hugged her and Charlotte cried a little while breathing down her boyfriend's neck.

The hug was stopped by a soft cough. Captain Murphy came to them, along with Eddie White.

"Hmm... Miss Gibbins," he carefully said. "I— I want to offer you my deepest condolences," Murphy uttered.

Charlotte didn't reply, she didn't know what to say. *This is really happening,* she thought. Her father was dead.

"Fred was a great, great man. I am—troubled, to say the least..."

Charlotte stared at the Captain, waiting for him to finish. She knew what was coming. She would have to answer questions and she would have to say that she didn't know anything.

"Detective White here informed me as to how you both discovered the body... I only have a few questions."

"Can't this wait?" asked Brian.

"No," said Eddie White.

Brian looked at White, annoyed.

"Let's get on with it," Charlotte heard herself saying. Her mouth was speaking for her.

"Okay... First, I need you to confirm this is really Fred Gibbins," said Murphy.

"Of course, it is," Brian almost shouted.

"Yes, that is my father," Charlotte quietly said.

Charlotte saw Murphy take out his pad and make notes. Murphy continued, in the most sympathetic manner he could manage. "Well, is it true that you came in and Detective White was already here?"

"Yes," she replied, almost robotically.

"Were you here last night?"

"No, I didn't spend the night."

"She was at my place," Brian added. "All night."

"All right. Then, you don't know what... We all witnessed you and your father the other night. I'm sorry to ask you this, miss, but do you think..."

He wanted to ask if she thought she had contributed to his suicide by her actions. What a question to ask.

"Did you and your father talk after that incident?" Murphy pursued.

"No," Charlotte replied. "I was at Brian's for the last two days. My father called me yesterday. I didn't answer. Then he sent me a text. Wanted to get dinner last night, but I never replied. I came in today hoping to... settle..."

"I see," said Captain Murphy. "Anything else useful you can tell me?"

Charlotte shook her head. *I am as shocked as you.*

"Did your father have a drinkin' problem?" asked Eddie White viciously.

"What?" Charlotte replied.

"Was he a sad man?" attempted to clarify White. "I understand his wife left him recently, yes?"

Brian stood up. "I think we're done here."

"That would explain a lot. Or maybe, as the Captain wanted to suggest, your poor choices may have had something to do with his... demise. I'm just trying to understand here. Which was it?"

"You fucker!" Brian yelled. He punched White in the face. The latter fell to the ground and blood started flowing from his nose.

Captain Murphy and a couple of officers tried to hold Brian in place.

"Can you take me home now?" Charlotte asked Brian.

Charlotte stood up and looked in her boyfriend's eyes. They were as cold as ice. She grabbed his fist until it unclenched. Brian finally sighed and looked at her.

"I think we've had enough," Charlotte said.

"Yes," said Captain Murphy, pulling White away. "Again, I am sorry, Charlotte."

Captain Murphy and Eddie White took a step back, leaving Brian and Charlotte alone. They soon left the apartment.

Brian kept cursing on the way home, things like, "I would have finished the guy off. Asking you that... Who does he think he is?"

And go to jail? Charlotte thought. He eventually stopped talking altogether, seeing that Charlotte was upset. He apologized to her and gave her some silence. She felt him taking and touching her hand, even massaging it softly as they kept walking through the streets.

CHAPTER THIRTEEN:

AT THE BEACH

Judy was very pleased. The resort looked absolutely magnificent and the people she had met the previous night seemed delightful. Her room was tiny but lovely, gazing out at the deep crystal-blue sea.

She woke up early on her first morning and sat on the balcony for a while before deciding to take a walk along the beach. She walked barefoot on the sand for an hour, watching the sun rise in front of her. She loved looking at the houses on the beachfront.

Some people really have money!

There were already a few people walking around at this early hour, which was nice. The ones she saw had smiles on their faces and warmly said, "Good morning!" as they passed one another. She saw a few people with dogs, but these were not people from her resort, they were locals. She knew Rush would have had the time of his life walking in the sand with her. He might even have been without a leash, a rarity for him in busy New York City.

Judy's mind was still busy with the Gregory case, her former police force duties as well as Fred's conflict with Charlotte. It would take a few days for her to let go and really relax and feel like she was on vacation. Maybe a few cocktails would help move her along that path.

She went for breakfast. It was an enormous buffet with eggs, pancakes, toast, bagels, fruit, potatoes, bacon, yogurt. Even with all this variety, though, Judy had a hard time finding anything vegan. She settled for some oatmeal with almond milk and toast.

She sat at a table and ate. It was already getting warm and it was still pretty early. Judy's eyes got lost in the depth of the radiant sea for a long moment. She saw women in bikinis strolling along the shore. Judy admired their forms and shapes. Brunettes with long hair and great big cheeks. Just her type. She suddenly felt warm inside. How cute they were! Maybe she would have fun here after all.

She wanted to have breakfast like this every day for the rest of her life.

The retired woman then decided to go to the beach again, grabbed a few towels on her way and looked for a long chair under a fixed umbrella to sit down. But they were all taken! There weren't any people sitting on them, but there were towels and bags there. These people must have woken up early, like Judy, and run to the beach to reserve their chairs before heading back to grab more sleep. Damn it.

She eventually found an empty chair, but without an umbrella on top of it. She wouldn't last long out here in the sun, it was already getting hot. *Also, I'm an old gal.* She went to her bag and picked up sunscreen, settled down with the intention of staying for an hour, and after that she was going to find something else to do, maybe go to the gym or the bar. Yeah, the bar. And maybe speak to some women. See if there were any singles with sexual fluidity. It was too early for that, though. Maybe she could find a spot to start reading her novel and drink more coffee. That sounded good.

As she went through her bag, she saw a glowing light. Her phone was beaming. Then she heard a ring. A call was coming in. She looked at it and saw three missing calls. All from dear Captain Murphy. What did he want? He knew she was on vacation, and she was also retired, wasn't she?

She called him back right away.

"Captain, this is Hunter!" Judy said firmly. It was like her detective role had never left her. She was too used to this.

Murphy answered in a melancholic and muddled tone. It didn't sound like good news, not at all. It was about Fred. Something horrible had happened.

CHAPTER FOURTEEN:

THE FUNERAL

The vacation ended abruptly. Judy took the first flight back to New York City the same day she heard the news. She couldn't stay away. This was her old partner, her dear friend, and he had supposedly killed himself. *Killed himself*. She repeated that to herself. *Killed himself? Fred?* That didn't make any sense. How could he? He loved life. Why the hell would he do that? He had a daughter who absolutely adored him. Sure, Charlotte and Fred had their conflicts, but nothing that could possibly lead to something like this. He had had a rough time with his ex-wife in the past year, ever since she filed for divorce, but honestly, he didn't seem all that affected by it. He had supportive friends; people from the precinct thought he was an amazing guy as well as a great detective. So, what the hell had happened? Did Judy miss something? She couldn't imagine how Charlotte must be feeling right now, especially after that fight at Judy's apartment. It was not her fault, she wanted to tell her. Absolutely not!

The retired detective got home and quickly unpacked her large suitcase. She then went out again and sped down the street to get Rush from the dog hotel. He was so happy to see her. He looked at her like she was the world, his goddess.

"You didn't think I was going to be back this soon, did you?" she said to him.

Neither did I.

Later, she gave Charlotte a call to convey her deepest condolences and to ask if she could help her in any way for the funeral. Brian answered and said that Charlotte had been sleeping all day, but she appeared to be doing fine. He then indicated that the funeral was to take place the following day.

The next morning, Judy left Rush inside the apartment and took the elevator down to the lobby. Outside, a black car with tinted windows was waiting for her. The ceremony was being held about two-and-a-half hours outside the city, in a greenish cemetery in Rockland, New York, the small town where Fred had been born.

The car rolled along the main street. Rockland was so small. The road was almost too narrow for two cars to pass each other. There were a few boutiques, an ice-cream shop, the bank, a grocery store, a pharmacy, an antique shop, a church, and a couple of tiny restaurants hiding in corners. People strolled casually along the sidewalks, not in any hurry.

The street soon ended. The car turned right and followed a short road leading into the countryside. Then Judy saw a long line of cars in front of the green grass of a cemetery. As her car pulled over, she observed all the black-clad people. Some women were wearing fascinator hats, with veils, hiding their crying faces. Judy didn't know that Fred knew so many people. She had never been to his hometown. All she had ever known was his entourage in New York—his ex-wife, his daughter, and his father, who had died a few years ago from cancer.

Judy tipped her driver for the ride, opened the door, brought her high heels to the pavement and put them on. She looked to the sky, which was gray and gloomy. It was going to rain, that was for sure. She asked the driver if he had an umbrella and he went to the trunk and kindly gave her one. Judy held onto her beige jacket tightly as it was chilly, and made her way across the grass, following the crowd.

Her emotions started to overflow as she kept walking down the short hill. She couldn't believe whose funeral she was attending. She had seen Fred three days ago, for God's sake! And now she was here to mourn his death with all these people she didn't know.

Glowing red hair suddenly shone in front of her eyes. A tall woman with a snow-white, angelic face was standing in front of an opened grave alongside a priest: it was Charlotte, looking to the ground, into the dark emptiness. Brian stood by her right side. Judy then saw another head of red hair get closer to Charlotte and begin talking to her, someone whom Judy immediately recognized as Charlotte's mother and Fred's ex-wife, Madelaine. She had come all the way down from Montreal, apparently.

Judy kept walking until she reached them. She stood next to Captain Murphy and a few officers from her precinct.

At the center of the crowd lay a closed casket. People began taking their seats as the service was about to begin. Madelaine finally finished talking to Charlotte, and Charlotte's mouth stayed closed as she ignored her mother and took her seat beside the priest. The latter began his speech.

"We're here today, on this sad and dreadful day, to celebrate the life of an incredible man by the name of Frederick Alexander Gibbins..."

The priest continued talking. Charlotte finally noticed Judy, her eyes went wide, and she gave her a smile. A depressed smile, but a smile.

"Of course, I did not know him. But people tell me Frederick was a respectable and honorable man. He was a great hero, and he was an amazing father to his daughter Charlotte and a good and kind friend to everyone who knew him," the priest said. "It is under tragic circumstances that we are here today. No one was expecting this. It reminds you how fragile life can be. One day our loved ones are here, the next they are gone."

Judy observed Charlotte as the priest uttered his words carefully. She was not crying. Instead, she was listening, almost nodding. Her mother, though, and a couple of others in the crowd started quietly whimpering. Judy could feel her own eyes filling with tears.

"You have to support each other right now. Be with one another. Share love and compassion with the people around you. Try to understand each other. Do not forget Fred, he lives in every one of you. Honor him. Share your stories and your memories of him, express how you feel and what you need. Come together and mourn his death. You are not alone, and you will never be."

That was a nice bit, Judy thought. The priest then moved over, and people lined up to throw flowers into the grave. One after the other, people either prayed or mumbled words over the grave and left the scene once they were done. It was Judy's turn and she mumbled the words, "I will miss you, buddy. Be well," and threw her flower. She paused for a moment, then began to walk away, looking back and seeing that Charlotte and her mother were behind her. Charlotte advanced slowly and stared at the casket. She was about to say something, but a roaring cut her off.

Judy turned, like everyone else, and looked at the road behind the trees. Making their way through the lines of limousines were a bunch of motorcycles. Men with leather jackets. A gang? Judy couldn't decipher what was written on the back of the jackets. Something to do with skulls. The motorcycles suddenly stopped. The man leading the motorcycle army turned his head towards the crowd. He had long gray hair with a mustache and a jaw beard. He was wearing black sunglasses and gripping a cigarette between his tiny lips. He hostilely stared at the crowd for a while. What were they doing here? Did they know Fred? Fred had not been known to appreciate gangs or motorcycle clubs when he was alive. In fact, he hated them.

After a beat, the silvery-haired gang leader turned his head away and restarted his engine. He rode away, disappearing along with his friendly colleagues.

Everyone thought the episode had been strange. Judy heard chatter echoing across the green grass. But then it died away as everyone realized this incident had interrupted Charlotte's turn to say goodbye at the grave.

A few minutes later, Judy approached Charlotte as she was getting into her car. Charlotte hugged Judy firmly, then tears started flowing, soaking both of their shoulders.

"Thank you for coming," Charlotte said.

"Of course," Judy said. "Listen—" She was suddenly interrupted by a crisp voice.

"Judy Hunter. Hello dear!" It was Madelaine, and she had a big smirk on her face. "I thought you were in the Turks and Caicos..."

"Punta Cana, Mom," corrected Charlotte.

"Yes, well..."

"I can't believe it either," said Madelaine. "He was a true joy, wasn't he? I—I don't know what to think."

Judy could see that Madelaine was struggling.

"If I had known how depressed and lonely he had been since... If I only had known, how foolish was I— Anyway, did you hear? Charlotte is going to your Academy." Madelaine forced herself to change the subject as she clearly felt guilt rising in her veins.

"Really? You decided?" Judy said, looking to Charlotte.

Charlotte nodded at her, giving her a polite smile.

"She's gonna be fantastic, isn't she?" Madelaine continued excitedly.

Judy did not turn away from Charlotte as Madelaine kept talking.

"A great way to honor your father," Judy replied. Then she stepped forward and looked straight into the young redhead's eyes. "Listen, this is not in any way your fault, Charlotte. It's not."

Charlotte lifted her head a little, listening. Judy caressed her hair softly and continued, "Believe me. You have nothing to worry about. Neither of you."

Although Judy didn't really know if it was true about Madelaine—the ex-wife may have had an effect on Fred's fate. Judy just felt she should keep that point of view to herself and try to make them both feel better instead of sticking the knife in. They'd all had enough sorrow for today.

Judy kissed Charlotte on the forehead, in a sweet, motherly way. She then shook Madelaine's hand, then Brian's. The trio stepped inside the car, leaving Judy standing on the pavement.

"So long, Judy," said Madelaine as she closed the door.

Judy could almost see Charlotte staring at her through the tinted windows. Somehow, she sensed that she had not completely convinced her...

CHAPTER FIFTEEN:

THE ENVELOPE

Charlotte already felt the cold wind on her body as she put on her black leggings. Summer was on its way, but it was still a bit chilly in New York City. She stood in the hallway of Brian's apartment. She snuck her long coat on, grabbed her keys from a shelf, and had started to leave when she heard a noise. It was coming from the bedroom. She hadn't woken Brian up, had she? Please no. Charlotte went to the door and started to turn the knob when she heard another sound.

"Where you headin'?" asked a voice.

It was Brian. Damn it. She knew she had made too much noise while putting on her clothes. He stood in the doorway, staring at her. He had a smirk on his face.

"Not trying to sneak off on me, are you?"

"No, no," Charlotte replied. "Just going to get coffee."

"We have coffee," Brian replied.

"Yeah, but I want a Frappuccino," Charlotte said.

"All right."

Charlotte smiled at him and he smiled back at her. He turned away, almost disappearing, but then his head popped back into the doorway. He came to her, grabbed her head and gave her the longest, most passionate kiss. When he finally let her go, he said, "Have fun at the gym."

"I am not—" Charlotte began.

"You could take a day off, sweetheart."

"I know, but—"

"Hell, a week off," he interrupted again, caressing her neck.

“I am just going for coffee. And then I’ll be back. I told you. You want anything?” she asked.

“You don’t have to prove anything to anyone, Charlotte. You don’t have to be tough and all strong right now, and act like nothing happened. It’s okay to feel sad and to stay in bed for a while. We’ll watch a movie; we have ice cream. You can have it for breakfast if you want!” Brian said.

Charlotte thought it was sweet, but...

“Sorry... I’ll be back in a while,” she said.

She turned away and was turning the knob when she felt a hand grabbing her.

“Brian?” she begged.

“You were about to forget these,” he said, handing over her boxing gloves.

She sighed. Oops!

Brian interrupted her once more. “Tell Joe I’ll be there at twelve. You better be gone by then and here in bed. Do you have water?”

Charlotte raised her water bottle and walked down the hallway. She could sense Brian standing at the open door, watching her go. *It’s okay, Brian, you can go back inside now. I’m fine.*

She was trying not to think about yesterday’s event. All those people, annoying her, wanting to know her feelings and reminding her that it was okay. She didn’t want to think about death or her dad either. She wanted this day to herself. Charlotte wanted to forget about it all and just carry on with her life.

As she walked down the street, she rubbed at a stiffness in her shoulder and felt something inside her coat. What was it? She put her hand inside and felt some papers in the inner pocket. She pulled them out. Envelopes—the ones she had picked up at her father’s place before she found him.

Charlotte looked through them one by one, most of them addressed to Fred. There was one from the bank, one from the phone company, and one was junk mail of some sort. Then she found a fourth envelope. This one was addressed to *Miss Charlotte Gibbins*. Charlotte was surprised every time she received an envelope with her name on it. She never received mail! What was this about? It was certainly not the NYPD Academy; she had only sent her application the day before she picked up this mail.

The envelope was odd. It had no address on it, no zip code, just her name. She stared at it for a moment before opening it. Inside was a small paper.

She read it, and quickly dropped it on the pavement in shock. She picked it up again and reread the first line:

YOUR FATHER DESERVED WHAT I DID TO HIM.

Charlotte stared at the note, reading it again and again. She began shaking.

CHAPTER SIXTEEN:

AT THE PRECINCT

Two days after the funeral, Judy headed back to the precinct: she had to empty her desk and pick up the rest of her things. She got a similar welcome to the one she had received at her retirement party. People seemed so happy to see Judy in their establishment again. But of course, everyone was also very down about Fred. Pictures of him had been put up on several walls. The late detective's desk was blooming with flowers. Judy looked at some of the pictures and stared at Fred's smile. One of the pictures showed him when he first started out. Young, without a beard, still with a baby face. Another picture featured him and Judy during one of their first days together.

A tall, muscular fellow approached Judy, a bit shyly: Officer Luke Tennessee. He apologized for making a mess in her bathroom after drinking too much at her party and then throwing up. Judy laughed it off before waving over at Erica Clay and Sergio Sanporo.

Erica Clay was a short blond with big shoulders and a strong, tough personality. She had a sarcastic sense of humor that Judy found so lovable. Sergio Sanporo was Portuguese. He used to have a massive mane of curly hair but had to shave it off once he joined the NYPD, almost five years ago now. His current army buzz cut suited him—kind of. Sanporo always had the biggest smile on his face. People sometimes called him Mr. Happy. Clay and Sanporo were both lovely beings, Judy felt. There were also a couple of other officers she was less familiar with.

Clay walked up to her and yelped, "Detective Hunter!"

"Not anymore, Erica," laughed Judy.

"You'll always be to me," Clay said with enthusiasm.

"What are you back here for?" said Sanporo. "Miss us already, huh?"

Judy laughed again.

"... Hey, sorry about Fred," Sanporo added.

"Yeah, we all miss the dude," said Clay.

"Thank you. It's kind of weird being here without him," Judy said. "Anyway, where is Captain Murphy? He told me I could come and get my stuff whenever I wanted."

"In his office, I think. Isn't your stuff still in your desk? I don't think anybody—" replied Sanporo before Clay interrupted him.

"Oh yeah, they did. Remember our new friend?" Clay said with an annoyed tone.

"Right. He wanted your desk real bad. Said he admired you a lot," continued Sanporo.

"Who?" Judy asked.

"That guy from Louisiana... Eddie White," Clay replied.

"Yeah, I know who you mean," Judy said.

"He got his nose broken on his first day," Clay added.

Judy gave a discouraged stare before replying, "I'll just go to Murphy, then."

"I wouldn't, Detective," Erica said.

"He's in there with Blondie and, huh... Charlotte Gibbins," cautioned Sanporo.

"Charlotte?" Judy then asked, surprised. "Why is she here?"

"Don't know, but she looked a bit off. She ran to Murphy and almost yelled at him. She looked stressed out," said Sanporo.

"Really?" Judy asked.

Sanporo and Clay both shrugged. Judy left them there and went to Murphy's office. Of course, with Fred's death, Judy could understand Charlotte being stressed, but why would she come to the precinct and approach Murphy like that?

Judy saw Captain Murphy through the thick glass walls of his office. He was sitting at his desk. A short blond man with a pigeon-like face and a white bandage on his nose stood next to him, putting his hair back in place with a comb. The man was wearing a tight black suit, and his vest was covered with blue patterns that looked like raging panthers.

Judy then saw Charlotte sitting in front of Murphy, talking. The conversation looked heated. The retired woman observed them for a moment. Then Charlotte was standing up and walking out of the office. Murphy was rushing after her, calling, “Miss Gibbins, please!”

But Charlotte didn’t seem to hear him. She went the opposite direction of Judy, not noticing her. Judy wanted to call to her but stopped herself. She instead approached Captain Murphy.

“Captain? What’s going on?” Judy asked.

“Hunter. Hello! What are you doing here?” Murphy replied.

“What was Charlotte doing here?” Judy retorted.

“Huh, you don’t even—” Murphy said before another voice spoke.

“Ex-detective Judy Hunter, wow, it’s you!” said the blond man standing in the doorway.

Judy looked at his horrendous suit again, then at his face. The man had an evil smirk. He came to shake her hand.

“You probably heard of me by now.”

“Edward White,” Judy said, ignoring White’s hand.

“My friends call me Eddie,” White said.

“Well... your reputation precedes you, as I’m sure you know.”

“Reputation. Ya, ya. Got one indeed. Good things you’ve heard, I’m sure,” White said.

He didn’t seem to mean this ironically. His mouth showed even more of his perfect white teeth.

“Just like I heard good things about you, great things. A lot of folks out here are fans o’ yours.”

"Uh, huh," Judy responded in a nonchalant manner. She turned to Murphy, "So, Charlotte?"

Murphy wasn't getting the hang of White either, that much was clear. He looked tired of him already. Poor thing.

"Yes, hmm... She found something in her mailbox," the Captain said. "A note. She thinks her father... Well..."

"What was the note?" Judy asked, interested.

"Just one of these weird things you send to your friends," White said, handing Judy the note.

She looked at it, her eyes widening. The note said:

YOUR FATHER DESERVED WHAT I DID TO HIM.

MORE WILL COME—

YESTERDAY IS NOT YET GONE.

FOLLOW THE PATH FOR ANSWERS.

"Gives you the frisk, huh?" White said.

As soon as she read it, Judy thought of Ethan Gregory. The note left by the actor's mouth had been written the same way and in the same tone.

"More will come...?" Judy said quizzically, showing them the note.

"Very cryptic, ain't it? I feel like I am in an escape room again. Do they have those here?"

Judy kept gazing at the note for a long beat. Then White started speaking again,

"As I said to our valorous Captain here and Gibbins's poor grieving daughter over there—and I'm sure you'll concur, Judy—it's a joke."

"What makes you think that?" Judy asked, raising her eyebrows.

"Well, it's clear, ain't it? Whoever sent this to her wanted to play with her suffering... Could be a bully at school, a bitch that didn't like her.

Or a... Y'know, as I said, she's grieving... It does weird things to ya. Hell, she might have written it herself."

"Okay..." Judy said unenthusiastically. She then moved on, "Have you found anything on the Gregory case yet, Captain?"

"As a matter of fact..." White said sneakily.

Murphy cleared his throat. Finally, he was going to say something.

"Detective White put a man... uh, behind bars," Murphy said.

"Yeah, he did," White said. "The Commissioner's all happy. Called me personally this mornin'! Wasn't expecting that on my first week."

"Who... who did it?" Judy asked.

"Guy was Hiroshi Yamato. Worked for the hotel as a bellboy. Caught him right on tape, going to the emergency stairs," White said.

"Is this a joke?" Judy asked, conflicted.

She looked to Captain Murphy, who was stern and serious.

"That's how you know he did it?" Judy said. She was almost laughing.

"Best of all, looked through his apartment and found a Japanese sword. They call it Katana, if you didn't know. The Asian guy named Price, of course, knows everything about them, and said it matched our murder weapon, and he even found DNA on it."

Judy took all that in. She tried to make sense of it... Wow... *Shake yourself awake, Judy...*

"Well, I guess your case is all settled, then," Judy said.

"Hey! As I told the daughter, Fred seemed like a good guy. Guess he was really depressed. Poor thing, nobody saw it coming. I really wanted to work with him... With a rope, jeez, that must have hurt bad. Your neck breakin' like that, ugh... Oh, well, guess he feels better now."

Judy knew that her face must be redder than Charlotte's hair at this moment. She took a deep breath and peered over White's bandage.

"Sorry about your nose, looks really bad," Judy said, copying White's evil smile.

She nodded at both men before continuing, “Captain, I was hoping I could pick up my stuff.”

“Yes, I’ll show you to it...” Murphy said.

Judy and Murphy walked away, leaving Eddie White behind. When White was at a safe distance, Judy began speaking again.

“You don’t really believe you caught the guy, right?”

“We have someone going to prison, Hunter. Case closed,” Murphy replied.

“Yeah, because of pure racism, not because of concrete evidence,” Judy said.

“Well, we got DNA.” Murphy said.

“Right... that.” Judy sighed. For all she knew, White could have put it on the sword himself. He looked that crazy.

“Look, I don’t want to believe it either, to be honest. But the Commissioner’s all over me, and after what the boyfriend did to White, I have no choice. Eddie wanted to sue or, even worse, get him arrested. He assaulted a member of the police force, for God’s sakes! It was either I let him do whatever he wanted or— Well, you heard White. The guy confessed, so...”

“I’m not following you. Who assaulted White?” Judy asked.

“Charlotte’s boyfriend, Brian. White said something offensive.”

“I see,” Judy said, not sounding surprised. She even felt herself smiling slightly. She grew a little jealous of Brian. “Still, an innocent man shouldn’t go to prison,” Judy added.

Murphy agreed. “Unless you can tell me something we’ve missed about Gregory, I can’t do anything,” he concluded.

Judy shook her head. Unfortunately, she had nada.

CHAPTER SEVENTEEN:

FINDING HER

Judy was hoping that Charlotte wouldn't make anything of the note. As much as Judy didn't want to believe Fred committed suicide, and think like that Eddie White character, she did not want Charlotte to get into trouble. She was hoping Charlotte would not try to find whoever sent the note. *Why her? Why send it to Charlotte? What did they want with her? Was it really a joke?* If it was, it was incredibly cruel. Judy hoped Charlotte would not "follow the path," whatever that meant. Judy had questions too, like why was it so similar to Ethan Gregory's note? Were the two connected? Had Fred really committed suicide? Even though she was thinking about all this, she fervently hoped the young woman wasn't.

She tried calling Charlotte's cellphone as soon as she got out of the precinct. No response. She left her a message, asking to call her back. She wanted to go to her, but she didn't know where Brian Haze's apartment was. She could find out, but she didn't want to assume things and get confrontational with Charlotte. She didn't want to barge into Charlotte's life and tell her what to do, it was not her place. But Fred wouldn't want Charlotte to get hurt, either.

Judy finally went back to her apartment and tried to call Charlotte again. Still no answer, so she sent her a text and decided to wait it out. Charlotte would get back to her and hopefully understand that Judy only wanted to help her ease her mind—even if Judy's mind wasn't eased. What if Fred had not killed himself? What if Fred instead had help? Why would a killer use a rope? Then an unwanted voice came to her, telling her to just forget it.

But she didn't let it go. Charlotte didn't call back, or reply to the text, and now Judy was worried. She spent the night alone with her thoughts, barely sleeping.

In the morning, the retired detective decided to call Charlotte again, but she still wasn't answering or returning Judy's calls. She called again a few hours later—still the same thing.

It was not until the next day that Judy's phone finally rang. However, it was not Charlotte. Someone with a low, raspy voice said, "Judy..."

"Hello?" responded Judy, confused, still not pinning down who the voice belonged to.

"Hi! It's Brian."

"Brian?"

"Charlotte's boyfriend."

"Yes, yes, I know. What's up?"

"I'm sorry, but Madelaine, Charlotte's mother, gave me your number. She said you could help. It's Charlotte."

"Brian, what is it?"

"She found this note telling about her dad. I don't know if you—"

"Yes, I heard about it," Judy replied.

"Well, she kept going on and on about it for the last two days. She acted kinda crazy. I kept telling her there was nothing to it. Probably some joke, right?"

"Yeah," Judy replied, even though she wasn't positive it was a joke.

"It's a suicide, I said. There is nothing telling us that it isn't, right? Fuck, I saw the body!"

"Is she with you?" Judy asked.

"No, no. That's the thing. This morning when I woke up, there were papers all over my desk, all over the floor. Her dad's things. She finally got them back from the precinct last night. It's a mess out here. I think she... she went to— I don't know where she is. I called the gym this morning, she isn't there either. She won't return any of my calls. Then I saw that my car was gone! I—I should have stopped her, but I was asleep and... I should have woken up—"

"Hey, hey, Brian! It's okay. It's not your fault, we'll find her."

Judy waited for a response, but there was silence. Was that crying she heard?

"Look, can you tell me your address so I can come and take a look? There might be something in all that mess that tells us where she went," Judy said.

Judy took down Brian's address, took a shower, and sped out of her apartment. She grabbed the first cab she saw.

Brian looked grim and dirty, like he was sick. Judy could smell alcohol on him.

"Come in," he said with a polite smile.

Brian didn't seem to know what to say, he just walked ahead of Judy down the apartment hallway. She followed him, looking around. The sunlight was beaming brightly through the windows. The apartment was toasty and warm, and she could still smell Charlotte's rose-scented perfume. The kitchen was empty and clean. There was a small but comfortable-looking couch not far away, and a TV. Brian continued to the end of the hallway and opened a door to an office. There were papers scattered all over the floor and desk. It reminded Judy of her former office, when she was working on complex murder cases.

"She must have been here all night," Brian mumbled. He took a beat and said, "Could I get you some coffee?"

"No, thank you. I'm fine," Judy replied.

She saw Brian out of the corner of her eye, sighing, then he left her by herself. She heard his steps moving back to the kitchen, and the fridge door opening.

Judy picked up some papers, looked through a few of them. It was mostly unreadable notes and some pictures. Pictures of Fred. There was nothing alarming about them, just Fred's old stuff. She had seen some of it on her partner's desk. She then caught a picture of her and Fred together, a rare shot. Fred didn't like being photographed. She stared at it for a bit, forbidding herself to become emotional.

Then Judy moved on to the computer. She quickly turned it on and looked through Charlotte's files. She saw nothing interesting, so she moved on to the internet. Judy clicked on the search engine's history bar and the list appeared. She read through the last visited sites. There was nothing outrageous or "adulty"—no porn sites. Then, as she went down a bit, she found something that caught her eye. It was about Rockland, where the funeral had been, the town where Fred was born. There were a couple of entries there: one was a search of the city on Wikipedia and then the search of a school. She clicked on the school, Rockland High. *Original*, Judy thought.

The retired detective looked through the site for a minute or two and then examined the history list one more time. Charlotte, or whoever had been using this computer, had searched the high school for about an hour or two the night before. There were multiple entries looked at different times. Then Judy deleted that page as she heard steps coming her way again. She quickly clicked on the Notes application on the Mac and saw the top entry, with the address of Rockland High written on it. There was obviously something there, Judy thought.

After a moment, the door creaked open. Brian was standing there, clearly waiting for an answer.

"You said she left with your car?"

"Yeah..."

"What's the brand and model?"

"It's a Nissan Rogue... Black."

Judy nodded, took note of it on her phone.

"Do you have a license plate?"

Brian touched his head, then went to the kitchen to get some papers with his license number. He gave it to Judy and then kept looking at her. His eyes were fatigued and stressed.

"I will find her, I promise."

CHAPTER EIGHTEEN:

ROCKLAND HIGH

Charlotte drove at high speed along the highway. She wanted to get there fast, she *needed* to get there fast. Rockland was two-and-a-half hours away. It was a long drive, and it felt like it. Unfortunately, there was no bus that went there so she had taken Brian's car. Hopefully he wouldn't be too angry with her. It was about her dad, after all. His death. The whole affair was muddled and she needed to clear it up. And now she had a serious lead. She hoped Brian would understand that and be kind and forgiving.

At about ten minutes before noon, the car arrived in Rockland. Charlotte checked her phone's GPS. It said she was less than three minutes away from Rockland High. This was the place where she would get all her answers. At least, she hoped so.

Her father had never really talked about his childhood or his teenage years. She never even knew he went to Rockland High or who his friends were during that time. Was he popular? Charlotte had never really asked him about any of that. It was sad, really. The redhead blamed herself a little, because now she felt as though she had been self-absorbed in her young life and had never cared about what her father had gone through before he had her. Now she wanted to ask him about his high school experience. Was it bad? Was it good? Or had it been somewhere in between, like hers?

After what she had found out the previous night, something told her she would know a lot more soon enough.

The Nissan Rogue pulled into the parking lot of a grainy brown building in the middle of nowhere. It was a medium-sized high school campus. There was a field on the left side, where students were playing soccer and cheerleaders practicing their choreography near the benches. On the other side were a bunch of picnic tables, where cool kids were "chilling." Charlotte had never been in that tribe, that inactive tribe. Well, maybe once or twice with her old girlfriends, but they had mostly wanted to "chill" to try weed behind the school. Otherwise, Charlotte had been one of those cheerleaders in the field, cheering for good old Kenny and his squad. Kenny had been the hottest guy in school and every girl had wanted to go out with him. Kenny had once picked Charlotte and they had had a hell of a time together. He was kind and funny, and a total gentleman. He had even come to dinner one night, and Fred and Madelaine had liked him a lot. But a week or two later it all ended, he moved on to another girl. And then another girl after that... and another. A real smooth Casanova he was. He had never talked to Charlotte again, even though she was still a cheerleader for his team. High school! It was less than four years since the end of her senior year, but it all felt like centuries ago.

The "chilling" kids turned their heads to look at Charlotte as she walked by them and they all went quiet. They looked at her as though they'd never seen an adult before. At least an adult that was close to their age but was not in high school anymore. Charlotte ignored them, fixing her eyes on the door. She pushed it open and walked in.

She was in a narrow hallway leading to some offices. On her way, she observed frames on the walls, class pictures of the different years. She didn't see Fred anywhere. Charlotte kept walking until she saw a black-haired woman sitting at a desk, typing. After a moment, she lifted her head to look at Charlotte. She seemed annoyed and breathed out a quick:

"Hi! Can I help you?"

"Yes. I..." Charlotte hesitated. She didn't know what to say, hadn't planned this. "I'd like to see your principal, please."

"Principal Black is on lunch break," the secretary replied.

"Oh, hmm... I'll just wait, then," Charlotte said.

"Can I ask what this is about?" the secretary added, looking even more irritated.

"I'm a reporter. I am writing a story about the school," Charlotte blurted out. "Is that okay?"

The secretary didn't respond. She wrote something on a notepad. Then she returned to her typing and sipped some coffee.

Charlotte took a seat in front of the desk. She waited there for about a half-hour. While she was waiting, she got a book out of her bag. It was a yearbook dated 1989. She had found it in her father's stuff from the precinct. She flipped through it. Again. She had done this all last night. The blue yearbook had not only revealed to Charlotte that Fred had gone to Rockland High but had also told her something important about his time there. So, after a lot of page = flipping, with her body beginning to shake, she had decided to come here. The panic got to be too much.

Suddenly, a body jerked out of an office beside Charlotte, and a woman with short hair and crooked teeth smiled at her. She was dressed businesslike but seemed to be trying to show she worked harder than she really did. She looked bored. The woman turned her head to the secretary and the smile faded.

"Annabella? Can you clear my schedule for the day, I have an appointment with my dentist at four. I think my children gave me another cavity," the woman said.

"Actually, Principal Black, there's a..." the secretary mumbled, not sure what to qualify Charlotte as.

"Mrs. Black! I am Heather Potter, for the *Tribune*. I'd like to ask you a few questions, if you don't mind."

"A reporter? Why, come in! Why didn't you tell me sooner, Annabella?"

Annabella shrugged.

"It won't take long. I promise."

Charlotte was shown into Fiona Black's office and took a seat in front of her desk. She looked around: a lot of space for nothing, she thought. A bunch of library books seemingly untouched, serving as decoration. A couple of ugly painted portraits stuck on the walls, all gazing at Charlotte creepily. A large desk, but not covered with papers, quite clean. The rest of the room was empty and unused.

Black seemed excited and kept smiling as Charlotte attempted to make herself comfortable.

"I'm writing an article on Ethan Gregory... I understand he went to this school?" Charlotte asked.

Fiona Black looked at Charlotte for a moment, observing her, analyzing her, not seeming very sure how to proceed. She had remained standing in front of her desk, arms crossed.

"Oh, yes. He apparently did... Wait, isn't he the movie actor who died recently?" Black asked.

"Yes, that would be him," Charlotte replied.

"I think I saw it in the papers... Yes. Another drug overdose, huh?" Black asked with a pompous tone.

"No, not exactly." Charlotte gave her a wry smile. "It was murder, actually."

"How terrible!" Fiona said, before going to a table and pouring herself some water from a filter pitcher. "Water?"

"Please," Charlotte said. She had not even thought about drinking for at least three hours. "I'm guessing you didn't know him?"

"No, no, my girl. I'm not very familiar with him or his work. I mean, I had heard his name on the news, like everybody else did, but I didn't think he was born here, let alone a player for the White Tigers."

"White Tigers?"

"It's our football team, of course!" Black replied, as if the White Tigers was the most famous high school football team in the country.

"Looks like your friend here was an accomplished player. One of the best quarterbacks we've had. As for the transcript I have in the system here, though..."

"Hmm... Interesting..." Charlotte replied, writing on her notepad.

"Who did you say you were with?" Principal Black then asked.

Charlotte saw her fixing her hair, almost nervously... or maybe excited?

"Er... the *New York Tribune*," mumbled Charlotte.

"Ah, is it associated with the *Times*? I read it quite often. Are you going to put my name in there?"

"It's another news outlet. And yes, if that's okay," Charlotte said.

"It is more than okay. Are you kidding? We never get any publicity out here."

The *Tribune* was not a real newspaper. It had once been, but it had died in 1966 after more than a hundred years of existence—a fun fact Charlotte had learned the evening before. And even if Charlotte was not a real reporter, she believed she could have made a good one. The young woman took another sip of water and continued, "So, about that transcript? What were you saying?"

"Oh, well. From what I see, he was not a very good student. But what can you expect from a wannabe actor, huh? I see lots of Cs, some Bs and a, huh... a D!" Black almost shouted. "How did they let that happen?" she added, speaking to herself.

Charlotte waited for a moment until Black was finished staring angrily at the transcript.

"Did he have any friends?" Charlotte asked.

"Friends? Well, I can't really see that, now, can I?" Fiona replied rudely. It was as if she was blaming Charlotte for the bad grades.

"No, of course not. Maybe you can get me a list of whoever was on that football team?"

“A list? Let’s see. I’m sorry, I’ve been trying to get my printer going all morning, maybe Annabella...”

“Can you name some of the players? I’ll take it down here,” Charlotte said. She held up her pad, ready.

“Right. Well, there was Ethan Gregory, the actor, Rick Carson, Patrick Miles, Viktor Kovachev, Xavier Rose, Zachary Smith, Julian Franco, uh... Sebastian Reed... Reed?” She stopped at that last name. Her face grew pale as a ghost.

“Everything all right?” Charlotte asked.

Black stared at her computer for a moment, dead silent.

“Yes, yes. That’s all I have here,” Black muttered.

“What’s the last name you mentioned? Is there something wrong?”

“No, no. I just... if you want to know anything else, you’ll have to ask the people who were here at that time.”

“And who might that be?” Charlotte said.

“It was Principal Batty who was in charge,” Black pursued.

“Any idea where I could find him?”

“I heard he lives in a beachfront house on the south side of the city. I don’t know the address. Never met him... just heard he was a pretty strict principal.”

“Thank you,” Charlotte said, standing up. She was about to shake Black’s hand when she gave her notepad a look and then inquired, “Fred Gibbins. What about him? Was he on the team?”

“Gibbins, you said?” Black said in a low voice.

“That’s right.” Charlotte nodded.

Black typed in the name on her computer and then nodded in turn.

“He was. He was our defensive lineman.”

Charlotte sighed.

“What about his transcript?” She couldn’t help herself.

Fiona made a few clicks, then typed again and said, “Great student.”

Charlotte lit up, so proud. She shook Black's hand and walked out of the office.

She exited the school with a slight smile on her face. She looked around. So this was where her father had been in his teenage years. He had played football here! Why had he never mentioned it? It was amazing. And he had good grades, too!

She drove Brian's car and went back into town. She stopped in front of a place called Granger's Coffee on Main Street. She was about to go inside when she heard a voice calling her.

Charlotte recognized that voice. She turned her head into the vicious sunlight beaming from the opposite side of the street. There it was, direct from New York City itself, the great metropolitan, a good old yellow taxi. And getting out of it was a tall gray-haired woman. Her smile faded from Charlotte's face as she saw Judy Hunter walking towards her.

CHAPTER NINETEEN:

GRANGER'S COFFEE

Charlotte didn't seem very thrilled to see her. No, not at all. Judy advanced towards her, Rush following on a leash. Judy attempted a gentle smile, but Charlotte crossed her arms.

"What are you doing here?" Fred's daughter asked.

"I could ask you the same thing," Judy replied.

"I was just... uh... admiring the city..."

"Great town, isn't it? Never been here before either... well... before the funeral," Judy added.

"Yeah..."

"You didn't answer any of my calls," Judy said.

"Right," Charlotte said timidly.

"Is there a reason?" Judy questioned, lifting her chin.

"I guess... I..." Charlotte began before shifting her tone. "Why is that cab waiting? Look, it won't work. I won't get in. Take it back with you and go," Charlotte said.

Judy turned around and looked at the cab. She seemed surprised too.

"Oh, I don't think I paid him, that's why!" Judy said, turning around. She walked back to the cab and gave him some money. She returned to Charlotte.

"So, you paid like—what?—two hundred dollars? For what? Why?"

Judy scratched her head. "Oh, no worries. It wasn't that bad. Anyway... Pension fund, taking a little advantage of it right now. Ha ha."

"Why don't you take Uber or Lyft, like most people do?" Charlotte said, condescendingly.

"Didn't think of that, and never tried it. Is it good?"

Charlotte barely nodded. "It would have been a little less expensive. A little..."

"Oh really? Do you think they might have also been nicer? It took three cabs before a driver would let me bring tiny Rush here!"

"Why are you here, Judy?" Charlotte cut through. The young woman crossed her arms.

"Just to grab coffee. Care to join me? " Judy replied.

"I'm not going back. I'm staying here. Whoever put you up to this—" Charlotte said.

"Is that a special coffee that they make here? If so, I want to try it. Can they make it with almond milk?" Judy questioned.

Charlotte didn't bother to respond and turned back around. She walked towards the entrance.

"Mind if we sit outside?" Judy proposed, pointing to Rush. "Not sure they'll allow him in."

Charlotte sighed and let go of the doorknob. She went onto the terrace, Judy following.

Judy ordered a café au lait with coconut milk and Charlotte ordered a Coke. They sat in silence for a moment. Judy kept peering around at the town and Main Street. Charlotte was nervously tapping her fingers on the table. The waiter brought water for Rush and caressed him. His name tag said *Stew*.

"He's so beautiful," he commented. "What's his name?"

"Rush," Judy replied.

"How old is he?"

"Just about four," Judy said.

"He has such nice hair!" Stew exclaimed.

"Yeah, yes he does!" Judy cried.

Judy saw Charlotte looking at Stew caressing the dog. She wasn't looking at the hand or at Rush but right at Stew. Analyzing him. Judy couldn't tell if Charlotte was annoyed by him or liked him. She was really staring, though. And who wouldn't? Stew was young, with dazzling blue eyes and a vibrant smile. His hair was long and dark, begging to be admired and touched. And he had a muscular body, too. He reminded Judy of that guy from *The Notebook*. That was a film her ex-girlfriend had loved. Judy had never understood why—she thought it was dull and poorly made.

"Anything I can get you ladies, in terms of food?" Stew asked.

"I'll have your veggie burger, if you don't mind," Judy replied.

"Perfect. Any sauce on there?"

"Only if you have vegan mayo," Judy said.

"We don't, I'm sorry. I keep telling the chef to get some because I'm vegan, too. It's really annoying that the restaurant doesn't have it." He added, "Fries? They're vegan and so good!"

"Sounds perfect!" Judy exclaimed.

"Great. What about you?" Stew turned to Charlotte.

Charlotte glared at him for a beat, frozen in time, before responding with a half-muted voice, "I'm all right, thank you."

"Have something, Charlotte, please. It's on me," Judy said, merrily.

"I'm fine," Charlotte insisted.

"You must be hungry, no?" Judy then asked.

"I'll just have my Coke, thanks." Charlotte crossed her arms with finality.

Stew nodded and walked away from them.

"Sorry, I didn't mean to push it. I just know the road was long for me and it's already past one. I barely had breakfast and I'm starving. I didn't want you to faint like I'm about to, that's all."

"How come you're vegan?" Charlotte asked. "I thought you and my dad went to a fish-and-chip place every day."

“Believe me, it was quite a shock for your dad when I told him. But he accepted me.”

“Right.”

“And teased me...” Judy added, chuckling.

She saw the ghost of a smile forming on Charlotte’s lips, but the young woman seemed to want to force the joy out of her body.

“I could never do it,” Charlotte blurted out.

“Sure you could, but do you want to, is the question.”

“I love steak and bacon too much,” Charlotte said. “A bunch of my friends are vegan and I admire them so much for it. But it’s like they have no choices and I see them struggle in restaurants and at people’s houses. It’s so complicated and restricted.”

“Yeah, I can see that. People can be annoying about it. However, when you are doing it for the right reasons, you don’t really mind fucking up the menu or eating only vegetables at dinner parties.”

Charlotte sighed. She didn’t look convinced.

The two women stared at each other for a moment before Judy shifted her head to look at Rush. She stroked the dog’s hair.

“So, how was the high school?” Judy finally asked.

“What?” Charlotte said. Blood was draining from her face. The young woman was turning white.

“You went there, no?”

Charlotte looked petrified. She didn’t respond.

“Well, did you find something interesting?” Judy asked.

“Something interesting?”

“You didn’t go there?”

Charlotte shook her head no.

“Huh... Funny how you can research something for hours and then go to the town where the thing’s at and just not go there.”

“What?” Charlotte said, looking even more confused.

“That’s where your father went to school, right?”

Charlotte gazed away for a second, clearly uncomfortable, and sighed again. "I knew it. He put you up to this, didn't he? Brian?" Charlotte said, almost standing up.

"No one put me up to anything," Judy replied.

"The bastard. I told him to keep quiet—"

"Charlotte—"

"I didn't find anything, okay?"

"So, you did go?"

Charlotte sighed again. "Yeah... I guess so."

"Why?"

"Why do you care? It's not— It's nothing interesting."

"Tell me." She reached for Charlotte's hand. It was trembling. She held it still, trying to keep the young woman in place. "I'm just here to help."

"Help? Really?" Charlotte said unbelievingly. "With what?"

"I just want to know why you are here."

"I told you, there was nothing that—"

"Did you find out something?"

Charlotte kept quiet.

"Look, Charlotte, you can tell me. I swear, I won't judge. I won't even comment on it if you don't want me to. I'm just curious."

Charlotte hesitated, then said, "You won't believe it, that's all."

"Try me," Judy said reassuringly.

The redhead took a moment, still unsure. Then she sighed and reached out for her bag. She pulled out the yearbook from 1989.

"1989? That's a while ago."

"I found it in my father's stuff!"

"Interesting. Is that—is that the year he graduated?"

Charlotte nodded.

"Cool!" Judy opened the book and began to scroll through it. "Cute pictures... What should I look for?"

Charlotte didn't say anything. Judy peered down and looked at it quietly. She then came to a bookmarked page and looked up. The redhead nodded.

Judy scanned the page. It was a picture of the graduating class of 1989. She looked through the people in the pictures. Then she suddenly saw a chubby boy with an energetic white smile looking to the camera on the far right. He had a comical but also tender expression that Judy knew quite well. It was undoubtedly Fred, although much younger than she'd ever known him. Judy looked at Charlotte with wide eyes. Charlotte didn't reply with a smile, she was still looking at the page. Judy returned her gaze to the picture. Something about it was disturbing Charlotte, and Judy could now see what it was.

Beside Fred were a few girls and boys. Judy kept scanning the picture until something caught her eye. *Is it really? It can't be.* Another boy who looked strangely familiar, who was super-handsome, with spiky pale hair. *Can it be?* She looked at the boy for quite some time.

"They were in the same class." Charlotte suddenly spat out.

Judy glanced up at her.

"Why didn't he tell me about it? He knew Ethan Gregory!"

"Charlotte—"

"It's him, Judy! His name and bio are on the other page. There's a record of him at the school."

"Wow!" Judy responded.

"They knew each other!"

"Apparently," Judy nodded.

"They were on the same football team," Charlotte added.

"I didn't know that either," Judy said.

"They were friends!" Charlotte insisted.

Judy nodded.

"And then the note! The note! It all makes sense!"

"Charlotte, I don't—"

"'Your father deserved what I did to him!' He killed him."

"What?"

"Judy! 'Yesterday is not yet gone.' It fits. This has something to do with the past. If my father and Gregory were friends, then—"

"What do you mean—he killed your father?"

"He didn't commit suicide, Judy. Whoever did this to Gregory also did it to my dad. I'm sure of it."

"Really?"

"You don't believe it. I knew you wouldn't!"

Judy wanted to believe it, but experience told her to be careful about jumping to conclusions. She didn't want to give Charlotte any encouragement. They didn't have any evidence, and Charlotte could not be involved in this... search... investigation... whatever it was going to be.

"No, Charlotte. Just explain yourself. Just tell me what you think happened."

"I don't know what happened. I just—I just know that it doesn't make sense!"

"Your father committing suicide, you mean?"

Charlotte nodded.

"And there was this boy Sebastian whatever, the principal was searching for—" Charlotte suddenly stopped herself.

"Yes?"

"Never mind," Charlotte replied.

"Who's Sebastian?" Judy asked.

"Who the hell knows..." Charlotte shrugged.

"I need to know everything you know, Charlotte. We have to tell the NYPD. What did the principal say?"

Upon hearing this, Charlotte stopped and stared for a moment. She looked enraged, insulted.

"I never said anything, forget it," Charlotte said, standing up.

"Charlotte, please!" Judy exclaimed, pulling the redhead towards her.

"Leave me alone, Judy! They didn't believe me back at your station, my mother didn't believe me... Brian... and you don't seem to either. I don't need you or the NYPD for help. Thank you very much."

"Wait, Charlotte, I never said—"

Charlotte made Judy let go of her hand and the young woman kept walking away. Judy looked around the terrace. People were staring at her now, but she didn't care. Judy stood up, left Rush there, tied to the table, and went after Charlotte. She reached the redhead in the street and made her turn around.

"Look, I want to believe you, okay? I don't want my ex-partner and good friend to have killed himself either! All right? I don't want it!" Judy raised her voice, getting emotional. "But I need to know more, to find out more, in order to make a case out of it! Yes, people won't believe it until they get proof, concrete proof. And a high school picture won't do it. It won't mean anything to them."

"It means they knew each other!" Charlotte exclaimed.

"Yeah, a lot of people know each other. It doesn't mean anything."

"But they were killed around the same time."

"Died, yes," Judy clarified. "Again, that proves nothing. We need a more tangible connection, more background information on the friendship. Why would a killer target them? Until we get that, your dad's death remains a suicide and Gregory is a separate, unrelated case."

"What about the note? Someone sent—"

"Yes, I know about that. That is not enough either. I need more," Judy said.

Tears filled Charlotte's eyes. She was slowly breaking down on the sidewalk.

"Start by telling me what you know." Judy said, gently. "Come on, let's sit down. What did the principal say?"

The two women returned to the table and Charlotte told Judy everything she knew: the little she had learned from Principal Black about the football team, about Fred's grades, and about how Black froze when she mentioned the name Sebastian Reed. She also told her that if she wanted more answers, she would have to go to the former principal's house. Judy in return conceded how similar Gregory's note was to the one Charlotte received.

"See, there is a link!" exclaimed Charlotte.

"We're still not sure it came from the same person."

Charlotte shook her head.

"Listen, I'll go to Batty and I'll come back. Tell you what I learned," Judy proposed.

"No," Charlotte said. "I'm coming. Or you can stay here and I'll come back to tell you."

"Charlotte—"

"It's my *father*. I am not going to stand here and do nothing," Charlotte said.

"It's not about that, Charlotte. It's about the note. The person who sent it to you clearly wants you in the game. I don't know why they targeted you or why they wanted you to have it. But I know it's dangerous. If Fred really didn't kill himself, then whoever sent you the note could be a cold-blooded serial killer. You don't wanna go near that. Let the police handle it."

"The sender wanted ME to do this, not you or the NYPD. I will deal with it," Charlotte replied firmly.

"Charlotte—"

"I won't be in danger; I can handle myself just fine. I don't need you or anybody to—"

"I'm sure you can, but—"

"But what?" Charlotte asked. She could read Judy, and Judy knew it. The ex-detective had no answer. "You can talk all you want. You don't have a badge, you can't arrest me, you can't shoot me. I am doing this whether your ego wants it or not."

"It's not about my... It's too personal to you. If this is about revenge, you might want—"

"It's not about revenge. My father deserves better. He deserves justice. It can't be a suicide, it just can't be. I can't have that on my conscience." Charlotte took a long breath before asking firmly, "Is there even an investigation I am stepping into?"

Charlotte waited for an answer, but Judy couldn't give one. There was no investigation into Gregory's case. It had been "solved" by the NYPD. The young woman understood that. She stood up and added, "Thank you for the drink."

She started to walk away. Judy stayed in her chair, watching Charlotte leave. She could try to force Charlotte back to New York if she wanted to, but did she really want to do that? Would Fred want that? If Fred had indeed been murdered, would he want the case to remain unsolved?

CHAPTER TWENTY:

BATTY

After searching online and finally finding an address for a Willis Batty, Charlotte got into Brian's car. She followed a road surrounded by the greenest forest the redhead had ever seen. The road continued for a few miles before Charlotte reached bright golden gates. The house behind them looked like a manor. As soon as she got out of the car, she sped to the buzzer and pressed the Talk button. She heard no answer beyond the deafening noise of the speakers. After a few moments of this, Charlotte wondered what to do next. She could either wait or jump over the fence. *I don't need the information that badly*, she thought.

Suddenly, she heard a sound and saw a black Toyota approaching along the road. She noticed the pink Lyft sign on the front window. The door opened and Judy and Rush got out. The retired woman thanked the driver, then turned to Charlotte and almost jumped in excitement.

"This thing is wonderful! All on your phone!" Judy exclaimed.

"Yeah..." said Charlotte, confused.

She gave Judy a look as if she was waiting for something to happen. This whole debate was exhausting her, she didn't want any more of it.

"What do you want now?" Charlotte finally asked.

"Like I said before, to help you. The NYPD arrested a man for Gregory's murder—an innocent man, I'm sure—and I am not about to let them get away with it."

The retired detective paced to the gate. Rush was wagging his tail, happy to meet Charlotte again. Charlotte was still unconvinced she wanted Judy helping her, but a small smile grew on her cheeks. She played with Rush's curly hair for a moment.

The two women looked at each other, and then Judy gave Charlotte a hug.

"We owe it to your father to find out the truth. If there is justice to be served, and if we have to turn the whole Gregory investigation around for the NYPD and they are mad at us for it, we'll do so. But I am not leaving until we find out the whole truth and our minds and souls are at peace with it. Understood?"

Charlotte was now beaming with excitement. She really liked what she'd just heard. She felt for the first time that someone believed her. No—believed *in* her. A team was formed.

The duo then turned to the speaker.

"Is he here?" Judy asked.

"No answer."

Charlotte pressed the speaker button again. They waited, and then they heard a voice, an old voice.

"Whatta ya want?"

"Mr. Batty? Willis Batty?" Judy said.

"Yes, that's me. Whatta ya want?"

"Sorry to disturb you, Mr. Batty. I—we just wanted to ask you a few questions about—"

"Questions, did you say? What questions?"

"About of few of your students," replied Charlotte.

"What students? I don't have any students. I haven't had students for nearly twenty-five years."

"Some former students of yours. Ethan Gregory and Fred Gibbins." said Judy.

Batty didn't answer. The two women heard only an exasperated sigh, then dead silence for a beat. A noise interrupted the silence and the golden gates flew open.

Charlotte and Judy drove along the paved, hilly road until they reached the entrance of the house. The property lay on top of the hill.

The house was pale blue, beautifully constructed and welcoming. And it was big. A wide green forest surrounded the gardens.

The door opened as they climbed the flight of stairs to the porch. A man with perfectly straight white hair stood there in a dressing gown, peering at the two women. He looked around eighty-five years old. Willis Batty peered at Judy for a second then turned to Charlotte. He stiffened immediately when he saw her. His mouth got wide.

"You look just like him..." he said to the redhead.

Charlotte was confused.

"There is no way you're not related to him," Batty added.

"What?" said Charlotte.

"Frederick... Are you his daughter? Granddaughter? No, he's too young for grandchildren... Are you?"

"Well..."

"Well, are you or are you not related to him?" Batty grimaced.

"Yes, she is. His daughter," replied Judy.

"Very nice to meet you, young lady!" exclaimed Batty, shaking Charlotte's hand, almost hugging her.

"Nice to meet you as well." Charlotte said with a warm expression.

"Please come in."

"Is it okay if he joins us?" said Judy, pointing to Rush.

"Absolutely, bring him in. I love my furry friends," Batty said. "What are your names?"

They headed into the Batty's living room and sat down.

"This is Charlotte and I am Judy Hunter, working for... Well, yeah, Judy and Charlotte," Judy said awkwardly.

"Did you know my dad well?" asked Charlotte.

"Oh yeah, one of the finest students we had at the school. Great footballer, too. He had a kind soul and was determined to make something out of himself, you could see it."

This made Charlotte smile even more.

"How is he doing?" Batty asked.

Charlotte's joy crumbled. *That was some question*, she thought. But then Batty kept going before either of them could answer, "After I learned about Ethan's death, I was devastated. I can't imagine how Fred must have felt, knowing how close they were."

"He... yeah, that was something," Charlotte replied, struggling.

"Actually, sir, that's why we're here," Judy interjected.

"Yes, it is so, so tragic," Batty said.

"Can you tell us how close they were?" Judy asked.

"Oh, they were close all right! I'd come out of my office and explore the grounds at lunchtime, and they were always sitting together, either studying or playing a game with some other friends. I would often find them in the field practicing football. They were on the same team, you know, helped us win a championship!"

"Yeah, we heard about their football days," replied Judy. "Can you tell us about some other friends of theirs? Who would you see them with?"

"They had many friends!" replied Batty with certainty. "There was that Sheldon girl. Melanie Sheldon, that is. And then there was... hmm... they hung out with Rick Carson, Julian Franco, Zachary Smith and uh... there was that Kovachev kid, maybe..."

"Sebastian Reed?" asked Judy.

"Oh yeah, he was part of their gang all right! I mean, maybe Frederick and Ethan were even part of *his* gang—the other way around. That's when it started."

"When what started?" Charlotte asked.

"Well... hmm, I don't want to assume. But I'd say Reed's recruiting, I guess."

"Recruiting for what?" Charlotte said.

"His... activity..." replied Batty, growing slightly nervous.

"I'm sorry, Mr. Batty," said Judy. "We're from New York City, we don't know exactly who Sebastian Reed is and what he does."

Batty opened his mouth and nodded. He stood up from his chair and started to walk around. "You'll probably see him in town, if you haven't already. He's... he's got this biker club, shall we say."

"A gang? Like a Hell's Angels type of thing?" asked Charlotte.

"Yes." replied Batty.

Judy and Charlotte stared at each other. This sounded a lot like the man they'd seen at Fred's funeral.

"How did Fred and this Sebastian Reed get along?" Judy continued.

"They got along fine. Reed was very controlling, though, over everyone. He was already a leader, even back in high school. Didn't like to be challenged."

"Right. Did they ever get in a fight?" Judy asked.

"I don't know. Probably. Nothing ever came to my knowledge, though. Reed probably didn't appreciate Frederick joining the police. Is your father still working as an officer?"

Charlotte felt herself shaking slightly. "He was a detective, actually," she replied.

"Wonderful! Did he retire?" Batty continued relentlessly.

"What?" Charlotte said.

"You said 'was.' What happened?"

Charlotte saw Judy look at her. Judy clearly wanted to help, but she kept silent.

"My father's dead," Charlotte blurted out.

"Excuse me?" asked Batty, clearly shocked.

"He's dead. He died less than a week ago..."

Batty froze. He looked at Charlotte with bewildered puppy eyes.

"My... my... Excuse me?"

He scanned Charlotte and Judy for a moment, searching for a sign that maybe this was some kind of joke. But it wasn't. They looked back at him, grim and cold.

Batty grabbed his head. "Why didn't I hear about this? Oh my God! I am so sorry, young girl..." Batty said. He thought for a moment. "Ethan and then Frederick... What is happening?"

"He apparently... we don't know..." Judy said.

"God!" replied Batty, now pacing furiously around his office.

"I was his partner in the NYPD," Judy added.

"Oh, you were?"

"He was a great detective."

"Of course he was," said Batty. "Brilliant kid, just brilliant."

"Mr. Batty, we... um... how do I say this? Is there anyone who would have wanted to hurt Ethan Gregory?"

Charlotte looked at Judy before adding, "Or my dad?"

"Hurt them? You think... Was Fred murdered, too?"

"We don't know, that's what we are trying to figure out."

"How can you not know?" Batty nearly screamed at Judy. "I'm sorry. Frederick was very dear to my heart. It's not often you come across such a child. Truly gifted."

"I understand," replied Judy.

"Three of my students in thirty years... unspeakable things happen to them."

"What do you mean three?" asked Charlotte.

"Viktor Kovachev. That happened back in my years as a principal... it was a long time ago."

"He died?"

"Probably..."

Judy and Charlotte looked at each other, confused.

"One day, after school, the boy never made it home. He... just never did. He was not at school either. Disappeared out of the blue. Nobody ever found him. Don't know where he went. We looked in the school, in the woods, all over town. We looked everywhere for days! He had just vanished, probably under our care, and there was nothing we could tell his parents. He was maybe fifteen or sixteen when we last saw him."

Judy looked at Charlotte again, disconcerted, then turned back to Batty. "And they were all in the same grade?"

"Horrible, right?" Batty nodded. "Anyway, that's another story. But to answer your question, I don't know. I'm not sure anyone would hurt Fred or Ethan, but with what you've told me, I can't be a hundred percent sure. Maybe there was something behind the scenes I didn't see. I was not in class with them, you see."

"Would Reed be the type?" asked Judy.

"Reed..." Batty shook his head. "I don't know. Maybe. If Frederick and Ethan offended him in any way, I guess... I don't want to assume here."

"Well, thank you, you've been very helpful, sir," replied Judy.

"Yes," said Charlotte.

"Please, find whoever did this. This is bloody awful!"

Charlotte saw Judy nod at Batty. The retired woman shook his hand and prepared to walk out the door. Then Batty came over to Charlotte and embraced her.

"I am so sorry," he said, with tears in his eyes.

Charlotte thanked him and said goodbye. She joined Judy and they walked out of the room, leaving the Batty manor the way they'd come in. Charlotte's heart was filled with both sadness and anger. What did this all mean? Who was this Reed character? She wanted to meet him and tell him what she thought. She needed to!

CHAPTER TWENTY-ONE:

DOWN TIME

Charlotte helped Judy find the nearest motel through an internet search on her phone. It was the only motel in the area, really. Judy wanted to go to a Sheraton or a Hilton and spend even more of her pension funds, but there wasn't anything like that in this town.

The old but clean and, thankfully, pet-friendly motel was positioned at the exit from the town. They arrived at the building, walked up to the desk clerk, and asked for a good room. Judy asked Charlotte if she wanted a separate room, but she just shrugged. Either was fine, apparently. They got a room together for a decent price and went straight up with their small bags. Judy carried Rush in her arms like a baby, to prevent him from licking every one of the motel's guests as they passed through the hallways and up the stairs to get to the second floor. At four years old, he had lost none of his excitable puppy energy.

When they finally arrived inside the room, Charlotte sat on a bed as Judy explored the room and poured Rush some water in his tiny bowl.

They then discussed what they had heard at Batty's house and concluded that they must try to find Reed tomorrow. Apparently, he was not a man who was in hiding in this town. He seemed, in fact, to be very present, and even perhaps feared. Judy could see that Reed might have hated Fred for being a cop, but why kill him? Had Fred threatened to compromise his presumed criminal activity? And why show up at the funeral and make a show? And why kill Gregory? Was the actor too arrogant, and had he been rude to Reed? Had Reed been jealous of his success? Some details were obviously still missing here, and Judy needed to know more about the situation. And until she had actual proof of something, she could only make assumptions, like she was doing at the moment.

Charlotte took a shower and Judy then proposed they go grab a bite. They went to the restaurant inside the motel, and the food was pretty awful. Judy barely found anything vegan on the menu, and she thought Charlotte might spit out her chicken as she struggled through a nasty burrito. They shared a good laugh about it, however, then they went back up to the room and lay in their beds. Judy quickly turned off her light, while Charlotte watched a bit of crappy television. Judy knew she would not fall asleep until the TV was off, so she eventually joined Charlotte and they watched some reality television together. When a commercial came on, Charlotte finally turned off her light. Suddenly, she was the one who was exhausted. Judy looked at her for a while and saw the sadness in her face. It was hard for her. Well, it was hard for both of them.

Again, thoughts began flowing in Judy's head. The ex-detective began debating if she should call Captain Murphy in New York and tell him what the two had learned about Ethan Gregory and Fred's relationship, as well as everything else. Charlotte would probably not like that. Judy didn't want to betray her trust. She could wait a little longer, at least until they got more information. The NYPD would have to know soon enough, especially if Judy could save an innocent man from going to prison. She needed to talk to Sebastian Reed first and see what kind of man he was and what he had to say about the deaths of his "friends." If she felt he had anything to do with their demise, she would take action.

Perhaps sleep would help. Judy let herself fall onto the pillow a short while after, and the two did not wake up until daylight hit the windows.

Charlotte was still asleep when Judy woke up early. She waited a moment, staring at the seemingly lifeless body in the bed next to hers. She decided to go for a run.

Judy ran through the town, exploring every inch of it. No one seemed to be up, the whole place was totally deserted. It was nice—she liked being up before everyone else. Judy could feel the cold of the night disappearing as the sun began to shine across the sky. Was it the sun that was so warm or was it her body getting hotter because of the jogging? She left Main Street and ran along a path through the woods until she reached a river. She sat there peacefully for a while. It was so beautiful there. After a few minutes, Judy stood back up and ran a bit more through the woods.

When she paced back to where she thought she'd come from, she got a bit lost, but she finally found her way back to Main Street and ran until she reached the motel. Charlotte was awake by now, but still lying in bed.

"I was starting to wonder," she said. "Maybe you'd left me and were working this case without me."

"Haha, no... and there is no case yet. But yeah, I wouldn't do that. I promise," Judy replied. "Otherwise, you would already be back in New York, and I would have made sure you stayed there."

"Sure!" Charlotte laughed it off.

"Just went out to clear my head. It's beautiful out there, great run."

Charlotte smiled and got up. She put on some clothes and makeup while Judy took a shower. When they were both ready, the two finally left Rush in the room with some toys and water and returned to Granger's for breakfast. They agreed they needed to get good food after the horrors of the previous night.

Charlotte ordered pancakes with maple syrup, which made Judy extremely jealous, because (a) she now wanted some and (b) Stew said they were vegan! *Damn it.* She wished she had ordered them. Instead, the retired detective had some oatmeal with fruit and a coconut milk latte.

As the two ate, Charlotte's phone kept ringing. Judy sipped her coffee as Charlotte kept dismissing them and then pushing her phone back in her purse. After the fourth ring, Judy finally asked, "Don't like talking on the phone, do you?"

Charlotte gave her a look, recalling that she had not answered Judy's calls either.

"Who's your secret admirer this time?"

"Brian..." Charlotte sighed.

"He's worried about you," Judy said.

"Yeah..."

"You should pick up."

"I don't think so, not now," Charlotte said.

"You stole his car..."

"I didn't steal it!" Charlotte exclaimed. "Okay... I borrowed it for a little while. He doesn't mind."

Judy frowned at her.

"Arrest me, all right?" the redhead grunted. "Go ahead, Hunter!"

But Judy relaxed her posture. *Okay. Let her be.*

There was a beat before Charlotte added more to the topic.

"We fought a little before I decided to leave for here. I asked him to look into the note with me, but he didn't want to help. I think, like everybody else, he thought I was crazy. So I did it on my own. I left and now I'm here." Charlotte let out a breath, frustrated. "I don't think anyone really thinks I have a brain, but sometimes I can see things that other people can't!"

"Maybe you're too smart for all of us." Judy replied. "It takes us time to get there with you."

Charlotte shook her head. "Anyway, here we are... maybe it's better this way. I don't have to worry about him pulling me down and stopping me."

"He seems like a good soul. You should still reassure him..." Judy began, and then stopped when she saw the angry look on Charlotte's face. "Or don't. Hey, do whatever you want."

Charlotte nodded but did not pick up her phone again. After a moment Stew walked over to their table and eyed Charlotte.

"More coffee?" he asked.

"Sure." She smiled at him and then touched his hand. "The food is really wonderful."

"Thank you!" Stew said gently. "I don't make it, but the chef will appreciate it."

Charlotte bit her lip. Her hand stayed on his for a moment, then Stew moved away and poured more coffee into Judy's cup.

"Hey Stew," said Judy. "Do you mind if I ask you something?"

Charlotte gave Judy that look of *What are you about to say?*

"What's up?" said Stew.

"Are you—what do you know about Sebastian Reed?"

Stew frowned, almost choking. He got rigid, dead cold, like a doorknob in a Canadian winter. Like everybody around this town when they spoke about Reed or heard his name.

"Well, that's quite the question... He is very well known around here."

"Yeah, we heard," replied Charlotte.

"What do you think of him?" Judy asked.

Stew did not seem to know how to answer that question.

"Does he ever come here?" said Judy.

"Hell no," said Stew.

"So where does he go for fun times?" Judy questioned, smiling.

"Hmm... I guess he hangs out with all the other Skullheads."

"The what?" Charlotte asked.

"His crew? That's what they call themselves?" Judy asked.

Stew nodded.

"Skullhead?" questioned Charlotte. "Like the Nazi band in the 1980s?"

Stew started to chuckle. "I thought I was the only one who caught that... history buff, you see."

Charlotte smiled. "So, are they singers? Nazis? Both?"

The history buff looked at her laughing again. They then kept looking at each other. Judy let this go on for a moment, but then she decided to cough.

Charlotte came out of her trance. "Probably just boys trying to appear tough..." she suggested.

Stew nodded again. Judy took a sip of her coffee.

"And where do these Skullheads hang out on your typical sunny day?" the retired detective asked.

That made Stew laugh again, and he said, "That would be two blocks from here, at the Rhode House bar."

"Think he'll be there for lunch?"

"Probably. It's Saturday, they like to party early," Stew added.

"Perfect! We like to party too!" Judy said.

Stew looked from Charlotte to Judy, confused.

"My dear Stewart, we'll take the bill now!" exclaimed Judy. "We'll explore the city for a bit and then head over to Rhodes to meet Reed when he arrives. Is it far?"

"Not really. Just two blocks, like I said," replied Stew.

"Perfect, we'll be on our way," said Judy.

"Wait—what?" Stew coughed.

"We need to ask him a few questions, too," said Judy. "Sound like a plan, Charlotte?"

Charlotte remained as silent as Stew in that moment. The two women paid the bill and headed out of Granger's to take a walk about the town.

CHAPTER TWENTY-TWO:

LEADER OF THE PACK

The Rhode House bar was only five minutes away from Granger's. The duo had two hours free to walk through Main Street, exploring the small shops and boutiques. Charlotte was bewildered and stressed about the whole situation. She wanted to talk to Reed, of course. But he was the leader of a biker club and what she had heard from Willis Batty and Fiona Black about the man was, without question, intimidating. Judy had had such a strong impulse at the restaurant about needing to talk to him—she didn't seem intimidated whatsoever.

"You wanted to investigate, right?" Judy asked.

Yeah, but I didn't know things would move this fast, thought Charlotte.

"Cops need two things," her father had always said, not knowing she was listening intently. "They need balls and brains." A lack of brains wasn't something she was afraid of here. Plus, Judy had done much of the thinking for her and she clearly had balls. So now it was time for Charlotte to test herself and see if she could grow a pair as well.

Charlotte wondered what she would say to this thug when she saw him. As much as she wanted to talk to him and ask him about her dad, she also feared she might be about to enter a war zone. She wondered how he was going to respond. She also hoped Judy was carrying a gun.

They arrived at the bar five minutes before twelve and sat on a bench, waiting. The bikers were not on time.

"So, what do you want to ask him?"

Charlotte shrugged. "I don't know. 'Did you kill my dad?'"

"How about something lighter first," Judy suggested.

"Like what?"

"I don't know... like what was his favorite subject in school?" Judy proposed, jokingly.

Charlotte chuckled nervously. She wasn't taking this so lightly anymore. She kept having the urge to walk away and never come back. She was becoming aware of the real world and the real consequences in it. She had never done anything like this before. But she would have to get used to this sort of situation if she was ever going to become a detective.

Grow balls, Charlotte, c'mon.

Might as well stay in your basement if you don't want to face danger, Charlotte.

It was part of the job. She had Judy. Judy had done this a million times. Judy had her back. It was going to be fine!

STOP FREAKING OUT! C'mon, Charlotte, you're a lot stronger and a lot braver than that. Shake him. Beat him if you need to. You're probably a lot more skilled than him—all them, really—in combat. You got this, so just breathe!

The two women had a few minutes of silence before they began hearing some noises in the background—aggressive engines shattering the wind. The bikes were on their way, and Charlotte could tell they were coming at high speed. The two women were still not able to see the vehicles, but they sounded like they must be very close. The wait lasted around thirty seconds before they finally saw emblazoned leather jackets roaring in.

Charlotte saw a sea of men rolling in on their motorcycles, looking like they were having an enormous amount of fun. Some of them were smoking. There were puffy clouds hanging out behind some of the bikes. The redhead looked for Nazi tattoos, but she couldn't see any. But these fellas weren't short of tattoos. They had many. Too many. One guy had his whole face covered with them. None of them were wearing helmets or any kind of protection, they were just hanging freely in the sun. It was as if they were at the beach, having a party and drinking beer, but on bikes. The men did not seem to care about any potential dangers of bodily injury, most of them driving with one hand. They were all shouting, looking back and front and sideways. And whichever way they were looking, they were looking tough.

The figures on the bikes now became distinguishable, and Charlotte took in the man at the front: long Tarzan-style salt-and-pepper hair, scars on his cheeks, and a cold and floppy smirk. It was the guy they'd seen at her father's funeral. He was wearing black sunglasses this time.

Was this Reed?

His crowd of men, boys really, kept following him until they all reached the bar. Then, Charlotte saw Judy stand up from the bench, looking fearless, and walk towards the parking lot.

Charlotte stood up and joined her. Judy stopped when she was close to the running engines. The motorcycle crowd kept chatting and entertaining each other for a good minute before they even noticed Judy and Charlotte. It was the silvery-haired man who finally turned his head around and glared at the women, first analyzing them, then smiling, and finally lifting his hand to silence his crew.

He stepped off his motorcycle and started walking towards the two ladies, more specifically Charlotte, staring at her as he approached. Charlotte didn't feel herself moving, she was like a statue. Judy took the initiative to talk first, *thank God!*

"Are you Sebastian Reed?" Judy asked.

As soon as she'd asked the question, laughter echoed across the field. Reed lifted his hand once more and the crew went silent. They were like a bunch of musicians who followed the cues of their conductor. Tarzan Hair kept looking at Charlotte, breathing heavily at her, but walked towards Judy nonetheless. He finally turned his head to the retired woman and lifted his chin.

"Well, are you?" Judy asked, unimpressed.

"Yes, ma'am. Who's asking?" Tarzan gleefully replied.

"Judy Hunter. Nice to make your acquaintance," she said.

"My acquaintance?"

The crowd roared again. Sebastian Reed stopped them once more.

"I should be the lucky one," he replied. "What are you two fine ladies up to? Wanna hang out?"

"Sure..." Judy replied.

"Really?"

"Yeah, really," she replied.

Charlotte gave Judy a look.

"We think you're really handsome..." Judy added.

The bikers laughed again, and Reed let them.

"Why, thank you!" Reed said.

"However, we're not cheap."

Reed lifted his hand in the air one more time. "Not cheap? Ha! Expensive whores are not really what we usually look for. They usually want some bullshit... they're complicated. Protection, no BJ, no aggressive sex... I mean, it's such a pain dealing with 'em."

Charlotte was offended by every word he'd just said. She could feel her blood heating up, slowly returning to life.

"We're different," Judy added.

"Oh, really? Alrighty, then..." Reed said. "Well, tell us. Sell us."

Judy approached Reed and whispered in his ear. "You give us what we want, and you'll get everything you need and deserve," Judy said, adding a flirtatious smile.

Sebastian Reed glared at Judy then turned his head to his crew, in excitement. He grabbed Judy by the cheekbones with his right hand.

"Hey!" Charlotte shouted.

Sebastian turned his head to Charlotte. He smiled at her. Then Judy mirrored his expression in return, and the latter finally let go of her.

"So, what is it you want?"

"Information," Judy replied.

"What kind of information?" he said.

"She wants to know about size, boss," one biker shouted from the back.

The crew chuckled.

"Yeah, what are you packing, Sebastian?" asked Judy.

Reed was not smiling this time. He started to frown at Judy, becoming very uncomfortable.

"A gun? Multiple guns? Something to hurt people badly?"

"Kill them, even?" Charlotte added.

Reed looked at her again. He licked his lips and showed his white teeth. The crowd wasn't laughing anymore.

"Do you have a lot of enemies, Sebastian?" Judy continued.

Charlotte could see in Reed's face that he did not like being called by his first name.

"You look a little pale," Judy added.

"I don't know what you're saying, lady," he said.

Charlotte jumped in. "Are you confused? Maybe you didn't use the right words here, Judy. Why don't I ask your friends here, maybe they can tell me. Have you guys ever hurt anybody?"

A couple of crew members got off their bikes, looking threatened.

"I mean, maybe not even enemies. Perhaps your wife, your kids, maybe even some friends of yours..." the young woman continued.

Silence.

"Nothing? Okay, what about you, Reed? Anything come to mind now?"

"Is that chick for real?" one gang member asked.

"Oh yeah, I am for real. See? I can even pinch myself." Charlotte said, with great assurance. She was growing more and more confident by the second, almost feeling unstoppable.

"I think..." Reed finally stepped forward. "If I could give you some advice, Red, now would be—"

"Shhh... just answer the question, honey," Judy interjected.

"I don't think you should be asking things like this..."

"Only a guilty man would reply like that," Charlotte said.

He looked at her again, licking his lips. "Well..." Reed started.

"Did you like Ethan Gregory?" Judy suddenly asked.

Reed now froze. His bright-blue eyes stared at Judy for a long and uncomfortable while. Charlotte thought Reed wanted to break Judy's neck.

"Who?"

"Don't play this game, buddy. We're talking about a high school buddy here. Don't you have more respect for him?" Charlotte said.

"Hey, boss. Isn't Gregory the guy from the news?" a biker shouted.

Reed closed his eyes. He looked as if he wanted to stab someone. He lifted his hand and silence reigned again.

"Gregory and me knew each other, yes," he replied.

"It's 'I.' Gregory and I," Charlotte pointed out.

Judy looked to Charlotte and gave her an amused look.

"You just 'knew each other'?" Judy asked.

"Yeah," Reed said.

"What about Fred Gibbins? Did you just know him too?" Charlotte asked.

Reed's expression shifted. He shook his head.

"Is that a no?" Charlotte asked.

"Yes, I knew Fred Gibbins."

"Great!" Charlotte said. "We know you were all besties, Reed. We know that y'all played football together."

"Sure," Reed replied.

"What I don't know is why you're so nervous right now," Charlotte added.

"Nervous?"

"Do the names Fred Gibbins and Ethan Gregory make you nervous, Sebastian?" Judy asked.

Charlotte knew Judy loved saying the man's first name. *Sebastian.* Because God, did it irritate Reed. It was hilarious to observe.

"No," Reed insisted.

"Do you know that they both died this month?"

Reed nodded.

"What do you have to say about that?" she asked.

"Yeah, they're dead," Reed said. "And?"

"And?" Charlotte then blurted. "Doesn't it trouble you more than that?"

"I'm grieving as much as everybody else," he said.

"Right." Charlotte sighed. "Do you know how they died?"

Reed shrugged again.

"One was murdered with a sword, the other with a rope," Charlotte clarified.

Reed didn't say anything.

"Can you guess which one was murdered with a rope?" Charlotte asked.

Reed stayed silent once more, until finally, "I don't know."

"It was Fred, he was the one." Charlotte said.

No answer again.

"Where were you at the time of Gregory's death?" Judy inquired.

"I was right here."

Charlotte didn't like that answer. "Here where?"

"Here! I am always here. He died in the city, right? I hate New York City. It's nasty and people are pretentious and rude. Why would I even go there?"

"To kill," Charlotte reinforced.

Judy looked at Charlotte then turned to Reed again. "Do you have any idea who could have done it?"

"Nope," Reed said, shrugging. He suddenly looked bored.

"What about Fred?" Charlotte asked.

Reed lifted his head to look at Charlotte, clearly confused.

"Did you do it? Did you kill him? Tell me!" shouted Charlotte.

Reed was taken aback. He didn't look afraid, just stunned.

"Answer me, goddamn it! Did you kill my father?" Charlotte shouted at him.

Then Reed smiled.

That set Charlotte off. She started pushing him, violently. When he tried to touch her, she punched him in the chest and kicked the back of his left knee. Reed fell and still she went for him, pushing him and kicking him on the ground. Even so, the gang leader was smiling throughout, as though they were kids playing a game.

"Charlotte!" Judy shouted.

"Did you kill him? Did he refuse to be one of your slaves? Was he not obeying your hand signal anymore? Did he want to put you in jail? Answer me!"

Judy pulled her back, steering her away from Reed. The gang leader was now laughing heartily.

"Your father? Fred Gibbins was your daddy? Ha ha!" he exclaimed.

"Yeah, he was."

"Awesome," Reed said. "Pretty girl! He must have been proud."

"You monster, I swear, if you touched him—"

Charlotte shrugged Judy off and went for Reed again. Reed smiled, made a sudden move and somehow got hold of her and threw her to the ground. Then Tarzan got on top of her, his lips curled wild and mad. His eyes were fixed on her, savagely.

"I didn't, sweetheart!"

There was a beat. Reed kept looking at Charlotte with his predatory eyes. He finally got back up and went back to his bike. His crew followed him. He started his engine.

"In case you haven't heard, your daddy killed himself!" Reed shouted through the noise.

Reed took his eyes off the women and followed his crew. The Skullheads drove off to the right side of the bar and parked their motorcycles there. Charlotte wanted to go after them, but she felt Judy holding her back, telling her for God's sake to just calm down.

CHAPTER TWENTY-THREE:

AUTOPSY

Against Charlotte's pleas, Judy stepped out onto the balcony of the motel and was about to call the NYPD. Captain Murphy needed to send actual working detectives to investigate this case, detached ones, with an objective point of view. Charlotte and Judy could no longer do this on their own.

"I wish you would have just shot at him," Charlotte had said on their way back from Rhode House. "That would have made him talk."

"I am not a cop anymore, Charlotte, and even if I was, that would have been against the law. I had no probable cause. You need to control yourself!" Judy had replied.

"I need to control myself? He grabbed you by the *face*, like... an insect."

"You should have stayed back!" Judy insisted angrily.

"You're the one who took me there in the first place," the redhead shouted back at her.

"Yeah. What the hell was I thinking? Your father would be ashamed of me for letting you near that man."

Charlotte shook her head. "I know that bastard did it, I know he did."

"We don't have enough to call Reed a murderer, Charlotte!" Judy added. "We should have never started this in the first place. I knew it was a bad idea. What the hell was I—"

Judy stopped herself, took a breath then continued, "Okay, I'll just give the information to the NYPD and they can figure out where to go from there."

"They're not going to do anything!" Charlotte was almost yelling. With difficulty, she lowered her voice. "They think my dad hanged himself like everybody else does. There is no case there for them. And like you said, they prefer arresting an innocent man because of his cultural background than investigating and finding actual evidence! They don't care!"

Judy stopped moving and stood on the balcony in silence.

"What about the others? My father's other friends. We still have them to interview. Maybe they can tell us something. Maybe—"

"We don't even know for sure that he didn't take his own life, Charlotte!" the retired woman blurted out.

Charlotte looked at her, bewildered. "Wow..."

There was a long silence.

"And Gregory?" Charlotte asked.

Judy took a moment. "We've done enough," she said finally.

Charlotte looked at her, truly disappointed.

Judy looked down. She knew this whole thing had been a bad idea.

She took a breath.

Judy didn't know what to do or what to believe. Part of her wanted to think she had done enough, while another part of her—she couldn't lie to herself—was intrigued by the mystery. The retired woman wanted to believe Fred hadn't killed himself, she desperately wanted to believe it, but there was no concrete evidence to show he hadn't.

She picked up her phone and thought about calling Captain Murphy and telling him everything. Then she felt guilt-ridden. She felt like a kid about to tell her dad that she had messed up. What would he say? Would he be angry? Or would he just be disappointed in her?

Then she just did it. She composed the number and it rang. Oh god.

"Hunter!"

"Hello!" a voice said.

"Captain?" said Judy.

"No Captain aboard this ship, ma'am!" the voice replied. "Just a kind and loving cruising officer. Not officer really. What am I saying? Sorry! How can I help you, ma'am?"

"Price?" Judy then said.

It was not Murphy but none other than the medical examiner, Vincent Price.

"That's me! Do we know each other?" asked Price.

"Yes, we do! It's Judy, Price!"

"Judy? Oh, Detective Hunter? Is that really you? I'm sorry I didn't recognize your voice. How are ya?"

"I'm good. Do you think I could speak to Captain Murphy by any chance?" Judy then said.

"No can do!"

"What?"

"He's not here at the moment, I'm afraid," said Price. "Can I take a message?"

"Where is he?"

"He's, hmm... Where is he again... Oh yes! His schedule says here that he is with the Commissioner and Eddie White."

"Why?" Judy asked.

"Commissioner Crowley wanted to have dinner with them to congratulate Murphy and White on solving the Ethan Gregory case."

"Right..." responded Judy.

Solving. Big word.

"Yeah, now he's on to the bride-killer case." Price said. "White's confident he will solve it. The Commissioner wants to hear all about that too. Happy as a puppy."

God.

"All right, then..." She was about to hang up.

"You sure I can't take a message?" said Price.

"No. That's all right. Ask him to call me back, though," Judy said.

"Sure thing," said Price.

Judy took a beat before giving up on the call, and she suddenly thought of something. "Hey Price?"

"Why are you in Captain Murphy's office?"

"Um," he hesitated. Judy had caught him.

"So?" she insisted.

"Oh, I wasn't doing anything bad, Mrs. Hunter... I was just..."

"You what?"

"I was just putting Fred Gibbins' autopsy report on the Captain's desk."

Fred's autopsy report? Judy paused herself for a second. It still was hitting her like a brick. That Fred was dead. Then, she wondered:

"Price?"

"Yes, Detective!"

"Is there anything you can tell me about Fred's autopsy?"

"Anything I can tell you?" Price mumbled, shyly.

"Yeah..."

"Well, what do you want to know?"

"This might be a weird question to ask, but was anything unusual discovered in the autopsy? Or was it definitely a suicide?"

"Looks like a pretty typical suicide," Price said.

Judy closed her eyes and heard herself sigh. But Price wasn't finished, "Although there was the brain..."

"The brain? Yes?"

"There was a lot of internal bleeding in there."

"So?"

"Well, I don't know if he hurt his head on his way to... you know... umm... the rope, but..."

"You think the bleeding was caused by him hurting his head?"

"That's usually what happens when you do so, yes. He suffered a severe concussion," Price said.

"What did Murphy say about that?" Judy asked.

"I told him about it—it's in the report. Didn't seem to care much about it, though. I don't blame him. Fred was really drunk. A lot of alcohol in his system..."

"I see." The retired detective took a breath. She had one more thing on her mind. "Could someone else have done it?"

"Excuse me?"

"Is it possible someone hit him?" she clarified.

"I mean... I don't see why that..."

"Could someone else have done it to him?"

Price didn't answer right away.

Judy pressed him, "Price!"

"Yes... that's possible, yes. But I am not sure why you would think that, Detective."

If someone did hit Fred in the head to knock him unconscious, then that same someone could have put a rope around her old partner's neck to make it look like a suicide.

A part of Judy wanted to run to Charlotte and tell her what she had just learned from Price, but she had to stop herself. Judy stayed on the balcony for a while, and looked at the radiant blue sky, thinking it all over. She didn't want another wild eruption coming from Charlotte right now. But it wasn't only Charlotte; Judy didn't want to act on impulse either. They both had to keep themselves from imagining things that weren't necessarily real, believing in them and then acting upon them. They were both in mourning, and it was affecting their bodies and souls, and maybe their judgments.

CHAPTER TWENTY-FOUR:

NIGHT OUT

Charlotte glared at Judy as she was on the balcony finishing up her stupid call, and then she saw her hang up. Judy stayed out there for a while after that. Charlotte couldn't see her expression as she now had her back turned to her. Finally, Judy moved farther away along the balcony, and disappeared. Charlotte stood up, went to the window, and saw Judy walking across the parking lot and onto the street with Rush, until they faded from view.

Charlotte stayed in the room for the afternoon and watched TV. Judy didn't come back to talk to her, and Charlotte was sure not going to go after her. She didn't want to think about anything anymore, she just wanted to relax and laugh at some mindless show. It was hard not to think, so she finally muted the sound of the TV, covered herself with the sheets, sank into the depths of the bed, and made herself forget about cverything.

She was awakened by a blaring ring resonating in her left ear. Charlotte sighed and grunted. Couldn't she have peace for one moment? She turned to the bedside table and saw a bright light beaming there. She picked up her phone and saw a picture of herself and Brian hugging. The caller ID said "Brian." *He's calling again! Ugh!*

Furious, she dragged the slider to the right as fast as she could and brought the phone to her ear.

"What?" she almost shouted.

"Charlotte?" Brian said in a gentle but upbeat voice.

"What do you want?"

"Where are you?"

"In bed, doing a gang bang. You're kinda disturbing. Can I hang up now?"

"Charlotte... I only want to— When are you coming home?"

"I'm busy, Brian!" she insisted.

"Are you all right?... Is everything okay?"

"Yeah... Your car is fine too. Okay? Bye."

But she didn't hang up.

There was a moment of silence before he said, "Are you watching the game?"

"No!" she grunted.

"It's the Knicks versus the Cavaliers! Guess which team is winning?"

Charlotte didn't say anything, not giving a care in the world.

"Your favorite team might be going to the playoffs this year."

"Okay, I'm gonna get off now."

"Charlotte, are you safe? Did Judy—"

"Oh, she found me all right."

"And what happened?"

"I sent her on her way. I'll do this on my own since nobody really cares about it except me."

"Charlotte, I didn't say— I—"

"All right."

"Did you find anything?" he said after a moment.

"Oh, is that you caring now?" she replied.

"Charlotte, please."

"You didn't believe me then, why would you believe now?"

"I—I think..." he said, and there was a beat. "I'm sorry, Charlotte! I do believe you. I'm sorry you felt that way. I just didn't want to..."

"You just didn't want to what, Brian?"

"Where are you right now? What have you found?"

Now he cares?

She didn't answer him.

"I miss you," he added.

She sighed and waited. She then heard a sound from Brian's end, a loud banging, and then something like wind. Some sort of machine.

"Are you in a car right now? I hear an engine running," Charlotte said.

"What?"

"Are you in a car?" she said again.

"No," he firmly replied.

Charlotte heard another noise, the sounds of wind again. "You are not coming to find me, are you? Brian, I don't need your help, I swear, if you..."

There was another moment of silence. Then she could swear she heard another voice.

"What was that?" she asked.

"Huh? Oh, nothing."

"You're not the one having a gang bang, are you?" she asked nervously.

"What? No. No, it was just, uh... it was—it was nothing."

Another bang.

"What are you up to?" she said.

There was no answer, just dead silence from his end.

"Brian?"

"I'm just sitting on the couch, watching the game."

"Right." That was a lie. "Don't come and find me, Brian, you don't want that. Stay away."

"I just want to know if you're all right, sweetheart."

"I'm fine," Charlotte said firmly. "You don't have to check up on me."

"Did you find anything?" he repeated. "Did your father really kill himself or not?"

What the fuck? Charlotte thought of Judy, of this horrible question he had just asked her. The redhead hung up and threw her phone at the end of the bed, screaming inside. She pulled the bedcovers back over her and sank into the bed again. She waited a moment.

She pushed back the covers and screamed. She leapt up and paced around the room. She looked out the windows, went to the bathroom and came back into the main room again. She stood in place for a moment, holding her head in her hands. She sighed.

Charlotte opened the closet. She glared at her clothes and flicked through them, finally picking a bright-yellow dress off a hanger. Filled with excitement, she ran to the bathroom. She put on the dress and stared at herself in the mirror. Then she smiled and started fixing her makeup.

The elegant-looking redhead walked down Main Street in her golden dress until she reached a bar called The Derbie. From the looks of the outside, Charlotte didn't expect it would be filled with drunks or biker gangs. In fact, it looked rather upscale—more than someone living on a tight budget could afford, but she didn't care. She just wanted to relax and have a few drinks, maybe get offered a few. The bar wasn't exactly packed, but there were a few people there. It wouldn't take long to fill up, it was Saturday night.

Charlotte walked in and immediately caught the eye of a few men. She didn't smile back but carried herself with confidence and class. She wanted to get more than noticed. She sat on a stool and asked the barmaid for some whisky. The barmaid gave Charlotte a look, then nodded. No, she wasn't into girly drinks at all. She liked what she liked, and that included good sharp whisky.

"Fancy seeing you here," said a masculine voice behind her.

Charlotte sighed. This was already looking like a bad idea. Damn it. She didn't turn around, just let things unfold as they would. She wanted to see how the man would proceed.

"Where's your friend?" the man continued.

Charlotte slowly turned her head and saw a familiar face. It was Stew. He had a denim shirt on. He looked good! He even had his hair up. Hot. Charlotte smiled at him.

"You!"

"Yes, me! Were you expecting someone else?" Stew asked.

Charlotte gave a quick look at the guys at the back, and Stew turned and looked at who she was looking at.

"Ah! Well, if you're expecting those guys to come here and buy you a drink, you'll wait for hours."

"Why is that?"

"For one, nobody goes up to people anymore to ask them out. Second, they're not exactly into women."

"Wow, really?" Charlotte chuckled. *What a day!*

She looked at the guys for another moment, then turned her gaze back to Stew. Her smile faded a little.

"Why are you here?" she said. "To find a date?"

"No, no," he replied, almost reassuringly. "I mean, I am not opposed to that... I'm pretty open... but I used to work here."

"Oh, ha ha!"

"I get discounts and I'm still friends with a lot of the bar staff, so... it's a nice spot, I like the vibe."

"Yeah, it is," she said.

He stared in her eyes. There was a short silence, and then, "So, where's your friend?"

"Just left her at the hotel. Partying is not really her style."

"I thought she said it was earlier," Stew said, laughing.

"Right, right. That was... something," Charlotte replied, taking a sip of her whisky.

"You talked to him?"

"Who?"

"Sebastian Reed."

Charlotte nodded.

"I get it. He's not your gentle joe."

"You could say that, yeah..."

"It's more of a facade than anything else, though. I think he just knows that people are afraid of bikers and he takes advantage of that."

"So, you think he's a sweet soul inside, huh?" Charlotte questioned, amused.

The night was turning good after all. He was sweet.

"I wouldn't say that. I wouldn't be friends with the guy," Stew laughed.

"Does he scare you?" Charlotte asked.

"I don't think so..."

"Playing the tough card, huh, Stewart?"

He laughed. "Is that whisky?"

Charlotte brought the glass up to his nose.

"It is!" he concluded.

"Want one?" Charlotte said.

"I mean, I don't want to bother you any longer, you seemed to be busy with the background crowd here."

Charlotte shook her head. "One for him, please!" she said to the barmaid.

The barmaid got a glass and brought over a bottle of whisky to show it to Stew.

"This is strong alcohol!" the barmaid exclaimed. "Are you sure about this, Stew?"

"Yeah, yeah," Stew replied.

The barmaid wouldn't pour, just kept looking at Stew as if to say, *Are you sure you can handle this?*

"Okay, just pour it, Tania."

Charlotte chuckled. Tania, the barmaid, finally poured into the glass. She shrugged.

"Watch over him," she told Charlotte.

"I will!" the redhead laughed again.

"Okay, okay. Just go!" Stew said to Tania.

Tania smirked at Charlotte before going back to her other customers. Stew tasted the whisky and made a funny face.

"Don't like it?"

"No, no, I do."

"What do you usually have?"

"A beer or two."

They both laughed, and then Charlotte suggested they go sit in a booth.

CHAPTER TWENTY-FIVE:

MADELAINE

Judy was feeding Rush his dinner when the sirens passed by the motel. She had wondered where Charlotte had gone. The redhead had left her clothes all over the floor and Judy saw an opened makeup bag filled with eye liner and concealer in the bathroom. She had not taken her phone, however—it was charging on the sink—so Judy could not call her and find out what she was up to. A night out, apparently that's what she was up to.

Rush was wagging his tail as he drank water. He'd had a good long walk. It had certainly helped Judy clear her mind a little. She knew what she wanted to do now, or at least she thought she did. She was going to inform Captain Murphy and, yes, that Eddie White character about everything she had learned and let them do what they would with the information. It was the right thing to do. She hoped they would also do the right thing and investigate. They had surely caught the wrong man for Ethan Gregory's murder, and hopefully they would soon realize that. She was not a detective anymore, so as much as she was free to speak her mind, she didn't have any power when it came to police investigations in New York City. Maybe Gregory's murder was related to Fred's death and maybe it was not, but either way, all she could do was give them the information and see what they came up with.

A call erupted from her phone, a number she did not recognize, but by the 514 area code she knew the call was coming from Montreal, Canada. It was Madelaine. Judy sighed, and picked up.

"Hello."

"Judy? Is that you?"

"Yes, yes. It's me."

"Oh good, good. It's Madelaine Gib— Bélanger. How's it going?"

"Madelaine!" she said, acting surprised. "I'm fine, thanks. How about you?"

"Not very well, Judy! It's Charlotte, she's worrying me. She's not returning any of my calls. And then this morning I call her at Brian's apartment and it's not her, it's Brian, and he says she's not available. Not available to talk to her mother, I say? What the hell? She's always available to talk to me! I press him and he says she's not home. I asked him where she went, and he says he can't tell me. I ask why and he gives me an answer that doesn't make any sense. I know he's lying. I can sense when people are lying. I press even more, and he says he can't tell me because Charlotte told him not to and I would probably go mad if I knew. And then I'm like, what the hell are you saying I'll go mad? He doesn't say any more, but I know it's something bad."

Madelaine suddenly stopped talking. Judy didn't know if it was her turn to speak or not, and then she heard what she thought was crying. Charlotte's mother continued,

"Look, I'm not okay with this. I know Charlotte, and this whole thing has been driving her nuts these past few days. I just want to know she's put herself into trouble."

"I understand," Judy answered.

"God, should I come down there?"

"No, no, Madelaine, it's fine. The truth is, she's with me."

Judy closed her eyes. She had to say something to reassure Madelaine.

"With you?"

"Yes... she... she's okay, Madelaine. Perfectly fine."

"What is she doing?"

"We're shopping," Judy said in a blatant lie.

"Shopping?... Downtown?"

"No, not downtown... Rockland," Judy blurted out, careful not to give too many details but not wanting to tell too many lies either.

"Rockland?" Madelaine questioned, sounding almost disgusted. "What the hell are you doing there?"

Judy took a moment to respond. "We're looking around..."

"It's not about Fred, is it? Good God. She's been crazy about the whole thing—"

"No, she just wanted to spend some time in her father's home town, that's all. She asked me if I wanted to come with her, since I was so close to Fred, and I said yes. Look, Madelaine, she's okay. You don't have to worry about anything. Really. We're fine."

Judy knew that Madelaine was okay with Charlotte wanting to become a cop, but no parent wanted to hear of their child putting themselves in danger.

"Okay, okay. Well, it's certainly good that you're with her. I was really worried, you know? It's good, it's very good. She needs a friend these days—we all do. Fred being gone and all, it's affecting all of us. It's changing our lives. I've been crying a lot, you know. I loved him. I really, really did... Crazy how tragedy makes you realize certain things, right? Oh, Jesus, here I go again. Patrice is so tired of hearing me talk about Fred. But he really was a great man."

"Yeah, he was," replied Judy.

"Anyways! I'm sure glad you two are all right. Is there anything... can I talk to her?"

"Umm..." Judy paused, trying to make up the most digestible excuse possible. "She's out, actually. Went for a run. And her phone is charging here."

"Went for a run? Really? Oh, wow! Gosh, she's getting back out there! I'm happy. Tell her to keep it up."

"I will."

"And tell her to call me when she has a chance, okay? Just when she has a chance. No pressure."

"All right," replied Judy.

Madelaine took a beat before adding, "Thank you, Judy. Really, thank you."

"No problem, Madelaine."

As soon as Charlotte's mother hung up, Judy felt a pain filling her neck and in her stomach. She didn't feel good at all about what she had just done. Lying to Madelaine was not the best idea. Who knew what Charlotte was up to? Maybe she really was in danger right now and Judy didn't know it. But Madelaine couldn't find out what was going on, that was for sure.

CHAPTER TWENTY-SIX:

THE THIRD MAN

Stew and Charlotte sat in the booth and drank for a while. Stew drank more slowly than Charlotte. The redhead would often turn her head and look around the bar, not really focusing on him. But after a while she began to relax and did take him in. And what she saw was pretty.

"What?" Stew wondered.

"It's funny to see you in this..."

"In what?"

"These clothes, without your cap on."

"Ha ha! Well, yeah. I don't spend my life in those clothes. I don't always work, you know."

"Don't you, though? You look like a guy who—"

"Who has no life? Yeah, thanks!" he laughed.

"No, I didn't mean that, I mean you seem to be a person who likes to work."

"I mean, I have a good job. I enjoy it. I like the people there, but I don't want to spend the rest of my life asking if someone wants a refill."

"Right," Charlotte said. "That's understandable. What do you want to do?"

"I'm saving for school right now. I want to go back and get my bachelor's in history."

"History... wow, right. History buff. Cool subject."

"Yeah."

"Lots of dates and names to remember," Charlotte said, discouraged.

Stew chuckled. "Yeah, I've always loved it, though, and I think I want to teach kids someday."

"A teacher, that's great! Much respect. Maybe you could give me a tour of the city sometime, tell me about the past."

Stew got excited. "I would love that, there's surprisingly much to tell about this town."

"Is there?" Charlotte asked skeptically.

"Oh, absolutely," Stew answered.

"You only have one street," Charlotte laughed.

It was almost the truth. It felt as if she had only been on Main Street since she arrived here. She hadn't seen much else.

Stew giggled at her joke. "No, really, I can show you so much. The Livingston's Manor, the railroad... The town was part of the Hardenburgh Patent! So interesting."

"I'm sure you can make the tour very long and interesting just for me," she replied.

Stew chuckled.

"No, I mean it, you seem very passionate!" Charlotte said. "It's great."

The man smiled. "What do you do?" he asked.

"Ah, me? That's a whole other affair!"

"Is it?"

"Yeah... Well, I just completed my bachelor's in chemistry."

"Oh, wow! Congratulations."

"Thanks."

"Where did you study?" he asked.

"Columbia!"

"Jesus!"

Stew high fived her. Charlotte stuck out her tongue.

"NYC. That's awesome."

"Yeah, well, I live there. So, it wasn't too much of a stretch."

"No way! That's awesome, I love the city. *That* I can tell you a lot about—it has great history," Stew said excitedly.

Charlotte agreed.

"That's why you two women didn't seem to be from around here..." Stew said, half to himself.

"What do we have to do to look like we're from around here?" Charlotte asked, drinking some more whisky.

"I don't know..." he said shyly.

"Maybe I should buy a leather jacket and a motorcycle," added Charlotte.

"Nope." Stew shook his head, laughing. "Nope."

Charlotte smiled.

"And what do you do now?" he continued. "You're going to go be a doctor or a scientist or something?"

Ah, the question! Charlotte thought.

"Nope..."

"What then?"

"I want to be police," she said.

"Police? Like a policewoman?"

"Sure," she laughed. "But more like a policewoman... detective."

His eyes went wide.

"No freaking way! A detective... Props to you. Detective Charlotte—what's your last name?"

"Gibbins," she answered.

"Detective Charlotte Gibbins, sounds great!" he exclaimed joyfully.

Charlotte smiled. Then she thought of what he had just said. *Detective Gibbins*... That used to be her father.

"Detective Gibbins, what do you think of this murder?"

She kept silent, still in her head. Stew studied her for a while, not saying anything.

"So... you have a boyfriend back in NYC?" he asked.

That took her out of it. Charlotte stared at Stew for a beat, not knowing how to proceed. She exhaled nervously and then they were cut off by blaring sirens. They turned and looked outside. They saw two police cars and an ambulance tailing each other, driving at high speed along Main Street.

Charlotte stood up almost instantly. She saw a crowd form outside. She glanced at Stew and then decided to go outside. Stew followed her and they both looked at the action on the street, the cop cars driving somewhere in a hurry.

This is too loud and too unusual for this small town, Charlotte thought. This wasn't New York City—people wouldn't even turn around if they heard a police siren back home. But they were startled here, and probably for good reason. This was almost certainly something more serious than a cat stuck in a tree.

"What is it? What's happening?" Stew asked.

Someone in the crowd turned to Stew and answered him. Charlotte heard the answer, "Apparently, something happened over at the docks."

"What?" Charlotte asked.

The man shook his head.

Charlotte asked Stew to take her to the docks, just a mile away. When they arrived, Charlotte saw dark-green water and dozens of boats, ranging from small rowboats to large yachts. On the nearby street, there were two cop cars, an ambulance, and a fire truck. The whole team united. Yellow tape was being placed around the scene.

Someone from the crowd shouted, "Isn't that Rick Carson's boat?"

Charlotte thought for a second, computing the name in her head. Rick Carson—she knew that name. Willis Batty and Fiona Black had both mentioned him. He had been friends with her father, and with Ethan Gregory.

CHAPTER TWENTY-SEVEN:

THE DOCKS

Just minutes after Madelaine's call had ended, Judy's phone started to ring again. The call came from an unknown number. She knew she had heard the voice before but could not figure out where. The voice then made itself known as Stew. Judy wondered how he had gotten her number and why he was calling. He proceeded to tell her that he was with Charlotte and that they were at some quay or docks. Then Judy heard Charlotte's voice hijacking the phone. The redhead urged her to come quickly to the docks at the end of town and said that something terrible had happened. Judy had to hold the phone a few inches away from her ear as Charlotte was almost screaming. The retired woman could have sworn she heard the words "murder" and "death" at least fifty times. She tried to make Charlotte calm down so she could hear her clearly, but it was no use. Judy finally decided to hang up and grab her coat, leave Rush inside the motel room, and head straight to the docks.

The retired detective arrived at the docks a little past seven thirty and, as she got out of the Lyft, immediately saw a large crowd surrounding the area. They were all trying to balance on their toes to get a glimpse of what was happening behind a yellow tape. Judy saw Charlotte and Stew rushing from the crowd, coming to her.

"What the hell happened?" asked Judy.

Charlotte looked odd and was breathing heavily. As for Stew, he looked red and unnerved.

"Rick Carson!" Charlotte answered. "He got him!"

"What?"

"He's dead," clarified Charlotte.

Judy stared into Charlotte's eyes and then wrenched her look away. She tried to look beyond the crowd and the yellow tape. Then she turned her gaze towards the police and the ambulance.

"I tried to talk to the Sheriff, but the officers wouldn't let me go to him. I told them I might know something about the murder. They said the Sheriff was busy inside the boat, but I could talk to him when he got out."

Judy stayed silent, observing the area.

"Judy!" Charlotte cried. "You know what this means, right? We were right all along. Something is happening here. Gregory, my dad... then this..."

Judy finally turned to Charlotte.

"Rick Carson was their friend. Batty said it. Even the new principal mentioned him."

"I know," Judy replied.

"So, what are we gonna do?" Charlotte asked desperately.

Judy stood for a moment, looking around. She thought about the whole business carefully, then took a long look at Charlotte before replying, "Nothing."

"Nothing? Are you mad? This confirms everything, our theory," Charlotte said as she stood there shaking, stressed and filled with adrenaline.

"I'll talk to the police, tell them what I know. Then I'll call New York and do the same." Judy said.

"What?"

"We've got a solid thing now, they'll believe it. They'll believe me."

"No! What about—"

"Charlotte, go back to the motel. I got this," Judy insisted.

"The hell you do! It was my thing, my discovery, my investigation. Ours. We should carry on with this thing."

"Charlotte!"

"Judy! I'm not going to let this go!"

"Yes, you are. Right now, you are."

"Why?"

Judy sighed, took a deep breath, then came out with it, "You've been drinking. I can smell it on you."

"And?"

"They're not going to take you seriously. You're agitated, out of breath. You can do whatever you want in the morning—go to the precinct, whatever—but right now, go rest."

"I'm doing this with you!"

"Charlotte, please. I will take care of it. I will tell them everything about your father and Gregory. They will know everything, I promise."

"But—"

"Stew, do you mind? Beverly Motel, room 212."

"Sure," he said, looking a little trapped.

Stew put a hand on Charlotte's shoulder, but she pushed it away forcefully, twisting his arm.

"You won't manhandle me, I'm staying here!"

Stew groaned in pain.

"Charlotte!" Judy shouted.

Charlotte held Stew's arm a little longer, twisting it even more. He groaned again. Then the redhead saw some people in the crowd looking at her, including some police officers. After a second she let go of Stew's arm and looked down, embarrassed.

A loud noise echoed through the crowd. The doors of a medium-sized boat opened wide. Charlotte turned her head to the crime scene, not caring about Judy or Stew anymore. Judy turned around as well and saw a middle-aged black man with a short white beard exiting the boat. He was wearing a uniform and had a badge on his chest. The Sheriff, Judy concluded. Then she saw a bunch of firemen and a few officers following him. Charlotte quickly stormed away from Judy and Stew, running straight for the exiting party.

"Charlotte!" Judy shouted again.

She stared at her, frozen for an instant, then went for her. She heard Charlotte scream at the Sheriff through the crowd, hysterically. Charlotte made her way through the people, who were looking at her curiously, and then walked up to the police officers standing beside the ambulance. The Sheriff stepped down off the quay and headed straight to the street. He finally looked at Charlotte, hearing her voice.

"Excuse me, sir. I need to talk to you!" she shouted.

The officers tried to keep her away for a bit, then the Sheriff crossed the yellow line and an officer went to him, mumbling something in his ear—probably explaining who that crazy shouting woman was and what she wanted. The Sheriff walked towards Charlotte. Judy finally reached them.

"Yes?" he said.

"I'm Charlotte Gibbins, sir."

"Yes, Ms. Gibbins. County Sheriff Newman Grant. What can I do for you?"

"I have something that I think is relevant to your case. I think this isn't some casual murder," she said.

"Murder? Who said anything about murder?" The Sheriff looked astounded.

Charlotte grew red. "Why? It isn't a murder?"

"Maybe..." the Sheriff said. "What is it to you? What can you tell me, young lady?"

"Well, sir, umm..." Charlotte began. "My detective friend and I have been investigating."

"Detective friend..." The Sheriff looked at Judy.

Judy smiled shyly.

"Who are you?" the Sheriff asked.

Charlotte turned, beaming at Judy. "NYPD," she announced joyfully.

Judy gave Charlotte a look.

"Really?" The Sheriff looked at her.

Judy finally stepped forward. Now she was the one feeling trapped. "Sorry, sir. Former detective of the NYPD, Midtown North Precinct."

"Midtown North Precinct?"

"Yes, I know," Judy said. "The precinct in the middle of Times Square. Very far away."

The Sheriff looked confused.

"Her name's Judy Hunter, Sheriff," Charlotte said.

"Judy Hunter?" he exclaimed.

"Yes, sir," Judy replied.

"Huh... I surely heard of you. Newman Grant. Nice to meet you." The Sheriff wiped his hand clean and put it out for Judy to shake. "You're famous, y'know. I've admired your work for a great many years. The Red Serpent case. That was you, right?" He kept smiling.

"You're not mistaken, yes," Judy said gratefully.

"Glad you put that psychopath away for good. What a terror! Should have gotten the death penalty if you ask me!"

Judy didn't know how to answer that.

"Well, excuse me, but why are you here?" he asked after a moment of silence.

"Just hanging around," Judy said half-jokingly.

"Really? I am sure glad you are, then. This is horrific, the way this guy died. Maybe you can see something I missed."

"How did he die, exactly?" Charlotte asked, pushing it.

Grant turned around and stepped back onto the quay. He raised the yellow tape and turned his head to Judy.

"Come this way," he uttered, his eyes cast down. He had a sad expression on his face.

Charlotte walked under the yellow tape and followed Grant down the path to the boat. Judy sighed and went under it as well. *Goddammit, Charlotte.*

CHAPTER TWENTY-EIGHT:

INSIDE THE BOAT

Charlotte kept walking alongside the County Sheriff, headed to Rick Carson's boat. After a beat, Charlotte asked, "Did you know the victim, sir?"

"I did, but casually," Grant said. "Small town, we know everyone. He was the nicest fellow. Always smiling and polite, always waving at us as he saw us on the streets. A model citizen, as far as I know."

"Right."

The little group kept walking and soon strolled onto the boat. It was a cramped old vessel with gray walls marred by oil stains and dirt. Judy and Charlotte followed the Sheriff down the stairs. He led them around a corner towards a door. It was closed, but it had a round window like a porthole so one could see inside.

The two ladies stood in silence, and the Sheriff turned to them.

"You might want to take a look inside," he said, pointing at the door.

Charlotte looked at Judy, and Judy looked back at her. They were both curious and hesitant. Nonetheless, they advanced to the door. Charlotte stood on tiptoes to look through the window. She saw three walls and a small, almost empty room in front of her. Then, there it was—a chair in the middle of the room and what looked to be a fat man sitting on it. His head hung down on his breast, with his wet, curled hair waltzing from it. By the looks of things, he was tied up with a white rope. Charlotte could smell the body even though the thick door was closed. She would have to get used to that, she told herself—the sight and smell of death. She put her finger on her nose.

Judy advanced, and Charlotte stepped aside. Judy looked intensely through the window at the body. The retired detective then peered down and stared for several seconds. What was she staring at? Charlotte went up to the window again. She looked around until she noticed something that looked like a fire extinguisher at the dead man's feet. That was no fire extinguisher, though; that much was clear to Charlotte. She could see the symbols on the canister.

"What the hell!" she exclaimed.

"I know, right?" replied Grant. "Funny business to me too."

"Can we go in?" asked Judy.

"No, you can't," replied Charlotte. "Not until it's safe."

"She's right. What's in there—it's highly toxic," the Sheriff added.

"It's gas," Charlotte clarified. "Why would anyone do something like that? Poor thing!"

Both Grant and Judy kept looking at Charlotte, who was peering at the canister. The redhead shook her head and gathered her thoughts.

"Horrible," she said. "Looks like carbon dioxide, carbon monoxide, maybe cyanide... Does he have burns?"

Judy and the Sheriff both looked at Charlotte with surprise. *Yeah, I didn't study science for nothing,* she thought.

"Oh, right, you don't know," she said, understanding their puzzlement. "You can't go inside. Cyanide burns your body from the inside... and out. Doesn't look like he has external burning, though—we would see."

"Yes," Grant finally replied after an awkward beat. "That's what the firemen said too, I think. Well they didn't know what *exactly* it was, but they were sure we couldn't go inside. So, nobody has gone in yet. We called in a team of people with protective jumpsuits that can go in, and they'll give us the go once it's cleared."

"Good," replied Charlotte. "Then you can call us in so we can figure out who and what did this."

"Sure..." Grant replied.

Judy gave Charlotte another look, then smiled slightly. "This is Rick Carson's boat, yes?"

"Yeah, it is. Not just his boat—he lives in here. He's a fisherman, you see. He loves the water and spends his days and nights out there in the wild."

"I see. That explains a lot."

Charlotte kept looking around the place. It was so dirty.

"Who found him?" asked Judy.

"A guy who was walking by, a local fellow. Works at the Wayborn Factory down the road. Was walking his dog, actually, and he said he heard some noise... some screams, and went in."

"What's this guy's name?"

"Wendell Pearson. Now, the interesting thing is that he claims he rushed to the boat. And that's when he saw the guy with the mask—"

"The guy with the mask?" asked Charlotte.

"He says he entered the boat and there was a dark figure in here... a man in a hoodie. The hoodie guy was hanging around in the boat and then got surprised by Mr. Pearson and automatically punched him in the face and rushed out. So, Wendell fell unconscious. When he woke up, he called us. He was hurt pretty bad, hurt his head on the wall when he fell."

"He saw the killer!" Charlotte exclaimed.

Judy was as shocked as Charlotte in that moment. The Sheriff nodded, then went on, "We got here at half past six. The door was closed and only Wendell was here. That's when my officers saw the tank. It was still spreading gas all across the room, and it continued for a good ten minutes after that! Nothing we could do, obviously. The guy was already doomed and most likely already dead."

Charlotte glared at Judy. The retired woman was thinking.

"Where is he now?" she asked. "This Wendell Pearson?"

"Hospital. Went there right away."

"Did he manage to see a face?"

"No, Pearson said the hoodie's face was fully covered with a gas mask."

"He was sure it was a man?" Judy asked.

"Yes, positive," answered Grant.

"Any other witnesses saw him?"

"Not that I know of as of now, but we're looking into it."

"All right," replied Judy. "Any next of kin we know of?"

The Sheriff scratched his head for a beat, then said, "Unsure... Carson had no kids that I know of... Maybe he had a girlfriend. I don't know. I'll check that out too."

Charlotte saw Judy pondering. Her detective mind was at work, and it was exciting to see. Charlotte could feel herself shaking a little, though; she wasn't used to all this. Interestingly, Judy was the calmest person in the room.

"What about Wendell? Did he see anything else? Eyes? How tall he was? Hair color? Was he white?"

"Maybe he did see something like that, but he didn't tell us. The medical team said he needed to get to the hospital quick. They were afraid of internal bleeding."

"Right, okay," Judy concluded. "Well, if it's all right with you... we could go talk go to him."

Talk to him? Really? Charlotte thought.

"Surely! Hell, I was hoping you'd do so. This is totally new to us. We've never seen anything quite like this, let alone a murder. Can't remember the last time I saw one."

Judy smiled politely. "Do you mind if we look around for a bit?"

"Yes, go ahead."

Judy took Charlotte with her. The redhead was beginning to see a new side of Judy, the experienced, professional side. Were they really doing this now? This case? Investigating her father's death?

Grant called out to them, "Ladies, sorry! Ms. Gibbins, if you don't mind, what did you want to tell me about this earlier?"

Charlotte and Judy looked confused.

"Behind the yellow tape. The thing that you thought was relevant."

Judy decided to take this one. "We don't know for sure, but we have strong reasons to believe that this might be related to some other deaths and murders that happened recently."

"Whose deaths?" he said with surprise.

"Fred Gibbins and Ethan Gregory," Judy answered.

"Gibbins... Gregory. Why do I know these names?"

"Gregory is a movie star," Charlotte said. "Both of them also grew up in this town."

"Yes, yes, I remember."

"You remember my father, Fred Gibbins?"

"Your father?" he questioned. "No, no, not a lot. But I can picture a face, sure." Grant turned to Judy. "Wasn't Gregory murdered? A week or so ago?"

"Yes, Sheriff," Charlotte replied. "And Judy worked on the case."

"Before I retired..." added Judy.

"Oh, did you now? And you think it's all related? How?" asked the Sheriff.

Judy looked at Charlotte again. They both sighed, took a minute, and started mumbling the story of what had happened back in New York and everything they had gathered since then—coming to Rockland and discovering the connection between the victims, and how they thought the first two deaths were linked with Rick Carson's. They continued with the notes that had been found—or left—with the victims. They told him about what they had learned from the people they'd interviewed, and they mentioned the name Sebastian Reed.

"Reed! Oh, God! He's involved in this?" Grant blurted out.

"Unsure yet," Judy said. "But he was also friends with Gregory and Fred, apparently."

"That belligerent scumbag! Mixed up with everything, all the time."

"He spends a lot of time in your jail, I suppose?" Judy asked with a smile.

The Sheriff laughed. "Of course not, he's got the greatest lawyers in town and he can't be nailed for anything. This might do it, though. That is... if you have proof."

"We don't, like I said," Judy replied.

"But we will," added Charlotte.

"Good. Can't wait. It sure seems like it's all connected, from what you've told me. I might have to call New York and give them my report."

"Not a problem," said Judy. "There is a man they arrested there who they think killed Gregory."

"But he didn't?"

"Nope," said Charlotte firmly.

"Okay. Well, you have my full cooperation. Since I have Detective Hunter here, I won't waste her. Anything you can do to help me nail Reed and resolve this thing I will gladly take."

While they were talking, a CBRN (Chemical, Biological, Radiological and Nuclear) team finally arrived at the scene and told Charlotte, Judy, and Grant they must exit the boat. The team went in and closed the door behind them. They wore yellow suits and had breathing equipment.

Grant asked Judy if they wanted to stay and check out the body once it was safe. Judy said yes. Charlotte was glad.

Judy and Charlotte waited patiently on the quay. Stew came back to see Charlotte. The redhead told him a bit of what had happened. He thought it was horrible and it took a moment for him to say anything. He then suggested that the gas used might also be Zyklon B, the gas that was used against the Jews in World War II. He said it was an effective killing method.

Charlotte took a moment and thought. World War II... Nazis. Skullheads... Reed? Had he done this?

She then came back to the present moment and thanked her history buff. Stew asked if he could do anything for them, but Charlotte said no and thanked him. She gave him a hug and told him to go and get some sleep. Stew hesitated but finally agreed and left them.

Thirty minutes went by and the doors of the boat finally reopened. It was late by then. The CBRN team members took off their masks one by one, and the woman in charge said it was all good. They had declared Rick Carson's boat clear of all potentially life-threatening gas and had given the green light for the search of the crime scene to begin.

The Sheriff thanked them and showed Charlotte and Judy to the boat.

CHAPTER TWENTY-NINE:

THE CRIME SCENE

Judy followed Charlotte once again as they made their way through the boat to the infamous door. Grant followed them.

The door was now wide open, and when they peeked in, they found Carson's body still tied up. Charlotte grimaced at the view; he'd looked better behind the glass. The man appeared to be literally torn apart. The dark circles around his dead, staring eyes were wide and deep. Blood was glued to his nostrils.

Seeing dead bodies was going to take some getting used to.

The Sheriff cursed. The smell was bad, too.

Grant took a step back and stayed in the doorway, watching from a distance.

"What do you think, Mrs. Hunter?" he said.

Judy looked closely around the room. The walls were as dirty as the rest of the boat. Then the retired woman moved to the body, analyzing every little detail. Charlotte observed her carefully. It was fascinating to see how Judy worked and how she approached things.

Charlotte suddenly peered down at the gas canister and looked at the label.

"That is hydrogen cyanide... exactly what Stew was referring to." The redhead continued, "In large doses, it prevents the cells from using oxygen, so the cells eventually die... and you die, obviously. Whoever got pleasure out of doing this is definitely sick in the head."

"No doubt about that," Judy exclaimed. "How the hell would someone get their hands on this gas?"

"I mean, you can make it yourself. From apple seeds, apricots, almonds... If you extract amygdalin from them, you can most certainly make your own hydrogen cyanide. You just need to know the right chemistry."

"Wow, okay..."

"Or this person could have had access to it through the military."

"Right," said Judy. She looked impressed by Charlotte's knowledge.

Charlotte starting walking around, until Judy interrupted her.

"What about the body? Do you see anything?" she asked Charlotte out of the blue. "What can you tell me about it?"

"Me?"

"You want to be a detective or not?"

"Yes. Of course."

"Then tell me what else you see."

"Hmm... He was tied up... and the killer turned on the gas... and then he died," the redhead said tentatively.

"Good, but besides the obvious..."

Charlotte felt foolish. "I guess..."

"Look at him," Judy said, helping.

Charlotte began to walk around the body. The young woman put her hands out as if she were going to touch it.

"Just look, no touching," Judy instructed.

Charlotte looked at the Sheriff, who gave her a kind face. She nervously put her arms behind her back. Judy saw her looking around the corpse again.

"The ropes appear kinda loose. He tried to free himself?"

"Who wouldn't?" Judy confirmed. "Try again... look near the head."

"It's red... Is that blood?"

Judy nodded.

"He was hurt?"

The retired detective nodded again.

"He hurt his head. The killer knocked him out before putting him in the chair!"

Charlotte heard Judy sigh, but she wasn't sure why. Was she missing something?

"His knuckles—they look bruised. He punched back?"

"Did he now?" Judy teased, but then she nodded. "Carson is quite a big guy. He probably didn't sit things out without a fight. The body looks fatigued... look. There is another bruise here, around the neck. I'm guessing the killer did everything in his power to put him down."

"That's not a bruise, that's a burn," Charlotte said.

"He Tased him?" Judy suggested. "Maybe."

"Right!" exclaimed Charlotte.

"Whoever did this had resources and knew what they were doing."

"I'm sure biking criminals slash Nazi wannabes have had plenty of practice and have plenty of barbaric tools to make a person suffer."

Judy nodded, but she still looked unconvinced.

"Well, who knew things like this could happen in a small town like this," said Grant. "You think it's quiet and you won't be doing much beyond issuing parking tickets or calming down a few domestic fights... Sure makes things interesting,"

"You wouldn't like New York City," replied Judy.

Grant sighed.

Judy and Charlotte walked around the boat for a bit, looking at the main cabin door and each of the rooms and areas. Aside from the dirt and the unwashed dishes, there were no signs of anything unusual—no weapons, nothing broken. The door didn't appear to have been kicked in, although the knob was broken. They would have to check for fingerprints.

After that, Charlotte and Judy thanked the Sheriff for allowing them to check out the scene of the crime. He told them to come to his office tomorrow to discuss the case further. He valued their help. Hunter and Gibbins agreed.

The two women finally went back to their motel.

CHAPTER THIRTY:

METHOD OF KILLING

Charlotte woke up with a heart-sickening headache. She wasn't sure if it was because of the booze she had had with Stew or the result of all the emotions she had been faced with over the past week.

Judy gave her two Tylenols. Charlotte took them and then the two went out for breakfast.

After she had a much-needed black coffee flowing through her system, Charlotte accompanied Judy on the short ride to the Sheriff's Office. Finally, they were off Main Street.

When they arrived, Judy made a comment about the building's size. Charlotte had noticed the same thing: Sullivan County's Sheriff's Office was almost as big as the building for a single precinct in New York City. This wasn't Times Square, obviously.

The building's walls were turquoise, seemingly freshly painted, unlike all the neglected buildings in the area.

Charlotte trailed Judy as they walked up the stairs to the entrance.

Grant welcomed them with a grateful smile and had them sit down in front of his huge black desk in his very small office. He offered more coffee and they finally began to chat.

"Pearson? Did he wake up?" asked Judy.

"Woke up—no. But the doctors say he will survive. He is in a stable condition."

"Great."

"I can take you to see him when he does regain consciousness."

"Okay, thank you," Judy replied.

Grant kept looking through his files and then said, "The thing I don't understand is this: if this is all linked, why has the perpetrator used different weapons? Gas, a sword and you said a... hanging rope?"

There was a moment of silence. They were all lost in thought, until Charlotte started laughing.

"We're so stupid!" she blurted out.

The Sheriff and Judy turned to her.

"Execution!" she shouted.

"What?" the Sheriff asked, confused.

"Execution. He's executing them. This also makes sense after what Stew said last night about World War II... gas chambers..."

The Sheriff leaned forward, begging for clarification.

"Gas, rope, sword... they are methods of execution," said Judy. "That's why the 'reckoning' was mentioned in the note—punishment. He's punishing them for something!"

"But for what?" the Sheriff asked.

"A personal vendetta maybe..." Charlotte suggested.

"Why?"

Charlotte didn't answer. She looked over at Judy. Judy glanced back at her and nodded approvingly.

"Yes," she said. She gently took Charlotte's arm. "Your father didn't commit suicide."

From her tone, Charlotte knew she now believed it. But she was troubled by something new. What did the killer have against her father? Why the hell would he want to punish him?

"Okay... so, execution," the Sheriff said. "And you think this Executioner... might be... Reed?" the Sheriff asked apprehensively.

Charlotte peered at Judy.

"To be determined," Judy answered. "But for now, we need to find the next possible victims and get them to safety."

"You think he might strike again."

"Maybe he's finished, maybe not. I doubt he is..." Judy said.

The redhead nodded at this.

"We can't take that risk," Judy Hunter continued. "If he's targeting friends of Gregory and Fred Gibbins, then we have to watch over all of them."

"And who might they be?" the Sheriff said.

"For now, he has targeted people in Fred's high school circle. Batty also mentioned a Melanie Sheldon, a Julian Franco and, hmm, somebody else... I can't remember the name... It's in my notes back at the motel."

"Melanie Sheldon?" the Sheriff repeated.

"You know who that is?" asked Judy.

"Yes, I do! Lovely girl."

"You know where I can find her?"

"She works at a bar not far from here."

"The Rhode House?"

"What? No. Nobody in their right mind works there. It's a coffee bar... place. Granger's Coffee."

"We know where that is!" Charlotte exclaimed.

She stood up and Judy was following her lead before something came to her.

"I remember now, the name we're forgetting. It was this kid who was missing at school, I think..." Judy said.

"A missing kid?" the Sheriff wondered.

"Apparently he went missing on his way home from school around 1989. It should still be somewhere in your files."

"Yeah, right," Charlotte said. "A Viktor..."

"Viktor Kovachev, you mean?" the Sheriff quickly asked.

"You know about him?" questioned Judy.

"Of course I do! Everybody knows about the Kovachev kid. I was a deputy back then. I remember the parents. They were utterly devastated. We couldn't find him. We questioned everyone. We looked for days and days... we thought someday we'd find a body, but we never have."

"Where was he last seen?" Judy continued.

"Apparently, he was on his way home. Yes—I remember now. Melanie Sheldon said he was heading home that day—they had left the school together. They were pals, I think. She was equally destroyed by this. She kept crying, saying that she saw him heading home... but he never made it. Nobody knows why."

"Weird," said Charlotte.

"If we could have some files on this, that would be great. Batty said he might have been Reed's friend," Judy said.

"You think Reed had something to do with this disappearance?"

"I don't know... I just get a strange feeling about it all. Maybe it's nothing, maybe it's something... If we could just have a little more info, that would be—"

"Will do, Detective Hunter." The Sheriff bowed slightly.

"Thank you, and please call me Judy!"

"And Charlotte!" the redhead said, smiling.

"Will do, Judy and Charlotte," the Sheriff said, chuckling.

As they left the room, Charlotte asked, "What do we now?"

"We go to Granger's, of course!" said Judy enthusiastically.

Charlotte was happy to hear that, and followed her eagerly.

CHAPTER THIRTY-ONE:

MELANIE

"You haven't received any more letters, have you?" Judy asked as they walked along Main Street.

Charlotte tossed her hair, shaking her head. "You would know if I had."

"Curious," Judy continued.

"You think he'll write again?" Charlotte asked.

"To be determined."

"We checked the crime scene and didn't find anything there."

True, Judy said to herself.

"Why do you think he sent the other one to me, instead of just leaving it at the scene?" Charlotte then asked.

"That's the thing I can't figure out," Judy replied.

Judy saw Charlotte looking around distractedly. It was a chilly day, and the street was nearly empty.

The two kept up their pace until they reached Granger's. The place was packed! It was Sunday morning, and it was brunch and pancake time.

"Maybe a bad time..." suggested Charlotte.

"We'll get coffee and then we'll see. Let's sit over there," Judy replied.

The two detectives sat down in the booth and ordered coffee as soon as Stew came around to greet them. He looked happy to see them but was also dragging a certain awkwardness from the night before.

"How are you this morning?" he asked.

Charlotte looked at him, she felt her face filling up with light. "Good. How did you sleep?"

"I've slept better. I kept waking up in the middle of the night."

"Yeah, alcohol does that to me too," the redhead replied.

"That, and I kept thinking of gas and how this guy died. Just... fuck. Freaking disgusting and horrible."

"I know."

The redhead and the history buff stared at one another for a few seconds.

"Heard any news about it?" Stew asked.

Judy and Charlotte looked at each other, then Judy shook her head. Charlotte followed her lead.

"What about you?" Judy questioned.

"Just that there is a different vibe around here, everyone I've met seems weirded out or concerned about it all. Something like that happening here, in Rockland...nobody thought it was possible."

"Not used to it?" said Charlotte.

"Hell no. Are you?" Stew asked, a little shocked by her question.

"Been around murders all my life, with my father and all..."

"Yeah, right..." he said, scratching his head.

"But being a detective and actually... smelling the bodies and seeing them in person... that's something new..." Charlotte added.

Stew nodded, seemingly glad he wasn't the only one weirded out by this.

"Hey, Stew, can I ask you somethin'?" Judy asked.

"Yeah. What's up?"

Judy looked around the room and then turned back to Stew, scratching her head as well.

"We understand that Melanie Sheldon works here?"

"Mel! Yeah, she does. Why? What do you want with her?"

"Is she working here today?"

"Yup. She's right over there, at the screen."

Stew pointed at a short, blond forty-something woman standing near the bar typing an order into the computer. She was wearing a striped black-and-red shirt. Judy immediately thought she looked really cute, although Melanie didn't seem too carefully put together. Her hair was all over the place. Charlotte turned her head to look as well.

"Do you mind asking her to come over when she has a minute?" Judy asked.

"Sure. Might take a while, though. Pretty busy right now in here," Stew replied.

"We'll wait. Not a problem."

"Just keep the coffee coming," replied Charlotte.

Stew bowed at her and went to the bar. Charlotte giggled. The two women saw him go to Melanie and whisper something in her ear. Melanie looked over at Charlotte and Judy and then turned to Stew, confused. Finally, she nodded and went back to her work.

Stew was right, it took a good twenty to thirty minutes for the rush to settle down and for Melanie to finally make her way to Judy and Charlotte's table. When she arrived, she looked slightly disheveled, sweaty, and exhausted. She wasn't wearing any makeup. Still pretty cute, though, Judy thought. By the way Melanie glared at the two detectives, she was clearly dreading this conversation.

"Melanie Sheldon?" Judy asked, as the woman approached.

"That's me," Melanie replied in a low, timid voice.

Melanie began scratching the back of her head, playing with her hair. Judy asked her to sit down. The woman hesitated then sat down next to Charlotte.

"How are you?" Judy then said.

"I'm good, how are you?"

"We're very good! Listen, Melanie, there is something very important we got to talk to you about."

"Okay..."

"My name is Judy Hunter. I used to be a detective for the NYPD, Melanie."

"Okay..." Melanie uttered again, clearly not knowing what to say.

"How long have you lived in this city?"

"Huh... pretty much all my life, I guess..."

"And you went to Rockland High?"

"Yeah." Melanie was trembling now.

"Melanie, you knew Fred Gibbins and Ethan Gregory, right?"

Melanie suddenly looked around the room, staying silent.

"And Rick Carson?" pursued Judy.

The woman didn't say anything. She looked down. A moment passed.

"Did you?" Judy asked again.

"Yeah, I knew them" she replied, almost too carefully.

"You were friends." Charlotte stated it as a fact.

Melanie turned to Charlotte and crossed her arms. "I knew them," she repeated.

"But you weren't friends?"

Melanie turned to Charlotte and crossed her arms. "I knew them," she repeated.

"But you weren't friends?"

Melanie looked at Charlotte, then seemed to dismiss her. Judy took the lead.

"You were all in the same class, yes?" Judy continued.

"Sure." Melanie shrugged.

"*Are* you sure, or..." Charlotte asked.

"It was a small school," Melanie answered. "Everybody of the same age was always in the same class."

"But you guys weren't friends?" asked Charlotte, smiling.

Melanie stared at them. She was so done with this—with Charlotte especially.

"You know that they're all dead, right? Fred, Ethan... Rick..." Charlotte threw this at her, making it seem very casual at the same time.

"Yes..." Melanie replied.

"Well, can you tell us anything?" Charlotte pushed.

"It was all over the papers. I was in complete shock, like everyone else."

"I can see that," Charlotte said, sounding incredulous.

Judy sensed as well that these words didn't ring entirely true.

"Melanie... Listen, we've been trying to figure this mystery out by ourselves," Judy said. "All the victims died in the past year. All went to Rockland High. All were killed within a few weeks of each other."

"Killed?" Melanie questioned, surprised.

"Yes," Charlotte said.

Oh dear, Judy told herself.

"Can you tell us anything?" Judy then tried, but there was no reply. "Look, some people told us you were part of that gang. That crowd. You were one of them."

Melanie was almost shaking now.

"Wait, who was killed?"

"Ethan Gregory, Rick Carson, Fred Gibbins..." Charlotte replied.

"Fred?"

"I'm sorry, it's complicated Melanie..." Judy said.

Melanie looked confused.

"We're still trying to figure it out," explained Judy.

"Didn't he commit suicide?"

"No!" Charlotte said, firmly.

"We're trying to figure it out..." Judy repeated.

Melanie looked disturbed by this, and even more confused than before.

"Melanie," Judy started. "Do you have any idea what happened? Why they are turning up dead?"

The woman looked down and sighed.

"You know, don't you?" Charlotte pushed.

Judy then said gently, touching Melanie's hand, "Please, Melanie if you know something..."

"I don't know anything," she replied.

"You sure?" Charlotte said. "Look, lady, we're trying to save your life. So, why don't you help us? Let's go!"

Melanie looked at Charlotte, utterly confused.

"It's true, Melanie," Judy agreed. "If you were part of that gang, for whatever reason the murderer is killing— you might be next on his list."

Melanie didn't flinch. She just froze.

"You don't exactly look surprised ... Do you know something we don't?" asked Charlotte.

Melanie remained without words.

"Does Sebastian Reed have anything to do with this?" Charlotte then said.

That broke Melanie down. She erupted in extremely strange laughter.

"Melanie?" Judy wondered.

"What's so funny?" Charlotte asked.

"You think I'm gonna—okay. Sebastian? Ha! I've had enough of this! All of it! Both of you, you leave me alone. Understood? I don't know nothing. They were my friends and I cared about them! I'm in mourning. Please leave me alone. Don't come back asking me questions, I won't answer them."

"Melanie!" Judy begged, touching the woman's right arm.

"Don't touch me, you don't understand a thing!"

Melanie stood up and started to walk away, but Charlotte went after her.

"What is it you said? We don't understand a thing? For your information, Fred Gibbins was my father! Her partner! You think we don't care? You think we don't mourn? We mourn more than anybody, lady!"

Melanie looked into Charlotte's eyes, both bewildered and deeply uncomfortable. The redhead kept her from moving away. Judy suddenly swept in and steered Charlotte away, before telling Melanie, "Help us understand. Please, Melanie. We want to help..."

Melanie glared at Judy for a moment. She seemed to be considering it all, but then looked down. She walked past Judy and Charlotte, leaving them without another word.

CHAPTER THIRTY-TWO:

AT THE HOSPITAL

A little while after they had left the restaurant, Charlotte stopped walking and peered at Judy as the ex-detective received a call from Grant. Judy put it on speakerphone so that the redhead could listen too. He told them that Wendell Pearson had just woken up.

The hospital was a mile away, so they walked there. It was a very small, one-story building that seemed more like a clinic.

The two women stepped inside and peeked around until they spotted the Sheriff at the end of the corridor. He looked slightly unhinged.

"Sheriff?" Charlotte asked, wondering what was up.

"Listen, I told him that you gals were all on it! He's quite the character—didn't care, really!"

Judy gave Charlotte a confused look.

"What's going on? Who are you talking about?" Judy questioned.

The silence echoed for a bit. The women's heads were totally clouded as to what was going on here.

Suddenly, a voice rang out loudly across the hallway. It was a man's voice. Strangely, it was also a familiar voice. Judy and Charlotte turned around. The two women couldn't believe their eyes. He was here! This wild chimpanzee, this baffling human who was one of a kind. This man who could have had so much charm and been so attractive if he had taken How to Be a Gentleman and How to Be a Respectful Human Being classes. He could have been so much better, if only he wasn't himself. Behind them was none other than Eddie freaking White, joining the party.

The duo stood there, open-mouthed, until White sneered and opened his dumb mouth.

"Judy! Charlotte! Happy to finally see you!" said the short blond man, who was wearing a tight green suit that made him look like the Riddler from *Batman: Forever*. Eddie White zipped his pants up and walked to them. "Interestin' you're here in this town," he said. "This ugly town, I might say. Very interestin'..."

Charlotte sighed. She then noticed the white bandage on his nose, with a red stain on it. She almost laughed.

"When my black brother over here called," White said, talking about the Sheriff, "I almost didn't believe it was you guys. Told the Sheriff here that it wasn't possible. Didn't you retire?"

He waited for an answer from Judy, but she didn't give him any, just smiled stiffly. White returned her expression and didn't seem irritated at all. "It's okay. I'm here now. Providing support to my black brother o'er here," he said, pointing to the Sheriff.

Both ladies rolled their eyes.

He didn't just say that, Charlotte thought.

The Sheriff waved at the women and walked down the hallway. Charlotte saw him approach a counter to speak to the hospital secretary.

The two ladies were stuck with the green suit. White continued, "Took more than three hours to get down here. Traffic was mad. People in this state cannot drive, I tell ya."

"Detective White! How are you?" exclaimed Judy, clearly faking her enthusiasm.

"More importantly, what are you doing here?" Charlotte contributed. She wasn't faking anything, she was showing genuine annoyance.

"Workin' on a case, obviously. There was a murder here."

"Yeah, we know," said Charlotte.

"Well, that's why I'm here, beautiful. Invited by my good friend here... what was it? Jamal? Terrance? Jefferson? Anyway, we're here to investigate... together."

"Newman—his name is Newman Grant," Charlotte said acidly. "You can call him Sheriff if the name's too difficult."

White sighed. He didn't give a care in the world. "Anyway, as I was saying, he told me all about your little finding and that you think it's somehow linked to Ethan Gregory's murder?"

"We do believe that, yes," said Charlotte.

"How is it related, might I ask?" asked White.

"Why should we tell you?"

"Don't. I'll figure it out on my own. I'm good with these things—my profession," said White.

"Sure," sighed Charlotte.

"Sheriff-friend here mentioned the names Gregory, Carson—or is it Cameron... the guy who just died? Well, that guy. And then he said something else about Fred Gibbins... it's probably me. I probably didn't hear that right. He ain't part of this—"

Charlotte wanted to say something, but she saw Judy lean forward. The retired detective sighed. "I'll save you the trouble," she said. "You heard right, Mr. White. We have strong beliefs that they were all friends: Gregory, Carson, and Fred Gibbins."

Charlotte was happy Judy had said it. And then, very quickly, she wasn't.

"Fred Gibbins?" White looked dumbstruck, and then he almost laughed.

"Yeah, he—" instinctively began Charlotte.

"It's not important," retracted Judy.

"Gee, I hope not," White said. "If you guys were paying attention, you'd know the dude killed himself."

"Not exactly," Charlotte interjected.

“Not exactly?”

Charlotte shrugged.

“So?” White asked.

“Why would we tell you anything?” Charlotte asked.

“So, he did kill himself. You just believed in some sad fantasy that your father was in a good place.”

Charlotte could feel all her muscles getting very tense. Her heart began beating fast.

“Mr. White,” warned Judy.

“That’s what grief does to you. Have you heard of the five stages of grief and loss?”

Charlotte felt her fist clenching.

Judy jumped in. “No, Fred Gibbins didn’t kill himself.”

White got a little pale. He seemed intimidated by the retired detective.

“How so?” He said, retracting a smile. He spoke tightly and timidly. “Explain it to me, then.”

“They were all killed in the same ways. We believe for the same purpose. His choice is very precise—“

Suddenly, Charlotte heard White laughing again. He really had a laugh a monkey would have.

“Sorry?” she said, doubting that any of this could really be happening.

“Killed in the same way?” he started. “A rope? Y’know he used a rope, right? He put it around his neck, stepped on a bench and jumped off it.”

“Not—”

“Not exactly? I’m sorry, Ms. Gibbins,” said White. “Please forgive me, where did your detective license come from?”

Charlotte’s face grew red. “I—I didn’t—”

"Then why are you here, sweet pea? I hope it ain't to spend time with me. If so, we can grab a drink after if you'd like, but right now I'm working on a serious matter—"

"Detective White!" Judy barked. "Like I was saying, we have very strong reasons to believe these murders, or deaths if you prefer, were all connected. A rope, a sword, and finally gas—all methods of execution."

"Execution?"

"Yeah, we think that's his MO."

"So, a serial killer, you mean?"

Judy nodded.

"You're really smart, aren't you?" joked Charlotte.

Detective White's face grew a little red, just like she wanted. But then the man smiled.

"Thank you, sweetie." He turned back to Judy, dismissing Charlotte again. "So, he's like some sorta judge? A punisher?"

"We thought of calling him the Executioner," added Sheriff Grant, rejoining them.

Charlotte shook her head. *That's not going to help.*

"Wow! That's so interestin'. And who is he, this Executioner?"

"Certainly not the one you have on trial in New York," replied Charlotte.

"We don't know for sure..." Judy said cautiously. "We think you might have the wrong person on trial," she clarified.

For the first time, Judy and Charlotte observed White at a loss for words. For the first time, perhaps in his entire life, he seemed to be thinking. Might we say, almost considering the whole thing.

"For what?"

Judy and Charlotte looked at each other, confused again.

"Why does he do it?"

"We don't know," Judy replied.

White remained silent for a second. "Okie-dokie. That was somethin'. Thank you very much for your help, detectives... no, that ain't right." He sneered. "*Ex*-Detective Hunter and... of course, Charlotte beauty."

Charlotte didn't want to look at him for another instant. She was beyond frustrated with his whole persona.

"I'll take it from here now."

"What?" the redhead said.

"Yes, it's all right now. Your considerations and thoughts have all been noted," White said, pointing to his head because he didn't have a notepad on him.

"You—"

"Don't worry, Charlotte, you ladies can rest. This must have been hard on you, on your souls. I'm so sorry you had to see that, the body and everythin'. Now, go rest. I'll take care of everything."

"This is our investigation."

"Is it?" said White. "'Cause if what you say is true and it's the same killer that killed Gregory, then this is my case. Gregory is my responsibility. I will find out who killed him."

"We've done all the work! Not you."

"Charlotte—" Judy implored.

"The Sheriff wants us here!"

"That's right," said the Sheriff, not as firmly as he probably intended to. "I asked them to stay."

"There you go," said Charlotte.

"If you wouldn't mind, Mr. White, having them here to investigate."

"I would mind. I think they would too. It's not their jobs. They don't wanna have that on their shoulders."

"We just told you—"

A nurse suddenly appeared from the room beside them. "Are you ready now?" she questioned. "Sheriff, you'll only have a few minutes.

He's still not in the best shape. Mr. Pearson was hit pretty bad on the head. He's lightheaded and coming back. He needs a little rest."

Grant nodded at the nurse, and she walked away.

The Sheriff looked at Judy, then at Charlotte, and finally at the smirking Eddie White.

"Well then, always a pleasure, ladies," said White. "I have things to attend to."

"Oh, we're going in," Charlotte announced.

Charlotte stepped forward and tried to move past White into the room, but Judy put a hand on her shoulder to stop her.

White nervously turned his head to look at Judy, wondering what she was going to do about this. He looked a bit afraid of her.

"It's okay, Charlotte and I will be on our way..."

"No!" shouted Charlotte. "The Sheriff brought us here, he promised us we could chat with Pearson. That's what we're going to do."

"That's right. I did say that, Mr. White," insisted Grant.

White glared at him.

"Please allow them," Grant said.

White was about to respond when Judy approached him. "Sorry, Detective, we don't mean to barge in. This is your investigation."

White looked surprised. She patted him on the shoulder.

Charlotte stepped forward and peeked inside the room. She saw Wendell Pearson in a hospital bed, a bandage on his head. She looked to Judy. *C'mon...*

There was a short beat.

"Mr. White," Judy then said, "we're sure you will do a terrific job solving this complex case on your own."

Charlotte made a face in her head. She was stumped as to what the heck Judy was up to. Judy continued, "You seem like a careful individual who doesn't trust easily, from what I can tell, and that's very intelligent on your part. Don't change! Don't trust anything but your gut, please. We just wanted to share our notes with you."

White frowned, and his cockiness seemed to fade.

"Look... would you mind if we go talk to Pearson with you? You can supervise if you want. It would just ease our minds, and we could provide you with notes of our thoughts again if you want. I promise it won't take long. Then we'll be out of your shiny and neat beautiful blond hair forever," Judy said softly.

Eddie White touched his blond fur and opened his mouth to speak, but Judy wasn't finished.

"We'll be back in New York tonight, I assure you. I'll even call the Captain myself and tell him what a fantastic job you're doing up here. He'll be so happy."

Charlotte could see something change in White's face as Judy said that. He had a sudden brightness in his eyes. This was working. Judy had hit the jackpot.

This is what Eddie White wanted. He had the Commissioner in his pocket, sure, but he didn't really have the 18th Precinct's respect or support. His own precinct. More than anything, he wanted to be accepted by his peers as part of the team. Like everybody, he probably didn't like feeling that he didn't belong.

A moment passed. Then White began straightening his yellow tie on his blue shirt. He cleared his throat.

"You're the lead detective here, Mr. White. Your call..." added Sheriff Grant.

"We're just going to take ten minutes, no more," said Judy.

White was considering it.

Judy said, "You can do all the questioning. We'll stay mute."

"Ten minutes never killed anyone," White uttered, smoothing out his hair with his black comb.

Judy stooped graciously. "Please, after you, Mr. White."

White nodded and marched authoritatively into the room. Judy winked at Charlotte as soon as White's back was turned. She grabbed Charlotte hand's in what the redhead thought was meant as a reassuring gesture. Charlotte replied with a happy face. All her worries now vanished from her face. The redhead knew that Eddie White would never solve anything in this town or with this case.

CHAPTER THIRTY-THREE:

WENDELL

Wendell Pearson had bandages covering his forehead. He was a fifty-year-old white man, with large eyebrows and fat cheeks, a little overweight. All in all, Judy thought he had a charming, happy expression that made you feel comfortable around him. He looked at the team of detectives and the Sheriff in front of him and chuckled.

"Where did ya find these folks, Sheriff?" he said.

"Wendell, these are Mrs. Judy Hunter, Charlotte Gibbins and—"

"Detective Edward White. How are ya, friend?"

Wendell turned to White, saw White with his hand out, waiting for a shake. Wendell looked slightly unsure and settled on a nod.

"Fine, thanks," he said, unenthusiastically.

"Now, what exactly happened to—" White barged ahead.

"I'm sorry, Wendell. Do you mind if these fine folks ask you a few questions?" Grant asked, seeing the awkwardness White was creating.

"Nope," Wendell responded casually.

"Thank you, Sheriff," the blond detective said, smiling. "Mr. Pearson, you saw the killer, right?"

"Yeah," Pearson answered.

"So, why didn't you stop him?"

Wendell looked confused, and so did everybody else in the room.

"I couldn't."

"Why is that?" White pushed on.

"Well... when I got there... well, the killer was in the kitchen, and—"

"And what?"

"Well, he saw me, and I couldn't do anything. I tried to go for Carson, but the door was already closed, then—"

"Then?"

"The dude stopped me. He ran after me and hit me hard in the head. Next thing I know, I wake up and he's gone."

"What about Carson?" Charlotte inquired.

"He wasn't movin' no more!" Pearson replied.

"Hydrogen cyanide usually takes ten to twenty minutes to kill..."

"Well, yeah. It must have been that long, 'cause when I looked at my phone to make the call, it seemed like a whole half-hour had passed."

"What did he hit you with?" Judy asked.

"What does it matter?" professed White, obviously outraged by the question and the fact she had asked a question at all. "The guy had a chance and he didn't take it. Lame."

"What are you saying, White?" asked Charlotte.

"He could have stopped him," replied White, looking uneasy.

"Like you would have done, you mean?" the redhead said with a smirk.

White stepped back, looked at his fists and began patting them together.

"Certainly!" White seemed quite sure of himself.

"Would have been easier for you to solve, right? If he had stopped him..." Charlotte said. "I mean, no actual investigation for you to do."

White looked at Charlotte, searching for a riposte, but Judy knew she had to interrupt before things got out of hand again.

"So, Mr. Pearson—if you don't mind, Detective..." She nodded to White, who slowly nodded back. "The killer was gone when you woke up?"

Wendell nodded.

"He didn't try to kill you, he just left you there?"

"I mean, I bet he tried to, he just didn't hit me hard enough..."

"Hmm..." Judy muttered. She wasn't convinced. "Did you happen to see what he looked like?"

"Looked like?"

"The killer, I mean."

"Well... no... He was wearing a—"

"A gas mask, yes, we know."

"Yeah."

"But what about the eyes? The hair? Did you see a color?"

"Hmm... the eyes. Yeah... they looked quite blue to me. I could be wrong, though," Pearson conceded.

"Reed has blue eyes," Charlotte uttered, turning to the Sheriff and Judy.

"Who's Reed?" asked White.

Nobody answered him. Instead, Judy continued talking.

"What about the hair behind the mask?"

"The hair was... I think it was brown. Maybe there was another color there..."

"A little gray?" suggested Charlotte.

Something sparked in Wendell Pearson's eyes, and he nodded. "Maybe. Yes."

Charlotte, the Sheriff, and Judy looked at each other again. Sebastian Reed fit that profile perfectly.

"Was it gray or brown? Or yellow? Or red?! I'm confused here," White interjected.

"It was all very quick... I—I don't really—"

"Right, but you're sure the eyes were blue?" asked Judy.

"Yes," Pearson said.

"Was he old?" said Judy.

Wendell shrugged.

"Tall?"

"Yeah. Or...average? I don't... remember..."

"It's okay," Judy said kindly.

Then they all heard a heavy sigh behind them. White was laughing.

"He got hit on the head, the poor fella, he doesn't even know what he's talking about," said White. "You sure it was even a man?"

"Yes," said Wendell, not finding it funny.

"At least that's something," said White.

"Did you see anything else?" asked Judy.

"Hmm... I don't think so... That's about it..."

"Thank you."

"I'm sorry I couldn't give you more... I mean, I'll think about it, detective."

"She's not—" White began, but he was cut off.

"Don't worry, Mr. White here will give you his card and you can call him whenever you think of anything," Judy reassured both Wendell Pearson and Eddie White.

"Right," said White, nodding.

Judy then touched Wendell's hand and patted it lightly in a friendly and empathetic way, reassuring him that everything was all right. Wendell Pearson smiled back at her.

"I hope ya find the guy," he said.

Judy nodded and walked out of the room. Charlotte and Grant followed her.

"Woah, where do you think you're headin'?" shouted White.

"Packing our bags, we're going back home. This is your investigation now, Detective. Well done and good luck! The Captain will hear good things."

Judy saw Charlotte smile back at White as she came through the door. The Sheriff quickly whispered into Judy's ear before White could follow them into the corridor.

"You'll be my first call if anything else pops up," he said.

"Thank you, Sheriff."

Two seconds later, Judy heard White walk out of the door and she and Charlotte turned around to look at him.

"Detective," Judy said, waving him goodbye.

CHAPTER THIRTY-FOUR:

BACK AT THE MOTEL

"We're not really leaving, are we?" asked Charlotte, as the two women got back to their room.

"Hell, no! Are you kidding?" exclaimed Judy.

Charlotte beamed. She ran to Judy and hugged her.

"I'm sorry I'm such a pain in the ass," she said.

"No, I'm sorry I didn't fully believe you in the first place. I should have."

"It's okay, I probably wouldn't have believed me either."

Charlotte sat on her bed, found a brush on the side table and started fixing her hair. Rush kept jumping around her, trying to get some attention. The redhead threw him his orange ball and he brought it back. As they played, Judy joined Charlotte on the bed.

"Your dad would be very proud, Charlotte," the retired detective said.

Now Charlotte was crying. For the longest time, she had wanted to become a detective, and for the longest time, she feared telling her dad. She dreamed of one day solving a case with him, catching the murderer with him. Now, she never would.

The redhead stayed quiet for a beat.

"I just want him to be here..." she murmured. "I just wanted him to—to see me like this."

"He is, and he's very proud, Charlotte," Judy replied, leaning in. "You know what he told me after that night at my party?"

Charlotte looked up.

"He told me that he was so happy you wanted to be like him, to be a detective. He wanted you to do this. He was so, so content and supportive. Maybe he had an angry reaction the previous night, but Charlotte, that's because he cared for you so damn much and the shock of those words... You were his little girl, and I think you becoming somebody that was a target for criminals scared him a bit. But I mean, what parent wouldn't react like that?"

The redhead nodded.

"He was so proud of you, Charlotte. He told me he thought you would be amazing at this, and he was right, you are."

Charlotte could feel tears running down her face. This made it all so much better. She had really thought her father didn't approve and was ashamed of her for not wanting to become a doctor or a scientist anymore.

Judy took hold of her once more and they sobbed in each other's arms. Then they let go of each other, and they began to laugh. They found themselves slightly pathetic. As Charlotte's stomach groaned loudly, which only increased their laughter, Judy suggested they order pizza and stay in. While they waited for the pizza to arrive, she could walk to the small liquor store that was a quick walk from the motel. Charlotte loved this idea.

The two women spent the evening eating and giggling together. Then they pulled out papers—notes on the case—and looked at what was on the table for them to puzzle through together. At this point, they knew three things for sure: one, the victims had all been friends; two, they were all killed by murder weapons that were used in executions; and three, Wendell Pearson had seen a man with grayish hair and blue eyes attack him and kill poor Rick Carson. So, there were three things they really didn't need to prove. They also had Sebastian Reed as their number one suspect, because of what Wendell Pearson had witnessed and because, from what they had heard from the community, he seemed to be manipulating, controlling, and feared.

"So, what do we do now?" asked Charlotte.

Judy didn't answer immediately.

"Could we go back to Reed?" Charlotte asked. "Ask him questions?"

"It's going to be hard with White around, but we can try. However, let's be honest. One eyewitness is not going to prove anything."

"But he clearly has—"

"He doesn't have motive," Judy softly insisted. "We don't know anything about his relationships to your father, Gregory, or Carson. We just know they had a relationship at one time. We've heard he was controlling, sure, but that's not enough."

"So... what?"

"Well, we need something more concrete. We need the backstory, the reason why this is all happening. Then we can identify a motive and start pinpointing individuals who fit."

"And how do we find that?"

"Not sure yet. We might need to talk to Melanie again."

"She's not going to tell us anything, she's stubborn as a mule."

"Maybe she's scared."

"Of what?"

"For one, she's on the list of potential next victims. Then, she might also know something we don't know about it all, and that might be the key to solving this thing."

"You mean maybe she knows who the killer is?"

"Yes, I think she probably does."

"Then we need to push her!"

"Yes, but gently." Judy smiled softly.

Charlotte nodded.

"We certainly have something we didn't have before, though."

"What's that?" asked Charlotte.

"We are now one hundred percent sure the killer is targeting high school friends of Fred and Gregory, so we can watch the next victims closely—"

"Before the killer strikes again," Charlotte finished.

Judy nodded.

"We find the victim, and the murderer will come," added the redhead. She took a breath as they agreed they were on the same page, and then asked, "So, who's left in the group? Apart from Melanie."

Judy took out a notebook and looked at the list.

"A Zachary Smith, a Julian Franco... and of course, if he isn't the killer... Sebastian Reed."

"We know where Melanie is, so that's a start."

"Yeah, we'll protect her."

"I had the Sheriff look into the other victims. Maybe I'll try calling him and see what he's learned. Let's just hope White isn't listening."

Then Charlotte jumped up from the floor where they were sitting and went to get her computer from her bag.

"Or we could just find out for ourselves and not rely on anybody," she chuckled. She then said out loud, as she typed, "Zachary Smith."

Dozens of names and faces appeared on the screen.

Charlotte looked at Judy. "Which one?"

The retired woman stood up and went for her bag, pulled out the high school yearbook.

Charlotte nodded, feeling dumb. "Or we could just narrow it down using their young faces..."

Judy grinned. As they looked through the pictures on Google, and matched them up with the high school yearbook, they finally found someone who matched Smith's profile. His picture was on a car company's website from Germany.

"Car salesman it is," Charlotte said.

Zachary Smith had gray hair like Reed and Fred, a chipped nose, and his face seemed to have gone through a lot of plastic surgery. Too much. Charlotte clicked on another page and let out a shriek.

"Fuck!"

"What?" questioned Judy.

"Come see this. The page says, 'On March 10th, our dear Vice-President and incredible American employee Zachary Smith left us. He tragically passed away.'... and then if we click on this news article link, let's see..."

Judy and Charlotte stared at the screen, reading the article before them.

"Electrocution... Zachary Smith died tied up on a chair in his apartment, 'we believe tortured to death with electricity,'" Judy read out.

"He got him too..."

"Damn it!" Judy exclaimed.

"What a maniac..." added Charlotte.

"Another method of execution..."

The redhead nodded. "So, that's four."

"That we know of... See if you can find anything on Julian Franco."

Charlotte nodded.

"There's nothing here that matches his picture from the yearbook." Charlotte said after a few minutes of research.

Judy took a breath, then said, "What about this... Viktor Kovachev kid? Can you find out anything about the way he disappeared? The Sheriff still has to get back to me on this one."

"You really think it's linked?"

"It's just... the way Batty was talking about him, and him being under Reed's 'reign'... Also, nobody just disappears. Ugh, I hate unresolved cases," Judy exclaimed. "They eat my brain like rats on cheese."

Charlotte found that hilarious.

"I just think it's all really weird, I don't know why," Judy continued.

Charlotte did as Judy asked and pulled up some articles. "There's barely anything on here, it's thirty years old. 'School Boy Gone Missing in Rockland, New York.' And here's another: 'Kovachev still missing. Parents' Lives Shattered.' Like the Sheriff said, it seems like they didn't find anything. The boy was just forgotten after some time."

"Right... We should talk to somebody close to the kid about it. Somebody that actually knew him."

"Like Melanie..." Charlotte suggested.

Judy nodded.

They sat on that for a while longer. Judy poured Charlotte some more wine. The redhead was starting to feel tired and tipsy.

After a while, Judy took Charlotte by surprise by asking, "Charlotte?"

"Yeah?"

"I have to know, what will you do once we find the Executioner?"

"What will I do?" Charlotte was surprised by the question.

"Yes."

Charlotte peered at Judy. The retired detective wasn't smiling, wasn't angry, she just had this stern, cold expression on her face. The young woman had heard that question being asked in movies and TV shows, and in novels she read, and now she was being asked the same thing. It was a cliché, she thought, but probably necessary for Judy to know. She probably wanted to make sure they understood each other.

Charlotte didn't really know what to say.

"Huh... well... we'll call the cops and they'll arrest him, obviously," replied Charlotte, a little scared.

Judy kept looking at her for a long minute, then finally flinched and went to the bathroom.

"Good," she said when she returned. "The desire for revenge is fine. But use it well. Use it as fuel to catch him, and once we do, we put him in jail, and you make your peace. It will all be over then. Your dad will be proud of you and you will be okay. Trust me. All right, Charlotte?"

Charlotte nodded. Frankly, she was concerned about what she would do, too. Her bones and her soul certainly wanted more than that, more than just putting the bad guy in jail. Her father's murderer. Charlotte wanted whoever had done this to suffer, to hurt. She wanted to hurt him. Bad.

CHAPTER THIRTY-FIVE:

A KNOCK AT THE DOOR

Judy watched as Charlotte fell asleep not long after their conversation had ended, and more wine had been sipped. It was dark outside and she heard rain pounding against the glass. The retired detective stared at the drops rattling against the window for some time. She drank some water and pet Rush, who was lying on her lap. Just passing her hand along the therapy dog's fur was calming her. She had many thoughts, some of them negative and painful. Even though she had done her police job for so many years, it was never easy to think about people getting murdered. It was never easy seeing their bodies and thinking of how much they had had to suffer before taking their last breath. However, the upside to this, if there was one, was that she was hopefully saving lives by doing her job and stopping the suffering and the pain from happening again.

She was looking outside, carrying these thoughts in her body, and suddenly she saw someone through the window, standing outside the motel room, looking at her. It was a dark shadow standing in the rain. Judy stood up from the bed. The shadow wasn't moving, it just remained there, staring.

The detective carefully stepped forward. She wanted to see who it was, but at the last second, before she came close enough to make out a face, the shadow vanished. She looked outside the window, then hurried to the door and opened it. The rain came down like a shower from the top of the door. Judy poked her head outside and turned it to the right and then to the left, looking along the continuous balcony. There was not a soul in the vicinity. She stayed outside for a beat, then finally gave up and closed the door. Judy turned around, sighing. *Who the hell was that?*

Several seconds passed, then she heard a knock at the balcony door. Judy turned, surprised, and sped to the door and opened it. It was a young man in a polo shirt, hiding under an umbrella. She recognized him as the motel manager.

"Excuse me, miss. There's a Charlotte Gibbins in here, yeah?"

Judy nodded, looking at Charlotte. The redhead was still sleeping. The manager spoke loudly, having to almost shout against the noise of the rain.

"I found this on my desk. There is no return address on it, but it's clearly for her."

Judy took the white envelope the manager gave her and looked at it. The label said:

To the lovely Charlotte Gibbins

Staying in Suite 212

The motel manager remained, waiting as Judy stood there apprehensively. She opened the envelope and read it. What was inside was even more disturbing than the inscription on the label. As she finished reading, Judy raised her head and look piercingly at the man.

"Who gave you this?" she asked.

"Nobody... it was on my desk. Found it after my five minute break."

"This just happened?"

"I— yes..."

Judy ran outside and into the downpour. She charged along the balcony, to the end. She then peered down into the street. There was nobody there she could see, only rain pouring on empty pavement. She ran down and looked around every corner of the hotel. *Where is he? Where did he go?* she asked herself, thinking she would go mad. She then sighed, realizing what she was doing. The sender of the note was long gone. And there she was in the rain, her clothes now heavy and her hair spilling water, waiting for somebody who clearly didn't want to be seen. *Was it him? Was it the killer? Was it him in the window?* Who knew? If only she could have gotten to the shadow in time, she would know who it was. She knew he was tall, that was about it.

She went back up the stairs and into the room. Judy closed the door and saw Charlotte, now awake, looking at her, perplexed.

"What are you doing?" the redhead asked.

Judy held up the envelope for Charlotte to see.

"Is that for me?" Charlotte said.

Judy nodded, handing it to Charlotte, and sat on the bed with her. The young woman seemed startled.

"Another note?" she asked fearfully.

Judy nodded again.

CHAPTER THIRTY-SIX:

CHARLOTTE, THE BODYGUARD

Charlotte could feel her hands shaking as she opened the envelope and read its contents. There it was again: all caps, bold letters, very personal—another of these damned notes. It read:

HOW DID YOU LIKE THIS ONE, SWEETHEART?

YOU HAVING FUN?

I AM.

THIS WAS MY FAVORITE TO DATE.

JUST WAIT FOR THE NEXT ONE, GONNA BE EVEN MORE FUN.

SHE'S A BAD GIRL.

"'Sweetheart'? What the fuck is this? Who does he think I am—his wife? This is sick," the redhead exclaimed, utterly disgusted.

She read the rest and looked at Judy.

"'A bad girl'?" Charlotte repeated. "'Girl'... like Melanie? Why would he tell us who his next victim is going to be?"

"My guess is... he wants to play."

"Play? Play with what?"

"With us... with you..."

"Why?"

"See who's going to get to her first..."

"Why?" Charlotte insisted, obviously disturbed.

"I don't know!" said Judy. "Killers can be very strange. Some of them love the thrill of police chasing them. Some of them like to have a nemesis and play the hero-and-villain game."

Fuck... Charlotte thought.

"This isn't a fucking comic book! Why the hell is he reaching out to me? I'm not even a detective, I'm not even supposed to be here."

Judy didn't answer.

"When do you think he's going to do this?" asked Charlotte.

"Who knows... it could happen at any time. The death timeline between the victims hasn't exactly been consistent. They either died days from each other, as we saw with Gregory and your father, or weeks, months, and perhaps even years apart if the Kovachev disappearance is part of this. The only thing we can do is protect the victim until he picks his day and time. That's our advantage."

Charlotte was still desperately confused.

She stared at the ceiling. After a beat, she heard movement and saw Judy reach for her phone and put it on speakerphone. She called the Sheriff's Office. The office transferred her to Grant's home. The retired woman told Grant everything and the Sheriff said he would put a patrol on Melanie for the night.

Later, he called back to say that the patrol had reached the woman's home and that she was fine and alive but hostile to police company. Judy thanked him and told the Sheriff she would go see Melanie first thing in the morning. Grant replied that he was getting Sebastian Reed to come in for questioning in the morning and that he wanted Judy there. Judy agreed.

Charlotte didn't sleep well that night. She arrived at Melanie's house at a quarter to eight. Judy had left her this assignment, to watch over the potential next victim of the Executioner, as the retired detective was going to the precinct to interview Sebastian Reed. Charlotte hadn't argued with this plan, even though she had wanted to. Judy had made it clear she didn't want Reed and Charlotte in the same room together for a while, which made sense. Plus, Charlotte was already angry, so why put her near someone who was likely to further irritate her? Judy had probably made the right call. Charlotte really wanted to know why the killer was leaving her these damn notes. Creepy notes! Why her? Fuck.

Maybe she could ask Melanie about it, maybe she could shed some light. But Charlotte needed to be patient and less aggressive—Melanie didn't seem very much like the talking type, especially when it came to this case. Maybe now, under the threat of her imminent death, the waitress might be a bit more chatty.

As she arrived, Charlotte saw the police car parked in the driveway and a deputy standing on the porch. The house was small but looked rather lovely. Melanie had built herself a nice garden on both sides of her white-painted house, with gorgeous flowers everywhere.

The deputy stared at the redhead as she approached. He didn't seem sure what to make of her. A cop in plainclothes? Or a civilian? A friend of Melanie's? Charlotte spoke first to clear things up.

"Good morning!"

"Hello," the deputy replied.

"Charlotte Gibbins. The Sheriff sent me to look over Miss Sheldon."

"Why? You a cop?"

"Kinda... Look, if there is a problem, I can always—"

"No, no, it's okay. Just messing with you. The Sheriff told me to expect you. She's inside. Not so happy to see us."

Charlotte nodded and the deputy pointed her to the door. She reached for the doorknob then decided to knock instead. She heard steps inside and saw a form approaching the window.

The door opened and there she was, looking both unnerved and annoyed. Melanie Sheldon was in her waitress outfit, half her makeup had been done, but her hair still needed some handling. As soon as she saw Charlotte, she started scratching her arms nervously.

"Yes?"

"Hi, Melanie. Remember me? I was at the café the other day. I'm a friend of Stew—"

"Of course, I remember you," she said briskly.

"Oh, good!" exclaimed Charlotte brightly.

But Melanie wasn't smiling. She appeared even more bothered than before. "Two cops are not enough?" she questioned. "I need a whole army at my house?"

"Oh, uh... I'm not a—"

"Whatever! Make yourself at home, I guess. The other one did."

Melanie stepped away from the door and started going back up the stairs as if nothing had happened. Charlotte entered the house and peered around. *Make yourself at home, I guess!* She looked into the living room and saw a second deputy sitting on a couch, watching TV and drinking coffee. He waved at Charlotte enthusiastically. Charlotte waved back shyly and kept walking.

The kitchen was a mess—dishes had not been cleaned, dirty plates on the counter, becoming a pile, same for the glasses. She spotted an ashtray filled with cigarette butts. A couple of cheap wine bottles were also on the counter, finished or half-finished. The room smelled even worse than it looked.

"You want coffee?" she heard a voice say. She turned to the deputy standing in the door.

Charlotte peered around the room again. The coffee machine looked as dirty as everything else. She turned back and shook her head. "I'm fine, thanks."

The deputy shrugged, walked in, and reached for the coffee machine. "She said she'll be down in a minute; she's getting herself ready for work. You still need us to watch over her while you two chat down there?"

"Nah, it's gonna be all right, I think," Charlotte answered.

"Well, from what the Sheriff has told us, this whole thing seems pretty serious. We'll be close by if you guys need us," the deputy added.

"Thank you," she said.

The deputy waved once more and slowly vanished from the room.

There were a few seconds of silence before the redhead heard some noise again. Melanie came into the kitchen. She was now fully made up, almost too much. She looked like a baby doll, but at least her hair was in order. The woman went to the fridge, ignoring Charlotte, poured herself some orange juice and emptied the glass. She then left it on the counter alongside the other filthy dishes.

"Are you driving me, or can I drive myself?" she asked Charlotte.

"I don't have a car, so..." Charlotte chuckled innocently.

"Oh, great!" Melanie said with almost a sigh of relief. She grabbed her keys, hiding under a plate, and left the room. Charlotte waited a few seconds before understanding that she was supposed to follow her.

CHAPTER THIRTY-SEVEN:

INTERROGATION ROOM

Judy barely had a sip of coffee before heading down to the Sheriff's Office. When she arrived, Grant handed her a cup of coffee and slowly walked her to the interrogation room.

"White isn't here? You sure?" Judy asked.

The Sheriff chuckled. "It was hard, believe me. I feel like the guy could sense something was up."

"Where is he?"

"I tried to send him back to New York, but no luck. He keeps sticking around..." added the Sheriff.

Judy didn't understand. So, was White still here? In the precinct?

"He's a real louse, isn't he?" asked the Sheriff. "I'm sorry about bringing him into the pot. I didn't know!"

Judy chuckled. "It's fine!"

"No, it's not. He keeps calling me 'my brother'." He kept scratching his head. Then, Grant asked, "Tell me, is that really him? The cop from Louisiana?"

"Sure is," Judy said.

"Man, that's just wrong," the Sheriff answered. "What he said... just wrong." He concluded, "I really want him gone."

Judy thought the same.

"Anyway, we finally got a location on Carson's girlfriend, Tia Blanche. I managed to send White to her. I'm sure he's gonna be quick about it, but we still have some time."

"Let's go, then!" exclaimed Judy.

Grant agreed. "By the way." He stopped at the end of the hallway before going inside the interrogation room. "I've looked into the other names that you shared with me... That Zachary guy, he died not long ago—"

"Yeah, we know. In Germany."

"Oh wow, okay. Well, do you know how?"

"Electrocution."

"You don't need me, then."

Judy laughed.

Grant continued, "Well, I've contacted the German authorities and asked them to send me some files on the case. Don't know yet if they'll cooperate."

"It's okay really, no rush. I know all I need to know for now about him."

"You really think the killer went across the world to find him?"

"It wouldn't be a surprise. Hate carries people to great lengths and distances. Some would do anything and go anywhere to settle their deeds."

"Any idea yet why he has to settle those deeds?"

Judy shook her head.

Grant took a beat and said, "Okay, well, I'll tell you if I learn anything."

"Sheriff, what about Julian Franco? Who is he?"

"Oh, yeah. Well, he's got something too. He's Reed's sidekick. He's in his crew... Really not the stable type."

"Great," said Judy, unenthusiastically. *Another character to handle,* she thought. "Have you looked into his alibi?"

"Oh, he's clean. His friends all said he was with them at the bar every time there was a death. Same for Reed."

"Right," Judy sighed.

The Sheriff finally ushered her into the interrogation room. Behind the one-way mirror, Judy could see good old Sebastian Reed staring at them with his piercing blue eyes. He had his leather jacket on. He already had the smirk on his face that Judy found so annoying.

"What did he say when you asked him to come?" she asked.

"Pfff... He said he had nothing to hide and was 'ready to help in any way he could,'" replied the Sheriff.

"Fantastic, should be easy, then," said Judy. "Let's go?"

"After you," the Sheriff responded, opening the door.

Sebastian Reed turned his head right away when he saw Judy. He didn't smile, but he wore a slightly cocky expression on his face. Judy could smell cheap cologne wafting from his skin. It made her feel slightly sick.

"Hello, Sebastian," she said.

Reed didn't open his mouth right away. Instead, he just kept staring at Judy, like he was analyzing her from top to bottom. "We met before, right?" he suddenly said.

"Glad you recognized me." She responded, maintaining eye contact with the gang leader. Reed continued staring at Judy.

"Yeah... you're the chick from outside the bar. Where is your friend, Red?"

"Just the two of us today, Sebastian. Me and you," Judy replied.

"Not using the wild card, huh?"

"Enough wild cards in this room already, I think."

Sebastian smiled at this. He seemed to love it. Judy decided to pull up the chair in front of Reed and sit. The Sheriff stood in a corner, arms crossed, and let her do her thing.

Judy glanced at Reed for a moment, then put her elbows on the table and finally spoke.

"I'm guessing you heard about Rick Carson?"

Reed shook his head, not as though he was indicating he didn't know anything about it, but more like he found the subject rather heavy.

"He was another one of your friends, right?"

Reed didn't do or say anything, just looked at the wall.

"Like Ethan and Fred?" Judy asked.

"Carson is a good guy, yeah. Haven't talked to him for months, however. What's happening with the guy?"

"Oh, so you don't know?"

"What? What don't I know?"

"He was murdered," Judy said.

"Murdered? Really? By who? What—what happened?" Reed proclaimed, innocently.

"Yeah!" Judy exclaimed, playing Reed's game. "Two nights ago. Didn't you see the papers? Or hear it from people in town?"

"Nope," Reed replied.

"That's weird," she continued in her smooth but vicious voice. "Well, the thing is, he was killed by gas in his boat. And someone named Wendell Pearson was passing by and heard loud screams."

"Really?"

"Yeah, and that Pearson man went into the boat and saw someone who we think is the killer. And he says that that someone had blue eyes, gray hair, and was very tall. Does that remind you of someone?"

Reed stared for a second and then laid back in his chair, sighing. "Nope," he said, crossing his arms.

Judy casually replied with a shrug. "Oh, look at that. Are these blue eyes, Sheriff?"

"Yup," replied the Sheriff.

"And that's gray hair, right? Or is my vision not good?"

"No, you're seeing fine, Hunter."

"And he's quite tall, isn't he?"

"Sure is," replied the Sheriff.

Reed's smile kept getting wider and wider. Judy stared him down and then she imitated the biker's expression.

"So, where were you on Saturday the 16th around the hours of five to seven p.m., Sebastian?"

"At the bar," Reed said.

"The bar?"

"The Rhode House. Ya know it?"

"Yes, I do know it. You were there all night?"

"Yup."

"Anybody other than your leather jacket friends who can vouch for you?"

Reed shrugged.

"Okay." Judy frowned. "How well do you know Melanie Sheldon?"

"Melanie?"

"Yeah," Judy replied.

"She's okay..."

"But I mean, you know her, right? Wasn't she part of your group too, at school?"

"My group? Hmm... if she says so. Sure."

"Do you talk to her often?"

"Not really. Where is she?"

"Okay, enough of this, Reed. I know you were all friends and that something is going on here. Either you tell me what is happening and who's doing it, or you watch all your friends die and I can't help you if you get the blame pinned on you."

Reed chuckled as if to say, *You're not that impressive or scary, woman!*

"Can I go now?" he asked.

"Melanie's next, Reed. He's pointed her out," Judy exclaimed, taking out a paper from her jeans. It was the third note sent to Charlotte. "See!"

Reed glared at Judy, then took his eyes off her long enough to glance at the note. Judy watched his face. For a split second she could almost sense fear in his eyes. Then his face went blank and she could see nothing more.

"What is going on? Just tell me," she pressed.

Reed smiled one last time and stood up. He looked at the Sheriff and then at the interrogation room door. "Free to go or...?"

The Sheriff looked at Judy, who nodded.

"Have a good day, Mr. Reed," Judy said as the Sheriff opened the door. Reed didn't turn back as he walked out.

"That went well," said the Sheriff.

"Better than expected," replied Judy.

The two came out of the interrogation room and started walking towards the exit.

"He's a cocky sonofagun, isn't he?" the Sheriff said.

Judy didn't respond. She was lost in thought.

"Did you learn anything?"

"A lot, actually," Judy replied.

"Really?" the Sheriff said.

Judy nodded.

"Well, he sure as hell answered like a guy who did it." Grant shook his head.

"That's the thing, Sheriff, I'm not quite sure anymore."

"What—"

They had almost reached the door when the two saw a cop car pulling up in the parking lot. From the passenger door, short, blond Eddie White got out. He immediately stuffed his shirt back into his jeans and put his hair back together. He also sniffed his underarm to see if he smelled.

As soon as she saw him, Judy quickly stepped back from the door so as not to be seen. The Sheriff was equally surprised to see White back this quickly.

"There's another exit at the back, right there," he said, rushing her away.

The Sheriff stayed where he was as Judy sped off to the emergency exit at the back. Outside, she kept walking until she was close to the parking lot. She hid behind the side of the building and observed White as he talked to the officer he had been in the car with. Then White's eyes focused on something in the distance. Not Judy, but Sebastian Reed, who was hopping onto his bike. Reed started the engine as White glared at him suspiciously.

Then, as if nothing had distracted him, White turned back to the officer and kept talking. They walked to the front door of the Sheriff's Office, where the Sheriff was waiting.

"Mr. White! Learned anything new?"

Judy sighed as White disappeared and went inside the building. She carefully walked away into the street. She was safe.

CHAPTER THIRTY-EIGHT:

TALKS AT THE CAFÉ

Getting Melanie to talk was not going to be easy. Charlotte drove with her to the café and Melanie went in through the back while Charlotte took the front door. Melanie still hadn't said a word to Charlotte about anything. She had driven, dead as a shadow, and then had exited the car without an expression of any kind. She had made Charlotte feel as though she wasn't even in the car with her. Melanie was carrying on with her work, not caring about Charlotte or anyone else.

Charlotte sat at her usual table and watched as the waitress greeted everybody and started working. Stew suddenly came over and locked eyes with Charlotte. Joy overcame him as he began talking. "Haven't seen you in a while!"

"Two days," Charlotte replied. "Feels like a long time, doesn't it?"

He laughed in agreement. "Where's Judy?"

"She'll be here soon, just taking care of some business."

Stew nodded. He cleaned Charlotte's table and poured her some coffee. "So, how's it going with the case?"

"Oh, it's going!" exclaimed Charlotte. "Yeah, it's going... Just looking into some people and some things, we'll see." She kept her eyes on Melanie as she worked.

The redhead didn't mean to ignore Stew, but she didn't really want to talk to him. Not right now. She was preoccupied. Stew finally left the menu on the table and said he would come back when Charlotte was ready to order. The young woman nodded and went back to watching Melanie. Nothing interesting was happening. The waitress kept serving her clients, talking to them, cleaning the bar and the tables, and going behind the counter. She was always in view.

Charlotte finally ordered an omelet and a bowl of fruit. She then looked at her phone and saw she had a text message from Brian. It said: *"Hey :) "*

Charlotte sighed and put it back in her pocket. She didn't want to give him any attention yet. He was clearly making an effort, and she wanted to make it right, but not right now. Maybe later she would reply... maybe tonight. Then she thought about it for a second and pulled out her phone again.

She unlocked it and typed: *"Hey."*

No emojis, nothing. Just *"Hey."* That would make him a little nuts. She smiled at her screen. Two seconds later, her phone started beeping.

"How's it going?" he had texted dully.

"Good, how about you?" she replied, answering dull with dull.

"Fine," he said before adding, *"I miss you."*

She could not tell herself she did not feel the same. Charlotte missed him, too. So bad. She could feel it now. Especially with Judy having come around and believing her now, Charlotte understood that it could take people some time, and she needed to give it to them. Maybe Brian had needed that time, and she could now give him a chance.

She typed *"I miss you too"* and sent it. Two or three seconds later, her phone was buzzing. He was calling her. She was about to pick up when Stew appeared and poured her more coffee. He smiled at her. It was the first time she really noticed how pretty his blue eyes were. They were the color of a bright blue sea.

"So... when are we touring the town?" he asked. "I made a list of all the historical things I want to show you."

"Did you now?"

Stew nodded. Charlotte thought it sweet and could not help but smile in return. He was making her blush.

"Well, hmm...maybe..." she began. Then the door of the café flew open and Judy walked in. She joined Charlotte at the table. She greeted

Stew and he went back to work, still starry-eyed from his encounter with the redhead.

"Anything new?" Judy asked.

"Nope, she's just been doing the usual. Nothing to be alarmed about."

"Okay, did she say anything?"

"Just the usual, as I said, being hostile at the idea of us surrounding her."

Judy didn't seem surprised. "So, nothing about the whole killer thing?"

"Not that I heard of. I tried to talk in the car on the way over here and she just kept turning up the music even louder."

"Great," said Judy. "Well, we'll need to talk to her at some point."

"You really think she knows something?"

"Oh, I think she knows a lot... She's probably just frightened out of her mind right now."

Charlotte nodded. "What about Reed?"

Judy filled her in on what had happened at the Sheriff's Office and how Sebastian Reed had reacted to the note. Aware of Judy's experience in the field and trusting her instincts as a great friend, and something of a sister figure, Charlotte still could not believe for a second that Reed was innocent. Her instincts were all pointing towards the gang leader. Not only the gang leader, but his buddies as well. They did that for a living, they were all criminals, so why not cold-blooded murderers?

Stew reappeared. "Are you having breakfast?"

"Yes, please! Haven't had any yet, just coffee. I'll take your vegan pancakes, as always!" replied Judy.

"Of course, my lady."

Judy thanked him and Stew left them. Then Judy saw Charlotte lift her head and look out into the crowd, then to the right. The redhead looked worried.

"Charlotte, what is it?" Judy asked.

"Melanie. I can't see her..."

Judy looked around. She couldn't see Melanie either, not behind the bar or at a table. She was gone.

CHAPTER THIRTY-NINE:

THE STORY

Judy stood up, hitting her kneecap under the table as she did so. She howled in pain. Charlotte went to help her and then they both flew off to look for Melanie. They moved towards the bar. Charlotte pushed herself up to look behind the counter, but Melanie wasn't crouched down anywhere behind there. Judy sprinted to the kitchen and peered around. The cooks and the other employees wondered what was going on. The retired detective kept going, moving farther into the cooking area. Then she yelled, "Has anyone seen Melanie? Anyone?"

No answer. Judy then came to a door at the very back and opened it. She stepped inside, but the room was empty. Judy found a bathroom next to it. She went for the door, but it was locked. She knocked and shouted for Melanie. She heard grunts from inside, then the voice of a man. Judy looked around the kitchen for another beat and finally heard a shout coming from the front, "Judy!"

It was Charlotte, waving at her to come. Judy quickly joined the redhead. Charlotte showed her to the front door, and they rushed outside. They turned a corner, going to the side of the building, and there she was.

Melanie was sitting on a bench, near some pretty flowers, having a cigarette. She was taking a break!

"Melanie!" Judy called out.

"Gosh, can't I have a second to myself?" Melanie replied, angrily.

"We were worried about you, we thought you had—"

"Don't need to worry, ladies, I'm still alive. No big monster came for me yet."

Judy walked towards the bench, gave a sigh, and then sat down next to Melanie. As for Charlotte, she kept her distance and remained standing, her arms crossed. The two detectives observed Melanie as she smoked her cigarette. Judy caught a glimpse of Melanie's shaking hand and glanced at the woman's face for a second. Melanie had black circles under her eyes. She looked like a woman who hadn't slept for days. A woman who was endlessly suffering.

Melanie resumed talking.

"You know, I knew this time would come someday."

Charlotte and Judy looked at each other.

"Nobody gets away with what we did. Nobody."

"What—" Charlotte tried.

"Life works in a weird fucking way, it really does. People who were done bad to in the past always find good for them in the future, and people who did bad in the past... well, they always find themselves with their tails between their legs in the end. That's how it works. There is retribution for everybody, good or bad."

"Melanie... what are you talking about? Have you done something?"

The woman kept smoking her cigarette, her hand shaking even more than before. Judy saw sweat dripping off her forehead.

"Doesn't matter now," uttered Melanie.

"Just talk to us. We can help you."

"No, you can't. Nobody can."

"What have you done?" persisted Charlotte. "Why is retribution going to come to you?"

"You folks think a bunch of cops surrounding me at all times and a couple of chitchats is gonna save me? It won't. Look at what he's done, the people he's already killed. The way he did it. Nobody can stop him."

"Who's him?" Judy asked.

"Reed?" Charlotte suggested.

"Sebastian Reed has nothing to do with this. He has a lot to do with a lot of things, but not this, no—"

"We have a witness telling us otherwise," said Charlotte.

"Fuck your witness! The one who killed Fred and Ethan wasn't him."

"But—"

"It wasn't him, do you hear me? It wasn't. If he goes to jail, then we all deserve to go with him!"

"What do you mean?" pressed Charlotte.

Melanie didn't answer. Judy stopped Charlotte with a stern glance before she could push too hard. Judy gently touched Melanie's shoulder and asked, "Then if it's not Reed, who is he, the killer? Who is he, Melanie?"

"I didn't say 'he'— I mean, I'm not totally sure if it is a girl or a guy..." Melanie responded.

"So, you don't know who it is..."

"I have some ideas, but I'm not a hundred percent sure. The only thing I'm sure of is why they're after us."

"And, why is that?" Charlotte asked.

"I told you, it's not going to help anything. They're going to get me anyways."

"No, not if we know who did it. We can stop them before they strike again," Judy said.

Melanie waited. Judy could see she was thinking about opening up.

"The thing you did, were Gregory and Fred involved as well?" Judy wondered.

Melanie hesitated again, and then quietly nodded.

"Rick Carson?"

Melanie nodded once more.

"Zachary Smith?"

"We all were," said Melanie.

"You know that Smith died too, right?" Charlotte then asked.

"Really?!"

She didn't know. She did not have a casual response to this. Melanie reacted like she had been hit on the head with a baseball bat. Then she started scratching herself again, growing nervous.

Judy nodded. Melanie put her head in her hands.

"He was killed..." Judy explained.

"But he's in Germany!"

"We think... the killer went there, too."

Melanie shook her head in disbelief. "Then he's done it. Almost killed us all. He'll kill us all!"

"All? Who are the others?" asked Charlotte.

"They are only three of us left..."

"You, Reed, and Julian?" helped Judy.

Melanie nodded again.

"What about that kid, Kovachev? Was he in it too? Did the killer get to him as well?"

Judy saw Melanie freeze. That name had struck a chord. The woman sat there in silence. Her two hands were now shaking. Not like when she had heard the news of Smith's death. No, this was much worse. Judy feared Melanie might collapse. But she didn't.

"Melanie?"

Melanie grabbed another cigarette from her pack. "No... he—"

"He disappeared, right?"

"Yeah," Melanie said after another long silence.

"Do you know anything about that?"

Judy heard Melanie chuckle. Charlotte and Judy looked at each other, not knowing where this reaction was coming from or what to do.

"Do I know anything about that? Do I know anything— Do I—" Melanie kept laughing, but not in an amused way.

They waited for more, but Melanie didn't spit it out just yet. The woman took a breath and then looked like she was gathering all her thoughts. Then Judy noticed a tear rolling down her right cheek. Charlotte uncrossed her arms and walked to the bench. She sat next to Judy. They listened to Melanie's breathing and crying until they heard more words coming out of her mouth.

"He was a very sweet guy, Viktor..." she said, before adding, "He was my friend." She took another short pause before continuing. "The guy came to Rockland in mid-November, or December, or whatever it was, in our junior year. Him and his family were all immigrants from Bulgaria, and he happened to move into the house next to mine..." she clarified, then inhaled noisily. "When I first saw him, I thought he was so cute. He had short hair that would curl, and beautiful brown eyes. He was smiling at me as he took out his bags from the trunk and helped his parents with everything. When he was done, he decided to come over and speak to me. He was nervous at first, and then he finally asked if we could hang out. I said sure. He had the weirdest accent I had ever heard in my life. But I thought it was great, and the guy seemed super kind."

Melanie smiled at the memory. "Then, while we were hanging out, he told me that he was going to this school called Rockland High the next day and he wanted to know if I knew it. I remember I said to him, 'Nope, never heard of it.' I think he didn't understand me at first and was, like, confused and everything. He kept telling me about it and how cool it was. He couldn't believe I didn't know anything about it. The school was like a dream for him! He wanted so badly to go there. Then I finally told him I was joking, and that Rockland High was the only school around so of course I knew it. I told him I even went there and was going to be in his class. He smiled at me, full of joy. We laughed for hours that day." Melanie smiled as she told that part. These were obviously fond memories for her.

"I kept messing with him. He was glad he found a buddy. I was glad too; he was nice. The next day, he got on the bus with me and asked if he could sit next to me. He was still a bit shy and his English wasn't that great. But I understood that he wanted me to show him around and make him feel less alone. He also wanted to meet my friends. At that time, I was hanging out with Ethan, Fred, who was a year older but was still my good pal, and another girl named Carla. They were my closest friends. They met Viktor and thought he seemed funny and that he was a good guy. They kept poking him, asking him questions about his country and why he was here. Not making fun, just genuinely interested. They were almost fascinated."

Melanie took another deep breath and put her cigarette back in her mouth for another puff. "Fred and Ethan were also on the football team, and they kept chatting about their next games and stuff and how excited they were during almost every bus ride. They were also wearing football jackets all day every day, like typical jocks. Viktor didn't ask right away, but I knew he was intrigued by the name. He kept looking at them, and even though he couldn't really understand the football conversation, he looked super intrigued by it all. One day he asked Fred, 'Why are you wearing the same clothes every day?' Fred looked at him, then looked at me and laughed. He explained that he was on a sports team and that's what people were wearing to represent it. Viktor, even more interested, kept bugging him to know more and Fred explained what football was and how important it was in our country. He even told Viktor about his ambitions to get a scholarship to college from playing football in the future. 'Football?' he asked, finally getting it. Viktor then told him he played a similar game back home, and they called it football as well in Bulgaria. However, they would play with their feet and kick the ball into a net to score points. He was talking about soccer! He then went on saying how good he was and how much he liked it. Fred and Viktor discussed the two sports and similarities and differences for a while. Viktor was astonished to hear about American football. Finally, Fred asked Viktor if he would try out for it and Viktor said yeah, he was so excited!"

"Reed, Franco, Carson, and Smith were also on the team, right?" asked Judy.

"Yeah, they all were. But that's not how Viktor first met them. We were all in the same class and they had encountered Viktor the first day he arrived at school. By the time he went to try out for the football team, Viktor had been, well... Sebastian and his whole gang that included Rick, Julian, and Zachary had made fun of him for quite some time in class before then. Mostly behind his back. He was the first non-white person to come to our class, to our school really, and... the gang were pretty... well, especially Julian. Julian didn't like him at all when he first met him, it was like he had been bit by something and caught the rage syndrome. Sebastian didn't really care, he just followed the parade like the others. So, Julian painted a target on Viktor's back and they all had fun taking advantage of Viktor and his background."

"They were racist bullies," suggested Charlotte.

Melanie clearly agreed. She didn't say anything, but she blinked.

"How surprising..." added Charlotte.

Melanie took another puff of her cigarette.

"What happened after that?" asked Judy.

"Viktor tried out for football... and he was pretty bad," Melanie continued, smiling a little. "Julian and Sebastian kept laughing at him all the way through the tryout, it was like they were watching a circus. But Fred didn't care, he liked Viktor and his spirit, so he convinced the team to give him a chance and said he would train Viktor every day if he needed to. With a lot of backlash, and some threats from Reed, the team finally agreed, and Viktor was on the team. He was very grateful.

"Fred did what he said. He trained Viktor every single day and the kid got better and better. He got so good that in his first game he scored two touchdowns for the team! Sebastian's furiousness started to blow off and he slowly accepted Viktor into the team. Viktor had a new group of friends, of 'bros,' and he was happy. We would all hang out together and go to parties as a huge gang."

Melanie took a long pause. Something else was coming, Judy could feel it, and Melanie was for sure not looking forward to telling it.

"Sebastian had a girlfriend, the most beautiful girl at school, Liv Porter. Cliché, I know, but still. In addition to being super handsome, he was the Captain of the football team and every girl wanted him—even though he was an asshole most of the time. Liv was not the slutty type, she was known as a good girl, almost too much of a good girl. The Miss Perfect who performed very well in school, the nerd who could do everything but was unattainable... well, unattainable until Sebastian got his paws on her. He wanted her. From the first day she had arrived at the school, he had decided she would not date anyone but him, and he made it known to everybody else in school. It took a long time for her to agree to date him, but weirdly, after some time, she did. Sebastian was very... let's just say... persuasive when he wanted to be. Nobody said no to him. And she did for a while, but that made him even crazier for her, and he kept chasing her until something switched inside her mind. The next thing we know, they're a couple, and they are kissing everywhere. Sebastian talks about her and walks with her like she's some kinda trophy."

She took another cigarette from her pack, still shaking. "Then, two years later, Viktor arrives on the football team. Sebastian and Liv are still dating. However, Viktor, not understanding English very well and being new at this school, does not know about Sebastian's claim on Liv. Even more than that, he doesn't know about Sebastian's gang and how much power they have cast over the whole school. When Sebastian or another Skullhead claimed a girl—yeah, they were using that name back then too—nobody was to touch her. So, one day Viktor is playing football and he sees this gorgeous girl on the field, hanging with her friends. He goes up to her. She says her name is Liv and he starts talking to her. They hit it off, and still Viktor knows nothing of Sebastian's relationship with her. And as Viktor becomes popular and starts going to parties with the football team, Viktor sees more of Liv and they keep talking. Suddenly, Viktor comes up to me and asks me if I think she has a boyfriend. I was shocked. I tell him about Sebastian, and he says, "How? They never kiss, I think they just friends." And I tell him, no. I also told him about Sebastian's character in every way I could to prevent him from making a mistake. Viktor looks at me sad, I never saw him so sad... ever. He looked like he was in love or something. He asked me if we could leave the party, and we hung out at my house that night, he was so shook up.

"The next day, we go back to school and he sees Liv, but he doesn't talk to her. He ignores her. However, she comes up to him and they chat right in front of me for a good ten minutes. Suddenly, Julian comes through the doors that morning and sees them together and he goes after Viktor and asks him what the hell. Then Sebastian comes in and Julian, like the vicious, manipulating snake that he was, explains to Sebastian what he saw and heard. Sebastian gets so mad that he throws Viktor into a locker and makes a whole scene. Liv tried to get Sebastian away and reassure him, but he was pissed."

"Jeez..." uttered Charlotte. "Why are boys so intense? Like chill, man."

Melanie continued, "Right! Well, it didn't end there. Fred finally came to defend Viktor, and Sebastian and the Skullheads ended up leaving. This whole thing created a mess in the school and in the vibe of the football team. Ethan, Rick, and Zack were now freaking angry at Viktor too. They all took Sebastian's side. You can argue that they had no choice.

"Things calmed down after a few weeks. By then Viktor returned to his shell, avoiding Sebastian and the gang as much as possible, and skipping most of the football practice, and certainly avoided Liv. He didn't even want to hang out with me and Fred. We suspected he was having lunch in the bathroom. Other than in class, we would not really see him. He looked so scared every time Sebastian and Julian came into the room.

"One day, we all hear some screaming in the cafeteria, it's Liv and Sebastian arguing. Sebastian keeps trying to get a hold of her, but she doesn't want him to touch her. The next day, after that argument, a rumor floats around the school that the pair broke up. This wasn't the first time we had heard that, for sure, but this seemed to be more definite than the other times. They certainly weren't talking to one another, even though Sebastian was clearly trying to. Weeks went by and suddenly we see Viktor coming to hang out again, and he now has a smile on his face. We ask what's up and he says that apparently Liv came to his house the night before and they hung out for a while. I didn't see this, 'cause I was out with friends that night. But I ask him why the hell did Liv come to his house and he keeps telling me that she said she was over Sebastian and that she wanted to go on dates with Viktor. 'Dates,' he said, 'dates.' I warned him it was probably a bad idea, but he didn't care, he liked Liv a lot. I think he even said he loved her. He told me she had kissed him when she came to his house and it was the best moment of his life. He was all red and smiley. I had never seen the guy so happy before."

"Did Sebastian know all this?" asked Charlotte.

"Fuck no! He would have—" Melanie stopped herself before going on. "No, no, he didn't."

"So... they dated in hiding?" said Judy.

"Oh, yeah. It was in hiding all right. The two didn't even talk to each other at school out of fear of Sebastian and company. But I knew, I knew everything. Viktor would tell me. She would go have dinner at his house almost every night and spend time there. They were so great with each other; I can't even tell you. The sweetest couple on Earth."

Suddenly, Melanie burst into tears. She couldn't talk anymore, she was crying so hard.

Judy put a comforting hand on her shoulder. "What happened, Melanie?"

"Nothing can save me from this. I'm gonna die."

"No, you're not. You are not. We will protect you. Whatever you did, we can—"

"No, you can't! You really can't! We're all fucking doomed."

"Melanie, please, I swear, I will do everything I can to find whoever is doing this and make him stop. Nobody deserves to die that way, whatever any of you did," Judy stated with conviction.

"Viktor didn't deserve it either!"

"What happened to him, Melanie? What really happened?"

Melanie cried a while and finally stopped. Judy handed her some tissues from her purse and Melanie cleaned herself up before continuing.

"A month and a half after they had started dating, something happened. Viktor came to me one day, shaking, not knowing what to do with himself. He was almost crying. Not entirely out of sadness, but not really from joy either. He really didn't know what to feel. Then I pressured him into telling me what was going on and he said it: Liv was carrying his baby. She was pregnant! I was shocked by the news, I couldn't talk. But he looked so happy even though he was worried about it all. He was seventeen and he was gonna be a dad. Yeah, they had decided to keep the child. When I saw them together at his place, Liv looked equally filled with joy. I became so happy for them too..." Melanie smiled briefly, and then said, "But then..."

"Sebastian found out?" Judy suggested.

Melanie nodded. "June came around, and it was the last month of school. Ethan asked me out on a date that first week and I said yes, so we started dating. I liked him, he was a good guy, and he treated me well. I felt like a princess around him. I trusted him. One day I decided to spill the beans on Liv and Viktor because I was enthused for them. I made him swear to not tell anyone, and he did... swear, that is. Then, on the following Saturday, he was going to a party with Fred while I stayed home to study. Julian, Sebastian, Rick, and Zachary were there. As the story goes, Ethan was talking to Julian, he got a little drunk and told him about Liv and Viktor. Ethan came to me the next day, realizing what he had done, and we argued for a while. I was so angry with him! The next Monday, we thought Viktor would get it, that they would come after him, but nothing happened. I kept quiet and I didn't tell Viktor anything."

Charlotte sighed, momentarily relieved.

"Weeks went by and still nothing. Then, me and Ethan just assumed that he hadn't really said anything, he had just had one too many and he *imagined* he had said something... but he had not imagined it. That sneaky bitch Julian had found out about it all from Ethan. He had just waited for the best opportunity to tell Sebastian. He had probably just waited 'till Sebastian was already in a bad mood. So, he told Sebastian, and the guy obviously freaked the hell out."

"Did he hurt Viktor?" Judy asked.

"He cornered him... us... me and Viktor were walking home. Suddenly we hear the sounds of motorcycles coming towards us. The Skullheads speeding, charging at us like mad men. Julian, Rick, and Zack shouting at us, Ethan following at the back like a lost sheep. Sebastian's face was deep red, enraged. He got off his bike and grabbed Viktor by the shoulder and pushed him into the woods. Julian grabbed the other shoulder and pulled too. They made us walk to the depths of the woods and then suddenly threw Viktor on the ground. Sebastian kept shouting atrocities at him. Viktor didn't know what was going on. He kept trying to stand up, but he was pushed right back to the ground every time. I begged them to stop, but they wouldn't. Then, Rick was finally the first to throw a punch, right on the nose, and Viktor starting bleeding. But Sebastian stopped him, he wanted a first go at him. After a few seconds of punching and Viktor crying, Sebastian smiled and invited his friends in. So, Zachary and Rick joined in. They went for Viktor with their feet and hands after that, me screaming in the background while looking at the horrible scene. Rick and Zachary finally stopped. They saw that Viktor had clearly had enough, but Sebastian kept going. I tried to stop him, but Julian got a hold of me and smiled. He loved all this. Then, suddenly, someone came running towards us from farther in the woods. The guy jumped on Sebastian and pushed him to the ground. It was Fred!"

Charlotte looked at Judy with tears in her eyes.

"I don't know how, but he found us. And now he was fighting Sebastian. But then Sebastian stood back up and punched Fred. Fred was now the target, and he was getting it bad. Suddenly Viktor got back up and jumped on Sebastian. And that's when it happened. Julian let go of me and grabbed Viktor, and pushed him away and started fighting him, beating him once more. So I mustered up some courage and jumped on Julian. Sebastian and Fred came and tried to tear us apart... it was fucking anarchy in there, everyone was holding and fighting each other! We heard something like a scream, then a huge bang, we didn't know what it was... and then we stopped fighting and looked around. It was Viktor... he was nowhere to be seen. I called for him, but there was no answer. After a few seconds, Ethan shouted. He pointed to a small hill beside us, leading to a hollow. And there he was. Viktor. Lying face down on the ground. We all called to him, but there was no answer. We rushed to him... I shouted again at him, and then finally went and turned him around. His eyes were closed. We all saw blood pouring from his forehead. Then, we saw a big rock on the ground beside him. There was blood on the rock. And Viktor... he was lying there, not waking up. I grabbed him by the neck and saw more blood pouring out of his skull. I was petrified. Everyone was. We didn't know what had happened. We weren't sure if one of us had done it or not—each of us looked as shocked as all the others. Even Sebastian and Julian. Everybody swore they didn't see what had happened. We just knew that Viktor was dead."

Judy took a heavy and painful breath.

"Then I heard Fred move around and shout at Julian and Sebastian, 'Look what you've done! You sons of bitches! Look what you've done.' Viktor had no pulse when I touched his neck. I kept asking him to wake up, but he wouldn't... he wouldn't... We stood there for a half hour, helpless. Sebastian kept telling us he wanted to hurt him a little bit, teach him a lesson, not freaking kill him... He was crying like a baby."

Melanie was bawling now. She was reliving every moment as if it was still happening. She then took a gulp of air, steadied herself and went on, "Then, Fred tried to go and find help, but Julian wouldn't let him. The guy pulled out a gun on us! He said we were all a part of this now. He told us that we needed to help them hide the body and wash away the blood on the rock. We were completely stunned. Even though we wanted to resist, we couldn't. He had a gun! He was going crazy! He said he had stolen it from his dad or something..."

Melanie was sobbing. She looked at Judy for empathy, but Judy was confused and disturbed by all of it.

"So, you just got rid of him and didn't tell anyone?"

"They forced us to! Julian said that if we were to tell anyone, he'd tell everyone that we were in it as much as them, and he made Zachary, Rick, and Sebastian swear to this as well. He even threatened to kill us if necessary. I was scared, and I didn't know what to think or do... so... I did everything they told me to. We hid the body, we cleaned everything, and we stuck to our story."

"Which was?" Charlotte asked.

"I walked with him after school, we parted ways, he told me he was going straight home, and I went to Ethan's, where all of us—Fred, Sebastian, Rick, Zachary and Julian—studied for our finals."

"Great studying, I'm sure," commented Charlotte sourly.

"Ethan's parents were travelling, so they couldn't say if it was true or not."

"And everyone believed you?"

"It's been thirty years now and everybody still thinks Viktor has gone missing."

"Nobody ever suspected anything?"

"Nobody ever saw anything..."

"Oh yeah? Then who's targeting you? Clearly somebody saw or heard something, because you're all on death row now. All of you."

Melanie nodded. "I don't know... maybe somebody from our class who didn't say anything back then, or... a local... someone walking in the woods..." She paused, thinking. Then she said shakily, "Look, I wasn't gonna throw my life away and go to prison... I was sixteen, for God's sake! I hadn't done anything!"

"What if it had just been an accident..."

"Yeah, an accident that had happened after we were all fighting each other, all getting bruised... an accident that had happened after Viktor had been viciously punched and kicked for a while before that!"

"Then it wasn't an accident!" Charlotte almost shouted. "You could've pointed the finger at Reed or at Julian, and that's it! They killed him."

Charlotte was shaking her head. Melanie looked awful; she was becoming white as a sheet. Judy understood that it might not have been that simple for Melanie at that time.

"Where did you hide the body, Melanie?" asked Judy, a lot calmer than Charlotte.

Melanie took a moment, hesitating. "We... hid it under a coffin at a cemetery..."

"Wow," replied Charlotte.

"It was Julian's idea."

"Of course it was..." Charlotte uttered sarcastically.

"He said nobody would look there..."

"So, you just let him rot there like he was nothing and made his parents go mad because they didn't know what had happened to him?!"

"I—I..."

Charlotte was furious. "It was a mistake, Melanie! You should have known that. Somebody should have—"

"I see that now. It ruined my whole life!"

"I bet it did. If you would have said something, then my father might have not—"

"Charlotte!" reprimanded Judy.

"I know, I know," replied Melanie.

"Why didn't *he* say anything?" Charlotte muttered bitterly.

"How good does it look for a cop to have helped his high school buddies, some of them now part of a biker gang, bury the body of his friend and maybe even have been responsible for his death? He couldn't. Even before that, he couldn't. He wanted a career, a life. We all did..."

"A life where you all carry a horrible crime on your conscience."

Judy shushed Charlotte before she could say more.

Almost a minute of silence elapsed before Melanie said, "Your father was a good man, Charlotte. Just know that."

This seemed to placate Charlotte.

The retired detective finally asked the question she'd been wondering about for a few minutes now:

"Melanie... what happened to Liv and the baby?"

"Liv went crazy when Vik disappeared," Melanie said. "She didn't believe for a second that Viktor had left her or had vanished out of the blue. She claimed that Sebastian had something to do with it. The police investigated, but they never found anything so they let it go. Her family finally learned about the baby and they threw her out of their home. She decided to move away, and we never heard from her again."

"Did Sebastian ever go find her?"

"No... he... she made herself clear and said she would probably kill him if he tried."

"Do you know if she ever had the baby?"

"I'm freaking sure of it," said Melanie. "Liv loved Viktor like no one else she probably ever loved before, and after that... she would never get rid of a baby that came from him."

CHAPTER FORTY:

IN SEARCH OF A KILLER

Charlotte stayed with Melanie while Judy called the Sheriff and explained the situation to him as succinctly as possible. Then, after the phone call ended, the two detectives waited for the waitress to finish her shift and they all walked back to the motel. Judy collected Rush and they headed back to Melanie's house. Melanie showed them in, and Judy and Charlotte sat on the couch, watching her. They kept talking about the case and tried to pick Melanie's brain a little more, but the woman was desperately exhausted.

It was almost dark outside when they heard a knock at the door. They all jumped.

The Sheriff came in, carrying a bunch of files under his arms. "That's all I could find."

He put the files on the table and watched Judy and Charlotte as they approached them and started eyeing everything inside.

"Dear me! I hope we find something. I need it quick," exclaimed the Sheriff.

"Why?" asked Charlotte.

The Sheriff sighed, scratching his head. "White is getting more and more suspicious. I think he knows I'm hiding something from him. If I don't give him a solid false lead soon, I'm afraid he'll catch on to us."

"He needs you to give him a lead?" replied Charlotte.

The Sheriff looked at her, amused.

Judy asked, "Sheriff, did you hear anything about Carson's girlfriend? White went to see her, right?"

"Yes, yes. I was gonna tell you about that."

The Sheriff stood there for a beat, then took a seat in front of Judy and Charlotte. Charlotte saw Melanie, in the kitchen, turn her head to look at the Sheriff.

"She said she saw some man spying on them two days before Carson got killed."

"What man?" asked Melanie.

"She said he was tall, and he was wearing a leather jacket."

"A Skullhead leather jacket?" Charlotte asked.

The Sheriff shrugged.

"Did it look like anybody we know? Sebastian?" the redhead pursued.

"She said he had sunglasses and the sunlight was heavy, she couldn't see his face well. All in all, she said he spent at least five minutes looking at them."

"Where?"

"They were sitting in the park, at lunch, having a picnic."

"It wasn't Sebastian!" shouted Melanie from the kitchen.

"Or it was, and he was just watching over his friend because he knew something was about to happen," said Charlotte. "He also could have put another Skullhead on him to simply keep watch."

The Sheriff nodded. Charlotte looked suspiciously at Melanie for a bit. She really hoped Melanie had told them the truth. It was an awful truth, but it could clear Sebastian's name. He was a jerk, nonetheless. Charlotte could never have imagined Melanie being involved with him. Having him as a boyfriend must have been a terrible drag. He seemed possessive and controlling, not to mention a little too violent for Charlotte's tastes. Never in a million years would she go out with a guy like that, and if she did, she hoped she would sense the red flags right away and break it off.

The Sheriff went into the kitchen and asked Melanie if he could get some water. She poured him some and he came back to Judy and

Charlotte. Judy was looking through the files. They were documents on Viktor Kovachev's disappearance.

"I looked for this Olivia Porter girl as well. The records say she hasn't been in the US for a very long time. Since 1996..."

"Where is she?" asked Judy.

"Dead."

Melanie stopped what she was doing and gave an astonished gasp.

"She died of cancer, two years ago," clarified the Sherrif. "She was staying in Bulgaria at the time."

Judy and Charlotte looked at each other.

"Was she with the Kovachev family?"

"No idea... It sure seems likely, however."

"One family rejects her, another welcomes her," said Charlotte.

Judy nodded. "Maybe. Either way, she's dead now, she's not a suspect..."

Charlotte saw Judy return her glance to the Sheriff.

"What about the child, Sheriff? Did you find anything? Did she have it?"

The Sheriff drank some more water. "There is a child registered to her name. His name is Damyan Kovachev. He'd be thirty now."

Charlotte was thinking all kinds of things. For one, Liv had kept Viktor's name, which showed that she clearly loved him. That reinforced Melanie's story. She was also thinking about him growing up in Bulgaria. It was not New York, the climate was so different there, not just the weather but the environment, the culture, the poverty. Damyan grew up without a father. Charlotte couldn't imagine growing up without Fred. Her father had played such a big part in making her the person she was now.

"That wasn't the only child of hers on record. There was also an Atanas and a Gavrail Ignatov, both from her marriage with a Borislav Ignatov."

Judy and Charlotte nodded. “Any other information on this Damyan kid?”

“Not much, just that he served in the military over there for quite some time.”

“Charlotte did say that you could get cyanide gas from a military background...” said Judy.

“You think he might be your killer?” asked the Sheriff.

“It seems most likely,” said Judy, glancing at Charlotte. “Well... it would make the most sense. At thirty now, he must have often wondered what happened to his father. And I’m thinking, maybe he learned the truth somewhere along the road. How? I don’t know.”

“Maybe his mother told him everything,” suggested the Sheriff.

“She didn’t know much, apparently, according to Melanie,” clarified Charlotte.

“You got a picture?” asked Judy.

“Hell no,” replied the Sheriff. “We’re not that lucky.”

Judy stood up and went to the kitchen to get some water as well.

“If it’s not in the records, then we might have luck calling the Bulgarian government. If he was in the military, then they’ll certainly have a picture of the man.”

“Good luck with that!” the Sheriff chuckled.

“Don’t worry, Sheriff. I’ll try calling them. If not, I’ll get someone from New York to do it.”

“You still have friends over there?”

“I hope so,” Judy laughed.

“If you don’t, then I was just about to suggest we could have White do it for you,” suggested the Sheriff.

“Sure, we would get it in six months. No, I’ll try my way first. Got a few sources at Interpol too. We’ll see.”

“I bet you do, Detective. Long career, a lot of achievements, great connections!” exclaimed the Sheriff. “I’m slightly envious.”

"Like I said, it remains to be seen how far I'll get." Judy smiled, then whispered so Melanie would not hear. "In the meantime, we need to verify Melanie's story..."

"How do you suggest we do that?" asked Charlotte.

"Well, first, the Sheriff and I will go on a hunt for Viktor Kovachev's body. You stay here."

"And do what?"

"Babysit. Watch over her."

"I've been doing that all day!"

"A few more hours are not going to hurt. I'll come back soon, don't worry."

The Sheriff nodded in agreement and began walking towards the front door.

"Ready?" he shouted.

"One minute, Sheriff. Wait for me in your car, I'll be right out."

Judy didn't speak until they heard the front door closing behind him. She gave Charlotte a smile. "You'll be fine."

Judy went to her purse and took something from it. It was shiny and looked heavy. Charlotte couldn't believe her eyes. It was a gun! The retired detective was handing her a gun. Why?

"Use it only if necessary. Aim and shoot. Got it?"

Judy was about to show her how to use the gun, but Charlotte took it from her hands and removed the bullets all by herself.

"Smith & Wesson... pretty."

"So, your dad did show you?" asked Judy, obviously a little surprised.

"Yeah, I know, he wasn't that disapproving and sexist after all..."

Judy sighed, slightly smirking. She then patted Charlotte on the shoulder. "Call me if there's anything."

"Will do," Charlotte replied.

The redhead watched as Judy left the house. She heard the front door close. Then she peered into the kitchen at Melanie, who was making herself dinner. Charlotte wondered whether she'd be making any for her.

CHAPTER FORTY-ONE:

CORPSE

The Sheriff drove with Judy down Main Street, heading for Rockland's cemetery. The small town was deserted at this hour. Some people were walking along the streets, but it was either to hurry home or to walk their dogs. As they kept driving down the hill, Judy peered at the full moon floating, at the end of the street, in the center of the sky before them.

They passed the park and kept on. Judy was looking around at the people when suddenly she saw someone she thought she knew walking along the sidewalk. He was tall and his face looked familiar. She asked the Sheriff to stop the car on the side of the road, got out, and crossed the street. She went up to the man, leaving the Sheriff in the car.

Oh, yes, she remembered now. It was Brian, Charlotte's boyfriend. What was he doing here? And why was he walking around so late at night? He looked equally surprised to see her.

"Judy!" he said uncomfortably. "Hi..."

He couldn't form any more words, Judy stared suspiciously at him.

"What are you doing here?" she asked.

"Uh... just hanging around..."

"Really?"

He took a deep breath, clearly nervous.

"Well, I didn't get any news from you guys, and Charlotte refuses to let me in on this whole thing..."

"What whole thing? What did she say?"

"I don't know. She honestly didn't say. I was just worried, you know."

"How did you find us?"

"Ugh... you weren't giving me any news, so..." he began anxiously. "I might have finally figured her password and tracked her phone here with the 'Find My Phone' app... I got a room at the motel and, uh..."

"Really?" Judy questioned, smiling.

Brian was getting increasingly uneasy.

"Have you seen her yet?" she asked.

"Nope... I—I..."

He obviously had no idea how to proceed.

"You should go catch up with her... I'm sure she would love to see you."

"Really?"

"Yeah. Isn't that what you came here for? Whatever argument you two had going on, she seems over it. Just talk to her, all right? Here, she's at Melanie Sheldon's house. I'll give you the address."

Brian thanked her, still obviously nervous. He handed her his phone and she added the address in his notes.

"Talk to her!" she insisted one more time, before waving goodbye at him.

She walked back to the Sheriff's car. Before she got in, she turned to look at Brian one more time and saw the young man leaving. Judy nodded to the Sheriff and they went on their way.

"Who was that?" Grant asked.

"Someone Charlotte's trying to avoid," Judy said. "Her boyfriend."

"He looks like a charm. Why is she avoiding him?"

Judy grinned at the Sheriff. "You should ask her," she said.

"Yeah... I'll let it go, then," Grant replied. The idea of getting involved in other people's romantic lives seemed to terrify him. "It's their business."

Judy chuckled.

There was a pause.

"How is she holding up?" Grant then questioned. "Her dad being dead and all."

Judy didn't know how to answer that. She stared into the night, thinking.

"How are *you* holding up?" Grant then asked.

"It's incredibly hard for all of us," she finally conceded. "Incredibly hard. We were partners for twenty years. We lived through everything together. Fred was really the best guy ever."

The Sheriff nodded. "Yeah, he seemed like he was... It's been a long time, but the kid and his parents seemed really well loved in town when I was a deputy." Grant sighed. "Do you think there might be a problem, though? If we get closer and closer to finding the killer?"

"I'm fine," Judy said. "I've lost a lot of people along the way."

"That's why I asked about Charlotte first... I'm not so much worried about you. But her—"

"That's why I'm here." Judy said firmly. "I think she's handling herself fine at the moment, but I'll let you know."

Grant nodded. He seemed to trust Judy.

"So, why did you retire?" he asked, changing tack.

"What do you mean?" Judy asked, surprised.

"I mean, you seem to be enjoying this... the thrill of it all!"

Judy shook her head, smiling.

"Come on, don't be ashamed. I see it. I feel the same way. Hell, I haven't had that many big cases in my career, but the ones I have had, especially this one— It's been fulling me with a sense of excitement and purpose. It's fun..."

Judy laughed.

"Of course, people die... that's not cool, as they say, but the puzzle and the journey of finding a murderer... Man! Why didn't I become a detective?"

"Yeah." Her face was bright. "I don't know... I was tired. New York and its politics... In our current climate, it's becoming harder and harder to really expose the truth. People just want things done quickly, they want to point fingers, get the murderers thrown away and move on..."

"Like White," he said.

Judy nodded.

"Something tells me exposing the real truth doesn't scare you, politicians surrounding you or not."

"It's time for a change. Honestly. I want to be free and play Jenga and do trivia nights with friends."

"Play Jenga, huh?" Grant nodded.

Judy smirked. "Why did you become a cop?" she asked.

"To put food on the table," Grant said wryly. "I was born in this town... and there aren't a lot of options to make ends meet. People are fishermen, waitresses, schoolteachers... I didn't wanna stand in a boat all day, waiting for fish to come. I didn't want to deal with food—I would eat everything on the plates before it ever got to customers! And teaching kids seemed dreadful... as you can see, they were a rough lot in this town..."

Judy nodded.

"I found the love of my life early on, and she wanted a big family. We had a lot of children in the house... all gone now, ha! They left us. But the point is, we had to feed them all."

Judy smiled understandingly.

"The thing is," Grant continued, "after I became a cop, I began to see the real darkness of this town. This county, but especially this town. I wanted other people to have dinner, too. To come home safe to their families. And with people like Reed rising up and the fear that it drew to this community, it became crucial that I do that for people. While everyone was scared, I couldn't be. They needed hope. That's what a cop is supposed to do: keep people safe, keep their hopes up. So, I made it my mission. I wanted to fight for the town I was born in. It's been hard, but I've never given up."

"That's very noble, Newman," Judy said.

Grant shrugged. "Also, one day, about ten years ago, I saw somebody on the news... a detective from the NYPD. He seemed to be doing the same thing for the big Red Serpent case... or was it a 'she,' actually?"

Judy beamed modestly.

"Anyway, she seemed to want to protect the people too, to want to battle corruption and throw out the fearmongers, and that gave me hope. It could be done."

"I'm glad to have helped," the retired detective said sincerely.

Grant nodded.

A moment passed.

"So, you said you had found the love of your life. Where's your wife now?" she finally asked.

"I won't tell you my address and you can't meet her. Okay?" He laughed. "Somewhere up north in Sullivan County... I keep my personal life personal! All right? Now, enough about me. Let's dig up a body!" exclaimed Grant.

"Hidden family, man of mystery..." Judy said. She looked at him appraisingly. "She's a lucky lady."

They both chuckled.

Grant was a good, kind man. He was also a great cop. She knew that, because she had met a lot of cops in her career, and in New York a lot of them were corrupt. He clearly wasn't.

They kept on driving along the muddy road. Then they entered the woods. As soon as she saw the tombstones, Judy got an odd feeling in her bones. The last time she was here, it was for Fred's funeral. This was the place where she had watched her old partner get buried underground. It seemed so long ago now.

They got out of the car and began walking down the wet, sloping grass. The Sheriff carried a shovel over his shoulder, along with a medium-sized flashlight in the other hand. He began casting it around the place to find the correct writing. They were looking for a particular name on a tombstone, a name that Melanie had provided to Judy. Under this tombstone, a casket containing the remains of a body was supposedly buried. However, unusually, underneath that casket was another body—the body of dead teenager Viktor Kovachev.

They looked around for quite some time until they found it, in a far corner of the cemetery. In the last line of tombstones, there it was: *Christopher Malikie 1919–1973. Beloved husband, and father of two.*

The Sheriff gave Judy the flashlight and put down the shovel. He then looked at her for a long moment before saying:

"You sure you wanna do this whole thing?"

"Do you have other interesting plans tonight, Sheriff?" Judy replied. "A date at the cemetery sounds good, no? We dig up a grave and then, when we find what we're looking for, we can even have a picnic. I might have some sandwiches in the car..."

Grant laughed uneasily. Digging a body out of a grave was most definitely not part of his regular duties. Judy was just as uncomfortable, but they had to do this to authenticate Melanie's story and get strong evidence that this whole murder investigation was related to Viktor Kovachev's disappearance—and probable death.

"We've looked so long for this kid, this might be the night we get some answers..." the Sheriff declared and pushed the shovel into the grass.

He dug and dug. Dirt piled up on the left side of the tombstone. Judy kept illuminating the Sheriff with the flashlight as he worked. Then the retired detective heard a dull thud. There was no more mud or dirt to pull out of the ground. The Sheriff had hit something, the casket.

"There we go."

Judy looked at the Sheriff and nodded slowly. He struck the shovel once, and then once more, and a third time, before the casket finally began to open. The Sheriff threw the shovel away and went down with his now-gloved hands, lifting the wooden door. It took a second, but he got it.

Inside was exactly what they had expected, a disintegrated corpse.

"All right. Let's get it out," said the Sheriff.

The Sheriff closed the casket once more. Meanwhile, Judy got down on her knees and reached into the hole to help drag the casket out. They certainly weren't prepared for this. The coffin was made of heavy wood. The Sheriff tried to get it out of the dirt, but it was stuck. He had to get the shovel again and create a larger space at the front of the casket for it to pass. He finally got a hold of the thing and was able to pull it up, slightly. Judy grabbed hold as well and helped as much as she could. Using all their remaining strength and energy in a great team effort, they eventually got the coffin out of the ground.

Judy and the Sheriff both fell back into the grass and took large gulps of air. They suddenly started laughing a bit crazily.

"That's why I want to retire!" Judy exclaimed. "If you were still wondering."

"You don't say!" the Sheriff shouted. "Now I'm the one thinking it might be time for the old man to hit the bricks and abandon ship. I feel my bones cracking, wanting to collapse. Thank you very much for the reality check. God!"

They kept giggling like four-year-olds for a moment. Then they both came back to the grim reality. The Sheriff gave Judy a hand and she got back on her feet. They looked at the opened ground before them and walked to the edge.

As they both looked down, they saw nothing but dirt. The Sheriff sighed and went back into the ground. He took the shovel and started digging once more. He dug for a long two minutes, then shook his head and looked up at Judy. There was no corpse down there, no Viktor Kovachev.

"Fuck!" she said.

"You sure it was Christopher Malikie?"

"Yeah, that's what Melanie said. I'm sure," Judy replied.

"Well, if the body was there, then somebody took it out. I can't think of another explanation..."

Judy kept listening to the Sheriff, glancing down into the cold ground. There was nothing there.

CHAPTER FORTY-TWO:

THE DOORBELL

"It was there, Charlotte!" said Melanie one more time after Judy had called them and told them they had not found a corpse under the coffin.

"Of course it was, Melanie. We'll find it, I promise we'll find his body, and the killer with it. We'll stop all this, I promise!"

They sat there for another moment before Melanie finally stood up and poured herself some wine. She offered some to Charlotte, but the redhead politely refused. The waitress then remained in the kitchen, preparing herself some food.

Did Melanie really have the right name on the gravestone? Had she forgotten to tell them something? Charlotte wouldn't know. Had Melanie told them the entire story? Or were they missing something? Was she hiding anything important? The redhead didn't think so. From her agitated body language and the honest expression on her face, Charlotte could tell that she was not being lied to. Melanie seemed as distraught as they were—even more so, because she was on the killer's list and could potentially die. What were they missing? They were definitely missing something!

It had happened thirty years ago. Was it possible the body had crumbled into dust since then? *No, buried bodies don't disappear like that!* Charlotte thought. *If they did, we wouldn't have mummies.* And Charlotte knew, from studying the human body in science, that bones don't just disappear. They last forever, that wasn't an option. So, had someone moved the body? Had the killer moved the body? If so, why? What would he have to gain by doing that? And if the killer really was Viktor Kovachev's son, would he disrespect his father like that?

Forty-five minutes later, the doorbell chimed. Charlotte saw Melanie quickly come up to her, on edge. Charlotte had been sitting on the couch, petting Rush. The redhead stood up and told Melanie she was handling it. She went straight for the door. She then stopped, came back to the couch, and picked up the Smith & Wesson. Charlotte held it tight in her left hand, close to her leg. She then drifted to the door once more. She couldn't see anything from the windows on the side, nor was there a peephole to look through to see who was there. After a brief moment, Charlotte called out, "Who is it?"

She received no answer. The redhead waited for a bit, then called again.

"Is someone there?"

There was another short beat, and then she finally heard a voice.

"It's deputy Nolan, ma'am. There is someone here to see you."

"He has pizza!" she heard another voice say.

Charlotte opened the door and behind it, standing on the porch, was Stew. She felt her eyes crinkle at the corners. He seemed glad to see her, too.

"Sorry, there was no vegan cheese left... I hope Judy won't be—"

"She's not here!" Charlotte replied. Her voice grew bubbly.

"Oh, well. Okay, then!"

Charlotte showed him in and was about to close the door when she looked at the deputy. "Didn't know you were still here."

"Following orders, miss. The Sheriff said it's important that we do, especially at night. Everything all right in there?"

"Everything's great!" Charlotte answered. "Please come in if you ever get cold or hungry. I'm sure Melanie won't mind."

The deputy nodded. Charlotte stepped back inside and closed the door behind her. She then looked at Stew, standing by the stairs.

"What are you doing here?"

"You told me you would have a long shift tonight... and I thought you might get hungry and, uh... if you ever needed company, well—"

"Absolutely!" Charlotte beamed. "Thank you!"

"Yeah." Stew looked like he'd hit the jackpot.

CHAPTER FORTY-THREE:

HEADING TO THE NEXT DESTINATION

Judy put down her phone. Melanie had gone hysterical in her ear. There was nothing hidden beneath the casket as she'd indicated there would be. What could the retired woman do?

She suddenly heard a noise not far away. Judy peered out into the cemetery. She couldn't see a soul around but she sensed someone looking at her. She did not know where to look, but she knew she was being spied on.

"Otherwise, she lied to you..." the Sheriff continued.

The Sheriff was about to get out of the grave and Judy knelt to give him a hand. She was still alert for sounds.

There was another noise. She looked again. The retired detective was now sure she saw someone staring at her. She stepped forward to see what it was.

"Judy?"

Judy reluctantly dragged her eyes away from the shadow and looked at the Sheriff. He was still waiting for her to help him back up.

"Come on!" she said, frantically.

She helped him to the surface. Then she looked back towards where she had seen the shadow and began moving in that direction.

"Judy?" the Sheriff asked again.

"I thought I saw... someone..."

The Sheriff's eyes followed where she was looking. "You sure?"

Judy stared for a beat and then gathered her thoughts. Whatever the retired woman thought she had seen was gone.

Was this the same person she had seen in the rainy window of the motel room? Was it the killer? Was he spying on her? Or was she hallucinating? She told the Sheriff about it. He thought it strange, too. Maybe someone was staring at her. But who?

They started putting the grave back in order. Then, after all this hard work and sweat for nothing, they walked back to the car. On the way, Judy kept looking around for the shadow, but it wasn't there. She then passed right by the spot where she swore she had seen it. Judy stopped there for a second and looked around. The shadow was nowhere to be seen, but something else was: the tombstone of Fred Gibbins.

Judy sighed, confused and febrile. What had the shadow been doing here? She loitered there for a second, looking at the name and the stone, before she heard the Sheriff calling her, "Judy?"

The retired detective sighed once more and then started moving back towards the Sheriff.

They were back on the road. Judy could hear Grant still trying to catch his breath. He was exhausted, and so was she. The Sheriff kept driving for a good mile before he finally turned a corner and they switched neighborhoods. The cemetery was behind them, and now they were passing through classy, luxurious scenery.

Displayed for them, as they drove by, was a series of houses with white picket fences and what appeared to be very carefully manicured lawns. Judy hadn't seen this posh side of Rockland until now. She looked around for a good moment, thinking how beautiful these homes were. People had so much space here compared with New York. The small town she was moving to in North Carolina—if they ever finished this case!—was quite like this, and that made her excited. She imagined Rush running around on the lawns, without a leash, having so much space to do whatever he wanted. She also imagined having her own garden and sleeping in a quiet room where she would not hear buses and sirens in the middle of the night.

The Sheriff suddenly spoke and Judy emerged from her dreamy state.

"I would live here if I was in Rockland—best part of town."

Judy agreed. This was awesome.

"Expensive, but so worth it."

Judy kept looking out the window for a moment. Then she had a thought, "Where did the Kovachevs live?"

"Hmm..."

"They lived in Rockland, right?"

"Oh yes, they did," he said tiredly. "From what I've read in my research and the people I talked to, they all went back to Bulgaria, though. But if you want, we can go look at their old house?"

"Just for a second, yeah," Judy replied.

He clearly wanted to be done for the night. He was covered in mud and dirt and looked exhausted. But he did know where the house was and he kindly agreed to show her. Judy felt she needed to see where Viktor Kovachev grew up. Maybe they'd find something—or someone important there.

CHAPTER FORTY-FOUR:

THE ACCUSATION

Charlotte and Stew went into the living room. Stew waved at Melanie, who was sitting at the kitchen table alone, and then sat down on the couch. The redhead joined him and immediately reached for the pizza. Melanie hadn't given her any supper, and she was starving.

Stew laughed. They devoured the pizza in under five minutes. Another couple of minutes passed. Charlotte's stomach was now full and hurting. She sipped some wine. Then she finally looked at Stew. She was happy he was here. This was certainly an unexpected visit, but it was so sweet. Charlotte wanted somebody to talk to. No, she wanted to talk to him, specifically. They always had these amazing conversations, deep or not, and he was always making her smile. She felt a strange connection with him, a connection she had never experienced with anyone else before.

"I wanted to take you on that history tour tonight, but you seemed to be pretty busy with this whole thing, so I didn't ask. And then I thought, hey, I'm just going to go see her anyway."

"I appreciate that!"

"How's your night been going?"

"Good... been taking care of Rush, watching some episodes of *The Bachelor* and, you know..."

Stew nodded. "How's she doing?"

Stew seemed to feel bad for Melanie, sitting there all by herself, eating and drinking wine.

"Nothing to worry about. She had a long day."

"She looks worried. Did something happen? You know, you never told me why you two ladies are creeping on her like James Stewart in *Rear Window*..."

Charlotte laughed. As she was about to reply, Rush came towards Stew, wagging his tail and looking at Stew with his puffy, deep eyes. The dog jumped onto the man's lap and lay down comfortably. Charlotte chuckled and made a soft *ahh* sound.

"He likes you," she said.

"He's so cute," Stew replied, scratching Rush between the ears.

They heard Melanie stand up. "Charlotte, I'm going to take a bath and then I'm off to bed"

"All right. Call me if you need me."

Melanie nodded as she passed the doorway and headed up the stairs.

"Good night," Charlotte added.

Stew said it too.

A moment passed as Stew kept his attention on Rush. Then Charlotte finally decided to continue the conversation.

"It's complicated... Melanie's... umm..."

Charlotte did not know how to say anything without revealing too much. She feared Judy's mighty hammer striking her down, so she said nothing. But Stew peered over at her.

"*That* complicated, you mean?" he questioned, pointing at the gun sitting on the couch, hidden behind Charlotte's left leg.

Charlotte sighed. She had forgotten about the gun. It was lying there, so close to her, as if she were about to use it on Stew.

"He's targeting her, isn't he?" Stew asked.

Charlotte gave him a look.

"I mean... you with the gun, you watching over her all day, and then the cops outside... I just assumed."

Charlotte nodded.

"That's a big thing to handle," he said, getting closer to Charlotte. "How are you feeling?"

"I'm fine," Charlotte said. "It's all I ever wanted," she added, chuckling.

Stew smiled understandingly.

"This job is not what I had imagined it to be... I mean, I knew what it was like with my father and all, but... when you're actually doing it, it's so different. People count on you. They really count on you to keep them safe. It's all on you. And if something were to happen—"

Stew grabbed a hold of her face and kissed her. She felt his warm, tender lips on hers. Charlotte immersed herself in it, closing her eyes and absorbing all the emotions and sensations that were now flowing through her. A minute passed before Stew moved closer. He was grabbing her legs.

The redhead thought she felt a hand sliding off her leg, moving towards the couch. Then she opened her eyes and gazed into Stew's piercing blue eyes. Something suddenly changed in her. She didn't see Stew anymore; she was thinking about something else. She was thinking about Wendell, about how he had seen the killer's blue eyes. Then she was thinking of Viktor Kovachev's child. And then she thought about the hand slipping off her leg, and she quickly grabbed the gun before he could and she aimed it at Stew's face. She cranked the hammer. Stew opened his eyes at the sound and peered at Charlotte, petrified. He took his hands off her body and lifted them up.

"Charlotte?" he said, looking confused and downright terrified.

The redhead didn't say a word. She carefully stood up from the couch and kept the gun pointed at Stew.

"Charlotte, please, what are you doing?"

"What are you really doing here?" she asked.

Stew looked even more confused. "What?"

"What are you doing here tonight?" she almost screamed.

"I—I..."

"Why are you here, Stew?"

"I came here... to see you..."

Charlotte wasn't satisfied in the least. "Where were you the night Rick Carson was murdered?"

"What do you mean?"

"Where were you?"

Stew started to stand up, but Charlotte flourished the gun and he sat back down.

"I was with you, at the bar... you know that."

"That doesn't tell me anything," said Charlotte. "Carson died long before you even came in, and even if Wendell said it was a little before seven, he could have been wrong, he was hit on the head. So tell me—"

"Charlotte—"

"Wendell said he saw the killer, and that killer had blue eyes..."

Stew tried to interrupt her once more, but she wouldn't have it.

"How old are you, Stew?" she asked, unexpectedly.

"What?"

"Just answer the question!" she almost screamed.

"Twenty-nine... I'm twenty-nine..." he quickly answered.

"He would have been born in 1988... or, no, 1989... nine months... around that time..." muttered Charlotte to herself. She continued, "Where are your parents, Stew?"

"My parents?" he asked, totally confounded.

"Where are they?"

"Umm... they... my dad... he died."

"He died?" Charlotte said.

"Yeah, last—"

Whatever Stew was saying, she would not hear it. The only thing that mattered was "he died."

"And your mother?"

"Charlotte, why are you asking me all these questions? I am seriously confused right now."

"Oh, you're confused? *You're* confused? I should be the one who's confused. No, not confused—distressed, sad... ashamed," she replied viciously. "Let's try this, then... Where were you on the night of April 6?"

"I—"

"The night Ethan Gregory got murdered!"

Stew didn't answer right away. He was thinking, struggling...

"Let's try this, instead. How about the night my father was found dead? April 9?"

Stew didn't say anything. He was shaking his head now, looking grim and almost mortified.

"Charlotte..."

"Stop saying my name! Just answer the fucking question, Stew!"

And he did. He shouted, "I was in New York, all right! I was going to see Gregory's show that opening night. April 7. My mom had gotten tickets, because she knew I was a fan and we were going to meet up. She lives there."

"Oh, really?"

"Yeah!" Stew cried. "But then I found out about his death. We were devastated."

"Were you?" said Charlotte.

"So, we just went out and had a bite to eat instead. Then I came back here and I was back at work the next day."

"I don't believe you!"

Stew finally stood up, angry. "Believe what you want, Charlotte. I told you the truth. Ask Melanie, she was there at Granger's the next day... You know what? Just shoot me! Do it, if you really want to. Do it! I have nothing to prove to you. I told you everything you wanted to know, all right? So just do what you have to do, Charlotte. Come on."

But Charlotte didn't want to shoot Stew. She was struggling to pull herself back together. She had gone completely overboard, and she knew it. She wasn't sure of anything anymore. Stew walked forward, and he even pointed the gun at his own chest, provoking Charlotte to do it. Holding her hands. However, before she could decide anything, they heard a scream.

"Melanie!" Charlotte shouted.

Stew looked at her, both gutted and completely stunned by what was going on. Charlotte moved the gun out of Stew's range and quickly ran from the room. She rushed up the stairs. Another scream echoed. An enduring scream.

CHAPTER FORTY-FIVE:

OLD HOUSE

The old Kovachev house wasn't far from where they were when Judy made her request to see it. However, it was not the same type of neighborhood. The white picket fences didn't exist here. It wasn't so much that this side of town was poorer or less appealing, it was just more embedded in nature. These were small farmhouses, though Judy couldn't see any animals wandering around. It was too late and too dark outside.

Judy and the Sheriff went down a bumpy road for a minute or two until they'd almost reached the end. There were only two houses left on the road, both on the same side. The Sheriff pointed to the first one. This was the Kovachev house, slightly smaller than the one next to it. From what Judy could see in the dark, the white paint seemed to be fading. That observation was proven to be correct when they got out of the car and started to approach the house. The paint was not only fading, it was begging to come off the exterior walls. The yard hadn't been tended to in a long while, and tree roots were growing from the ground. The house clearly hadn't been renovated for a very long time and was apparently uninhabited. However, that last observation proved to be incorrect. Judy and Sheriff Grant noticed a car parked in the narrow driveway.

"I thought you said nobody was living here..." remarked Judy.

"That's what I thought... but then I don't come here often," he replied.

Grant pointed his flashlight at the car. It was a vintage 1967 Chevrolet Impala, in one of the strangest colors an Impala could ever wear: a nauseating yellow-beige. Judy didn't know how you could decide on that color in a million years, never mind the fact that it was even on the market.

The flashlight moved away from the car and swept the surroundings. The Sheriff pointed it to the lawn and then went to the other house on the right.

"Was that Melanie's house?"

"If I remember correctly, yes."

Judy looked at the other house. That one was a bit more her style and looked better cared for than the Kovachev one.

"Who lives there now?"

"Hmm... a lovely young couple... the Andersons. They're not here most of the time. They own a place in Barbados if I remember well. That's their chalet, as they call it."

"Fancy!" Judy said.

"Instagram influencers, you know..."

Judy nodded. Their driveway was empty. The Andersons were on the beach now, surely. Like she was supposed to be.

Then the Sheriff moved his flashlight back to the Kovachev house.

"You have an idea who lives here?"

"Absolutely no clue."

Either way, they would find out soon enough. The Sheriff pointed the light at the windows of the house. It was dark inside; whoever lived there had gone to bed. They carefully approached the porch and looked carefully through the windows when suddenly a light came on inside. They then looked back at the house. They could now see the kitchen very plainly. It was also painted white. Everything was white—the cabinets, the drawers, the fridge. It looked like a hospital, Judy thought.

They heard a noise. Judy saw a shadow move through the hallway. The retired detective stepped back. Then they heard steps coming their way. Judy slowly shifted to the front door and stood in front of the screen. It was a tiny woman who appeared, with long white hair flowing down to her hips. She wore a blue shirt and brown shorts. The woman was very old, and looked at them with a stern, almost creepy look. They were more shocked to see her than she was to see them.

"Who are you? What are you doing here?" she said.

The Sheriff approached the screen and looked at her. He realized that he knew her.

"Lilyana? Is that you?" he exclaimed.

She looked at him, puzzled.

"I'm Sheriff Grant. I—I investigated your son's disappearance. I was a deputy at the time."

Lilyana didn't flinch. She stared back, looking dazed.

"Don't you remember?"

"I remember," she finally answered, in a very cold tone.

"You're Viktor Kovachev's mother? The Sheriff said you went back to Bulgaria..." Judy interjected, surprised.

Lilyana seemed very annoyed.

"Vy are you here?" she asked again, in her thick accent.

"Mrs. Kovachev, can we talk to you for a second? Do you mind?"

Lilyana laughed. She looked at the Sheriff, then at Judy. The retired detective was now the confused one.

"Do you know vot time it is?"

"I understand, ma'am... but the matter concerns your son."

"My son?"

"Yes. That's right," said Judy.

The old lady started chuckling again. "My son?"

Judy nodded once more. Lilyana kept laughing.

"Ma'am, would you mind if we come inside and talk about it?"

"Ve're going to talk about nothing," Lilyana said. "It's late. I haff to get back to bed. Good day."

Lilyana turned around, started walking back towards the hallway. Judy approached the screen more closely.

"Ma'am, it's really important. We might know what happened to him."

Lilyana stopped and stayed frozen in place for a second. The Sheriff gave Judy a look. Then the old lady turned around and walked back to the screen.

"Vot did you say?"

"We think we know what has happened to your son."

Lilyana started laughing again. "I don't haff a son. I haff not had a son for thirty years," she said, before looking at the Sheriff. "Now you know? *Now*?"

"Lilyana... I'm..."

"Get away," she said.

"Ma'am, can we just come inside and discuss—"

"You have varrant?" she asked.

"No," Judy replied.

"Then get away. Now!"

Judy wasn't discouraged that easily.

"Your grandson... he's killing people. Do you know that? He's killing people."

"My grandson?"

The old lady approached the screen.

"Damyan Kovachev. He's the one we're looking for."

Lilyana dragged her eyes to the ground, looking sad and worried at the same time.

"Can you help us find him, please?" Judy said. "He's dangerous, ma'am... and I think you know it."

The Kovachev grandmother didn't say anything. She was looking more worried by the second.

"Please, he's hurting people. Terrorizing citizens... He needs to be stopped. Can you help us find him, please?"

Lilyana took a moment. She finally lifted her head and looked at Judy and the Sheriff again.

"My grandson is dead."

"Dead?"

"He died in Bulgaria. One year ago. He was soldier and there was explosion."

"Really?" the Sheriff asked.

"I'm sorry..." said Judy.

There was a silence. Lilyana didn't look like a soulless individual anymore, she looked like a depressed, ruined, and mourning woman.

"I'm sorry to do this, but it is essential for our investigation. Would you mind if we come inside and ask you a few questions?" Judy asked. "If not, do you happen to have a picture of your grandson that we could see?"

"I can't help you. I'm tired. Sorry."

"We can come back tomorrow if you want," Judy insisted.

But the old lady didn't answer her. She turned around and closed the front door in their faces.

The Sheriff sighed. "I had no idea she was still living here..."

"Yeah..."

"What do you want to do now?"

"Nothing... I'll go back to Charlotte."

They walked to the car. Judy turned around and glanced back at the house one last time. It was pitch-dark now. It looked uninhabited once again. She opened the car door, sighing deeply.

CHAPTER FORTY-SIX:

THE CLIFF

Charlotte got hold of the stair railing as she reached the second floor and turned a corner to get to Melanie's room. The room was empty. Then she heard another scream. *Bathroom, right. Melanie was taking a bath. Of course.* The redhead rushed to the bathroom. She stepped onto the white tiles and her eyes immediately looked to the window behind the bathtub. It was wide open. Charlotte ran to it and heard more screams. She looked outside, down at the ground and saw a dark figure dragging Melanie across the backyard.

Charlotte yelled out to Melanie, but it was no use. The killer forced her onto his motorcycle and then got on it himself. He started the engine and gave Charlotte a look before speeding off into the distance.

"No!"

The redhead, not knowing what to do, stood there for a second and then ran back to the stairs. Stew was standing there at the bottom.

"Call Judy!" shouted Charlotte. "Call the Sheriff, say he's got her and I'm going after them."

"What?!" replied Stew.

Charlotte sped out the front door and stopped abruptly. Lying in front of it, on the carpet, was the deputy. He was unconscious.

"And call an ambulance!"

She looked towards the street and saw a cop car parked on the other side. Charlotte knelt down to the deputy and grabbed his car keys from his belt. She then ran for the car. She unlocked the door and got in.

She drove at high speed, looking for the motorcycle. Her efforts were quickly rewarded. It was right there, just past the trees. He was waiting for her! She sped up, and the killer started his engine and rushed away in a screech of tires.

He was fast. Charlotte passed every car in her way, honking like a madwoman. She finally figured out how to turn on the headlights, and then the cars let her pass more freely.

She kept driving down the long road, and then suddenly entered a narrow path—a path that led to water. She couldn't see the motorcycle anymore.

She kept driving along the path. Charlotte found herself in the middle of rugged hills. Should she have made a turn somewhere? Where was she going? She didn't know. She just kept going, enraged now.

She heard screams, and then she spotted him. The dark figure had parked his motorcycle at the side of a cliff and was now standing at the edge, the river below him, holding Melanie. Melanie had her hands tied behind her back and a bandana covered her eyes. The waitress was screaming at the top of her lungs. Charlotte parked her car, not too close to the motorcycle, and got out.

The redhead pointed the gun at him. And then she saw him lifting Melanie up.

"Let her go!" Charlotte heard herself shout.

She moved towards them. The dark figure pushed Melanie closer to the edge of the cliff.

"Don't do it, please! Let her go!" Charlotte panicked.

There was a beat where all Charlotte could hear was the blood rushing in her head. She was ready to shoot him. She had her gun pointed straight at what she thought was the killer's heart. But then her arms started vibrating. Shaking. She wanted to shoot, but her body wouldn't let her.

"Let her go!" she said again, her voice trembling.

She could not do it. She could not shoot him. Then she noticed the dark figure's clothes. He was wearing a leather jacket with *Skullheads* written on it. She peered at the man's hair and thought she saw gray.

Charlotte moved forward again. But still she couldn't do it.

The dark figure's head finally turned to look directly at her. He gave Charlotte a look, and then a faint smile.

And before Charlotte could respond, he let go of Melanie. Melanie fell into the darkness, screaming.

Then, seconds later, Charlotte heard a splash.

Charlotte froze, in complete shock.

The killer ran back to his motorcycle and started it up. The redhead finally shook off the horror that was paralyzing her and she went for him, but she was too late again. Before she knew what was happening, he was speeding off into the distance.

"No!" Charlotte shrieked, and let a bullet fly in the killer's direction. He turned his head and kept going.

Charlotte really wanted to shoot again, but the killer had vanished. She put down the gun and screamed at the top of her lungs. Then she ran to the cliff and peered down, as if expecting to see Melanie still alive, hanging onto something, just like in the movies. But Melanie wasn't hanging there. Her body was impaled on the sharp rocks below.

CHAPTER FORTY-SEVEN:

AFTERMATH

Falling from unknown heights. That was the way they were getting rid of prisoners in Iran. And as Stew added, this method had previously been used at the time of Ancient Greece and during the Roman Empire. That was Melanie's fate. She was dealt with in one of the most barbaric ways imaginable.

The girl they had sworn to protect was dead. Judy shut her eyes and gathered her thoughts as she sat in the ambulance. The killer had succeeded again. Another death, another punishment had been meted out. A fall, gas, a rope, and a sword. *All terrible ways of losing your life! He is such a soulless maniac.*

She was angry. Not just angry, she was frustrated, boiling up, and about to explode. She had to do something! She had to stop this. Then she thought it was all her fault. After all, she had left Charlotte alone with Melanie. If she had been there with them, this might have not happened. Melanie might have been alive right now if Judy had not decided to go with the Sheriff to find a dead end, and then gone on to find another one when she chose to check out the Kovachev house.

The retired detective sighed as she looked down the cliff. She saw the ambulance workers down there, collecting the body. Judy turned her head away from the scene and looked down at Rush on his leash, sniffing around. She then moved her glance to Charlotte, sitting at the back of the ambulance with a blanket over her. Stew was standing by her side, not saying anything.

"She's a tough cookie," the Sheriff said. "She'll be all right."

Yeah, Charlotte was tough indeed. Truthfully, Judy wasn't so much worried about her as she was worried about herself and what she might do next if she stayed in this raging state. She left the Sheriff standing there at the edge and drifted towards Charlotte.

"How's it going?" she asked the redhead, and immediately realized how ridiculous the question was.

"How am I supposed to feel?" responded Charlotte, frowning.

Charlotte was obviously as furious as she was.

"I don't know, Judy," added the redhead, sounding defeated. "He was right there. I had him and... I didn't do anything. I just let

him—"

"Hey, it's fine," replied Stew, putting a hand on her shoulder.

Charlotte looked at him strangely, as if she didn't want to be reassured or comforted. Judy thought she looked as though she wanted to push his hand away, or even strike him.

"What did you see, Charlotte?" the retired detective moved on to ask.

Charlotte didn't answer right away. She stared at the cliff's edge in front of them, disappearing from the conversation. Judy was about to ask again when they heard something in the distance, coming towards them. Lights appeared in the road. A muffled sound hit their ears, a piercing sound. It was a car. Its headlights were pointing right at them, and the sound was the muffler coughing like a cat desperate to get rid of a hairball. It was an old, gray car. The driver was none other than someone everybody knew and liked so very much: Mr. Eddie White.

Shouts echoed from the windows as a blond and slightly attractive, but incredibly annoying, individual pulled into the crime scene.

"What in the world is goin' on out here?"

White got out of his car and rushed over. Judy and Charlotte—they were still here!

"Hello, Mr. White!" greeted Judy.

White gave her a dreadful look. He had stupidly believed her when she said she would leave town, and now he was either angry or full of shame, or both. Either way, his face was plain red.

The Sheriff ran over, holding his hands up, trying to calm things down before a bloody war broke out.

"Eddie! How are you? Look—"

"Why wasn't I told 'bout this? Why wasn't I called?" he said in a brusque tone.

"Look, Eddie we... I—"

"What the heck are they doin' here? Weren't you supposed to be gone? You told me they were— This is *my* investigation, understood? My investigation. Now, somebody will have to start talking or I can't even tell you what's about to happen!"

Judy looked at Charlotte as he said this. They were both stunned by everything that had happened in the past few hours and really didn't know how to proceed with this man.

"Mr. White!" said Judy once more.

"Stop it with the Mr. Whites, okay? I've had enough of your dumb bullshit! I've had enough, all right? I've told you this already. Don't you know how it works, Mrs. Hunter? This is my case. You are infringin' on my investigation. Mine!" White looked at them with slightly mad eyes. "Now, you two are gonna tell me what is goin' on here. Somebody is going to talk, otherwise—"

"Detective, I'm so sorry," began Judy, very calmly. "But Charlotte got another message from the—who we think is the killer, and—"

"Oh... really? That again? The killer. The so-called Executioner, right?"

"Yes," replied Judy, refusing to take the bait.

"And what did he say?"

"He said he was going to go after someone... Someone we knew, so..."

"And who might that be, exactly?"

"Melanie Sheldon."

"Sheldon? Never heard of a Sheldon. What has she got to do with this? You know what, I don't even wanna know. I don't care. You two—and where is this Sheldon now, huh?"

Judy pointed to the edge of the cliff.

"He just threw her down there!" clarified Charlotte, irritated beyond belief.

"Threw her?"

Charlotte stood up and faced White, with dead, cold eyes. "Yeah! She had her hands tied behind her and her eyes covered with a bandana. And like she was a fucking prisoner on death row, he pushed her off this cliff and she fell face first to her death, and he didn't look back."

White kept his head turned towards the cliff, waited a beat, then decided to walk to the edge and peer down. He stayed there for a moment and then came back, looking as pale as a ghost.

"Well," he said, now in a very temperate tone. "That is... unfortunate, to say the least."

"Yeah," said Charlotte. "And if you hadn't intervened, if you had believed us and given us the resources to investigate and interview more people, we wouldn't be here, discussing this. Instead, we had to tiptoe our way through this village and find out what we could on our own while you were up to God knows what—probably jerking off in that disgusting four-wheeler of yours while waiting for some miracle to solve this fucking case for you."

White stared at her as if defying her to go on.

"Mr. White..." Judy tried once more. "Detective. If you could at least let us explain ourselves, what we've found out and who we think did this, we could then—"

"Who did this?" White demanded.

"Damyan Kovachev," replied Charlotte.

"Damyan who? Who is that now?"

"We believe he is Viktor Kovachev's son," said Judy.

"Who are these Kovashun guys?"

"*Kovachev*. He's the kid that disappeared mysteriously, years ago," replied the retired woman.

"Okay, we can discuss this scribble all later. It's too cold here," White said.

Judy and Charlotte looked at each other, thoroughly tired out by this guy.

"And he was here, this Kova dude?"

Nobody answered. The retired detective turned to Charlotte, waiting for her to provide the answer. The best the redhead could do was, "Well..."

"Charlotte?" Judy nudged. "What did you see? Who did you see? Did it look like it was him? Young and—"

Charlotte stayed silent for a minute. She looked at Judy with big puppy eyes, ashamed.

"Just say it. What did you see? Tell us."

"He was driving a motorcycle..." the young woman said, nervously.

"Uh-huh," said White.

"And he had a jacket..." she added.

"A jacket?" White said.

"Yeah... a leather jacket..."

Judy started to understand and looked away from Charlotte. She knew she would regret pushing her into telling the truth. But it was too late now.

"He was wearing a leather jacket that said *Skullheads* on the back..."

The Sheriff looked shocked by this revelation. Judy didn't know if White had understood, but one thing was sure: he would understand in the very near future, and that wasn't a good thing. He kept staring at them, looking confused, not replying.

The retired detective suddenly felt something moving behind her back. Then she realized Charlotte was giving her back her gun. Judy took it, careful to keep it hidden from White. She put it on her belt, under her coat. The redhead looked at Judy again, apologetically.

CHAPTER FORTY-EIGHT:

UNEASY SLEEP

Detective White sent the two women back to their motel and told them to come back to the Sheriff's office in the morning for more questions. Exhaustion was starting to overtake Charlotte, but she couldn't get any decent sleep. Shock and dread were stinging her, and a lot of remorse. If only she could have saved Melanie. But no, she had just stood there and let the poor woman die. She should have done something! Well, she did, at the very last minute, and then missed her shot.

She thought about this for a while, tossing and turning. Then she finally got up as she thought her agitation was probably disturbing Judy. She went into the bathroom and sat there for a while.

She began to think about her father and how he would have handled this. How could someone live with confronting death all the time? She had seen Fred at home, how he managed working on murder situations and being around killers, she had seen him mentally suffer, being somewhat depressed at times. It wasn't only mental suffering, either. More often than not it also took a toll on his body. Besides the occasional wounds he got in confrontations with criminals, Fred would often complain about his neck or his back hurting. Charlotte knew this wasn't just because he had been physically active, fighting crime, but he suffered from anxiety as well, and that weighed him down more than anything else. She sure understood him better now. She understood the stress of the job, and she understood why he was the way he was sometimes at home. This wasn't late night puzzle-solving with good (and possibly drunk) friends, this was real life—hard, painful, and sometimes dangerous. This all extended her love for him so much more.

Had Fred ever been helpless like that? Had he ever watched someone innocent die a violent death? Yeah, of course he had. Viktor Kovachev. How had he handled his death? Had it given him enormous stress? Did he feel guilty all his life? Then more and more questions kept arising in her head, driving her further from sleep.

After a good twenty minutes sitting on the side of the tub, she heard a knock at the door.

"Charlotte?" Judy asked. "Are you all right?"

"You can come in!" the redhead answered.

The retired detective opened the door and approached her.

"Tough night, huh?"

"I was just wondering how you can do this job..."

Judy sat next to Charlotte on the bath. "Is this about Melanie?"

Charlotte nodded.

The retired detective took a moment, sighed, and said, "My first day on the job, someone killed himself in front of my eyes."

Charlotte frowned.

"I was an officer back then," Judy continued. "My training officer and I went to an office on Wall Street where someone had a gun to his head and was threatening to shoot himself."

Charlotte seemed mesmerized by Judy's tale.

"I tried to tell him to stay calm and look at me. I tried my best to tell him that it was going to be all right, that life was not that bad even if he thought so in the moment. That whatever he was going through right now, it would pass." Judy shook her head. "But that was not the thing to do. He just laughed at me. Told me I was an idiot. That he wasn't a victim and didn't need my pity. I asked him to put down the gun, but he wouldn't. I again tried to reason with him. Then I suddenly saw a picture on his desk of him with his wife and kids, tried to ask him about them. Asked him how they would react right now if they saw him like this. If they would miss him."

Judy stood up, her back to Charlotte. This was clearly tough for her to recall.

"I asked him how they would react if he wasn't at dinner tonight with them," Judy said. "What his son and daughter would do without their father there, how much they would cry. How much they would feel abandoned."

Judy turned to Charlotte. "He finally looked at me and smiled. 'You're so right,' he said. 'I should be there with them.' He kept on smiling as he closed his eyes and pulled the trigger."

Charlotte looked stricken and confused.

"His wife and kids were dead," Judy said. "They were killed in a car crash a year before... but I didn't know that. Nobody told me that."

Judy came back to the tub and sat again. "That was my first death... the first one that I felt responsible for. I thought about it for years. I had made a big mistake. I made it worse and I watched him die."

Charlotte felt even more upset now.

"The point is you—"

"I made a mistake too!"

"No, Charlotte! The point is you can't know what you don't know. You didn't know that as soon as you left Melanie alone, she would be taken. You didn't know."

"But I could have prevented it. I knew that somebody wanted to kill her. I could have been with her if I had not been with Stew."

"Maybe. Maybe not," Judy said. "Maybe the killer would have managed to take her anyway. Even with you there. You don't know that."

Charlotte stared down at the tiled floor. "And then I was right there, and I had a shot, Judy, and I couldn't even do that properly."

"You're going to lose people along the way, Charlotte, it's inevitable," Judy said. "That's the job. It's not all sun and rainbows. We're not the almighty saviors. We're not gods. We can't save everybody we want to save. You can't pick and choose, and you certainly can't go back and change things. The best thing you can do for yourself and your mental health is to move forward and learn from your mistakes. Then you try to save the next person and the next person."

The two women talked a little bit more. Judy had managed to ease Charlotte's mind a bit. Then they moved back to the main room and tried to get some sleep.

CHAPTER FORTY-NINE:

GRILLING

At eight o'clock the next morning, on the dot, Judy heard a knock at their door. It was a deputy, coming to get them. They had to go to the Sheriff's office, where Charlotte would be further questioned by White.

Judy and Charlotte got ready. Then Judy took Rush into her arms and decided to take him with her to the Sheriff's office. She could sense their time with Eddie White wouldn't be short.

Charlotte followed the retired detective out to the deputy's car.

When the two women arrived, they were told Eddie White wasn't in yet. Surprise, surprise... While waiting, Judy informed Charlotte about what they had discovered at the cemetery and the Kovachev house. She told her that Lilyana Kovachev was still alive and that she had revealed to Judy and Grant that her grandson, Damyan Kovachev, was dead. Charlotte wasn't happy to hear that but Judy hadn't given up on finding out the identity of the killer. She knew better. This was just a small bump in the road they had to work through.

Charlotte asked what she was thinking, and Judy said she didn't know what to think right now. She just knew someone was either lying or hiding the truth to protect themselves. Maybe it was the Kovachev grandmother, maybe it was Reed, maybe it had been Melanie. Maybe Damyan Kovachev was really dead, maybe he wasn't... Maybe they were way off and somebody else was committing the crimes, somebody they hadn't thought about. Maybe... She didn't know who it was, but something was clearly not fitting in this whole story and they needed to figure out what it was.

White finally arrived and did a little morning stretch and yawn as he walked in. He greeted Judy and Charlotte, then took Charlotte straight away to the interrogation room. The Sheriff arrived and said good morning to Judy. He looked disheveled. He proposed they go into the room overlooking the interrogation room: they could see the young woman through the one-way mirror and keep their eyes on Eddie White.

As he stepped into the room, White was carrying a notepad and a pen. The blond man put them down on the metal table in front of Charlotte. He took off his brown jacket, tucked his yellow shirt into his beige pants, and finally sat down in front of the young woman. Judy thought he was done with the preliminaries, but then he took out a comb and put his hair back into place. He returned the comb to his pocket and stared at Charlotte like a hungry fox.

"So..." he started.

"Yeah?" asked Charlotte.

It was like White was waiting for her to begin, but Charlotte didn't say anything. He finally got bored with the silence and took charge.

"Can you tell me exactly what happened? What you saw?"

"Didn't I tell you back at the crime scene?" Charlotte said.

"I feel like I'm missing some details here," White said. "You saw the killer, right?"

"Like I told you, yes..."

"Oh, wait! Your name for the record, please."

"You know my name."

White's smiled widened, he loved this. "It's the procedure, miss."

She frowned and rolled her eyes. Judy did so as well from behind the glass. Then Charlotte finally spat out, "My name is Charlotte Gibbins."

"Nice to have you with me, Miss Gibbins. Now today I'm gonna ask you a few questions. It's regarding the death of Melanie Sheldon on Monday, April 18..."

"Nineteenth."

"Huh?" White frowned in turn.

"Nineteenth. It was Monday the nineteenth and it's the twentieth today."

White kept frowning, then shuffled through his notes, trying to find something. Finally, he went to his pants and took out his phone and looked at it.

"Ah, yes! April 19. You're right."

Charlotte seemed more and more irritated.

"So, Miss Gibbins," he continued. "You were at a crime scene last night?"

"Yes," Charlotte answered.

"You witnessed the death of Melanie Sheldon, right?"

"Murder, yes."

"And why was that? Why were you present at the event?"

"It wasn't an event, you dumb—"

Smooth, Charlotte, stay smooth. I know it's hard, thought Judy. *But stay smooth.*

"Uh-huh. Just answer the question for the record, please. And use respectful language, please."

Charlotte sighed. "I was there because I was investigating the whole thing."

"Investigating? But you're not a detective, you're not even police. Is that not correct?"

Judy heard Charlotte sigh one more time. "Sure."

White frowned.

"I'm not police," Charlotte clarified.

"So why were you investigatin' this whole thing?"

"You know you're wasting a lot of time here, right? You could be looking into something more concrete, like interviewing suspects and finding evidence so you can find the actual killer and stop this whole thing before another murder happens."

White tapped on the table again. "Question, please."

Gosh, he is unbelievably annoying.

"Fine. I was there because I received a note saying that Melanie was the next target. So, we went to Melanie's house and watched over her. Then the killer came out of the blue and took her away, and—"

"A note, you said? Now, who was this from?"

"The killer?"

"He signed the note 'Killer,' yeah?"

"Well, no."

"So, how did you know it came from him?"

Charlotte rolled her eyes deep into her skull. "I know it came from him because he actually did what he said he would do in the note. Kill Melanie Sheldon."

"Interesting. He said Melanie Sheldon, specifically?"

Charlotte wanted to die, right then and there. This was unbearable and stupid.

"No."

"No? Then what?"

"He said, 'You'll like this next one even more. She's a bad girl.'"

"'She's a bad girl'? So, how did you—?"

"Because Melanie was fucking friends with my father, Ethan Gregory, and Rick Carson."

"Language, please! And you said your father—that is Frederick Gibbins, yes?"

"Of course it is."

"And he committed suicide last week, right?"

"Two weeks ago, and like I said before, he didn't commit suicide, he was killed by the same murderer that Melanie Sheldon, Ethan Gregory, Carson, and Zachary Smith were killed by!"

"What's the last name you said?"

"Zachary Smith..."

"And he's another victim?"

"Yeah, he was murdered in Germany."

"Germany, you say?"

Charlotte nodded.

White paused and then chuckled. "Okay..."

He kept laughing. Judy looked at the Sheriff. The Sheriff seemed as irritated as she was. But what else could they have expected from Eddie White?

White finally settled down. He brushed saliva off his tie and went back to being serious.

"Well..."

"Well what?" Charlotte scowled.

"They were all killed by the same murderer, you said?"

"Yeah..."

"Well," the man said again.

Charlotte looked at him, confused. Judy was too. *Well what?* she repeated in her head for the young woman.

"A great theory!" he said.

"Not a theory! The truth!" Charlotte hurled.

White wrote something on his notepad and sighed. "Miss Gibbins, you seem a little heated right now. We'll go to another question, a more easy question now if you want..."

"Sure."

"You saw the killer last night, yes?"

"Yes."

"And? Who was he?"

“I don’t know who he was... I didn’t see a face.”

“Ha! How so?”

“It was dark and he had his back turned.”

“Hmm...” White muttered, writing.

A pause. Charlotte waited for him to finish.

“So... what did you see?”

Charlotte didn’t answer right away.

“Ms. Gibbins!” he smiled, annoyingly.

“I was at Melanie’s house. I heard some noise from the living room, where I was, and went upstairs, and through the bathroom window I saw a guy on a motorcycle holding Melanie. He forced her onto his bike and took her to the cliff. I followed them there.”

“Hmm... why did you follow them?”

“Because I didn’t want him to kill her, obviously.”

“And how would you have stopped him? With your hands? You’re not a detective, not even a trained deputy. How would that have happened? Do you do karate or somethin’?”

“I had—”

But Charlotte stopped herself. She couldn't answer that. The young woman peered down at the metallic table for a moment, then her eyes drifted to the one-way mirror. She was looking at Judy.

Charlotte had used a gun. A gun that Judy had given her. That was how she would have stopped him, and she tried. But she couldn’t say that. Charlotte wasn’t a detective; Judy wasn’t a detective. Neither were allowed to carry a gun.

Charlotte stared for a long beat, seemingly begging for help from Judy.

“Oh, they’re not gonna help you...” White said. “You’re all alone with me, sweetie.”

Charlotte shook her head. She peered down again and then finally looked back at White. She crossed her arms.

"I don't know..." the redhead sighed.

He seemed amused. "Wow, fascinating!"

Charlotte nodded.

"So, that killer? Who was he?"

"No idea," Charlotte replied. "I didn't see his face. Just his jacket. It said *Skullheads* on it."

"Isn't that the emblem of gangsters here?"

"Oh, now you know!"

"Of course. I remembered all along. Miss Tia Blanche said something 'bout that."

"Who's that?"

"She's a..." He hesitated, then looked through his notes. "Yes, she's Mr. Richard Carson's girlfriend. Sweet lady. Very pretty."

"Awesome," Charlotte answered.

"So, you saw the mafia gangster. Can you say that on the record?"

"He's not in the mafia, he's part of a motorcycle club."

"Right..." White replied nonchalantly. "So?"

Charlotte sighed. "I didn't see Sebastian Reed, if that's what you're asking."

"Who's Sebastian Reed?"

"He's the leader of the Skullheads."

"Hmm... that fits!"

"I just saw a jacket! And it couldn't possibly be Reed or a member of his crew. It would make no sense."

White took a note, mumbling the words, "Sebastian Reed." Then he looked up at her. "And why is that?"

"Because he was involved in the death of Viktor Kovachev."

"And who's that?"

Charlotte painstakingly explained to White what Melanie had told them before her death. Eddie White listened to it all, or half listened. Of course, he asked more awkward and idiotic questions.

White finally finished with Charlotte and they left the room. Judy and the Sheriff were waiting in the hallway.

"Mrs. Hunter. Sheriff. This young lady tells me you've vandalized a cemetery?"

The Sheriff and Judy looked at each other.

"Well, that's not exactly—" the Sheriff started.

"What the heck did you do that for?" White interjected.

"Like Charlotte said, we tried to find the body of Viktor Kovachev."

"And did you find it?"

The Sheriff's shoulders slumped as he glanced at Judy and Charlotte.

"Sheriff? Did you find it?"

Grant hesitated.

"No," he then said.

"Mrs. Hunter. Did you find it?"

"No."

White shook his head. Then a smile grew from his cheeks.

"A good story... but just a story. The waitress got ya! She was crazy, no doubt about that. There is no body that exists. The kid just—"

"He didn't just disappear!" shouted Charlotte. "Nobody just disappears! Talk to Reed, I bet he'll tell you!"

"Thank you, Charlotte. I will talk to Reed. One hundred percent."

"We already did," said Charlotte. "He said he didn't do it!"

"And you believe it?" White shook his head. "I will talk to him about the murder of Melanie Sheldon and the fact that you saw him push her to the edge."

"I didn't see him!"

Judy spoke up. "She's right. She just saw a jacket. Nothing else. You have nothing on Reed."

"I do, actually. Tia Blanche said she saw a man just like him, wearing a jacket, spying on them for the last week before Mr. Carson got killed."

"That's not enough!"

"It will be, once I make Mr. Reed talk!"

Judy laughed.

Eddie White gazed at her, dumbfounded. "Is there something funny?"

"Nope, just good luck, friend!" She patted him on the shoulder.

White stared at her suspiciously. Then a deputy came up to the Sheriff.

"Reporters are here, sir!" he said.

"Reporters, you said, my good friend?" White questioned, smiling broadly. "Awesome."

White followed the deputy to the front of the building. Judy, Charlotte, and the Sheriff looked at each other. White was going to meet the media? God no!

CHAPTER FIFTY:

THE REPORTERS

The two women stayed where they were while the Sheriff followed White in an attempt to stop him. Charlotte couldn't imagine what was about to happen.

A deputy helpfully turned on the TV in the waiting room and the women were watching the interview happening live on the screen.

Grant was on camera.

"Anything you can tell us, Sheriff, about the murders happening in this town?"

"We have everything under control," the Sheriff started. "Nothing to worry about. Thank you."

The Sheriff was trying to drive the reporters away, and get himself off camera as quickly as possible, when suddenly a hand grabbed his shoulder and pulled him back. It was White. The detective was now smiling at the camera, holding the Sheriff by the shoulder.

"That's not entirely true, pals!" Eddie White began. "You should be worried!"

The crowd of reporters was stirred up now.

"But not for long! I'm taking care of all of it!" shouted White.

The crowd got a bit quieter.

"Who are you?" asked a reporter.

"Me?" White responded. "I'm Edward White of the NYPD. I'm here today to say that the great and incredibly smart Sheriff Newman Grant of beautiful, sunny Rockland, New York and I are on our way to solvin' the biggest series of murders you have ever seen. It all started with Ethan Gregory, the Hollywood man, as you know, and then it moved here with Richard Carson, and then Miss Melanie Sheldon."

"You're saying they're all connected?" asked another reporter.

"That's exactly what I said, sir!"

"Who figured it all out?" This question came from a different reporter.

"I did!" White was smiling proudly. "Yes, that's right, me!" he stressed. "Edward White of the NYPD..."

Judy was shaking her head in disbelief. Charlotte was shouting at the TV.

"Do you have a suspect?" Each newsperson had questions for White.

"At this time, we're lookin' at a fella by the name of Sebastian Reed, a gang member, really well known in this town. Known to cause fear and to be extremely dangerous! A real psycho. But don't worry, I'm on it! I'll stop Reed and put him in jail!"

White kept beaming. The reporters got loud again.

"Don't worry, everyone," he added. "The amazing Rockland will be safe soon; I'll personally make sure of it!"

White didn't offer further answers. Instead, he turned and started to walk away, waving his hand and smiling like a president about to board Air Force One.

Charlotte looked at Judy in awe and shock. They both seemed to have the same thought. *What the freaking fuck?*

CHAPTER FIFTY-ONE:

NO, HE DIDN'T!

Judy watched White walk back inside the sheriff's office with Grant. As soon as the men entered the precinct, Sheriff Grant cornered Eddie White and started arguing with him. Rightly so, too. White had just used Grant, a black man, as a mascot to potentially heal his reputation.

"This is my reputation too," the Sheriff yelled.

But White didn't care. He was damn proud.

Not only had he used his speech to build up his own reputation, but he had also taken the credit away from the two women. Who the hell did he think he was?

Judy approached Charlotte and the redhead stood up from her seat. They both stared at White in agitation. White saw them and smiled.

"Oh, Mrs. Hunter!" White said.

"Can we go now?" Judy asked. *You've done enough. And we've had enough.*

"No, I'm afraid you can't," said White.

Both women stared at White.

"You're staying here. Your ride will arrive soon."

"Our ride?" Charlotte asked.

"You're gettin' outta this town, and if you come back, you'll get arrested for interfering with a crucial police investigation. Mrs. Hunter, do you understand me?" cried White, adopting an authority he clearly didn't have.

"We need to get our things at the motel," said Judy.

"Your things are comin'. A deputy will be picking 'em up too, along with that filthy car of yours that I saw. Keys please?"

White looked at Charlotte. Charlotte hesitated and frowned. But after a beat she reached inside her pocket and put the car keys into Edward White's hands.

The two women waited it out in the Sheriff's office's waiting room. Judy held Rush in her arms and Charlotte tried to sleep a little. They had to wait until 11 a.m. for the car to arrive. When the time came, both Eddie White and the Sheriff came to see them. White looked at Charlotte for a moment, and Charlotte tried to ignore his creepy stare. Then the detective went for the front door and they saw him walk into the parking lot, where he started shouting, greeting the people stepping out of a car. It was an NYPD police car. What was it doing here?

"Good morning! Please, come in!"

Judy saw who it was coming from the car, and then Charlotte noticed too. Her jaw fell open, shocked.

"Mom?"

Madelaine got out of the NYPD car, flipping her wild red mane over her shoulders. She put her sunglasses on in the blinding sunlight. Then Judy saw someone else get out of the car. It was Brian!

Why is he here? Judy thought. *And with her?* Hadn't she seen him just last night in Rockland?

"Where the hell is she?" they heard Madelaine ask White.

Charlotte glanced at Judy with incredulity. Neither of them could believe their eyes. White had made her mother come here all the way from Montreal? *No freaking way.*

Judy immediately followed Charlotte out and into the parking lot. The redhead was rushing down the few stairs, looking white as a ghost, most likely petrified to see her mother here. Brian stayed frozen in place. As for Madelaine, she sped towards her daughter.

"Brian? Mom?" Charlotte said in shock. "What are you two—"

"Charlotte!" cried Madelaine, as though she had not seen her daughter in decades. She hugged her close. Judy observed that

Charlotte was not really hugging back. Brian was also smiling at Charlotte and hugged her as if it had been a long time. So, had he not shown up at Melanie's house the night before, after Judy spoke to him? Why was he just manifesting himself now? And was he going to pretend he had just come to town with Charlotte's mother?

"What are you doing here?" Charlotte asked, looking at both Brian and Madelaine.

"What am *I* doing here? Why are *you* here, Charlotte? I was so worried for you, sweetie!" Madelaine answered breathily. She added, "Mr. White called me and said that you were almost killed last night!"

Charlotte turned to look at White when she heard this. He looked back with a big smile on his face.

"That's not—" she attempted, before Madelaine continued.

"Charlotte! Look at me!" Madelaine said. "Is it true? Is it true what he said?"

"What did he say?" Charlotte replied.

"That you've been crazily investigating murders and tracking down an evil serial killer!"

"Mom... I—"

"Is it true?" Madelaine asked again.

Charlotte didn't answer right away. She looked at Brian, who didn't offer any help. Then Charlotte turned to Judy, who nodded.

"Yes, Mom, it's true! But—"

"Jesus Christ, Charlotte!"

"Jesus Christ? Are you serious right now?" Charlotte burst out. "You both have been so supportive of my career choice for the last year, and now that I'm doing it—doing what I love, by the way—you are acting like this? What the actual fuck, man?"

Madelaine looked taken aback and was momentarily at a loss for words.

"What are you really doing here, Mom? Judy and I were fine! We were fine! We don't need anything from you. Anything. I'm fine, I'm safe. No, I didn't nearly get killed last night. If anybody was going to fucking die, it would have been that killer. I had him, Mom, I nearly had him."

Judy saw that White was getting a little bit more interested in the conversation. She stepped in before Charlotte said too much, especially before saying that she had pointed a gun at the killer the night before.

"Madelaine! I—I'm sorry. It's true—"

"What the hell, Judy? You told me you were just visiting Fred's town and getting familiar with where he grew up."

Charlotte gave Judy an appreciative glance.

"Charlotte is right! She's not in any danger, I was watching over her. If you want someone to blame, blame me. I kept Charlotte here. I kept her by my side, and we investigated Fred's death and others' deaths. It was all my fault."

Madelaine looked disoriented.

"I assure you, Madelaine, I would never let anyone hurt Charlotte. Never. Please, blame me for all this."

"No! I can take care of myself. Everyone needs to understand that!" shouted Charlotte. "Nobody makes decisions for me. If you want to come after me, come after me. But I'm twenty-two and if I say I'm going to investigate a murder, I will do so. All right?"

Charlotte gave her mother a cold look. Madelaine looked at her for a moment before replying, "I'm sorry. I am the one freaking out. Brian believed you were okay and... I don't know, I just..."

Madelaine came up to Judy. "I'm sorry, Judy. I just wanted to know my daughter was safe."

Judy beamed at Madelaine and hugged her.

"Is there anything we can do? To help with your case..."

"Hmm..."

Before Judy could explain the situation, the valorous Eddie White stepped in.

"No, no, no!"

They all turned to him. Brian stepped forward, looking mad as hell.

"Nobody is gonna help them with anything," said White. "I said you're outta here. These ladies are not detectives. I am. Now, if you all want to get arrested, that's fine, but—"

Madelaine chose to simply ignore White and continue to talk to Charlotte.

"Is it true? That your father didn't take his own life?"

"Yeah, I—"

"No! Of course it's not true, you damn fools," screamed White, furious that his plan looked to be crumbling. "Like I said, millions of times: your father, Frederick Gibbins, was a drunk and was suffering from severe depression, and everyone who knew him told me so. But at least he had the courage to see that he had a problem and did somethin' about it, not like all of you!"

Madelaine was now looking at White in a less favorable light. She turned to Charlotte. "Who killed him, Charlotte?"

"No one!" uttered White.

"You only believe that because you don't want me or Judy involved in this," said Charlotte, calm but firm.

White scratched his head, trying to figure out his next step.

"We don't have a name yet, but we call him the Executioner," said Charlotte.

"The Executioner? Ha ha!" giggled White. "That's a nice theory. A false one, but a nice one."

Charlotte turned away from him.

"What motive does this gangster have, anyway, to be this Executioner?" questioned White.

"Exactly," said Charlotte. Was White finally seeing the light of day?

"It doesn't fit, Miss Gibbins!"

"Yeah, that's what I've been saying!"

"This is purely mafia business!" White uttered, laughing. "Not some personal vendetta... Just business. How can you not see that? Everyone can see that. They are dangerous people and they kill everyone who does bad business with them. That's what is happenin' here. And your killing method theory, well, that's how the mafia get rid of folks: drastic measures. There's nothing more to it than that. They don't care how they do it—gas, swords, cliffs... They don't care, they just do it! That's how psycho they are. But don't worry, these people don't scare me. I'll make that Reed guy talk."

As soon as White had finished his speech, Judy saw two cars arrive from the main road and pull into the parking lot where they standing. One was a Sullivan County Police car and the other one was Brian's car, being driven by a deputy. They had come back from the motel. Eddie White saw them too. His face brightened up again. He had brought in the whole cavalry to help him and it was clearly a moment of glory for him.

"Look! You can finally be on your merry ways," the yellow-haired detective said. "Your beautiful four-wheeler is here." White smiled graciously.

But Charlotte wasn't finished with the conversation. "Not the mafia—Reed isn't in the mafia, you idiot. My father was not dealing with the maf—"

"Look! What did I tell ya? She's a lunatic."

"But he's part of it! Not the mafia, but the serial killings—my father was killed by the Executioner too! Like all of them!" Charlotte cried, sounding a bit like an angry child.

"Again with the father!" White said. "I told you—"

"He's part of this too, you dickwad!"

White shook his head sadly. “You’re making a mistake, dear. I am the detective here! I know what a suicide looks like when I see one. Okay?”

Judy felt he was trying to convince himself more than them.

“Now that that’s settled, you can go back to your crummy little apartment in New York, okay? You have nothin’ to do here, your daddy is not involved.” White began to walk away.

“What about Melanie’s story?” Charlotte shouted at his back. “That fits!”

“The ‘story’?” he repeated, laughing. “That’s just a story, darling. I bet she told you that just so you would protect her because she knew that the mob was after her. And great job you did protecting her, I might say!”

“You... It wasn’t a story! And we—” Charlotte was beside herself. “Fine. What about the notes, then? Your story is filled with holes, you imbecile!”

White shook his head. “Maybe Reed just likes you! You went to see him, right? Maybe he just has a crush on you and likes playing! Like a player! That’s all. Don’t you want him? I can understand him. Jeez! He’s got taste.”

Charlotte was ready to strangle White. She rushed towards him, but Judy pulled her back.

“Oh, my dear! These women, I tell you. They think they can do a better job than the men. But they cannot. You know why? Because you are just too emotional, and when you go after something, you don’t think, you just do it. Well, if you weren’t this emotional, you would have thought this through, and you also would have figured out how delusional you both are. Neither of you have a badge and neither of you—well, maybe Judy a bit—but Charlotte doesn’t know how to defend herself.”

“Oh, yeah?” Charlotte shouted.

Charlotte raised her hand and was about to go after White again, but Judy stopped her once more.

"Charlotte!"

"None of you appear to have brains, so what can you expect, really," White continued. "I thought the mother would have her senses, but no— and let's not even talk 'bout the boy toy over here," he added, pointing at Brian. "He's violent as hell but he's got nothin' else besides the muscles. Expected, really. I gotta explain everything to everybody—many, many times—because they're all idiots," he said, shaking his head with regret. "Who knew we would come to this point, in this society? Sad, really. That damn Barack Hussein, it's his fault—"

"That's enough! I'll show you who's an idiot, you mother—" shouted Madelaine. Judy had to physically restrain her too.

"No!" the retired detective said. "That's enough!"

"That fucking piece of—" Madelaine began.

"Madelaine—get back in the car. Charlotte, take her, please. You too, Brian."

Charlotte hesitated but did as Judy had asked. Madelaine was still struggling to go after White, but she finally listened to Charlotte's pleas.

Judy waited for the doors to close, and then walked over to Eddie White.

"I'll arrest you, if you come back. Do you understand this, Hunter?"

The Sheriff's face grew angry. "You won't!" Grant said.

White turned to look at the Sheriff. "Excuse me?"

"I won't let you!"

"You won't let me?" White chuckled.

Before the Sheriff could say another word, Judy stepped forward. "It's okay, Sheriff, we'll go. He's right. We're not cops. And this is his investigation."

The retired detective approached White. "Mr. White, it was... a pleasure. Just keep in mind, Mr. White, that if you ever say things like that again, things that are disrespectful of either my late friend or his family, never mind me, I will not only do everything in my power to expose your racist, sexist, and overwhelmingly shameful and dishonorable police behavior, but I will also kick your fucking ass to the ground and you won't be able to stand up for months. And you can tell everybody that it was a woman who did that to you."

She was about to get into the car when Judy heard White babbling something he shouldn't have babbled, "Fucking dykes, I tell ya!"

She smiled softly to herself, turned around, and walked back to White. Judy stared into his eyes once more and then lifted her hard hand, now made of unbreakable stone, and jabbed it onto White's fragile and already broken nose. The yellow-shirted detective fell to the ground, crying like a baby.

"You should be happy there are no reporters in here, Mr. White!" Judy exclaimed. "Please, don't say another word. For your own good."

And he didn't.

Judy nodded at White and then waved goodbye to the Sheriff, who smiled supportively at her. She got inside Brian's car and triumphantly yanked the door shut. She wished a reporter had caught that.

CHAPTER FIFTY-TWO:

BACK IN MANHATTAN

"Rockland! There is nothing remotely cute about this town," Madelaine kept whining in Brian's car. "I never liked this place. Fred brought me here a lot when we first started dating and I dreaded it! Everyone is sleeping with each other, catching diseases. Everyone knows each other, no room for mistakes—believe me, they won't forget it. Plus, they're all bitchy to outsiders. If you come in with a different opinion of how things go and how things should be, the hell with you. They're going to crucify you and send you right back to where you came from... or, worse, torture you until you weaken and assimilate. What a lame piece of trash of a town."

Charlotte was sitting in the front, with Brian. They were not talking, just holding each other's hands while Brian drove with his free hand. Judy was the one with Madelaine in her face. The retired detective didn't care, she was tired. She didn't have to respond, and she didn't. Madelaine just kept talking, not the least bit offended that she was doing so alone. But Judy did feel restrained; the car was too tight and too small for all of them.

Brian drove for an hour and a half before they entered New York City. Finally, here they were, back in the big city. New York had not changed. It was just as busy as always, the traffic still unbearable. People continued to cross at street corners even though the pedestrian lights weren't on and cars were bearing down on them.

It took a while for Judy to adjust. New York City was not Rockland. The streets here were never empty, there were tens of thousands of people about at every minute of every day. And in those thousands of people, hardly anyone knew anyone else. As Madelaine grudgingly expressed, in Rockland, you saw the same faces all the time. Not here.

Brian took them one by one to their apartments. Judy was first on the list. She got out, holding Rush in her hands. The whole lot—Charlotte, Brian, and Madeleine—got out with her to say goodbye.

The retired detective hugged Charlotte and Madelaine. She then told Charlotte not to worry about anything and that she would call if she had any news about the case. Charlotte clearly wasn't satisfied with that, but waved goodbye resignedly. Madelaine thanked Judy again for taking care of her daughter. Both mother and daughter closed their doors behind them.

Brian was about to get back in the car as well when Judy pulled on his arm. "Brian?"

He turned around, surprised.

"Didn't you go see Charlotte last night?"

"No... Well, yeah, I did."

"Which one is it?"

Brian smiled, embarrassed.

"Look, I just noticed you were a little distant and you... acted as if you haven't seen her for weeks."

Brian shook his head before replying, "Yeah, I did go... I didn't want to say anything... but... she doesn't know."

"She doesn't know?" Judy said, confused. "How come?"

Brian paused. "I—I saw her with somebody else... they were... kissing. I saw through the window of her friend's house."

"Really?" Judy said, surprised.

"Yeah."

"Wow... Well, I'm sure it's nothing. Maybe you saw wrong. It might have just been a mistake. I know you've been through a rough patch because of this case, but… Charlotte seems to love you a lot. Those hugs and kisses showed that in the car. Be gentle with her."

Brian nodded and turned back to the car.

"Brian?" Judy called once more.

He turned around.

"Did you happen to see anyone else when you went to Melanie's place that night? Someone maybe hanging around the house? In a leather jacket?"

Brian thought about it and then said, "There was a policeman outside the door."

Judy nodded, expressing disbelief that the policeman outside the door had anything to do with the murder. He had been unconscious when Charlotte went after the actual killer on the motorbike.

Judy went up to her apartment. She closed the door behind her and didn't look back. She just wanted to sleep in her own bed now. She was desperately worn out by this whole situation.

PART TWO

CHAPTER FIFTY-THREE:

THE FOLLOWING DAYS

Charlotte barely slept the night she got back from Rockland. She was lying in bed next to someone she hadn't slept with for quite a while. It felt so strange, especially after what had happened in Rockland with Stew. Brian didn't seem to feel the same way, or even to notice the change in her behavior. He had her in his arms all night, holding her tight to him. It was comforting to be hugged and loved so much but she wished she could return the favor. She didn't feel that way right now. With everything that had gone on, she couldn't. She didn't feel like that same sweet and dreamy girl, so filled with love, any longer; she was someone else. Charlotte had become what she had always wanted to be: a detective. Realizing one's dreams was supposed to improve a relationship, it was supposed to make it stronger. She was no longer a girl struggling to find confidence and approbation. She had those things. Well, she still had to become a real cop with a real badge, and real credibility, but it didn't feel like an unreachable goal now. Whatever happened, she hoped she wouldn't feel the same way after a few days. She hoped she would be able to reconnect with Brian. She loved him, she knew she did.

She waited until dawn before getting up. But as soon as she began to slip out of the bed, he dragged her back.

"Where are you going?" he asked.

Charlotte acted confused, and then she noticed his smile. He moved to kiss her. She hesitated for a bit and then resolved to do the same. Maybe this was a good start to renewing what appeared a little lost. Sex followed, and even though it was not the best they had ever had, it still felt good. It was a step in the right direction.

Brian then insisted on making her breakfast. He whipped up her favorite: chocolate chip and banana pancakes. It was very kind of him. He poured her some coffee and they sat at the table staring at each other for a while. Brian couldn't stop smiling.

He began, "So?"

The redhead looked at him. "So... what?"

"What's next? What are you going to do now?"

"Here?"

"Yeah..." he replied.

Charlotte shrugged, unsure.

"Are you gonna still do this? Pursue this case of yours?"

"I don't know. I want to. I just need to figure it out with Judy... if she wants to or not."

"You like her, Judy?"

Charlotte smiled. "I don't think I would still be here without her. She's taught me so much in so little time. I—I don't know... She believed in me when nobody else would."

Brian gave her a look.

Sorry, I didn't mean to—"

"No, it's fine. You have the right to say that. You were right, I freaked out for nothing. I knew you were good at this. I knew you could take care of yourself and that you didn't need me or anyone else to protect you, but I still went—mad. I'm truly sorry, Char."

Charlotte smiled. "It's okay. 'We all go a little mad sometimes.'"

Brian was amused. "He was right," he said.

"Well, Norman Bates killed people," Charlotte replied. "Dressed as his mother, I might add. It wasn't exactly a good mad."

"So, mine was a good mad. Perfect."

Charlotte bent in two. Brian held her hands, then kissed them. He seemed so grateful for her forgiveness.

Another moment passed, and he added, "You should really do this. Don't let that coward ruin your ambition. Only you can really solve this."

"Can I?"

"Yeah, you can. Believe me."

Charlotte thought of this, staring at the wall.

"There wasn't even a case before you started, right?"

"Well, there was Gregory. But... yeah, that was going somewhere nobody wanted. So, I guess."

Brian nodded as if to say, *There you go.*

"Call Judy," he then said.

She nodded back and he stood and kissed her forehead. It felt good that he believed in her too. She liked that a lot.

Of course, she wanted to call Judy. Even though it had been difficult, and Judy wanted to give up, she needed to finish this. They needed to finish this. She just didn't know how the retired detective would feel about it.

She then received a call from Madelaine. Her mother was staying at the Mandarin Oriental, one of the best hotels in town. She could have stayed with Brian and Charlotte, but Madelaine had told Charlotte she didn't want to disrupt their reunion and that she found the hotel more luxurious and comfortable anyway. Charlotte was not too offended by that.

Last night, after they got back from Rockland, Charlotte's mother had stayed with them for hours. They had ordered Chinese food and Madelaine talked and talked and talked. Finally, Charlotte had to say she was tired and needed some sleep. When Madelaine finally called a cab to take her back to her hotel, a wave of relief swept over the apartment. Clearly, Brian had had enough too.

And then, this morning, she had asked Charlotte to come and have breakfast with her at the hotel. The redhead told her mom that she had already had breakfast and that Brian made her pancakes. A sound of disappointment had echoed in Madelaine's voice, so Charlotte said she would come anyway and have coffee, and she did. They had another long conversation about her future and her life plans. But Charlotte didn't mind. She was feeling more energized, even though she still hadn't slept much the night before. She was happy to have her mother by her side, and Madelaine was delighted to have her daughter too.

A few days went by. Charlotte didn't hear from Judy or anybody else about the case. She hung out with Brian, having breakfast with him, and later usually going shopping with her mother. It was all good, but she still wanted to know what was happening. For one, had Reed talked to White? What was she thinking? It was impossible. Nobody in their right mind would think that was ever going to happen. If someone was going to weaken in these investigations, it was sure not going to be Reed.

She really wanted Judy to call her, but she didn't know if the retired detective wanted to get back on the case or if she had given up on the whole thing. Part of Charlotte wanted to give up. She felt discouraged and hurt. But she couldn't, she really couldn't. Somehow, she had to find a way to uncover the truth. She kept looking through the notes that she made for hours on end and looking at images and articles on the Internet. But she found nothing new, nothing that could help her move forward. Charlotte felt depressed by it all.

Her mother left for Montreal after a few days in the city. She said she had to get back to her husband and her other kids. She asked Charlotte if she wanted to go back with her, but Charlotte said no, maybe soon but not now. She made up excuses that she had appointments to go to and friends to see. But really, she wanted to stay in New York for Judy, so they could get back to the investigation.

The days slipped away, and she kept herself occupied: getting back into her New York routine, going to the gym, and punching bags she imagined were the faces of Sebastian Reed and Eddie White, combined with the unknown face of her father's murderer. Finally, her mind felt clean and crystal clear. Charlotte was left with one recurring thought in her head: she needed to find the murderer and close this case. She finally thought she would call Judy. If they don't come to you, go to them, right? It didn't matter if Eddie White was having little panic attacks and threatening them. It didn't matter that everything was pointing to Sebastian Reed. It didn't matter that she wasn't a cop, legally. She was a detective at heart, and a damn good one, too. She had to finish this, for her father's sake and for hers. No matter what. *Get back on the horse, Charlotte! A little fall won't kill either of you. And if it does, then you'll go out with honor and bravery.*

It turned out that Judy was on the same page when Charlotte finally gave her a call. They decided to meet up the next day at a café a few blocks down the street from Brian's apartment to see how they would proceed.

"Sorry, I should have called, but I figured with your mother and Brian, you might want some time with them," Judy said to Charlotte when they sat down. "And to be honest, I didn't know if you still wanted to do this."

Charlotte gave her a look.

"Don't kill me!" Judy smiled.

"Are you mad? Have you met me? Of course I want to do this. I thought *you* didn't want to. Look, until we're done, there will be no doubt in my mind that I want to see this through to the end."

"Okay," the retired detective replied.

"At whatever cost. Even if it means breaking someone's nose a third time!" Charlotte exclaimed.

Judy laughed. "Let's not do that again."

"Are you kidding? It's amazing that you did that. He totally deserved it."

Judy shook her head. "How's your mother?"

"She went back to Montreal to take care of her kids. She loves them more than me."

Judy smiled wryly. "That's not true."

"We had some good times, I guess. I'm glad she was around. I will definitely go to Canada once we're done. I need to see my brothers... well, meet them, really. I have only seen them on FaceTime."

"And I will return to Mexico."

"Oh yeah, you're right. I might need a vacation too, after this."

The two women settled with joy into being together again.

"And Brian? Is he happy you're back?"

"He's over the moon about it. Never been held so tight in my life."

"You told him about Stew?"

Charlotte gave Judy a cold look.

"He called me. The Sheriff gave him my number. Stew said he doesn't have yours."

"What did he say?" Charlotte asked.

"He apologized and said that he wanted to talk if it was possible..."

Charlotte shook her head. "He has nothing to apologize for. It was all me."

Judy looked skeptical.

"I... I made a mess of myself..."

"How so?"

Charlotte felt ashamed of it all. She looked down before speaking again.

"He kissed me, and I freaked out and I—I then accused him of being the killer."

Judy was taken aback. "Stew?"

"I *know*. He has blue eyes, he's tall, fits the age description of what Damyan Kovachev would be right now, and then he told me he had been in New York a day before Gregory died... and I freaked out! I pointed the gun at him... I almost shot him. Then I realized I was wrong, and before I could make it right, I heard Melanie scream and I didn't get a chance to fix it."

"Right..." Judy nodded. "What told you that you were wrong?"

"Nothing in the moment. I just lost myself, I didn't know what to believe anymore. But looking back, he was nothing but honest. He wasn't hiding anything. He had an alibi for Gregory's murder. He was aware of how suspicious it looked that he was in New York. He was also with me when Carson died. It's just me that went completely bonkers. He's just so sweet and kind, how could anyone think of him as a murderer?"

"Have you told him that?"

Charlotte looked down again and shook her head. "Brian loves me. He's so great too. He helped me become the woman I always wanted to be. He trained me, he taught me how to fight and defend myself. He taught me how to become strong."

Judy grinned. "I didn't know that... How does he know how to fight?"

"He's a coach at a gym, where he teaches different martial arts and kickboxing."

"Wow!" exclaimed Judy.

"Yeah, we spent hours and hours in there so I could learn to throw a punch properly. He wanted so badly for me to get it right. I was reckless and weak before he met me. Really."

"Sounds like he really believed in you," Judy observed.

"I would be nothing without him. He never doubted me for a single second. He is the one who made me believe I could stand up to my father and tell him I wanted to become a detective. He wanted me to become a cop like no one else ever has." The redhead took a breath and then said, "I don't want to let him down now... not after everything he's done for me. He's got no one else around to take care of him."

"Where are his folks?"

"His parents died when he was young, back in Albuquerque. Their house caught fire and he was the only one who survived the flames. Horrible."

Judy looked shaken. "Poor kid."

"I know... he's only got me. I just can't leave him alone. Things have been so good lately. Even though he messed up, I was so glad to see him come to Rockland with my mother. I was so proud to show him I had done it. *We* had done it. I was finally a detective."

CHAPTER FIFTY-FOUR:

GOING AROUND TOWN

Judy observed Charlotte carefully as she explained how much Brian had cared for her and how much he loved her. The retired detective believed that Brian had a lot of love for the redhead, but she wasn't exactly sure Charlotte was feeling the same way about him. It was almost like the young woman was trying too hard to convince herself that this was the truth.

No matter, it wasn't Judy's business. *Let it go, Judy. Let it go.* However, at her core, Judy just wanted to see Charlotte be the happiest she could be. Judy didn't have any children of her own, but it was as if she did with Charlotte, and she wanted to protect her.

The two then decided to speak about the case. Judy even texted the Sheriff to get some news. He said he couldn't talk at the moment but would get back to them when he had a chance. He likely couldn't talk because of Eddie White: he didn't want White to know that Judy and Charlotte were still in contact with him.

Judy then had an idea. She suggested they go back to where the murders started. They were in New York, so why not take full advantage of that? It had all started here, in this city, with Ethan Gregory's death. Hunter told Charlotte that she and Fred had barely questioned the movie star's entourage following his death because she was retiring the next day. Maybe Fred had—he was still in service in the days after her retirement—but now that she knew about Fred and Gregory's relationship, the late detective might not even have bothered. He may have already felt a sense of doom.

Judy didn't know if the people she wanted to interview were still in town or if the Broadway show was still happening. Charlotte did a quick Google search and learned that it was. And as they got to the theater, this was confirmed. The marquee still featured the show's name and its star. It was still called *Highway Nine*, but of course the name of the actor wasn't the same. Ethan Gregory had been replaced by another movie star, someone Judy Hunter surprisingly recognized. It was none other than Daniel Craig, Mr. James Bond himself.

The two women went in, passing a few men dressed in black carrying walkie-talkies, guarding the entrance. There were a few more security guards inside, dressed the same way. They stood with their arms crossed. Nobody wanted another star to get murdered, especially not Daniel Craig. Judy smiled awkwardly at them, and she and Charlotte moved to the ticket office. They asked if they could talk to some of the cast about Gregory's murder. The ticketer asked to see a badge.

Judy had thought about this and had brought one just for the occasion. Charlotte looked at her like she was some crazy woman. She *was* a bit crazy, she said to herself, but so was this whole case, so why stop now? Hunter had anticipated that the ticketer would only need to see it for a second and then Judy would flip it back, and that's exactly what happened. It was a toy badge she had bought at the grocery store, and the ticketer hadn't noticed.

Judy then added, "I already talked to them three weeks ago. They know who I am."

The ticketer paused, then nodded and went to get her manager. The bald old man, by the name of Hector, joined them after a few seconds and immediately recognized Judy from when she came in with Fred.

"You again!" he uttered, half-annoyed and half-smiling.

"Yes. We're here to see Mr. Bond," she laughed.

Hector looked at her with an odd expression on his face and then Judy said it was a joke. He slightly chuckled. "You should know how many people come here each day and say the exact same thing you just said."

"Ha ha! Really?" she replied.

"That's impossible," added Charlotte. "We're his only fans."

"Right!" said Hector, shaking his head.

"No, seriously, do you mind if we ask a few questions to your available crew and cast?"

"The night show is starting in two hours, you know that, yes?"

Judy and Charlotte looked at each other and then nodded at him.

"We'll be really quick!" Charlotte replied.

Hector still didn't look sure. He was frowning.

"We promise," said Charlotte, batting her lashes.

Hector stared at her for a second and then finally accepted under the condition they be *really* fast about it.

They didn't get to meet Daniel Craig that day. They were told he came in very close to showtime. Charlotte really wanted to see him and tell him how much she loved him. Anyway, they weren't here for him. Hector first took them to director George Mickelson, whom they found in a dressing room with a cast member, going over lines. The director, a medium-sized man with long, curly black hair that went down almost to his waist, looked very surprised to see Judy but didn't appear the least bit annoyed by her. He jumped straight away from his chair and greeted them with enthusiasm.

"Detective! Is that you?"

"Yes. Judy Hunter. You remember—"

"Oh, of course I remember. So, is it really him? That Asian man?"

"Excuse me?"

"They arrested somebody for Ethan's murder, no?"

"Ah, right. Well, umm..."

"I knew it, I knew! These racist fuckers. What has this world come to? Right?" he exclaimed passionately. "Please excuse me for my language. I just thought it was so, so bad. And God, I was wondering if you would ever come back here. They barely talked to us... Damn, I was right. So tell me, did you catch him, the real killer? Please."

This is a breath of fresh air, Judy thought.

"Not yet," she said. "But we're working on it."

"Good, good!" replied Mickelson. "Ethan was such a kind man, and generous... such a generous and talented actor. He doesn't deserve a half-baked investigation."

Charlotte smiled. "We're not letting that happen."

Mikelson turned to Charlotte, stars came over his eyes, "Oh dear! You!"

"Uh... what?" asked Charlotte.

"Aren't you a pretty one! Oh jeez! Please, tell me you're good at acting."

He waited for an answer, looking so sure he'd made a great discovery, but Charlotte had to set him straight.

"Thank you for the compliment. But no... I wish. I've never acted in my life."

Mikelson's excited face then flushed a little. "Oh, I'm sure we can do something anyway... It doesn't matter, it really doesn't. You're probably a natural. What are you doing tonight?"

Charlotte was nonplussed.

"My friend and I are shooting a movie next week, and we are still painfully looking for a redhead. Chastain is not available; Stone doesn't like the script... but what does she know? And... yeah, others are not... Anyway, you are perfect! Just perfect, my dear. You really are."

"I'm genuinely flattered."

Judy had to interrupt. “Mr. Mickelson, if you don’t mind. Like we discussed, we haven’t caught a killer yet and we’re pretty sure he may strike again. So, I’m afraid we’re on a tight timeline. Do you mind resuming your conversation later?”

Charlotte looked a little sad. Her moment had ended!

“Sure! Oh, for sure. Sorry, I just got carried away. Please, ask me anything you want to know.”

Judy nodded. “You said we barely talked to you. What did you mean by that? Do you have something you didn’t tell us?”

“Oh, yes!” he replied immediately.

“And that is?” Judy asked, surprised.

He hesitated for a moment, then said, “I must get Sofia for this. She experienced it. She is the one who called your precinct, several times, and they never called back. Do you mind?”

“Of course, not,” replied Judy.

George Mickelson stepped out of the room and closed the door behind him, leaving the two women by themselves.

“Sofia?” asked Charlotte. “Like Sofia Marlow?”

Judy nodded affirmatively.

Sofia Marlow was the other star of the show, whom Judy had met before with Fred for questioning. From what Judy knew of her, she was one of the biggest stars Broadway had ever known. She saw the blood leaving Charlotte’s face as she confirmed it was indeed her that was coming to talk to them.

CHAPTER FIFTY-FIVE:

MARLOW

They were about to meet Sofia Marlow, *the* Sofia Marlow, and Charlotte was not the least bit unhappy about it. But she feared she might pass out from excitement and nervousness. This was certainly the most nervous she had ever been in her life. Even though she had never participated in theater activities because her youthful time had largely been devoted to science, that hadn't stopped the redhead from becoming one of the biggest theater fans New York had ever known.

She and Judy waited a few minutes before the door of the dressing room opened and Charlotte finally caught a glimpse of Sofia Marlow's beautiful green eyes and stunning face walking through the door. The five-foot-five Italian woman was just breathtaking. Charlotte thought she saw Judy's jaw drop too. She really was a goddess. In fact, she was even more goddess-like in person than on the screen.

The redhead gasped as she took in Marlow's elegant, business-like black suit and the splendid beret she was wearing. Another woman followed her, carrying a makeup bag. As the star kept walking, the makeup artist was still trying to apply powder to her face. Marlow recognized Judy immediately. Her gloved hand reached out.

"Detective Hunter, isn't it?" Marlow said. "I'm glad to see you here."

Judy nodded and shook her hand. "Good afternoon, Mrs. Marlow!"

Marlow turned to Charlotte. The redhead was beaming at her. Charlotte thought her face must be beet-red. Redder than her hair. She was almost guilt-ridden to be this nervous.

"Hello!" greeted Marlow. "How are you? We didn't meet, did we?"

"Umm... no... we didn't." Charlotte had to force the words out of her mouth.

"Sofia Marlow! Pleasure to meet you."

Judy must have seen the stress that Charlotte was experiencing, and she intervened. "This is Charlotte Gibbins, Mrs. Marlow. She's helping me with this case."

Charlotte felt her lips form a smile. After an awkward pause, Marlow moved her eyes back to Judy.

"This case... you're still on it?" the actress asked.

"Yes," replied Judy.

"Oh, good. They told me you retired."

"I did. But I am... I guess I'm still investigating anyway," said Judy, clearly not sure how to answer.

"I don't care!" exclaimed Marlow. "I'm sure glad you are. Whatever you're doing, keep doing it. At least somebody cares..."

Marlow sighed and walked to the dressing room mirror. She sat on a chair in front of it and let the makeup artist finish her work.

"I called your precinct so many times last week, you don't even know. Every time, they said they'd call me back, but they never did. Then I finally talked to the detective in charge, which I thought was you, and he told me that whatever I had to say didn't matter, they had already caught the killer and that was it."

Charlotte and Judy exchanged a knowing glance.

"Eddie White?" asked Charlotte.

"That's his name! There you go. I've been calling him Detective Zero all week because I didn't remember what he said his name was."

Both Charlotte and Judy chuckled.

"He was so condescending! Damn!" Marlow added. "Does he *really* work for the police force?"

"I'm afraid so," said Charlotte.

Marlow shook her head. Charlotte was getting such a good vibe from the actress. She had always been warned never to meet her heroes in person, and she was sure that saying applied to most heroes, but not this one.

"Anyway, I needed to share some details with you guys about Ethan's death," Marlow announced. "Something I've never talked about before."

"Okay," Judy encouraged. "Go for it."

"I should've said something before. I was just afraid, y'know... the way they killed Ethan... it's horrible."

The two detectives nodded.

"I just didn't want that to happen to me!"

"Don't worry," reassured Charlotte. "You can talk freely. I promise, nothing will ever happen to you."

Charlotte then got this weird sensation driving through her fingers. She was getting her nerves back. She had promised Melanie Sheldon the exact same thing. Judy saw the redhead's expression and nodded, indicating that she understood, and it was okay.

"Yes, Mrs. Marlow. You'll be fine."

Marlow nodded as well and went on, "The night Ethan died, he didn't exactly go back to his hotel room alone."

"You were with him?"

The actress nodded again.

"Why?" asked Judy. "Were you guys seeing each other?"

"Oh, no, no! Nothing like that. I mean, I *wish*. But Ethan was gay."

"What?" Charlotte heard herself exclaim. She was slightly disappointed to hear that.

"Yeah, right? No, he just wanted to rehearse his lines with me that night. The premiere was the next day and he was so nervous. I could understand—the guy had never done a full-on stage performance before this. He had always been in front of the cameras, and had multiple takes and angles to get things right. Plus, he wasn't used to having an audience that might laugh at him if he fucked up. I mean, he asked me to help him out, because I'm used to this and he trusted me. And it was a pleasure! He was such a great scene partner."

"Right," replied Charlotte. "Of course, he trusted you."

Marlow smiled at her. "So, the night it happened, I was leaving Ethan's hotel room around eleven, and I was walking down the emergency staircase and I saw a guy coming up."

"You took the staircase?" Judy asked.

"Yeah, it led to the parking lot downstairs and I exited there."

Charlotte saw Judy give Marlow a confused face. That was a lot of stairs!

"I always went through that exit," Marlow explained. "I didn't want to be seen coming out of his hotel room and start all these rumors of our being together or sleeping together and all. People are really quick to assume things, and the paparazzi are really quick to catch on and harass people."

"Sorry," said Judy.

"Not to worry," reassured Marlow.

"So, you said you saw someone?" the retired woman moved on.

"Yes. I went through the doors and rushed down the stairs and I saw this man coming up. When we crossed paths, he stopped and stared at me for a moment, then continued to go up. I didn't do anything or say anything, I just kept going down the stairs."

"You sure he was going to Ethan's suite?"

"No idea, he kept going up as I kept going down, like I said... but he did look weird."

"Weird how?" Judy asked.

"Well, very creepy, to say the least. I didn't smile or anything, but he gave me this quick, cold look."

"What was he wearing?"

"He had a black hat on, was dressed all in black, and he was carrying some kind of long bag."

"A long bag?" Charlotte said.

"Yeah, it wasn't large, just long. Like he was carrying a stick in there or something. A sound pole..."

"Or a sword..." Charlotte uttered.

Judy nodded at this. Marlow looked at both women and became very agitated.

"Damn it," the actress said.

"You hadn't seen him before? The man," asked Judy.

Sofia Marlow shook her head. "At first I thought he was a friend of Ethan's, but he didn't exactly look friendly. He looked very rough around the edges... intimidating."

Charlotte frowned.

"You sure his eyes were brown?" Judy insisted.

"Yeah!" replied Marlow, without a bit of hesitation.

"No gray hair?"

"No, he was young. Very young. Early thirties maybe."

Judy nodded. "And what was he wearing?"

"He was dressed in black: black shirt, black pants. Everything black. No other colors."

"So, he wasn't wearing a leather jacket with markings on it?" asked Charlotte.

"Nope," Marlow said firmly.

Charlotte and Judy both sighed. That was not a description of Sebastian Reed or a Skullhead.

Suddenly, Marlow starting crying.

"If had done something, and not stayed frozen there, then maybe I could have warned Ethan... I should have!"

Charlotte went to her and put a hand on her shoulder tenderly. "It's all right," said the redhead. "It's all right, it's not your fault."

CHAPTER FIFTY-SIX:

MURPHY

"What do you think?" Charlotte asked Judy as the women exited the theater.

"I don't know," the retired detective said.

"Do you think it was him, the killer? The man she saw?"

"Perhaps."

Judy really didn't know what to think. Marlow's version was definitely interesting. The actress had seen a man with a long bag. If it was the killer, what Marlow saw was him holding a bag containing the murder weapon—the katana.

"Well, now we've got different descriptions. One clearly corresponds to Reed, mine that goes with whoever, and the other... fits with that Damyan Kovachev thing. You really believe in that story, right? Melanie's?" Charlotte asked.

"I don't think she had any reasons to lie, do you?" Judy asked.

"No," Charlotte said. She then paused for a moment before asking, "So, you think he's alive, Damyan Kovachev?"

"I think Lilyana wasn't fully honest with us, yes," Judy said.

"Do you want to go back there? To push her?"

"No, we've done what we needed to do there. Now we need to look into Marlow's lead. And to do that, we're going to need to see footage from the parking lot and the Four Seasons again... and she's going to do a sketch of the man she saw for us."

"How do we get this footage?" asked Charlotte.

"We have to go to the NYPD."

Charlotte shook her head. Judy also sighed—an exhausted sigh.

As the two women stepped onto Broadway, Judy's phone rang. It was not the Sheriff calling back, but somebody else at the force. The ID said: "Precinct." *Speak of the devil.* Her old precinct was calling her. Judy Hunter hadn't spoken to them for the longest time; the last conversation she had with them was when she talked to Price. He had told her about finding lesions on Fred's brain that indicated he had been pushed around and that he had knocked his head before getting the rope around his neck. Then, before she could reach out again, they had sent White to Rockland, and that had been a bit awkward and strange to say the least, so she stayed out of the way. They wanted him investigating, not her or Charlotte. Well, they were calling now. What could they possibly want?

"Judy!" said a fast-paced, aggrieved voice.

"Captain?"

"Yes, how is it going?" replied Captain Murphy.

"I'm good."

"Listen," he said, trying to sound authoritative but ultimately getting caught up in his words like a nervous bulldog. "I heard you were down in Rockland."

"Yeah, I was."

"White was really not happy about it..."

"Wasn't he?" Judy smirked.

"This is not a joke, Judy. All right? He has a right to be not happy. It's his investigation. What the hell were you even thinking? He—"

"I get it, Captain! I was just trying to help and steer everybody in the right direction."

"The right direction?"

"Yeah."

"So, what is the right direction? The Sheriff called me personally and told me all about your thoughts on the investigation."

"Did he now?"

"Yeah... do you really believe all the things he said?"

"Well, what did he tell you, Captain?"

"That you didn't think Mr. White had the right suspect on his hands."

"Hmm," replied Judy, annoyed. *Now you care?*

"Do you believe that?"

"It's White's investigation, Captain. The Commissioner's own boy. I'm not a detective anymore, my opinion doesn't matter."

As Judy kept talking, Charlotte ordered them a Lyft.

"Don't you play with me, Judy. The Sheriff told me you believe a serial killer is doing this. You call him the Executioner or something. You believe it was linked to a high school grievance. You even believe Fred Gibbins was part of it."

"That's correct, Captain."

"You really believe all that?" he asked again.

"I do."

"Well, Eddie doesn't."

Of course.

"I can't say I blame him. It's weird and slightly crazy..." he said. "But then again, you're my best girl, Judy. You always have been the best detective I had."

Judy felt her heart being warmed by this thought.

The Captain didn't say anything for some time. Judy heard him sigh. Meanwhile, the Lyft arrived and the women got inside.

"I heard Charlotte Gibbins was with you too?"

"Yeah, she was."

The retired detective took a seat and put the Captain on speakerphone so Charlotte could hear the conversation.

"Does she really believe all that stuff?" asked Murphy.

"What part?" Judy said.

"Everything... that her father was part of it and also killed?"

"Yes," Judy replied right away.

"Really?"

"If I remember correctly, you are the ones who didn't believe her. She came to you with it, remember? That note she received."

"Right..." he said. "I do remember that..."

They heard him pause and take a breath.

"I'm truly sorry about that day. We were a little harsh on her."

Judy looked at Charlotte. *A little harsh?* she almost heard Charlotte say in her head—and out loud, as she saw the expression on her face.

"It's okay, we were all harsh on her."

Captain Murphy asked, "Does she still get them? Those notes? White mentioned something about that—"

"Yeah, she does. Before every murder."

Captain Murphy sighed. "What the hell? What do they say?"

Judy told him about every one of the notes and what they said. She added that the killer looked like he wanted to play games.

"Why her? Why send them to her? What the hell does this bastard want?" Murphy implored.

"I don't know," said Judy.

Murphy sighed one more time before concluding, "Well, if another one comes up, I wanna know. I trust you, Judy, always have. We must find him and stop this! Right away."

Charlotte looked at Judy. The redhead was smiling.

"Agreed," said Judy.

"I wanna know more," he then said. "Who do you think could be the next victim?"

"According to what we know, there is only one person left before Sebastian Reed, and that's a guy named Julian Franco."

"Who's that?" Murphy asked.

Hunter briefly told Murphy about Julian. She then informed him about the other victims and their links to each other. She said she suspected the killer was trying to put it all on Sebastian Reed. Murphy found it all very interesting. She didn't know if he believed her or not, but she didn't care. He had the information now, at least.

"Who are your suspects?" he asked.

"I actually don't know at this point, Captain... we have a few. One of them is Sebastian Reed, but like I said, we don't believe he's done it."

"Okay... Well, either way, if he has done it or not, he's not telling us. He's not telling us anything, as a matter of fact. He seems like a tough nut to crack. White told me he's in the mob?"

Judy saw Charlotte roll her eyes.

"Not in the mob! He's the leader of a bikers' club," Judy clarified.

"Right... Jesus..." the Captain muttered. "Well, White interviewed him. He won't say a thing. He was with his lawyer the whole time. I thought White sounded a little scared by him. He acted tough, but his voice was cracking. He didn't know what to do."

Judy heard a small chuckle coming from Charlotte.

"Right," Judy replied. "But we're pretty sure he has nothing to do with this, Captain. We think the killer is framing him for some reason. The reason, we don't know yet."

"Interesting... what other suspects do you have?"

"Actually, we're looking into a lead now..."

Judy also explained the Marlow situation to him, and the Captain told her he would see Marlow the next day and check the security footage from the Four Seasons. Judy asked him if they could come take a look. She didn't want him to miss anything.

"I wanna believe you, Judy, I really do," the Captain responded. "But until we find real evidence, you have to stay out of sight of the NYPD and of White. The Commissioner is always looking over my shoulder. White told the Commissioner all about you guys, and Crowley keeps calling me. He said White's his guy. He wants him to investigate, nobody else. If he finds out you guys are still on it, the Commissioner ordered me to arrest you for infringing on an investigation. He even sent guys to look over the precinct—his own trusted cops. They can't see you here and he can't find out that I'm helping you. We have to be careful."

"Fine," she said. "But let us know what you find."

"White really hates you, doesn't he? What did you do to him?"

I broke his nose a second time.

"Still trying to figure it out," she said. "Everybody usually likes me."

The Captain cracked up. "Well, he's wrong not to," he stated.

Judy smiled at this and then decided to thank him, grateful for his support. The conversation ended and the retired woman put down the phone.

"Well, that was nice," Charlotte added, half-sarcastically, as Judy hung up the phone.

Judy agreed.

"And White is really a paranoid fucker."

"He's right, though," Judy said. "We're not going to give up!"

Charlotte broke into a wide, contented smile.

CHAPTER FIFTY-SEVEN:

THE INVITATION

On their way to Judy's apartment, Charlotte invited her to have dinner with her and Brian at their place, and Judy gratefully accepted. The retired detective did so, one, because she was tired and did not want to cook for herself and, two, because Charlotte was so persuasive, promising there would be an excessive amount of wine to drink. And there was even a third reason: this would give her the perfect opportunity to observe Charlotte and Brian together.

The Lyft took them to Judy's apartment, where she picked up Rush. Then they called for another car and were soon on their way to Brian's place. As they arrived, the door of the apartment opened and the tall man, with his dark hair and brown eyes, emerged. He hugged Charlotte as hard as he could. He spoke in his soft, sexy voice and kissed her lovingly. Brian had the biggest smile on his face, and so did Charlotte.

Then he greeted Judy warmly. He let them pass like a gentleman, and they went up the stairs and into the apartment. After they sat down, Brian poured them some wine. They all started talking, not about the case, thank God—Judy had had enough of that for tonight. They talked about life in New York, politics, Madelaine's visit and her love for Charlotte, and how Brian and Charlotte wanted to go to Montreal soon. Judy said she had been, and it was a great city: a lot like New York, great entertainment, great walking, but also very cold in winter—way colder than New York. But all in all an awesome place. And the food was apparently amazing up there. The couple looked excited by the prospect. As the conversation continued, they eventually found themselves talking about the case. Charlotte told Brian about Marlow.

Then the redhead stood up and said she would make dinner. Brian and Judy sat alone now.

A minute of silence echoed. Judy kept sipping her wine, and then Brian said, "I never thanked you, by the way."

"What for?"

"For taking care of her like that, for protecting her."

"Well, she sure doesn't need my protection. She's a strong one. The toughest woman I know, really."

"Yeah, she really is," Brian agreed.

"Apparently, you had something to do with that," Judy added.

"Me?"

"She told me you're a martial arts expert."

He giggled.

"You're not?" Judy asked.

"No, no, I guess I am. I hate the word 'expert,' though. Nobody's an expert at anything... I guess I know my way around, yeah."

"Well, you certainly do. From the little I saw you've taught her well."

Brian smiled. "She's a real fighter."

"Oh yeah, she is!" Judy chuckled.

Brian followed suit. Judy then took another sip of wine before asking, "So, where did you learn it all?"

"What?" he asked, looking surprised.

"The fighting."

"My... uh, father. He owned a gym back in New Mexico. He is the one who taught me all of it."

"Wow... runs in the family, then."

Brian nodded, and took a slow, pensive sip of his wine.

"She told me about your parents."

Brian put down his wineglass and stared at Judy, frowning slightly.

"They died tragically, right?"

"Yeah, there was a fire when I was young. It was horrible. I was the only one who survived," he said, very quickly.

"I'm sorry," Judy said.

He didn't like to talk about it. He even looked a little unnerved.

Judy reached for his hand. "Truly sorry," she added.

He smiled at her, but not with the same smile he gave them when they came through the door. This smile was forced.

Brian stood up and went to the kitchen and joined Charlotte for a bit.

"Anything I can do?" Judy heard him say.

Charlotte shook her head, and he kissed the back of her neck. Then the redhead turned around and kissed him back. While the make-out session was going on, Judy looked away and scratched Rush in between the ears. She finally let her eyes swivel back to them, and they were still kissing, looking as far into each other as two people can possibly look. Charlotte turned her attention back to dinner and started cutting the potatoes. He stayed behind her, kissing the nape of her neck. Then Brian decided to step away and turned to the sink. Judy saw him take something out of his pocket. It looked to be his phone. He looked at it for a second before putting it back in his pocket. All of a sudden, he opened the kitchen sink cabinet and took out the trash can.

"I'll take this out and be right back," he said.

Charlotte barely turned around. "Sure."

Brian left the kitchen, holding the garbage bag. He looked at Judy and kept moving, passing her. She saw him go out the apartment door and head for the stairs.

Judy stood and told Charlotte she was going to use her bathroom. Once inside, she went immediately to the window. The view was of the street. She looked down through the glass and waited a moment. Then she saw Brian walking along the sidewalk, holding the trash bag. He put it in the dumpster where it belonged, and then stayed there. He took his phone from his jeans pocket and put it to his ear. A few moments later, he began speaking. But this wasn't English. It was some foreign language—not French, or Spanish, or any language Judy recognized. This language sounded strange, clunky.

Then it all started to add up for her. He had dark hair, brown eyes, and was extremely tall. He was speaking in a foreign language. He was in his early thirties. She had seen him in Rockland at the time the murders were being committed. His excuse that he had been worried and looked up Charlotte's location on his phone had seemed a little off to her at the time. It felt a little rehearsed. Then there was the fact that he didn't go to Charlotte but showed up out of the blue when Eddie White called Madelaine into town. His later excuse, about seeing her and Stew through the window, didn't matter, he had just said that to throw Judy off the scent.

And then there was his past. He had apparently lost his parents. His explanation of their deaths felt rehearsed too.

It was not Charlotte and Brian and their relationship she needed to be observing. It was just Brian. She had suspected something for a few days now, ever since he came to Rockland unannounced. Something was not right with him, she'd sensed. She waited for the pieces to come together, and they slowly had.

Was she crazy? Was Judy Hunter out of her mind? Maybe she was. Nevertheless, it all fitted, and she couldn't ignore that.

Judy felt dizzy. She almost fell off the toilet seat as she sat down. She held her head in her hands. The right thing to do would be to tell Charlotte. A huge part of her wanted to do that right away, and even confront Brian. But she had to stop herself. What if she was wrong? Charlotte would hate her forever.

The retired detective finally took out her phone and texted Captain Murphy and asked him to look into Brian Haze. Once that was done, she stood up and looked out the window again. Charlotte's boyfriend was yelling in that foreign language now. He was yelling at whoever was on the other end of the phone, in an aggressive manner that seemed unlike the Brian she'd known until now. He looked like a raging lion.

She wasn't wrong. She knew it. She knew it was the truth. Brian was the man they were looking for.

CHAPTER FIFTY-EIGHT:

DINNER

Charlotte finished preparing her new-found garlic mac-and-cheese pasta recipe. The garlic had been roasted in the oven, the pasta had been cooked, the sauce had been made with almond milk, and she was now ready to put it all in the pan. She then noticed Judy coming back from the bathroom, touching her head. The retired woman seemed to be in pain.

"You okay?" Charlotte asked.

Judy jumped a little at the question. She snatched her hand away from her head quickly.

"Yeah. Yeah. No, I'm fine. Just a slight headache, that's all."

"Too much wine?"

"Yeah, and I'm kinda tired, too."

Charlotte nodded and was about to say something else when the apartment door burst wide open. Brian appeared, touching his head as well, looking really disturbed.

"Oh no! You're not hungover too?"

Brian lifted his head, surprised. He gazed blankly at the two ladies for a moment, then his grim expression changed into a wide smile. "I'm all right! Actually, I was about to open another bottle. Is that okay?"

"Good! I thought I was going to be the only one drinking, getting hammered," Charlotte said.

"We don't want that, now, do we?" Judy chipped in. "No, you won't be alone. Quick, Brian. Get that thing opened."

Brian turned to Judy, nodding.

“This smells so good, right?” asked Charlotte.

“Hmm, hmm!” Judy nodded excitedly.

Charlotte finished turning the wooden spoon in the pan; the sauce and the pasta were now combined.

“Is there anything I can do?” said Judy.

“If you could bring the plates from the table, that would be great.”

“Sure!” Judy said, reaching for the plates.

Charlotte poured her creation onto everyone’s plates and brought them one by one to the table. They finally sat down and started eating. The room stayed silent for a while. Everybody was tasting the pasta, enjoying every bite of it.

“This is so good, Charlotte!” Judy said.

“I know, it’s wonderful,” Brian added.

“Well, thank you, guys,” Charlotte answered. “Babe, what is this wine?”

Brian slowly turned the bottle for Charlotte to see. The redhead looked down at the label.

“No way!” she exclaimed. “You didn’t!” The redhead goggled at Brian, both confounded and thrilled. Excitement took over his face. Charlotte picked up the bottle and examined it.

“What is it?” Judy questioned.

“I thought... you wanted to keep it...?” Charlotte said to Brian.

“I did.”

“For a special occasion, I mean!” Charlotte clarified. “Judy, this is an Opus One. I can’t even tell you how expensive it is. Brian got it as a gift from my mother when she came to New York. I guess she felt bad about her reaction and everything. She bought it for us. It’s really fucking first-rate wine. I looked it up afterwards and called her to say this was too much!”

Brian kept radiating joy.

“Why did you open it?” Charlotte asked.

"This is a special occasion," Brian answered. "Honey, you made us the most amazing pasta, my favorite. You killed it, honestly! Since you've been back, you've made me feel like the happiest man alive. I've never loved you so much." He then turned his attention to Judy. "And we're with your incredible friend over here, who helped you so much after your dad's death in ways I never could have. She made you *you*! I am so eternally grateful for this night!"

Charlotte looked at Brian, tearing up.

"And on top of everything else, here's the cutest dog I've ever seen!" he added, as Rush jumped up, wanting to jump onto Brian's lap.

Brian pet him and Charlotte giggled.

"By the way," he said. "Your mother didn't buy this—I did. She sure gave me the suggestion, though, after I told her what I wanted to ask you. I'm glad, because it's a hell of a wine!"

"Ask me? What did you want to ask me?"

But her confusion didn't last long, because Brian got up from his chair, went to a drawer, and opened it, grabbing a small black box inside. Charlotte put her hand to her mouth. *NO FREAKING WAY!*

She caught a glimpse of Judy doing the same thing. The retired detective appeared equally stunned.

Brian went down on one knee before Charlotte and opened the box. An enchanting diamond ring revealed itself. Charlotte wouldn't have predicted her reaction. A word came out of her mouth as if of its own accord, without her even thinking about it.

She said, "Yes."

CHAPTER FIFTY-NINE:

THE WALK

"I love you so much!" Brian said, pulling out the ring and putting it on Charlotte's finger.

This isn't happening! It isn't happening! Judy kept shouting to herself.

Her fingers and toes were vibrating, shaking from bewilderment. Was Charlotte really not seeing anything? Did she truly want to get married to this man?

The redhead stood up with him and kissed him. She then gazed joyfully at the ring and started jumping around. She turned to Judy and showed it to her. The ring was made of pink gold and had an unusual flowery shape, and at the center of it all lay the most elegant and striking diamond. The retired detective made sure to smile and take a moment to admire the diamond. She wanted to tell Charlotte right now that this wasn't a good thing. But of course, she didn't. What if she said something and then later found out that she was dead wrong in her suspicions?

The festivities lasted a while longer, and then Judy was finally able to say her last congratulations and leave. She ordered a cab and went home. She felt nauseous and tried to take deep breaths. She arrived home sometime between ten and eleven. The retired woman went straight for her bedroom. Rush followed her and jumped on the bed. Judy got on the covers too and sat there, staring at the wall. She was shaking. When she finally pulled herself back together, she looked down at Rush and lifted him up. She took off his leash and undid his purple harness.

She told Rush to stay on the bed and quietly shifted to the bathroom. She looked at herself in the mirror, splashed water on her face, then dried it off. When that was done, she brushed her teeth and took some Tylenol.

The retired detective took off her clothes, left them on the chair next to the bed, and got under the sheets. She took one more deep breath. Whatever she was planning to do, she could do it in the morning.

Get some sleep, Judy. Get some clarity.

But then she thought of Charlotte. Was she safe? What if she had left her young friend with a sociopath? What if they got into an argument tonight and he lashed out?

Charlotte can take care of herself. She's strong. She can defend herself. Not only that, she's smart. She will see through his game eventually. If there is one. There is one! Stop denying it, Judy.

The game! The only thing she couldn't figure out was why Brian was sending Charlotte those notes if he was the killer. Why play with her like that?

She finally took another breath and tried to force herself to forget about it all. She wanted to fall asleep, but the cloud of thoughts kept coming at her, growing bigger and bigger by the minute. She was turning in bed every few seconds. She was getting sweaty, and her heart rate was not calming down.

Fuck it! She rose and grabbed her aching head. Then she looked at Rush, sleeping soundly. But suddenly he lifted his head and looked at her with wide, confused eyes. She pat his small head and gave it a kiss. Then she looked away and sighed.

She reached out and grabbed her phone from the cabinet. She hadn't looked at it since she had left Brian's place. There was a missed call. Captain Murphy. Judy quickly unlocked it and listened to the voicemail.

"Hunter. It's Murphy. I got your message and did what you said. But... I can't find anything on Brian Haze. There is nothing in our criminal records under that name. And there is no one registered as Brian Haze in New York. There's one in Miami, age 12, one in Colorado, age 56, in California, age 75, New Hampshire, age 43. That's it. Which one do you want me to look for? I sent you the pictures in an email." Then he asked, "Hunter. Why does this name sound so familiar? Who is he? Let me know if you have more information or anything else you can give me. I'll be at the office in the morning. Bye."

Judy looked through the email Murphy had sent. None of these men looked like Brian Haze. She put down her phone and grunted. *So, no Brian Haze around age 29 or 30, from New Mexico or living in New York. How so?*

Judy couldn't even consider getting back in bed. She turned on the lights, put on some night clothes, and sat on a chair. She sat at her computer and Googled "Brian Haze." At the top of the search page, a number of pictures came up. One old man with no hair and half his teeth missing, another that had red hair and glasses, a businessman trying out a perfect smile but failing, and finally a twelve-year-old with his green hoodie pulled over his head.

Then she checked Facebook. Nothing there either. She found Charlotte Gibbins and looked through her profile. There was not even one picture of him on there. Judy clicked on her Friends list. No Brian in sight. It seemed he was deliberately avoiding being featured anywhere public.

Maybe Brian Haze was a made-up name. And if he lied about that, he could be lying about everything else. He didn't really grow up in New Mexico. He was not American. He was really... someone named Damyan Kovachev.

Judy Hunter spent a little while longer looking at her computer before deciding to give up. She put it on the floor and went to take a shower.

She had a coffee and some food before the clock finally showed 3:00. She decided to take Rush for a walk. The city was still alive at this hour, unsurprisingly for locals.

She turned the corner and walked down 59th. She walked all the way to Times Square, where Rush decided to do his business right in the middle of the crosswalk. Judy sighed and quickly took out a bag to clean it up.

She kept walking along 59th until she reached Hell's Kitchen. She turned the corner and decided to head for 38th Avenue, the street where Brian's apartment was located.

Rush was getting tired, but she kept going. She gave him some water on the way.

After another fifteen minutes, Judy arrived. She crossed to the other side of the street and found a bench on the sidewalk. Judy sat there, holding Rush on her lap and staring at the apartment. What was she expecting to see? Everyone was asleep, the blinds were on—she couldn't see anything or anyone.

She sat there for another half-hour. It was now 4:40. Judy waited another ten minutes before deciding to stand up. She put Rush down and started to walk back home. Suddenly Rush froze. Judy looked down: he was peeing. Then she heard a noise. A car was coming down the street.

Judy looked. She knew that car!

It stopped in front of the apartment building.

Could it be him? Lo and behold, it was.

Under a baseball cap, she could make out his face. Brian immediately went to the trunk.

After a second, she looked again and Brian was holding something on top of the trunk. It was a gun. He was putting a silencer on it and cranking it. Who was he going to kill this time?

Hold on—his lips were moving. He was talking to someone. Was someone in there? In the trunk?

Brian pointed the gun inside the trunk.

He then slammed the trunk shut. Brian sped up the stairs of the apartment building and disappeared through the door.

Fucking hell! He really was their guy.

Judy took a moment, looked around, and went straight for the other side of the street.

Please don't come back right away. Please don't.

When Judy reached the car, she went for the trunk. She tried to open it. Of course, it was locked. Who the hell was stuck in there?

What could she use to open it? Her first instinct was to reach for her belt.

You don't have a gun, Judy... You should have brought one.

God, she wished she had brought one.

She could hear sounds from the trunk. The person was trying to scream. Their mouth must have been covered.

Then the apartment building door opened. Brian was back. Judy quickly bent down and ran to the other side of the street.

She hid behind a tree.

She picked up her phone and unlocked it.

She heard Brian's voice. He shouted something in the dark. He seemed angry again.

Rush started wagging his tail as he heard the voice. Judy tried to calm him down. He barked at her. The dog pulled on the leash. Rush wanted to see Brian! He barked again. Judy saw Brian look in her direction and she quickly hid again and desperately kept Rush quiet.

Had he seen them? She held Rush tight to her, almost closing his mouth with her hands so he wouldn't bark or cry.

After a few seconds, she peered out, but Brian had disappeared. Was he inside the car? She couldn't see him through the windows. The retired detective scanned the dark street to see if she could spot him.

Then she felt her hand move. Rush was pulling on the leash, jumping, his tail wagging feverishly. He barked again, louder than before. Judy turned around... Brian was standing there.

A sudden electric shock sprinted through her body, but she just had time to spot the Taser before she blacked out.

CHAPTER SIXTY:

ANOTHER NOTE

Through the sunshine, the diamond sparkled and brightened her face even more. The ring was so beautiful. Charlotte sat at the end of the bed by the window for a while, looking at it. She couldn't believe it. She had not expected this to happen, not in a million years. Or not right now, anyway. Not ever, really. Brian had said more than once that he didn't believe in marriage, that it was just an old-fashioned tradition for people to get access to their partner's finances and be able to survive in time of crisis or after their partner's death. He said multiple times that everyone used love and "the celebration of love" as an excuse to hide their true motivation for getting married. It was a bit extreme, but Charlotte couldn't deny he had a point. The redhead also believed that some people really did marry for love, because she was one of them. She had always wanted to dress up as a princess, have a wonderful wedding, and celebrate love with her family and friends, and of course her true soulmate. She wanted to be called a wife one day and be able to refer to her partner as her husband. She wanted the real, everlasting thing. And marriage was the symbol of that for her.

Maybe it was clichéd and too dreamy to be true, but she didn't care. That's what she had always wanted, and that's what she was going to do. And she couldn't care less about getting access to Brian's account! She was going to build her career and make her own money. Charlotte never wanted to be dependent on anyone else.

So, this was definitely a surprise! After Judy left them, Brian had spent the night telling Charlotte how much he loved her, how happy she made him, and how he didn't want to lose her. He said she was his home. Charlotte's trip to Rockland had apparently made Brian realize that it didn't matter that he had an apartment or a wonderful job and worked with great people—he didn't feel whole, his place didn't feel like home, if Charlotte wasn't there. He wanted her by his side forever. She was his family, his peace and quiet, his soul. He wanted to live with her, to have kids with her, and to grow old with her. That put a smile on her face, she was so excited.

Charlotte was caught by surprise when she found herself saying yes. Maybe it was just out of impulse—the idea of getting a flashy ring making her say yes. But she wanted what he wanted, someone who was her home. She also wanted children, and someone wonderful to raise them with. She wanted someone by her side, supporting her, caring for her, completing her. But if she was perfectly frank with herself, she had never really thought that Brian was that person.

But now, with a ring on her finger, she felt differently.

Or did she? Was he really her special someone? She had already said yes, so she really had to figure this out—quick! Still, this was just an engagement, it was not the real thing... yet. If she ended up deciding that it wouldn't work between them, she could still break it off.

The truth was, he made her feel like home too. She felt comfortable around him, safe. She felt she could tell him anything and do anything to him and he would still stay by her side always, and that was nice. What made her happiest, though, was that he said he felt like she was family. She knew how lonely he had been for all these years since his parents had tragically passed, and for him to say that meant a lot.

Then she suddenly shifted gears and was thinking about Stew, and that made her smile slightly fade. She felt sorry for him. He truly was a wonderful, kind-hearted soul. He had been so nice to her. He had been such a good and supportive friend this past month. Charlotte knew he cared for her, and probably as more than a friend. When he found out about the ring and the engagement, he would be crushed. He probably wouldn't accept her friendship anymore. She would lose him, and that made her sad.

Brian had left the apartment early. He had probably gone to the gym for an early kickboxing coaching session like he did every Wednesday morning. As for Charlotte, she would go to the gym too, but for a 10 a.m. session. It was now ten to nine. She stared at the ring for a few seconds longer and finally stood up and went into the bathroom. She put her gym clothes on, had a hot breakfast, and coffee.

By nine thirty, she was out, and arrived at the gym sometime after ten. She saw Steve, another kickboxing coach, carrying a sports bag on his shoulder, reaching the door at the same time. He was a short man, not particularly handsome, but he had a genuine smile and always seemed excited about life.

"The little miss redhead coming our way again today?" he said, greeting her.

"Of course! I don't miss a day, Steve!" she replied with enthusiasm.

"Well, I don't know, we didn't see you for a while before the other day, so I didn't know... maybe you decided to try another gym."

"Ha ha! Brian would kill me... literally."

Steve chuckled and moved to open the door for her. He followed her in, and they looked around the room. The place was already packed. The gym was filled with mostly women, kicking and hitting their coaches with their rage-filled gloves. As Steve kept moving, Charlotte stood still for a moment. She couldn't see Brian anywhere. She followed Steve to his office and glanced into the office next to his, Brian's office. He wasn't there either.

She asked Steve where Brian was. He shrugged. *Strange*, thought Charlotte. Her fiancé had told her he was teaching today. They didn't have a session specifically scheduled, but he did say he was teaching other people. *Oh well.*

The redhead moved on to the locker room. She greeted a couple of women she knew from the group lesson and said she would join them in a minute. She opened her locker and was lifting her small bag to put it inside when she saw something there. It was a folded piece of paper. As she reached for it, her body started shaking, as if it knew what it was.

She unfolded it and read:

HOW ARE YOU ENJOYING BEING BACK IN NYC?
I AM SURE IT'S PLEASANT.
BUT NOW I HAVE GOT ANOTHER SOMETHING SPECIAL FOR YOU.
MORE BLOOD WILL BE SPILLED.
HE'S A VICIOUS TRAITOR TO OUR BROTHERHOOD...
STILL HAVE BALLS TO CATCH ME?
ROCKLAND WON'T WAIT FOR LONG.
YOU HAVE 2 DAYS.

Charlotte was not shocked this time. Instead, she was annoyed, even a little bit depressed. *What the actual fuck, man?* How did he know she was back in New York? This was creepy and insane. And why did he want Charlotte to catch him? *Why me?* Why does he want to be caught in the first place? And it said "our brotherhood"... A brotherhood like the Skullheads? Was Judy right, was the killer really trying to frame Sebastian Reed, or was it him all along? But why would he want to get caught if it was him?

Charlotte dropped the note on the bench behind her and phoned Judy right away. She got no answer. She tried again, but still nothing. She tried a third time, then texted her instead. She waited a good ten minutes but there was no response. It was ten in the morning! Was Judy still sleeping?

CHAPTER SIXTY-ONE:

THE EXECUTIONER

Judy woke up from the most uncomfortable dreamy state. Had she been drugged? There was a bad taste in her mouth. Her body felt numb. Her eyes swayed all over the place. They kept pointing to the ceiling for a long time before she was finally able to tilt her head back to normal position and look in front of her. As she did so, she saw a gray, filthy wall. Then she saw Rush attached to a pole, drinking water. She couldn't reach him, but he seemed all right. Nobody had hurt the little beast.

She turned her head to the left and saw a set of stairs leading up. Then she felt her uncomfortable bum. The retired detective understood she was sitting on the floor—a grainy, cold floor of cement. She was in a basement. This couldn't be New York. Was it? She kept looking around for clues. Her head was buzzing. She was sleepy.

She thought some more. His apartment? No, he wouldn't dare.

Then what? Was she back in Rockland? The basement at the Kovachev house? Most likely. Was Lilyana here? Was she letting Brian do this? Then the retired detective tried to stand up, but her hands and arms wouldn't let her. Judy had been tied up with a strong rope. It would take some out-of-this-world strength to get her hands free. She went back to looking around the room. She was definitely alone.

Then she looked to the floor and saw a long black bag that appeared to be full and heavy. Judy was sure what it was, she had seen them a lot in her career: a body bag.

Who was in this one? Who had Brian killed this time?

She heard a noise. Light came at her from above. A door had opened. Then, spiraling down the basement staircase came Brian. He had his shirt off and was covered with what looked like mud—and maybe blood.

"Does Charlotte know?" he asked fiercely.

"Damyan, is it?" Judy said with a feeble voice.

"Does she know?" he asked again, more strongly.

Judy didn't answer. She just stared at him.

"I hope she doesn't," he said. Brian stared at her for a while.

"Why, because you'd have to kill her too?"

Brian's eyes were dark, very dark. He looked like a man without a soul. He looked like some type of demon.

"I would never do that to Charlotte! Never!"

The killer kept pacing back and forth. Judy looked down at the body bag.

"Who's in there, Brian?"

Brian stopped pacing, looked at Judy and smiled. He went to the body bag, bent down beside it and unzipped the top.

Judy looked. It was a woman.

She stared at the face for a while, and then realized it was Sofia Marlow.

That's who was in the trunk. *Fucking hell... Jesus Christ.*

"That's what happens when you fuck with my plan!" Brian snarled.

Judy was mortified.

She was still alive in the trunk! I could have saved her.

Judy immediately wondered if that's what was going to happen to her in the next few moments.

"Why, Brian? Why her? She had nothing to do with this..."

"You know why!"

"I guess murder is normal for you now... huh?" Judy said after a few seconds of silence.

"When someone deserves it, yes!"

"The horrible things you did to them... your victims, Brian!" Judy exclaimed. "Gas, swords, throwing them off cliffs..."

"They had to pay," Brian muttered.

"I understand," said Judy. "But killing them was not the way."

"Of course it was, Judy!"

"What does your grandmother think of all this? Is she here? Does she know about this?"

"She is. And she wants me to make things right. They destroyed my family, Judy! My grandmother's life," Brian echoed, pointing upstairs. "Left my grandparents wondering for years, my mother alone with a child... For thirty years they just lived their lives like nothing had happened. Like my father never existed. Nobody cared. The police tried to find out what had happened to him, sure. For a minute. Then they gave up and everybody forgot about him. And these people who did this... these maniacs, they went on and lived happy lives."

Judy, again, wondered if Lilyana was hearing all this.

"Some of them, yes," Judy agreed. "Ethan Gregory was a movie star, sure. Fred was a great detective. But you didn't meet Melanie, did you? You just killed her. Did it look to me like she was having a happy life? No. Your father's death ruined her life. She couldn't get over it, what they had done to him. It destroyed her. She paid for it all her life."

"Why didn't she tell the police, then? Why didn't she come forward with it?" Brian challenged, red-faced.

Judy couldn't answer that.

"If she was so depressed by it and felt so guilty, then she should have said something and relieved herself of that guilt, no?"

"She was scared..." Judy said.

"Pfft..." Brian barked. "Scared? Please..."

"Brian, you don't have to keep doing this, you can stop now. I'll bring you in and you won't be hurt."

"Ha! Right, hurt. You plan on hurting me, Hunter?" Brian chuckled. "And I'm just supposed to stop and let Julian Franco and Sebastian Reed go free? You know what they've done in their lives, these men? Do you know? Do you really think they lived with guilt? Hell no!" Brian shouted. "The women they've raped! The people they've stolen from over the years. The folks they've killed. Do you think they have guilt?"

"Perhaps not. Perhaps they do. Either way, Brian, killing them won't end your suffering, it will only—"

"Oh, please, spare me that corny revenge speech!" he replied, getting angrier by the minute. "It will end my suffering! My father will be avenged!" He grew stern. "Justice will have been served and he will finally find peace in his grave. I will be happy. I will marry the woman of my dreams and will have nothing more to worry about than to love her and bring her happiness."

"You think she'll marry you? Really? After this? No, she'll detest you. She'll think of you as nothing more than the cruel monster who killed her hero of a dad."

Brian took a beat. This clearly hurt.

"What do you think she'll do once she finds it was you who killed him?"

Brian frowned.

"You killed her *father*, Brian..."

He shook his head, very fast. "Charlotte will never know about this! I will make sure of it."

"Of course, you will." Judy decided to move on. "How did you even find out what happened to your dad?"

Brian turn his head and curled his upper lip. "My mom never believed my dad just disappeared. She always thought something had happened to him. She had mentioned the name Sebastian Reed several times, she hated the man like crazy. She also had mentioned who he was friends with back then, she had named the members of his 'clans.'

So, after my time in the army, I had some free time and I started investigating and found most of them..." His excitement kept growing. "And the closest one to Bulgaria happened to be sweet little Zachary..."

"In Germany." Judy nodded.

"I went there and questioned him about my father. He denied knowing him at first, but I had a few convincing methods in my bag from the army, and he finally spilled the beans."

"Then you killed him."

"It was so satisfying, you can't imagine." Brian raised his voice.

Judy was disturbed. "So, why now? Why kill Fred now?"

Brian looked confused.

"Haven't you been with Charlotte for the past year? Couldn't you have done it before then?"

Brian didn't answer. Instead, he turned around and faced the wall.

"You were in love, that's it!" Judy exclaimed. "You wanted to do it but couldn't. You fell in love with your enemy's daughter."

She saw Brian nod.

"I was going to kill him when I first arrived in New York, but then I saw that he had a daughter, and when I saw her, my heart just stopped. I couldn't move. She was so..."

"Oh, what love does to you."

"We talked and she was just amazing. We connected on so many levels. She understood me like nobody else ever had before."

"And then you killed her father! And now you've lost her."

Judy could see Brian was getting angry. *Very* angry.

"I thought about sparing his life, for Charlotte. She admired him. She loved him, and I didn't want to kill somebody she loved. But after what happened at your party, there was no going back. I'm glad I ended up killing him. Not only did he kill my father, but Fred was a bad man. Just the way he reacted to her wanting to be a cop should tell you that.

A fucking stubborn, traditional old coward. Humiliating her like that in front of everybody... She doesn't need him in her life. She's fine."

"He wanted to protect her, Brian, like any father would his daughter!"

"Protect her? No, he didn't believe in her. Well, guess what—she's gonna be the best detective there ever was. You've seen it. She can kick ass like nobody I know. She's the best student I've ever had. She doesn't need protection from anyone."

Judy tried to process this all. It was hard to empathize with Brian. Fred had been her partner, and he killed him. Not to mention that everything Brian was saying about Fred being a bad man was so patently wrong.

"Her father was a good man," Judy said. "Fred tried to protect Viktor Kovachev, your father. They were great friends. He defended him against Sebastian Reed and his crew when nobody else would."

Brian looked at her, bewildered.

"Smith didn't tell you that, did he?" Judy continued. "Brian... Fred didn't kill your father, he was trying to protect him."

Brian didn't look at her anymore. He had his eyes fixed on the floor. *Maybe he does have feelings after all.*

Minutes passed. Brian kept himself from speaking. The retired detective continued to look at him. He was now cleaning the blood off himself. She still had many questions, many unresolved things to ask about. She began with something that was very confusing to her.

"So, why the notes? And why send them to Charlotte?"

"Because she's the only one who will do it—solve this case!"

Judy gave him a confused look. "Solve this case?"

Brian nodded.

"And arrest you?"

Brian shook his head and gave a crooked smile. "Not exactly. That was never the plan. I just needed to find somebody they could point the finger at. And I realized that I needed to hurry, because you guys were getting close to me. But, it turns out, I didn't have to look that far. The easy target was right there to take it all for me, and I barely had to do a thing."

Judy thought for a moment. *Easy target?*

"Sebastian Reed..." she realized.

Brian nodded. "She will put him in jail," he said.

"Why?"

"I don't know... for everything he's done over the years. Being a biker and hurting people while partying like a madman. For killing my father. Even if he has nothing to do with these killings, he still belongs there."

"But why Charlotte?"

Brian started moving again, growing annoyed. "You didn't hear me, Judy? Charlotte is going to be the best detective. She will solve this case by herself." He held his head high. "Plus, by putting Reed away, Charlotte will be respected forever. Do you know how many people want Reed in prison? How much they've tried to do it over the years and couldn't? She's going to be remembered forever for what she did for the police."

"Really?"

"Yeah! Exciting, isn't it?"

"But now she also knows about your father and his murder, and that he had a child. She suspects Damyan Kovachev to be the murderer."

"Sure, like I said, you guys got close... I didn't think Melanie would talk to you, but she did. The Damyan Kovachev thing... there is really nothing for her to find. I'm supposed to be dead. Melanie's story will just be a story."

There was silence. Brian kept cleaning himself, trying to get a stain off his well-built body. Judy processed as much as she could.

"Okay. Let's say this works. Let me add this up," Judy resumed. "You make Charlotte a detective, you get away with murder in the process, get revenge for your father and then live happily ever after with your fiancée, with no one bothering you... is that correct?"

Brian nodded once more, carrying a sly grin on his face.

"Hmm... only one small problem, Brian."

"Which is?" he asked, frowning.

"Charlotte is not that dumb. She might be caught in your honeymoon, romantic boyfriend fishing hook right now. But she will get out of it. She won't forget about Kovachev. Granted, Sebastian Reed might have done some bad shit in his life, but no one will believe he did this. Anybody with a brain will see that it doesn't add up."

Brian's glow faded, transforming into an angry sneer.

"We'll see," he said, walking to the stairs. As he reached the first step, he stopped.

There was a noise coming from upstairs. It was a door clacking. Steps moving, making dirt drop from the ceiling. Rush started barking.

"There she is!" said Judy, smiling. "Charlotte."

The look on Brian's face was priceless. He looked crushed.

"She's come to get revenge for her dad as well."

Was it really Charlotte? Already? Judy didn't know.

Rush kept barking and barking away.

"Shut him up," Brian whispered roughly.

Then they heard a voice coming from upstairs, but it wasn't a woman's voice.

"Detective Hunter! Judy Hunter! I know you're in here! I can hear your little doggie."

Judy instantly recognized that voice, high-pitched and aggravating. It was Edward White.

The retired detective immediately screamed at the top of her lungs.

CHAPTER SIXTY-TWO:

MISSING

Charlotte waited for half an hour before calling again. The phone rang four times before it finally went to voicemail: "This is Detective Judy Hunter's phone. I am not available to take your call at the moment. For emergencies, please call the New York City Police Midtown North Precinct at 646-555-2827, or simply call 911. If it is a personal call, I will get back to you as soon as I can. Thank you."

She tried again and again, to the point where she could repeat Judy's message word for word. Where was she? Why wasn't she picking up? Every time Charlotte had called her before today, Judy had answered right away or called her back within five minutes.

She texted her again. That wasn't producing results either.

They were supposed to meet today, at one in the afternoon at a coffee shop on 47th Street. Charlotte left the gym, without having done a workout, and spent another hour strolling the streets. Finally, she decided to go to the coffee shop and see if by any chance Judy showed up for their appointment. Maybe there was something wrong with her phone.

She arrived at the coffee shop at a few minutes past one. There was no gray hair in sight, just a young, vibrant crowd. Charlotte sat down at their usual spot with her coffee. After another fifteen minutes she checked her phone, but there was still nothing. She tried calling again and texting. Nothing.

So, she decided to call someone else: Brian. But he wasn't picking up either. That was nothing new. She didn't know why he even had a phone. She sighed, frustrated.

Eventually, she decided she needed to call somebody about Judy. The only people she could think of who might help her were the police. Maybe they had talked to her. If not, then they should be able to help find her. She could call Grant as well as the NYPD. Who was less scary to talk to? She tried Grant.

The Sheriff picked up instantly. The number that Judy had left her must be the Sheriff's personal number. He sounded tired.

"Hello."

"Sheriff!"

"Yes, that's me. Who's this?"

"It's Charlotte!"

"Charlotte? Jeez, no phone call from you guys in more than twelve hours! That's somethin'."

The redhead forced a little laugh. "So, you haven't talked to Judy either?"

"Judy? No. Why?"

Charlotte explained. Then she mentioned their appointment that Judy had missed. Grant found it all very strange. Then he told her that he was meeting with Sebastian Reed and his lawyer again today to discuss some newly discovered evidence. The redhead, surprised, asked about the evidence. The Sheriff said he had gained access to the security cameras on the pier where Rick Carson had been killed and had caught someone wearing a leather jacket running out of the boat sometime after the murder.

Charlotte asked if the footage showed the face of the murderer, but the Sheriff said no, the individual wore a gas mask just like Wendell Pearson had described to them.

"Anything on the Kovachev story?" Charlotte inquired.

"Yes!"

That answer surprised her.

"I was just about to inform you guys before you called. We got a picture, from the Bulgarian army. It's him, Damyan Kovachev."

"Really?"

"Yeah... he's dead, though, died years ago. Like the grandma says, in the line of duty."

Charlotte sighed. *Fuck.*

"Sheriff," she continued. "What does he look like?"

"He could be your brother," the Sheriff observed.

"What?"

"It's not the most usual thing that you'd expect of a Bulgarian, but he's a redhead!"

"Wow..."

That didn't fit with Marlow's description at all.

Charlotte took a minute to register that and then went on: she informed the Sheriff about the other note she had gotten in her gym locker. The Sheriff asked what she thought it meant and she told him exactly what her thoughts were.

"Well, for now, we gotta look at the evidence," he said. "It's all pointing not just to Sebastian Reed but to any of the Skullheads. I plan to check them out first, all of them. Interview them one by one if I need to, until there is a crack."

Charlotte didn't like that, but what was she going to do? They had no other leads.

"What about White? What does he think?" she dared to ask.

"I haven't seen him this morning. I find that unusual, to say the least. He's always there yapping at my ears and destroying my sanity first thing every morning."

"Wow..." *Where are all these people*?

"I'll start with that Julian Franco, I think. See what he knows and why they would want to kill him, if he really is the next on the list."

Charlotte didn't speak for a moment, lost in thought, then managed, "Well, good luck!"

He thanked her and hung up.

Charlotte put her phone down. It was almost two. She waited another five minutes, drumming her fingers on the table. Then she finally stood up and went to make a last-ditch attempt.

She walked for fifteen minutes before reaching Judy's building. She rang the buzzer, but again there was no answer. Then she waved at the concierge. He opened the door and she told him she was Judy's friend. He remembered her from the party and let her pass. Charlotte took the elevator upstairs and knocked frantically on Judy's door.

"Judy? You in there? It's Charlotte."

Charlotte stopped and waited for a few seconds. Dead silence. Not even a bark from Rush. Where the hell were they?

She sat near the door, enraged and increasingly anxious, for another five minutes before picking up her phone. The redhead dialed the Sheriff again.

"Sheriff, about Julian Franco—"

"Yeah, I just gave him a call to come in. He wants nothing to do with us. The man's a real pain to talk to. I then told him about the threat to his life. He says he'll be fine on his own... not surprising."

The redhead paused. "Yeah... well, if you interview other people and continue to look at evidence, maybe I could help!" Charlotte heard herself saying. "We're kinda stuck here in New York."

The Sheriff didn't answer right away. Then she heard a cough.

"No, I'm all right," he said. The Sheriff gave another little cough and didn't say anything else.

"Please, Sheriff, I have to see this through," Charlotte insisted.

He took a moment before explaining, "You can do whatever you want, Charlotte. You know I like you and I trust you, but if something happens again, and if White or the FBI tell you to go, I won't be able to do anything—"

"The FBI?"

"They'll be here any minute now."

"Why the hell are they going to Rockland?" asked the redhead, baffled.

"Once they heard Reed was our prime suspect, they wanted to know everything. Reed and his gang have been on their watch list for years. So, they've decided to take over."

"Great," said Charlotte sarcastically.

"Yeah, I don't like it any more than you do..."

The redhead pondered for moment before stating, "I'll be fine. Be there in two hours!"

She hung up the phone, stood, and walked out of Judy's building. If the retired lady showed up, or called back, she would let her know where she was. But until then she sure wasn't going to sit around all day, wondering when and how Julian Franco was going to die.

Charlotte ordered a Lyft and headed straight for Rockland.

CHAPTER SIXTY-THREE:

WHITE TO THE RESCUE

Judy kept screaming until Brian rushed towards her and pointed a gun directly at her eyes. Even then, she didn't stop right away.

"Shut up! Shut up!" Brian kept whispering aggressively.

Judy continued until Brian gagged her. Rush kept barking. Brian went to hide under the stairs. They both waited for the basement door to open and for Eddie White to find them.

After a few seconds of silence, they finally heard a creak. The door slowly opened and there he was: Eddie White was pointing his gun in front of him and coming quietly down the staircase.

"I know you're in here, Hunter!"

He didn't see her right away, but after he'd taken a few steps down the stairs, he and Judy finally met eyes. His face went white as he saw Judy on the ground, tied up and gagged.

"What in the hell is this? You playin' a game with me, Hunter? Who did this to you?"

White quickly came down the stairs. He went to her to ungag her, but before he could do so, there was a cracking noise. Eddie White turned his head to the staircase and saw someone coming out from under it. The detective saw Brian's face and froze instantly.

"You!" he shouted.

Brian cocked his eyebrow and added a smirk.

"What are you doin' here?" White asked. "What is this, Hunter?"

Judy tried to scream to warn White, but almost no sound emerged. Nevertheless, two seconds later White understood. He looked at Brian's right hand and saw that Charlotte's fiancé was holding a gun. White's face grew as white as a ghost.

"Just the man I was about to go see!" Brian said.

"Me?"

"I was about to kill you for taking the credit away from my girl."

"Kill me?"

Brian held the gun even higher. "You almost ruined it."

"I knew there was something wrong with you!" White shouted. "I knew it!"

White tried to shift his gun towards Brian, but as he moved to do so, the detective stumbled upon something: the body bag. He crouched to it, looked to Brian for a second, then at Judy. Brian nodded casually, as if to say, *It's okay, you can open it, pal.*

White took a breath and began unzipping the bag. He saw the high-heeled shoes. There was a foot in there... a person. He kept unzipping until the body of Sofia Marlow was in full view.

He gasped. "What the hell is this?"

"Your destiny!" said Brian.

White tried again to stand up and point his gun at Brian, but as he did so, White suddenly fell to the ground. The detective had fainted.

Brian burst out laughing.

Judy couldn't believe it either. She found herself shaking her head. She knew that White was an oddball, but she didn't know he would react like that in a stressful situation. His wild personality had led her to believe he had a backbone.

But, come to think of it, she had punched him in the face very easily...

When Judy was calm again, Brian removed the gag from her mouth and started up the stairs.

"So, are you going to kill us or let us rot down here with the rats?" Judy questioned.

"No rats down here, I promise." He came back and crouched down to Judy's height. "Him, yes. But you..." The madman grimaced. "You gotta see this through with me first. You've been her guardian angel just like I have. You've helped get her to where she's going."

Judy looked at Brian, not sure if she should thank him or call him crazy.

"And I'm grateful for it," he continued. "That's why I chose you."

Chose me? Then the answer came to her. It was true in a way that it was Brian who had partnered Judy with Charlotte. He was the one who called the retired detective and made it seem like he was worried sick. He had made her his helper.

Judy found herself closing her eyes and exhaling.

"I knew she would get in trouble at some point, and I needed somebody who had a little experience in the field. Somebody who would believe in her case. And you happened to be close to Fred, too. Plus, she already loved you. I chose you and look how great this has turned out." He looked proud. "I'm not the only one who made her a detective, Judy. I can't let you miss seeing her succeed. And maybe, by the end, you'll see the light of day. You'll understand that I'm not evil. Reed and his gang are. And then you'll finally appreciate what we've done."

Judy brought her head down and said, "That's the thing, Brian. If you really believed in her, you would see that she was born a detective. She doesn't need you or me, or anybody else's help, to become one."

Brian pretended not to hear this. He remained for a while with his back turned to Judy. Then he suddenly grabbed his gun and pointed it at White, about to shoot him.

"Don't kill him either!" Judy blurted out.

"Why?" Brian said, irritated.

Think quick, Judy.

"Not yet," Judy pleaded. "I mean, look at him, you can't kill a man in his sleep. You'd be a coward."

Brian tilted his head.

"And after all he's done..." she added. "The way he talked to your fiancé... don't you want him to suffer first?"

"Torture?" asked Brian.

"Like you did to Zachary Smith..."

That was sick, Judy. You sound like a monster.

She really had his attention now.

"Fine!" the killer concluded.

Brian moved White, who remained unconscious, and tied him to the pole next to Judy.

"I'll be back soon. Hopefully, the racist will be awake then."

The killer grinned and exited the basement. Judy sighed. *That was close.*

CHAPTER SIXTY-FOUR:

AT THE SHERIFF'S OFFICE

"Charlotte! Glad you're here!" exclaimed Sheriff Grant as she entered his office.

"Are you really?" replied Charlotte, deeply unconvinced.

"And so is the FBI."

Charlotte thought about this for a second.

"They said they wanted to talk to you."

"Me? Why?"

"Because of you being a witness to a murder. They want you to tell them everything you saw that night. If you are able to identify Reed."

"I told you, I didn't see a face," exclaimed Charlotte.

"Yeah, well..."

"I thought eyewitness testimony was not taken into account anymore."

"Oh, it is... it's just not valid and strong-enough evidence for arrest."

This was starting to frustrate Charlotte a lot. Everyone wanted so badly to put Reed in jail without looking at any other possibilities.

"So, what? They just want me to say yes, I saw him kill Melanie, and then they do what? Nothing? Wait for something to come up that is strong-enough evidence to arrest him?"

"It's not the only thing we have," the Sheriff clarified. "CSI found fingerprints all over Rick Carson's boat. On the teapot, on the chairs, in that room where he died. Fingerprints that all belonged to Sebastian Reed."

"You got a match and the face that came up was Reed's?"

The Sheriff nodded. "Feds are also inspecting everything for DNA as we speak."

"Okay... well, maybe Reed visited Carson one lovely afternoon for tea. They were buddies, weren't they? That doesn't prove anything."

"Right... but still, he was there..."

"Fine, maybe he was..." replied Charlotte, annoyed. *What do you want me to do?*

"We'll need to ask Reed about it," said the Sheriff.

"And when does that happen?"

"As soon as the FBI gets in; they want to be in charge."

The Sheriff told Charlotte she could observe the questioning through the one-way mirror. Either way, the FBI wanted to question her and to get her two cents on the situation.

The young woman sat in the waiting room— the same room that Eddie White had made her sit in with Judy for hours on end until her mom picked her up—and drank some coffee.

She still had not heard from either Judy or Brian. It was awfully strange. She tried Judy again. Nothing. Then she went to the Sheriff. She asked him to call the NYPD and anyone else who could help look for her. She tried to think of places she could be or if the retired detective had said anything about an appointment or something. But there wasn't an appointment—Judy was supposed to meet her. *That* was the appointment. Fucking hell.

Maybe the killer has taken her.

But why? Had Judy found out who the killer was?

She heard a ring... but it wasn't Judy. It was Brian. She let out a sigh of relief and picked up.

"Where are you?" he asked before she could say anything.

"What do you mean? Where have YOU been?"

I should be asking you that question, dummy.

"Oh, you know, just needed to take care of some business..."

"What business? You weren't at the gym."

"No, no... I was downtown. Jack is having surgery in a couple weeks and he wanted to know if I could cover for him and coach his clients during that time. We were checking our schedules at a coffee shop."

"Right," replied Charlotte. "You left early."

"Yeah, went to the gym first, did my workout and then went to meet Jack. You know those nights where you want to sleep more but just can't, so you just get up and start the day? That's what I did."

"What do you mean you didn't sleep well? You got engaged to me last night. You should have slept like a baby!"

She heard Brian chuckle. "What have you been doing?" he asked her.

"Mostly looking for Judy. She hasn't been picking up her phone and we were supposed to meet earlier today."

"Wow. Maybe she's just... busy."

"Yeah, well, she would still call me back. I don't know, Brian... something doesn't feel right."

"How do you mean?"

"It's not like Judy to not be on the ball like that... It's starting to worry me."

"Hmm... What's the last thing she said to you?"

"The last thing she said?" she repeated, confused. "Hell, I don't know... 'Goodbye'? 'Good night'? It was at the apartment when she left us last night."

Brian seemed relieved for some reason. She heard his sigh.

"What?" Charlotte asked, puzzled.

There was an awkward silence. Charlotte waited for him to say something.

"So, what are you doing now?" he asked.

"I just came back to Rockland ..."

"Rockland? What are you doing there?"

Charlotte explained the situation with the FBI.

"Jesus, this is insane. What are you going to do?"

"I guess they want me here now so I'm just going to stay until they tell me to leave."

There was dead silence.

"Brian?"

"Yeah, I'm here!"

"You okay?" she asked.

"Me? Yeah, I'm fine..."

Silence.

"You know what? You should come!" Charlotte suggested. "We could hang out and I could show you my world. Plus, I could really use the support."

No reply.

"Brian?"

"Great!" he answered enthusiastically. "Yeah, I will."

"Yeah?"

"Give me a couple of hours and I'll be there."

"All right, fiancé!"

He laughed joyfully as he hung up. The redhead was smiling. She was starting to like the idea of being engaged to this man. They could have so much fun.

Before she could pursue those thoughts, she heard a voice calling her in the background.

"Here they come!" exclaimed the Sheriff.

Charlotte turned to look out the window and saw two SUVs pulling into the driveway. Rushing out of one of the cars were a man and a woman with emblazoned blue jackets. The FBI was here.

CHAPTER SIXTY-FIVE:

DEALING WITH THE FEDS

Charlotte thought of Judy again. Still no news. She was really worried now.

She took a breath and stood up from her chair and waited to be introduced. Grant walked to the door and showed the FBI in. The first agent was a black woman, with beautiful curly hair, almost Charlotte's age. She had great energy but also seemed a little severe. The other agent appeared to be Hispanic. He had long hair and was shorter than his partner, which for some reason Charlotte found funny. He was also much older.

The Sheriff introduced himself and then pointed them to Charlotte. The male agent seemed thrilled to meet her.

"Miss Gibbins! The name's Javier Del Torres, FBI."

Charlotte nodded and shook his hand. "Nice to meet you!"

"I knew your father very well. We solved some cases together back in the day."

"Did you?"

"I'm sorry for your loss."

Charlotte thanked him. He then introduced Charlotte to his partner, Beatrice Wallace.

The group moved into the hallway to get to the interview room, chatting.

"This is a wild case you got on your hands, Sheriff. Quite the serial killer!"

The Sheriff nodded.

"It's huge for a small town like this..." Del Torres continued. He stopped walking and looked around the precinct. "Excuse me, Sheriff.

We were told there was a detective here from New York also investigating. Is that correct?"

"Yes, Detective Edward White," responded the Sheriff.

"The racist from the news," Del Torres whispered to Wallace. "You let him use you like that, Sheriff?"

The Sheriff frowned. He wasn't happy either.

"Can't believe the NYPD hired him." Del Torres looked baffled. "And where is he now?"

"I don't know. I just tried to phone him; I haven't seen him all morning." The Sheriff shrugged.

"Interesting," Del Torres responded. "Oh, well, it's our case now. When he returns, you'll let him know, Sheriff."

The Sheriff nodded again.

Charlotte was still confused. "I'm sorry, Detec— Agent," she interjected. "Why do you want me here, exactly?"

"Didn't he tell you? We're going to question Reed, possibly arrest him, and you're going to testify against him."

"For what?"

"You've seen him do the crimes, haven't you?"

"I didn't see a face."

"Fine!" said Del Torres. "But we still have video footage of a guy in a biker's leather jacket. We have fingerprints, we have your letters—"

"My letters?"

"Hasn't the killer been sending you letters? That's evidence."

Charlotte looked at the Sheriff with disappointment as Del Torres said this. *You told him about my notes?*

"What did that last one say again? Something about them, their tribe?" Wallace asked.

"It was brotherhood," Charlotte responded. "'He's a traitor to our brotherhood.'"

"There you go!" Del Torres exclaimed. "And that traitor is Julian Franco, right?"

"Yeah, but those notes don't mean anything. For all you know, they could be framing Reed for the crimes."

"They?"

"I don't know—the real killer, I mean."

"That's evidence, Miss Gibbins. Now, unless Reed has a strong alibi for these crimes and can prove that he wasn't there, he's in serious trouble. We could build a solid case against him."

"But it doesn't make sense."

"What doesn't? From what the Sheriff told me about what you found out, he had a thing for terrorizing his friends and people who annoyed him. He was a bully."

"Being a bully doesn't make him a murderer!"

"They all start that way, Miss Gibbins," Del Torres said.

Charlotte was getting exhausted by this. It was like having a useless argument with Eddie White all over again. Yes, at first she had wanted to believe Reed was the one doing it, but after hearing the Kovachev story from Melanie and finding out more information with Judy that swayed them in that direction, she had gained a whole new perspective on the case.

"Why would he send those notes, then? Why would he point to himself as being the killer?"

"Some killers like to play games. They don't care so much about getting caught, they just like toying with cops," said Agent Wallace.

Charlotte was starting to get annoyed with this kind of explanation.

"So, are you staying for the interview?" asked Del Torres.

Charlotte shrugged. *I guess.*

The redhead stayed behind the one-way mirror as Agent Wallace and Agent Del Torres took on Reed and his lawyer. Sebastian Reed's lawyer seemed like a crook. A crook who had come all the way from New York City, Charlotte was told. *I guess Reed still has ties to the Big City even if he says he doesn't.* One could tell this wasn't the lawyer's first rodeo, he had been around the block many times before. *With Reed?*

The lawyer was wearing a black suit and his hair was tightly and methodically put together. He smiled, playing with a toothpick.

"My client told you repeatedly that he's not the one doing this," the lawyer said.

"We understand. We still need to ask a few questions following some new evidence that came to light," said Del Torres.

"New evidence?" The lawyer looked surprised.

"Some fingerprints were found in Rick Carson's boat," clarified Agent Wallace. "Fingerprints belonging to your client."

"My client? That sounds absurd. Why would my client have been to Rick Carson's boat?"

"That's what we're trying to find out. Maybe he had something to do with the death of Mr. Carson," said Del Torres.

"And what evidence do you have of this?"

"We have video footage, after the crime was committed, of a man in a leather jacket—" Wallace began.

"I've seen the footage," said the lawyer. "It doesn't prove anything. We don't even see a face."

That's what I said, Charlotte thought.

Sebastian Reed, who had from the beginning of the interview sat frozen in place with a mischievous grin, now started flinching. "It's all right, Lucas!" he said. "What do you wanna know?"

"Sebastian..." the lawyer attempted.

But Sebastian Reed didn't react. He kept staring at Wallace.

"What were you doing in Rick Carson's boat?" Wallace asked.

"I was visiting him. I did that often. He was a high school buddy and we were still good pals. His girlfriend is a fun gal, too."

This seemed to shake the room up a little bit. Clearly, Agent Wallace and Del Torres weren't expecting this.

"Was she there too?"

"Most times."

"What about that time?"

"What time are you asking about? I went there almost every week," Reed responded. "I mean, you can ask her if you want. She likes me a lot. We connect."

Del Torres was struck again. He didn't like this at all. "So, you had tea with him? With Carson?"

Reed looked confused.

"Your fingerprints were all over the teapot that we believe Rick Carson got hit by several times before he was strapped to a chair and died from a gas attack."

Sebastian Reed took a moment. He stayed frozen in place again. Then he finally grunted and grinned. "I like tea. Orange pekoe is wonderful. They also have nice tea at the Rhode House. What's your favorite, Agent Del Torres?"

Del Torres smiled but didn't seem that content.

As for Charlotte, she was really enjoying the show.

"What about Julian Franco?" Wallace asked.

"And what 'bout him?" asked Reed.

Wallace explained to Reed and his lawyer about the last note Charlotte had received. She also informed them about Julian Franco, Reed's fellow Skullhead, and why they thought he might be the next victim.

"Surely you see how insane that is! Don't you?" the lawyer asked. "Sebastian loves Julian like a brother. Clearly, somebody is trying to set up my client."

What I said, Charlotte thought again.

CHAPTER SIXTY-SIX:

A SAD MAN

Judy could feel her head throbbing even more now. She was thirsty too. Her lips were dry and cracking already.

Suddenly, she heard a sound. It was someone breathing. She looked next to her and saw movement. Eddie White was raising his head.

He searched around the room just as Judy had done, trying to orient himself. Then he sighed and looked like he was trying to go back to sleep, when he caught Judy's eye.

"Are you all right?" Judy asked.

"I all wet," White said. "There is saliva all over my face."

His voice was calm and relaxed, as if he had been filled with sleeping pills and was trying his hardest to come back to this world.

"Well. You weren't feeling too well and had a small fall."

"Ugh, did I?"

Judy nodded. White rolled his neck around, grimacing.

"I thought I saw your friend's boyfriend. He was holdin' a gun and you were tied up. I think he wanted to kill me. He looked dangerous. I knew there was something fishy about him," he professed. "I also thought I saw a dead body..."

"I assure you, that wasn't a dream."

"Huh..." White looked confused.

"He...Charlotte's boyfriend... he's killing those people. And that's Sofia Marlow in there, the actress. He killed her."

White looked stunned. Was he about to faint again?

After a moment, he tried to get up on his hands. "I can't move."

"Yeah, we're tied up."

"Where?"

"In the basement, where you found me," Judy answered.

"Huh," he uttered again. White then asked, "What are you doin' here? I thought I told you to go."

"Yeah..."

"You're not the best listener, are you, Hunter?"

Judy laughed for the first time at one of White's lines. "How did you even find me?" she asked.

"Great question. You'd think I'd be dumb enough to forget about you guys, but I didn't. I was waiting. Patiently."

Judy was really smiling now. This Eddie White was a riot.

"I was having my good-enough breakfast. And then I saw Brian up there pass by in an old car. I knew if he was here, then one of you gals should be close enough too!"

"So, you just jumped out of your seat and followed him here... to save me?"

"I thought I could get up quick enough, but I couldn't. I spilled coffee all over myself."

Judy could make out the stains on White's shirt. She started giggling.

"I nearly burned myself." He smiled proudly. "Then, when that was over, I grabbed my donut, did my best Flash impression, sped to the car and rushed to him. I nearly lost him, but then I drove back a little. Got to the muddy road and finally found the car, parked here."

"Good job!" Judy exclaimed.

White grinned. "I mean, I could have gotten us both out of here if I hadn't—"

"It's okay. Don't worry about it. You did great."

After a moment, White continued. "So, he's really the murderer?"

"Yeah."

"Yeah, I thought it couldn't be Sebastian Reed. It didn't make much sense."

"Did you?"

White stayed silent for a while. It seemed that either he had no clue what she was talking about or he was as distraught as she was.

"They all scare me, either way..." he confessed. "Why did they do it?"

"Brian is Damyan Kovachev, Viktor Kovachev's son!"

"Oh, wow!"

"Yeah!"

"Must be fun to be right, Hunter!"

Judy laughed out loud now. White followed her lead.

"Why is he keepin' us down here? Why aren't we dead?" White then asked. "Like her?"

"He said he wanted to torture us," said Judy.

Only you. He wants to torture you, Edward. Which I suggested. The only thing I could do to buy us time.

White's face went pale again. "He thinks he'll get away with it?"

"He will. He's going to frame Reed for it all."

White chuckled under his breath. "I heard Reed is a bad guy... that he has done a lot of damage in his life, but this guy up there, he's... somethin' is not right in the head. Dude's bonkers! He needs to be off the streets."

"Glad we agree on something," Judy answered.

There was a moment of silence before White said, "I don't think I'm really meant for this job, to be honest. All this paperwork, interviewing weirdos, and often very cruel and terribly bad sinner folk, the running around all the time..."

"Getting punched in the nose," Judy cheerfully added.

White looked at her. He wasn't smiling, in fact he was trying to look angry, but in a very comical way.

"That hurt!"

They both chuckled.

"It really did."

“Sorry...” Judy tried to dampen down her laughter.

“I’ll tell you, your punch is not as weak as him,” he said, looking towards the stairs. “Surprisin’ for a wo—”

“Let’s stop there,” Judy said firmly.

White smiled uncertainly.

“You deserved it, the punch. I’m not sure I’m sorry. You’re pretty mean.”

White lowered his head. Judy was unsure if he was ashamed or just tired. Then he raised it and stared at her. He looked sheepish.

“I know, I know... 2020, I shouldn’t be talking like that. I keep makin’ mistakes... I know what you must think of me: another old-fashioned, racist Southern white man.. I’ve heard it. Again and again.”

Judy didn’t say anything, just watched and listened.

“My pop was like that. He hated immigrants—feared them like wildfire. He hated black people, he always said they stole America from us. That it was our country and they had no right to be here. His pop was like that too. My grandfather’s dad was a plantation owner and once the blacks got freed, he raged. He took out his anger on my grandfather, who then took it out on my father... who took it out on me.

“It’s just hard to get out of it sometimes, with all these new rules. I just have a hard time figuring it out,” he added.

“It’s an ever-changing world. We all have a hard time with it,” Judy replied. “Even women make mistakes—we’re not perfect.”

White smiled shyly. He then nodded, not sure what to say for once.

“How was your mother?” Judy inquired. “Did she work?”

“You probably already know the answer to that. No, she didn’t. She stayed in the kitchen all her life.”

Judy didn’t reply. She was a little embarrassed she had asked in the first place.

“She was a great lady... so was my pop. He used to take us to church every Sunday when we were kids. He’d laugh and joke around. He’d notice the priest and make fun of his long robe and his haircut. He would say, 'How long do you think it takes him to get ready in the mornin'? Do you think he ever trips on his robe when he walks, Ed?'"

Detective White looked in a dream state as he marveled at these memories.

"He was a fine fella. He had so much respect for me when I became a cop and found it so amazing that I was serving my country. 'Finally, one of my sons who is doing somethin' right.'"

"How did he die?" Judy asked.

"He died of a heart attack a few years back," White replied.

"I'm sorry."

"It hadn't been his best years before then. He was drinking a lot, my mom and him got separated, and one of my brothers, Charlie, died in a car accident two years before."

Judy now really felt for White.

"And you won't believe it, it was a black dude in the other car. He caused the accident. Illegal turn. This pissed off my family, but my pop especially, as you can imagine. And he got himself into a lot of trouble with the law, trying to get revenge for his kid. He even got arrested at one point... I told him I could help, but he didn't want it. He was frustrated with cops and said we weren't doin' anythin'. He didn't like me very much at that point."

White took a deep breath. This was obviously hard for him.

"He destroyed himself, and I couldn't stop it."

"I'm so sorry, Edward."

Judy wanted to say something more than sorry, but she couldn't find other words. She was processing all this as it came. She understood him so much better.

"And now I've managed to do the same shit. I've destroyed myself, too."

Judy turned to him, curious. "Is this about what happened back in Louisiana?"

"Yeah... I made an even bigger fool of myself there. When he died, I was angry and... it doesn't account for what I said to that lady... but I felt so miserable back then."

White was gulping his breaths now.

"My wife won't talk to me—she wants a divorce. My kid... ugh... My daughter, she just turned five, she's starting school in the fall and I can't even see her. My wife won't even let me talk to her on the phone."

"I didn't know you had a wife and a daughter," said Judy.

"Yeah... well, they're the best things that ever happened to me. They make me so damn content. You don't even know."

Judy saw White smile like she hadn't seen him smile before. He really meant it.

"Listen, Eddie. You'll talk to them. You will. Even if your wife doesn't want to listen at first, you keep on trying. You get your life back together, all right? Eddie White doesn't give up. He's a detective for the fucking NYPD. He's about to solve one damn important case and put a vicious serial killer in jail. He's a great, successful man. Sometimes a jerk, and your wife knows that, but lovable... in time."

Eddie White chuckled gratefully.

Judy concluded, "We just need to get out of here first..."

"How do we do that?" he asked her.

CHAPTER SIXTY-SEVEN:

THE TWO LOVERS

"It was our case, Brian. Mine and Judy's! *Our* case," exclaimed Charlotte as they were walking down Main Street. "They didn't believe us for a second, and now that we've brought them enough proof, they are hijacking it and messing everything up! They literally have nothing, it's so stupid. It was embarrassing even. You should have seen their faces when Reed responded to their questions. He gave reasonable explanation for everything they had. So did his lawyer."

Brian kept walking, listening to her talk. He had just joined her after his long trip from New York City. Charlotte had proposed they go have dinner together.

"You really believe it isn't him?" asked Brian, feigning genuine interest.

"It just isn't logical, that's all. Why would he go through all this trouble of killing like that? With ways that are used in executions? That doesn't go with Reed at all."

"How so?"

"Well, it just doesn't fit. He's a gang leader, a nasty biker. If he was to kill someone, I would assume it would be with a simple baseball bat or something like that. A knife maybe. Or even with bare hands," Charlotte went on, getting caught up in imagining the possibilities. "He wouldn't think that much about it."

Brian nodded. "Fine, maybe that's the key, then. Maybe the detective was right and *you're* thinking too much about it."

Charlotte stopped and looked at him. *Careful, Brian.*

"He just picks up whatever is at hand in the moment and strikes. Look no further than that!"

"Really? He just found cyanide gas lying around, like that?"

Brian didn't reply. He looked puzzled.

"It doesn't fit, Brian. The killer is someone with a plan, someone with a desire for vengeance. He wants to punish people, not hurt them for pleasure."

"So, maybe Reed has a desire for vengeance," Brian tried one last time.

"But why would he want to punish those people?"

"Maybe he's the victim. Maybe he's the one that's been bullied in high school and now he's getting back at them."

"The victim? Sebastian Reed?" Charlotte frowned. "Have you met him?"

"Then maybe there is no purpose, he just likes killing and he likes being methodical when he does it. It's fun for him. He's a cold-hearted serial killer."

She looked at him skeptically.

"You also said his crew was named after Nazis, right?"

Charlotte just kept staring him down. Her heart and gut were pumping a booming thunder storm...

"Why are you so determined to make me believe it's Reed?"

"I'm not!" Brian replied quickly. "I just want you to consider all your options here."

"I've considered all my options, thank you very much," Charlotte said coldly.

The Kovachev story works. It's the only thing that makes sense in all this. If only we could find that psychopathic son!

Brian didn't say anything else. He knew that Charlotte was getting angry.

"Unless they find Reed actually chopping up a body in front of them, I don't think they'll find anything on him," the young woman carried on loudly. "They are the ones that need to start considering other options... like mine."

Brian nodded in support. He had gone silent.

"And where is Judy, anyway? I need her right now. Fucking hell!"

Brian didn't react.

"What if something bad happened to her, Brian? What if I'm not seeing something? What if I'm missing something? Did she say she was going somewhere? Did she mention a lead and got fucking caught by someone?"

Charlotte looked at her fiancé. Brian didn't react. He shrugged.

The redhead stopped walking and tried calling Captain Murphy again. She had asked the Sheriff to let the NYPD know, but she hadn't heard anything from anyone. No answer. She then called the NYPD itself and left a message with an on-duty sergeant.

The couple kept walking down Main Street for half a mile until they reached a closed door. The restaurant was called Tiffany's. It appeared very grand and high-class from the outside, but there was no one inside. No servers or diners. *What the hell?* Charlotte looked through the window and then rattled the door.

"Damn it," she said.

Charlotte had really wanted to dine here. The menu seemed great and everything on it looked so appetizing.

"Hey, maybe we'll find something else down the street... It doesn't need to be fancy," Brian said consolingly.

"Fine."

They walked a little more, Brian holding her hand. His hand was warm and smooth. She did feel somewhat bizarre doing this. It was strange being with Brian right now, in this town, with everything that had happened here.

The two of them passed a few places, but none of them were restaurants. Then Brian suddenly stopped. She looked at him and he pointed to the other side of the street. He was pointing to Granger's—the one spot she had been wanting to avoid. Fuck!

Charlotte shook her head, let go of his hand and kept walking. But then she turned and saw that Brian was crossing the street. Either he hadn't seen her rejection of the café or he just didn't care.

"Brian!" she shouted.

Her fiancé half turned and waved at her to come to him. Then he turned away before Charlotte could show her disapproval again.

She sighed. Then, when she saw that she couldn't dissuade him, she abruptly decided to cross the street. As she stepped out, a car almost hit her. Charlotte yelled at the woman driving and rushed aggressively towards Brian.

"Brian!"

"Let's go in! They have cheeseburgers. It seems nice in there. Cozy."

"No!"

He gave her a confused look.

"It's not..."

"What?" he asked.

Charlotte didn't respond. Instead, she peeked inside Granger's to see if there was someone in there she didn't want to see. He didn't appear to be there. But she was sure he'd be there, he was always working!

"Why don't you want to go in there?" questioned Brian.

He seemed to sense that something was wrong. Charlotte needed to change gears before he figured it out.

"Okay!" she exclaimed. "Let's go!"

Brian grinned.

And then there they were—sitting at Granger's, which had been a happy place for Charlotte before but was now a minefield. Maybe she was in luck: she couldn't spot Stew's face anywhere. Their waitress was a woman she didn't know. She looked somewhat like Melanie, which made Charlotte twitch and played on her nerves even more. Brian ordered pancakes for dinner, which made Charlotte laugh a bit, but she kept looking around, worried.

"Everything all right?" he finally asked.

"Yeah," she said chirpily. "Everything's great!"

She stared at the waitress for a bit then went to her phone. Still dead silence on there. Charlotte put it down.

As soon as she did that, it started to ring. "NYPD," it said.

"Hello?" she nearly shouted.

"Miss Gibbins?" the voice asked.

"Yes. Who is it?"

"It's Captain Murphy, how are you?"

Finally.

"Captain! Hi."

"I'm sorry to bother you, but I received your message. We haven't heard from or seen Judy either. You still haven't been able to reach her?"

Charlotte rested her head in her free hand. "She hasn't picked up her phone or called me back all day."

There was a cold moment of silence before the Captain murmured, "Well, that's weird..."

"Yeah..."

"I tried calling earlier too," he said. "She was supposed to call me back after last night."

"Last night?" Charlotte wondered.

"Yeah. I left her a message yesterday, because I looked something up for her."

"Damn, really?" she said.

Another silence.

"What were you looking up for her?" she asked.

There was a pause, and then Murphy asked, "Where were you guys at with the case?"

"Not anywhere concrete... where we were yesterday when she talked to you."

"Okay."

She informed him that she was supposed to have met up with Judy earlier today to continue the investigation. Then she explained that she was in Rockland, and why she was there.

"The FBI?" he responded.

"Yeah!"

"Fucking hell!" he almost shouted.

Murphy paused and then mentioned something else, "I also have Sofia Marlow coming in later today or tomorrow to provide us with a sketch of the man she saw. Her manager said so, anyway. Busy woman—I can't seem to reach her either."

Marlow? She had said she was going first thing in the morning to the precinct. What had happened with that?

"Anyway, we're still reviewing the footage from the Four Seasons to see if we can find anything, but so far no man who matches her description is seen. If it really was him that she saw—the killer—he knows exactly where the cameras are and when to hide. He's like a ghost."

"Great," the redhead replied sarcastically.

"Lucky that Marlow saw him!"

Charlotte took a breath, processing this. After a few seconds she asked, "Captain, what did Judy want you to look up?"

"Oh... just a small thing... nothing very—"

"Captain!" she begged.

"Well, sorry, Charlotte. I'm just finding it all very strange what she asked for, and to tell you... it's even more strange."

"What did she ask you for?"

"Look, it was just some easy, dull search, nothing to be frightened about or anything. Cops do that all the time."

"What dull search?"

He sighed. "She wanted me to search your boyfriend, Brian. Well, I didn't know he was your boyfriend. The name was familiar, but I didn't recognize it at first."

"Why?" Charlotte said brightly, taking care not to alarm Brian and let him understand what they were talking about.

"Excuse me?"

"Why would she ask you to look him up?"

"I don't know," Murphy said. "Look, it's nothing. I shouldn't have said anything... I'll just look at things, track Judy down, and call you back when I know more, all right?"

"Sure," Charlotte answered. "Please do."

The redhead hung up. She looked at Brian, who glanced at her questioningly. Then she moved on to looking at the restaurant. She desperately wanted to ask him why he thought Judy had asked for information on him, but she didn't know how to proceed.

The waitress came by to ask if they were ready to order, but Charlotte said they had changed their minds and they had to go.

The two fiancés walked out onto Main Street. Charlotte didn't say anything to Brian, and they just kept strolling. She sensed he was looking at her weirdly. She kept her head down and began to rush along. Suddenly, she bumped into something. Or not some*thing*—some*one*.

Stew.

CHAPTER SIXTY-EIGHT:

TIGHT ROPES

"These aren't my mother's sewing threads. These ropes are strong!" exclaimed Eddie White.

"Yeah, I can't get out of them either... they're not loose enough," said Judy.

A couple of hours had passed since the last conversation between Judy and Eddie White. Now they were both thirsty and hungry. Judy couldn't feel her legs anymore, and her bum hurt from sitting on the rigid, cold floor. Not to mention her arms: being tied up like that for hours on end, with her arms behind her, in an upright position, was no trip to Disney World.

Rush was about fifteen feet away from them, tied to another column, and he had mostly been staring at them, but now he was sleeping. This had not been a good day for him, either. Judy had begged Brian to bring him food, but he hadn't yet. He had brought the dog water, at least, but Judy knew that Rush was getting famished.

They needed something sharp to get out of these ropes. But there wasn't really anything in this room. There was very little furniture, just a table. And then the floor was bare. It was so clean Judy couldn't see a speck of dirt. It was a cold floor, too. When they got out of these ropes, if they managed to find a way, they would need to get their hands on a weapon as quickly as possible. Because if Brian were to find them free, he would wreak havoc on both detectives. The only weapon available was White's gun, and Brian had taken it upstairs with him. Well... they could probably get lead pipe from the wall and hit him with it. Whatever way they chose to go, they would need to be careful.

Then, as Judy was gazing at Rush, she had an idea. She looked at the basement door, then at White, and finally at the ceiling.

She did nothing for a moment, just staring quietly.

"What is this?" Eddie White asked. "What are you doin'?"

Hunter kept staring at the ceiling.

"Hunter?!" he blurted at her after a few seconds.

"You don't hear anything, do you?"

"What?"

"He's gone!" Judy exclaimed.

"Gone?" frowned White. "Who is?"

"Brian!"

"Oh, that guy. Where is he?"

"Well, not in this house, dummy."

White looked at her naively, like he understood nothing of this world.

"Now, we need to get out of here!"

"Out of here?" White repeated. "How? I thought we already talked about that. I say we can't! There is no way for us to get out of these ropes!"

"I know!" Judy exclaimed. "But I think I've figured it out."

White looked extremely muddled. He peered at her hands for a moment. No, she didn't have an object to slice the ropes off or anything like that. Judy gave him a smile and then looked at Rush.

"What?!" he asked.

"Our ropes are tight. But *his* isn't."

White stared at her, confused. What was she talking about? Then Judy pointed with her head towards Rush.

"Yeah?" questioned White.

"This is Rush, Eddie," she answered.

"Yeah, you have a dog. I know that. So what?"

She ignored White and instead called out, "Come, buddy! Come!"

Rush moved. He was still tied up, but the leash around the column he was tied to was getting loose. He tried frantically to get to Judy, but he couldn't. She called him again. Same thing—the dog was stopped by the leash. She grew frustrated, but tried one more time.

"Rush! Come!" she shouted.

Rush gave one more tremendous effort, and finally the leash undid itself. He sped to Judy, wagging his tail.

"Good boy, good boy!"

Rush was licking her face and jumping on her. Then he went to Eddie White and began doing the same, but the detective didn't seem to appreciate it.

"So, what now?" Eddie White cried. "What was even the point of this?"

"We have to try," Judy said, sounding determined. "Now that I got him loose, he has to do the same for us."

Eddie White looked at her like she was crazy.

CHAPTER SIXTY-NINE:

RHODE HOUSE

As soon as she laid eyes on him, something in her body changed. Charlotte's hands went behind her back and, as quickly as she could, she got her engagement ring off her finger and put it in her jeans pocket. She didn't know why she did it; it was instinctive. She couldn't get a word out, either. Charlotte felt as if she had been caught by her mother doing something forbidden.

"Hey," Stew said, casually waving at her.

He looked at them both with his beautiful blue eyes, appearing as confident as ever. He was carrying a bag on his shoulder and had his work clothes on.

Charlotte still couldn't get a word out. It took her a few seconds to come to her senses, at which point Brian held out his hand and began introducing himself.

"Name's Brian. I'm Charlotte's—"

"Friend," Charlotte uttered without thinking.

"Actually—" Brian tried.

Charlotte could see Stew getting puzzled.

"From New York. So, I'm back! How are you, Stew?" Charlotte interjected.

"I see you're back!" Stew said, playing with his hair. "Well, everything's fine. I was wondering if you guys were still here. You left without saying goodbye."

"Did I—did we?" Charlotte gave a forced and over-the-top laugh.

"Yeah... you're still working on the case?"

"Yeah, yeah, yeah!" Charlotte said, brashly and awkwardly.

"Awesome," he said. "Where's Judy?"

"She's not far." Charlotte smiled.

Stew kept looking between Brian and her. Finally, he nodded. There was a short silence.

"Well, I gotta go to work!"

"Yeah, of course."

He forced a smile. "Nice to see you, Charlotte."

He passed by them and continued walking down Main Street. She had never seen such a sad smile in her life.

The second he walked away, she wanted to talk to him more, to explain, but she couldn't. Her body wouldn't let her. And... there was Brian. Beside her. Staring.

She couldn't tell him anything either. She just kept walking.

Charlotte walked in front of Brian, leading the way. She didn't know where she wanted to go now. She was getting tired. Maybe they should get a room at the motel, she thought, so she started heading there in total silence.

Two or three minutes passed before she heard a harsh noise behind her. It sounded like an engine of some kind heading their way. Charlotte turned around and Brian followed suit. There were two motorcycles coming towards them. Two men and a woman, laughing hysterically. Charlotte suspected they were all drunk. They were also speeding. The woman was wearing a white dress and had a vodka bottle in her left hand. She was holding onto a skinny man with flat, shiny black hair that was blowing wildly in the wind. The man had a long, sharp nose and tiny lips, thick eyebrows, and a mole on his right cheek, right under his eye. He turned his head towards Charlotte and smiled as he passed her. His eyes were slit, feral, and somehow hollow. He looked like a serpent riding a motorbike.

The other man was alone on his bike. His hair was a mix of white and orange, and he looked to be tiny. Both men were wearing leather coats. Skullheads.

"That's fucking right, Julian!" she heard the short man yell. "That's fucking right, dude."

They kept on laughing and speeding away until they disappeared.

Charlotte felt as if her brain and her guts were on fire. She began almost running down the street after them.

Charlotte heard Brian shouting at her back, but she didn't care. She was heading right for the street where the bikes were turning. They were probably going to that dive bar named the Rhode House. Yes, that's exactly where they were going!

The redhead turned the corner and stared into the distance. The two bikes had stopped. She could hear the boyish laughs of those two Skullheads. The woman was hooting even louder, really forcing it. She was likely just trying to avoid getting hurt, but Charlotte had the impression nothing would prevent Julian Franco from hurting her or anyone else. Just from his appearance, she knew this was the man Melanie had described to them. She couldn't see a soul behind this man's eyes.

Charlotte hurried towards them. The two men and the woman were heading for the Rhode House doors. It was like a saloon door from the Old West. The trio disappeared into the place, laughing uproariously.

The redhead sped through the doors. Yes, this was definitely the Old West: women everywhere, sitting on men's laps, all of them dressed provocatively. The men were wearing leather jackets, all of them Skullheads, except for the bar employees, who dressed a little more formally. As she peeked around, Charlotte recognized most of the men. This was the same crew that had breathed down her neck and violated her with their savage eyes as she was confronting their leader, Sebastian Reed.

She couldn't see Reed anywhere. Maybe he'd taken a woman upstairs or was giving the old ass-licking to his lawyer in the bathroom down there. She didn't care. She didn't want to talk to him. Julian was the one about to die, he didn't seem to give two shits about it, and she wanted to know why.

Charlotte stared for a bit, staying grounded. Then she felt a hand on her shoulder. She turned her head. It was Brian.

"Char, what are you doing?"

"Just the usual—finding a place to get a drink and pour my feelings into it," she replied.

She started walking away, not caring about Brian, just doing her business. She sped to the bar and put both hands on the counter. The bartender took a second to notice her, but the second he did, there was no going back. For the first time since she had come into the bar, she felt like an intruder.

He came over. "Can I help you?" he said, sounding almost frightened.

"Whisky, please," she replied. "On the rocks."

There was not an ounce of fright in her voice, which made the bartender even more uneasy. He nodded and turned away. Charlotte looked around her. A couple of guys in leather jackets turned their heads, noticing her. Their gaze was not going away, either. She smiled back at them, more confident than ever.

She felt a hand on her shoulder. Brian again. She sighed.

"Charlotte, please," he said.

" You're not scared? Are you?"

Then she felt a hand on her other shoulder. It was the bartender with her drink. She grabbed it and smiled. She gave him a huge tip and he stared at her like she was an insane person. She just kept on smiling and headed for Julian Franco. He was sitting with the woman from the motorcycle on his lap. Charlotte could see that guys were standing up and staring at her. She sensed some of them moving towards her.

"Charlotte," she heard Brian say again.

Julian finally noticed the redhead.

"You're Julian Franco! Aren't you?" Charlotte yelled.

The whole room went silent. Charlotte looked around. All the men were now standing, arms crossed, glaring at her. She turned to Julian again.

"And who might you be, sexy?" Julian said.

"Someone who doesn't understand you, buddy."

"Excuse me?" he said.

"You're partying like there is no tomorrow, your own mate is being accused of murder and about to be arrested for it, and you're all doing nothing. Just fucking around and drinking, and... laughing at your own gags."

"Oh, I know who you are! You're that detective girl that Seb keeps talking about. I think you're his type. He likes you. Are you looking for him? I could call."

Charlotte felt disgust coursing through her veins.

"What are you doing here, honey? This doesn't seem like the right bar for you," he said. "Clearly."

The whole crowd of men started laughing. Julian stood, leaving the woman seated on his chair. He came up to Charlotte and began circling her.

"Or maybe it is..." Julian cackled. "Careful where you go with that outfit... Seb is not the only one who's gonna start running after you in here... We all believe in brotherhood and all, but I mean, man! He was right, you are gorgeous!"

"And feisty!" she said. "Don't you dare touch me!"

"Okay! Okay," he said, keeping his hands away.

"You know that the killer has targeted you next, right?"

Julian didn't seem to know if she was talking about him. He kept staring at her, and realized she was.

"Seb might have called and mentioned it to me. So what?"

"You don't care if he gets to you? The killer?"

"Babe, it's not like I haven't had a threat from someone before. Look at me. Look at us."

Charlotte looked at the whole bar. He had a point.

"Plus, I have my buddies to protect me!"

"Okay, but what about Reed? You're not going to let him go to jail, are you? You all know that he hasn't done it, so why would you let that happen?"

"Seb is gonna be fine," Julian opined, going back to his seat.

"No, he's not!" Charlotte shouted. "I've sat in for that FBI thing. They almost have him. They have fingerprints, they have footage, they have notes."

"All bullshit, as he told me," Julian replied. "They can't prove a thing. And they won't be able to, 'cause he didn't do nothin'."

"But what if they do find something?"

"They won't."

"You can't let them—"

"Look, honey. He didn't do it. So let it go."

"Then tell me who did. Come with me to the precinct and tell them. Tell them that the Kovachev story is true. That you buried him. Tell them everything."

Julian was surprised by this. He didn't react right away. He looked around the room to make sure no one else had heard her. Charlotte looked at Brian and smiled. Brian wasn't as joyful as his bride-to-be.

"They'll start looking for someone else and we can finally solve this case and put the right guy in jail..." Charlotte added. "We can protect you, too. Keep you out of the killer's hands."

Julian stayed rooted for a moment, his back to Charlotte. Then she heard a laugh.

"Please go back to where you came from, sweetie."

"Just tell them everything, please! You don't have to die. He'll get to you, believe me!"

"He won't!" Julian shouted angrily. "I'm not helpless and pathetic like Melanie!" He turned to face Charlotte. "And we don't need a fucking woman's help! We're doing fine on our own."

Charlotte grew angry and started towards Julian, wanting to punch him. Hands grabbed her. Then the hands were pushed away as Brian arrived and began swearing at them and fighting back.

"Leave her!" he shouted.

"Look at that!" Julian exclaimed. "And who might you be, muscle man?"

Brian and Julian stared each other down. Brian was raging, and Julian found it amusing.

"Seb's gonna be disappointed! Oh wait, no, I heard that you were hanging with another, actually... Stewart is gonna be very disappointed when he finds out that you have a boyfriend."

Charlotte went for Julian again.

"Yeah, nothing's going to happen to you, you're right," said Charlotte. "At least Sebastian would let himself be hit. He would go to jail for all of you if he had to. I know that now. You, on the other hand, Julian! You're just a pussy. You're a sociopath, sure, but that doesn't make you a fighter. You control people, you have them in your pocket. That's all well and good. But if you had to fight back, one on one, you wouldn't be able to. You'd be crushed. You'd be on the ground crying your eyes out."

Julian almost puffed out his chest after hearing that. He then gave her a threatening look.

"You're not scary," she continued. "You don't scare me. You might have scared Kovachev for a little while with your creepy eyes and judgmental tone, you might have had him killed, but you're nothing besides a fucking pussy. I sure hope God protects you. I hope the killer doesn't come and find you when you're all alone at night. You're not going to survive this, and it's almost sad."

Julian kept grinning at her. But she knew she had struck a chord.

"Celebrate well, Julian!" were her final words before she stepped back and went for the door.

CHAPTER SEVENTY:

TUG OF WAR

Rush kept jumping on Eddie White and licking the man's grumpy face.

"Tell him to stop," the detective implored. "For heaven's sake, tell him to stop!"

Judy chuckled for a bit and let Rush give White some love.

"Hunter, please!" he begged. "I'm allergic."

"You're not. Nobody is allergic to cute puppies. How can we be? They're the best!"

Judy let Rush lick White's face for another short while before she finally called him.

"Rush, come here!"

But Rush kept on licking White, whose face was growing redder and redder.

"Rush! Here."

Finally, he obeyed. He had a hard time doing so, though—he liked White so damn much. He must have sensed that the man needed love!

Rush scampered over to Judy and sat down beside her, looking adoringly at her.

"Come here," she said once more, indicating with her head to come to that side. He did. Now she tried to make him see the ropes, holding them up and turning her arms. Once he noticed them, she made him come to them.

"Fetch," she said to him.

Rush looked at her blankly.

"This isn't gonna work, Hunter..." White said. "You're wastin' your time."

"Fetch, Rush..." Judy continued. "Fetch! C'mon!"

The dog kept staring at her.

“I told you,” White said.

“Come on, Rush! Grab the ropes! Play!”

But the dog wouldn’t move. White was now laughing. Judy was not going to give up that easily. She lifted her tied-up arms behind her back and began shaking the ropes so that Rush would be interested in playing. She did it again and again, until the dog finally got excited and took a tip of the rope in his mouth.

The dog started playing tug-of-war with the rope, pulling on it, and that was all Judy wanted.

She saw White shaking his head and giggling. “Come on, dog!” he said encouragingly.

But as soon as he spoke, Rush dropped Judy’s ropes and looked at White.

“No, Rush, keep going!” Judy said. “Keep going, play!”

But Rush just stared at White.

“Now what?” said White, appearing a little scared. “What’s he doing?”

Rush kept staring at White.

“Come on, dog!” White said, lifting his ropes in the process. “Play with the ropes!”

And Rush obeyed. He went to White’s ropes and bit on them hard. White screamed.

“Not me, not *my* ropes, you dummy! He bit my finger!”

Judy lost it and starting laughing.

Rush kept on playing tug-of-war with Eddie White’s ropes, wagging his tail. He was even giving a cute little growl now.

“Come on, Rush! Come on!” Judy kept on saying.

Rush was biting and pulling on knots, loosening them. Slowly but surely, he was freeing Eddie White’s hands.

When it was loose enough, Judy began asking for the rope, "Come on, Rush! Give it to me! Give it. Here!"

Rush grabbed some of the rope in his mouth and brought it over to Judy. She took it in her hands and began pulling it, untying White. A few seconds later, he was free. White liberated his hands entirely and stood up, groaning.

"Fuckin' hell! This hurts!" White said. "And I need to pee... badly!" He began moving towards the stairs.

"Hey, wait! Untie me now!" Judy said.

"I will. I just gotta grab my gun first in case he comes back!" Eddie White started up the stairs.

"White, you can't just— We need to come up with a plan! He's gone, but maybe his grandmother is still—"

"This is the plan" the detective shouted, not listening.

Judy sighed. This was a bad idea, letting him do things on his own. Really bad.

CHAPTER SEVENTY-ONE:

CONFRONTATIONS

Charlotte didn't want to talk about it—any of it. She just wanted to get some quiet time in bed and sleep it off until morning came. She had had beyond enough with this day, with all these people and with this case.

"Charlotte, please talk to me!" Brian begged, following her down the street towards the motel.

She didn't answer.

"What's up with you? Why would you even do that? Are you crazy?"

"They weren't going to touch me, Brian!" she muttered, not turning to look at him.

Then he grabbed her and made her turn around.

"Leave me alone!" Charlotte shouted.

"No! Charlotte, you're not hearing me!"

She glared at his hand on her arm.

"That was dangerous," he said. "Those men!"

"Wow... you're a lot like my dad, aren't you?"

Brian pulled his hand away. He looked ashamed. "No, I'm not!"

"Oh yeah, you are! You're the same way he was, all hypermasculine, all protective. Like I always said to him, I can protect myself, I can make my own decisions. Here you are again! What about what you've taught me? What about my fighting skills? Are they not enough for you?"

"Of course, they are, Charlotte. I didn't mean—"

"Right, you didn't mean it."

"That's not the point I'm trying to make, Charlotte. I know you can fight! But there were *hundreds* of men in there. You can't fight all of them."

"Can't I?" she said, frowning.

"Do you know what they've done with their lives? The people they've hurt? They're criminals. Assassins. You don't just go in there and do whatever you want."

Charlotte shook her head. "You're funny. Like I said, fighting was not the plan. They weren't going to fight anyway. Fuck me? Maybe. But not fight. Like I said, not the plan. I had it under control."

"Charlotte—"

"I don't need a fucking father, Brian!" she shouted. "All right?"

Brian didn't say a word.

"I had one, and he was great," she added. "He's dead now." Charlotte felt tears welling up. She turned and walked away, quickening her pace. She wanted to get in a warm bed as soon as possible.

They finally arrived at the motel, and Charlotte hurried to the office to get a room and a key. The manager recognized her right away and said he was happy to see her back and hoped she was enjoying her time in Rockland. She smiled at him respectfully. He gave her a key to room 205. Outside the door, she glanced at Brian and kept walking. She went up the stairs, found the room, turned the key and left the door open as she walked in.

Charlotte got into bed immediately, turning out the lights. She didn't care if she was wearing her clothes, she just needed to sleep. She heard Brian close the door and come slowly to the bed. After a few seconds, he sat on the bed and sighed. Her fiancé waited a bit before saying, "What was that guy talking about? At the bar?"

Charlotte did not answer.

"Stew? Is that his name?" Brian continued.

Charlotte's face flushed.

"He's the guy we saw earlier, right?"

She kept quiet.

"He's more than an acquaintance, isn't he?"

Charlotte sighed.

"Do you love him?" Brian asked.

She didn't respond. She couldn't. It hurt too bad. Charlotte felt sweat dripping from her cold arms as she held the sheets tight in her hands. She remained still, pushing her head against the pillow, pretending to sleep.

Brian didn't say another word.

After a minute or two, she heard him get up and move to the door. He opened it and left the room. Charlotte felt her heart pounding. This conversation hadn't been the best.

CHAPTER SEVENTY-TWO:

THE ATTEMPT

Judy heard the basement door close behind Eddie White. Now he just needed to grab his gun and come back to untie Judy before Brian returned. Judy looked up, hearing footsteps above her. Christ, he needed to hurry.

A few seconds went by... a minute... two minutes. What was he up to? The retired detective kept hearing steps and other movements. She calculated another minute, and then another. She tried to shout with her dry mouth, “White!”

No answer.

“Come on! What are you doing?”

But it was hopeless. Had he really stopped off in the bathroom? *Right now?*

Judy didn’t hear anything for several minutes. Finally, a noise—a bang. And another! It was loud and heavy. A gunshot? *What the fuck?* BANG!

Judy wondered if White had been hurt. Or had he run into a chair or a table, or maybe just fallen on his way outside? She hoped it was something like that. Please, not a gunshot.

This didn’t seem to be coming from within the walls of the house, but from outside. Then there was silence again.

What had happened out there? Had Brian come back?

After a minute came another noise, a door opening and then slamming. Rush began barking. The dog ran up the stairs to the door. And then...

BANG! That was definitely a gunshot. *What the fuck?*

BANG! What in God’s name was going on out there?

She heard a scream. More screams. Loud slamming and smashing.

Then everything went quiet again.

Finally, Judy heard steps. Rush started barking and running around in the stairs.

The footsteps were approaching the basement door. Judy thought she could see a shadow under the door. The doorknob started to turn. It stopped, and then the door began sliding open. Rush backed away, moving down a couple of steps, still barking.

A shadow appeared in the door frame. Then the face came into the light...

It was Eddie White. He looked a little bruised, but not as bad as she had feared.

"Eddie?"

He held a woman in his arms. Judy realized it was Lilyana Kovachev.

"Who the hell is this?" White asked.

Damn it. Judy had hoped the woman was sleeping. She had tried to warn White about her, but he had left so abruptly.

Still standing in the doorway, White put the body down.

"Is she alive?" Judy asked.

White put a hand on the old woman's neck to feel her pulse. After a second, he looked up. He was very pale.

Suddenly, Judy made out another figure in the dark. A tall figure. Before she could say anything, the figure shoved Eddie White down the stairs, screaming. White fell face-first to the bottom, groaning.

The figure came into the light. It was Brian. The killer went directly to his grandmother, touched her neck. He stood there for a minute, breathing loudly. The old woman was certainly gone.

Viktor Kovachev's son looked into the basement and started down the stairs.

Eddie White attempted to stand, seeing Brian coming for him. The serial killer kept moving down the stairs, got a hold of White's body, and dragged it ferociously along the floor, towards Judy. The detective wanted to fight back, but Brian held him down.

Brian smiled strangely at White. The detective threw a terrified look at Judy, still trying to get out of Brian's grip.

"Leave him be, Brian! Please!" Judy begged.

But Brian just smirked at her. He turned back to White and stuck his tongue out. The hungry wolf and the scared sheep.

"You were right about letting him live. Now this is the perfect kill!" he said to Judy mischievously.

The next second, the smile was gone. Brian had turned. He didn't look entirely human anymore. He started to slam the detective's head on the ground. From Dr. Jekyll, he'd become Mr. Hyde.

White screamed. He screamed until the light in his eyes was gone and a massive amount of blood was covering the floor.

Judy was in complete shock. Her face couldn't move, her mouth couldn't speak. She just kept staring at White's eyes. His panicky, frozen eyes, still looking at her, unseeing.

A couple of minutes passed before Brian stood and turned to Judy. He didn't speak, but he approached very near. He looked down at her with a carnivorous smile. Then he crouched and she felt his breath on her neck. His eyes were filled with hate.

After a few moments, he stood up and went behind her. He tied her up again. Then he tied Rush back to the pole, much tighter this time. He wasn't going to kill them. Not yet.

Judy didn't make one protesting move.

A beat of silence occurred, and then Brian smiled at Judy again.

"Guess what, Judy?" Viktor Kovachev's son said. "Tonight's the night!"

He started for the stairs.

"And it's gonna be awesome!"

Judy shouted at the top of her lungs, "Brian! No!"

But Brian ran up the stairs, slamming the door behind him. There he was, on his way to cause doom, and there wasn't a damn thing she could do.

CHAPTER SEVENTY-THREE:

THE RECKONING

Charlotte woke up very abruptly from the gloomy clouds as her phone rang into her ears. She opened her eyes and turned towards the windows. The sun was rising. There was nobody beside her in the bed.

She looked at her phone and sighed. She wanted to throw it off the table to shut it up. Instead, the redhead quickly answered. The number was unknown.

"What?!" she croaked.

There was no immediate reply, just breathing.

"Hello?"

A voice finally made itself heard. "A terrible thing is about to happen," said the low voice, which appeared to be electronically modified. "Julian Franco will die... judgment is here."

Charlotte shot up, tense, and alarmed. "Wait," she said.

"Bradford Road," the voice continued.

"Wait!" Charlotte tried again.

"You have ten minutes."

The voice hung up. Charlotte looked at her phone, confounded and panicked. She dropped it on the bed and dressed as fast as she could.

She ordered a Lyft and met the car outside in a hurry. The young woman got inside and shouted at the driver to move quickly.

Charlotte had only six minutes left. She couldn't waste them or she would have another death on her hands. She made a call to Grant and told him the situation.

"Charlotte, I understand... We'll be there in less than ten minutes, please wait for us."

"He'll be long dead, Sheriff!"

"Please, Charlotte. Don't do this on your own. Wait for back—"

"I got this, Sheriff!"

"Charlotte—"

She hung up. As she did, she saw something else on her phone, a notification she hadn't seen before. A missed call from New York, specifically from the Midtown Precinct. Murphy. He had left a message:

"Miss Gibbins. I just wanted to follow up on our earlier discussion," the Captain said. "I have tried to track down Judy. Her phone says it was in her apartment. I tried calling again, but nothing. Then I authorized my men to look through her apartment. She isn't there. The dog isn't there. She just left her phone behind, so we can't use that to track her. We're still trying to look everywhere for her. Doing our best..."

Charlotte put down her phone and processed this. She then looked at the Lyft's GPS. She was three minutes away. She needed to do this first.

She put down her phone and again told the driver to hurry, reinforcing this by saying it was a police matter.

They travelled fast along a country road a bit out of the central part of town. The road was bumpy, but the terrain was flat. The pavement had been seriously neglected.

After a minute, the car finally turned. Charlotte saw the sign saying *Bradford Road.*

There was a minute and a half left to count down. Charlotte looked around desperately. She couldn't see a house or anything else that would show her where Julian might be. There was just an open field with hay and grass, a bunch of cows and sheep lying around, and some horses.

The redhead made the driver stop. She got out of the car and told the driver to go. The car left her.

She kept quiet for a moment. Only the sound of the wind blowing. Nothing on the horizon. Was this not the place?

After a few seconds, she heard a scream. Then a man shouting. It was coming from the right.

She ran to the sound as quickly as she could. She rushed through the long yellow grass, trying to find the source of the noise. Charlotte kept looking around, but the noise had died.

Then it started up again and she finally saw something a little farther away. She ran to it. She had very little time left.

As she got closer to the screams, she saw what was going on. There were four horses, standing at four different corners of a space in the hay. A man, naked, was tied to them. She recognized him immediately. It was Julian Franco. Then, as she rushed towards him, she saw somebody next to him. A tall man. He had gray hair. Julian was screaming at him. The tall man had his hands on the ropes.

Julian's four limbs were tied up separately, each to one horse. This man was about to perform a damn dismemberment on him.

Charlotte grabbed a stout piece of wood lying in the grass and brought it up, ready to hit the killer.

"Hey!" she shouted.

Julian turned his face, noticing her for the first time.

"Help! Please!" he screamed.

Then the tall man turned around. It was Sebastian Reed!

Charlotte shook her head and shouted again, moving towards them.

"You gotta help us, please!" said Julian.

Help both of them?

"Reed, get away from him!" Charlotte ordered.

"Can't!" he shouted.

She moved closer, raising her club. "Move!"

"You don't understand!" Reed shouted. "We don't have time!"

Charlotte looked at them, confused.

"Untie me, lady!" Julian shouted at her. "Quickly, help!"

Without any more hesitation, Charlotte advanced and did as she was told. She put her hands on the ropes and began untying his right arm. Reed was occupying himself with the left one. These ropes were so tight.

"Did you see a face?" Charlotte pressed. "The killer?"

"He hit us from the back and put bags on our heads!" Reed rushed. "Though I could have sworn I saw a reflection beforehand. He had dark hair and I'm sure he was tall."

Same description as Marlow's, Charlotte thought.

"Did you see a face?"

Reed shook his head.

"Fuck!" Julian shouted. "Just untie me!"

They were both still struggling with the expertly tied ropes. Reed was getting frustrated.

"You got a knife or something, Red?" Reed quickly asked.

Before she could say no, they heard something from the woods in front of them. A gunshot!

Charlotte let go of the ropes as the horses started moving, running.

"No!" Julian screamed.

Charlotte had to turn her head away. She heard dreadful sounds of horror, until she heard none.

When she finally looked, Julian's body had been spread across the field. It wasn't Julian anymore.

In shock, she looked at Sebastian Reed. Blood was covering his face. The redhead could see such sadness and terror in his eyes.

Charlotte then heard another noise from the woods. She was sure these were footsteps. She ran towards them as fast as she could. Then she stopped suddenly and turned to Reed.

"Get out of here!" she yelled at him.

But Reed didn't move, he just looked at her without a single expression on his face, stunned. She turned back and kept running towards the woods.

She ran and ran, not seeing anything. Then she stopped. She couldn't hear the footsteps anymore. She waited for a minute or two. She then ran in another direction and stopped again and did the same. *Where was he?*

It was all in vain. She heard and saw nothing.

She screamed in frustration and moved back in the direction she'd come from.

As she was returning, she heard sirens. When she finally arrived in the open field again, several police cars were arriving at the scene. FBI SUVs followed them. Deputies rushed to the horses and the ropes. Sebastian Reed was still there. He hadn't run as she'd told him to. Why?

He seemed frozen there, kneeling, looking at what was left of his friend, his brother, his high school sidekick.

Deputies and FBI agents moved in, pointing their guns at Reed. One of them held handcuffs. They were arresting him.

CHAPTER SEVENTY-FOUR:

RETURN OF THE BEAST

Judy had spent the entire night sitting on the floor, waiting for something to happen, for Brian to return from his macabre adventures. God only knew what he had done now. Judy feared what might have happened. She was also more frustrated than ever. She was raging. Half the night she screamed, hoping somebody would hear her and come save her. She felt so helpless. The once-great detective who had rescued so many people in her life and career was now tied to a pole, reduced to agony and despair, with no way out. The world would need to help itself.

About an hour after she began seeing some light through the basement door, she finally heard some noise. A door slamming. It took a few seconds for him to come to the basement, but when he did, he rushed down the stairs, limping. His leg seemed to have been wounded. He carried some bandages in his hands.

God, he had done it.

His clothes were dirty as hell, and there were bits of grass or foliage on them. He had the most unsettling smile on his face. His face was the most joyous she had ever seen it. He was almost dancing around. Oh, god!

She didn't say anything. She didn't know what to say. He had just killed someone, and he liked it.

Brian grabbed a chair and sat on it. He finally calmed down a bit.

"So, what now?" she heard herself saying.

"Now?"

"You killed him, didn't you?"

"I'm celebrating!"

"What about Reed?" she asked. "How are you going to get him?"

Brian smiled broadly. "Get him? Oh, that's right, lady! You didn't hear the news! 'Cause you were down here, of course! Ha! They got him! My plan worked."

Judy's heart skipped a beat.

"Perfectly, I might add. And Charlotte was there. Oh! My heart! She was there, and they're gonna thank her for it all. It's all on her," he babbled. "Yeah, it's all very... it's all very wonderful!"

The retired detective was speechless again.

"Sebastian Reed is gone. He is paying for his crimes. Damn, I've never seen the FBI so happy!"

The FBI? They had come here? To Rockland? *Jesus fucking Christ!* And they now had Reed?

"Ah, it was no easy task, though. Had to get my way through a couple of their goonies to get to Julian, gave them the beating of their lives... and then I had to go get Reed somewhere else. Turbulent night, I tell you.

"Now he's doing time for his crimes," Brian continued. "Hell, if we were in another state, he might even have gotten the death penalty. Then the Executioner's plan would really have been on a hundred. Well, you know. Some say life in prison is even worse than death... I'm just glad he's away."

Brian shook his head, but not in an annoyed way. "Anyways, I think I'm gonna get some sleep, maybe see a doctor before that, yeah... and then grab lunch with my fiancée! It's so well deserved."

As Judy kept trying to understand what was going on, Brian looked at his leg, and he finally put a new bandage over it. Had Julian or the other Skullheads given him a run for his money?

"What about—" Judy began.

"You?"

Judy looked at the ground, at Eddie White.

"What if I don't talk?" Judy said.

Brian looked intrigued.

"I appreciate what you... what we've done, Brian. Reed is dangerous and deserves to go to jail. And you—you've suffered a ton. It's sad that you had to grow up without a father. What Reed and the rest of them did, it's just... awful. They deserve what they got."

Brian stood up, looking more than satisfied. "You really want to?"

"Yes. I'll do it," Judy said. "Charlotte won't know a thing. She'll believe Reed did it."

Brian couldn't get the smile off his face. He moved to her ropes and started playing with them.

Judy couldn't feel them getting loose. Then she heard Brian chuckling under his breath. He came back in front of her.

"Nice, very nice," Brian said. "I almost believed you." He let out a laugh. "C'mon, Judy. You're never gonna shut up about it. You think I'm a maniac."

"I don't," Judy replied firmly.

"Well, it's okay. I get it. We don't see justice the same way. Difference of opinion, that's all. I respect you."

Brian started for the stairs.

"Don't worry, you and Charlotte will soon see each other again..."

Judy was confounded.

"You'll be another victim of Reed's. I've arranged things... a plan for her to have real closure when it comes to you. I'll be back soon. In the meantime, say your prayers or whatever it is you do."

CHAPTER SEVENTY-FIVE:

CASE CLOSED

Charlotte kept yelling at the FBI to stop—Reed was not the murderer. She ran to them and tried to prevent them from handcuffing the Skullhead leader, but it didn't work. Charlotte followed them to the police cars, shouting at them all the way. They finally put Reed in the car and drove away.

The FBI took Charlotte back to the Sheriff's office after a quick debriefing. The redhead tried to tell them about the gunshot in the woods and how she chased the sound. They took her remarks into consideration, and even had a search party look through the forest, but they found nothing. Then it all stopped when an officer found a pistol buried in the hay. The cartridge was missing a bullet.

The feds suggested that Charlotte might not have heard the shot coming from the right direction. Sebastian Reed might have hidden the gun and taken a shot while Charlotte wasn't looking. Charlotte protested that Julian hadn't indicated that Reed was his enemy, nor was Reed acting hostile towards Charlotte. She then told them about the description Reed had given them of his assailant. Agents Del Torres and Wallace took notes of all this, but they weren't enthusiastic about everything the redhead was saying. There was too much on Reed now, and whatever Charlotte could say felt like it didn't matter.

She was so frustrated. What did she know? She was not in a position to make decisions. Charlotte wasn't a detective; she wasn't even police. They looked at her very bizarrely as she tried to argue with them. The redhead felt as if she was some crazy person who was seeing things and hearing things.

When the SUV finally dropped her at the Sheriff's office, Charlotte didn't feel like talking anymore. This whole morning had shut her down completely. She had done everything in her power to defend Reed, to believe he hadn't done it, and he had still been arrested.

She stepped through the doors of the building and was greeted by the Sheriff, who showed her to a desk so she could wait. He said she would probably get debriefed again. Del Torres and Wallace walked in a few minutes later, and came immediately to Charlotte.

"Miss Gibbins!" Del Torres began. "We're heading back to New York, and we'll take care of Reed and the case from there."

Charlotte nodded.

"Your father would be very proud," the agent continued. "Thank you so much for your help with this."

She gave them a polite smile.

"Listen, we'll look into everything you told us, we'll make calls, we'll send folks down here. If something comes up, you'll know!" he said.

Yeah, I'm sure you will. After getting that more-than-awesome promotion for capturing Reed, you'll sure think of little crazy Charlotte Gibbins whom you saw twice in the very small and unimportant town of Rockland. Yeah, sure.

"Viktor Kovachev, right?" Del Torres continued. "That's the dead kid you were talking about?"

"Yeah," Charlotte replied, getting interested again.

"Well, our agents found a body... mere bones, really... it's really old. But the bones were tiny... it was in Sebastian Reed's home, in his basement."

Charlotte kept silent, trying to process this.

"Guess he's really been killing his friends for years, huh? Who knows what we will find out next." Then Del Torres concluded, "You did a great job out here. I'm sure the NYPD will be happy to have somebody like you. I'll give them a call, and the academy, and give them my recommendation."

"Thank you," Charlotte heard herself say. Even though this didn't make her feel happy right now.

"Reed is somebody that we really needed to catch," Wallace added.

Charlotte turned to her and watched the agent as she placed a file on Charlotte's desk. The redhead glanced at it. It was labeled "Sebastian Reed."

"Do you need a ride back to the city?" Del Torres inquired.

Charlotte didn't give them an answer. She just stared at the file.

"We'll be in the lot for another five or ten minutes. Let us know."

Charlotte nodded. She watched the FBI agents leave and head outside.

She kept staring at the file that had been casually dropped on the desk. Charlotte was about to make a move to open it when she felt a hand on her shoulder. She turned and there was the Sheriff, grinning at her. His short beard appeared to have grown a bit whiter since the day before. He looked as though he hadn't gotten much sleep in the past few days. He looked like someone who had endured being yelled at and told what to do.

"Hey, sweetie!" he said. "How are you feeling?"

"I'm all right." She forced a small smile.

"I know... not what you wanted."

"I just feel like this isn't right," said Charlotte. "That there is something we've missed along the way."

"Like what?"

"I know Reed didn't fire the pistol. I know he didn't do this, Sheriff!"

Grant glanced at her, then at the floor. He nodded. She knew he believed her.

"There's nothing we can do now," he said. "They've shut down everything. It's a federal investigation now, and if we interfere, we'll be jailed."

Charlotte sighed. This really sounded like the end. Grant gave her a kiss on the right cheek and then hugged her.

"You're wonderful, Charlotte!"

Grant then stepped away and left her on her own.

She looked around: at the Sheriff's precinct, at the FBI dragging Reed and putting him inside one of their SUVs. She peered at the Sheriff and saw him going back into his office, where he made himself coffee and then sat at his desk and started picking up the phone and writing things on his notepad. He was back on the job. He didn't look at her again.

She then thought about Judy. What would she do in this situation? Would she just give up? Would she be ready to keep going? Would she undermine the FBI's authority? How would she proceed? She needed her right now, more than ever. Where the fuck was she? Why hadn't they found her yet? She had to find her. That was her priority.

She heard her phone beeping in her pocket. It was a message from Brian—he wanted to have brunch with her. She didn't know what to say. She didn't want another awkward and infuriating conversation right now.

She finally moved her eyes to the elephant in the room: the file. Charlotte slowly undid the rubber band wrapped around it. She opened it and scanned through. Right from the first page, horrible details popped up. The report said:

```
UNDER INVESTIGATION
Victim Name: Jenny Davidson
Date of incident: January 17th 1998
Crime/Incident: Attempted rape
```

Brief description of incident: Young woman (27), Jenny Davidson, claims a man by the name of Sebastian Reed drugged her and attempted to rape her on the night January 17th 1998 near the Rhode House bar. Davidson claims there was no consent. She says she managed to get away before the assault took place.

Charlotte turned the page and moved on to another one:

Victim Name: Natalie Richard
Date of Incident: September 21, 2001
Crime/Incident: Sexual Offense/Rape/Battery

Farther down, Charlotte read:

Case on October 1st, 2001. Mrs. Richard dropped the charges on Mister Sebastian Reed.

Charlotte read through all the other reports—dozens of women reporting sexual assault and worse. Most of them dropped the charges in no time. But there weren't only women in this, there were men too. Not a lot, but some men who reported battery and assault on them. Then the redhead got to the worst part of the file, the suspected murders:

CLOSED CASE
Victim: Rupert Fringe (Deceased)
Suspected cause of death: Battery.
Brief description: Deceased was found in bar near Kensington Road. Found in dumpster. Deceased was beaten before death. (Suspected Initiation)

Prime Suspect: Sebastian Reed and the group known as the Skullheads.

Case closed on July 13th, 2004. Man by name of Jackson Pierce (construction worker) was found to be guilty of murder.

And another:

CLOSED CASE
Victims: Mariana Sanchez and Frederica Sanchez. (Deceased)
Suspected cause of death: Asphyxiation and battery.
Brief Description: Deceased were found in house on Roland Street on the night of December 25th 2006. Mother and daughter. Mariana Sanchez (39) was married to Mr. Sebastian Reed. Frederica Sanchez was 10 years old.
Prime Suspect: Sebastian Reed.

Case closed on February 14th, 2007. Skullhead member by the name of Kenny Long was found guilty of the murders.

After this one, Charlotte finally decided to close the file. She couldn't handle it anymore. This was all very nauseating. She thought about Reed and how he had physically intimidated her in their first meeting. If she had been alone with him and had not been a skilled fighter, what might have happened?

She took a moment to gather her thoughts, and then Charlotte heard a voice calling her.

"Ms. Gibbins?" It was a deputy. "The FBI wanted me to let you know they're about to leave."

Charlotte nodded and left the file on the desk. She grabbed her jacket and began walking to the parking lot. It was time to return to the Big Apple. She couldn't do anything more.

CHAPTER SEVENTY-SIX:

JUSTICE

Rush kept looking at Judy with begging, pitiful eyes. He wanted to get out of here to eat, drink, run around, and to smell the air around him. So did Judy. Her hands and fingers were hurting, numb as hell, her bum was destroyed from all this sitting, and her whole body felt so dry she thought she would soon to turn to ashes.

She waited for Brian to come back, to tell him her answer. She was sure he would appreciate it, enthusiastically.

After a few minutes of waiting, the basement door opened and Brian shuffled in. Judy was now feeling more scared than ever. It was time.

"Hi Brian," Judy said calmly.

"I'm sorry, Judy. It's time! Charlotte just called. It's over. I'm meeting her back in New York. Thank the fucking lord," Brian said cheerfully. "I hope you did everything you had to do. Prayers and all. Charlotte's gonna miss you. You really were like a mother to her!"

Brian took a gun from behind his back and pointed it at Judy. The retired detective took a breath and closed her eyes. So this was it, the end. He had won. They had lost. This was how she was going to meet her fate.

There was a long pause. Judy knew the gun was pointed at her. She wanted to do something, but she couldn't. She was about to die. Then it would be Rush. He would probably take her dead body, get her out of this place, and stage her murder where it would match with Reed. Sebastian Reed would be her killer. Charlotte would be angry, but she would eventually move on. She hoped the young woman wouldn't forget, but Brian was so good at turning things to his favor that it could happen. She might very well move on.

Judy waited some more. When was it going to happen? What was he doing?

Then she heard him sigh.

"Don't worry," he said. "I'll take care of her... I promise."

Judy was ready for the gun to fire any moment now.

"I take care of myself!" a voice cut through instead.

Judy opened her eyes and looked at Brian. He looked at her. They didn't know where it was coming from.

Then Judy looked up the stairs and thought she saw an angel through the shining light of day. Charlotte was at the top of the stairs, pointing a gun at Brian.

Brian took a moment, processing this. "Charlotte?" he said, looking petrified. "What are you—"

"What am I doing here?" the redhead replied. "Your plan was perfect, honey. Only some very, very small mistakes... that turned out to be kind of big." Charlotte paid him with a smile. "Thanks to you, I managed to finally solve this case. Turns out we really needed your help after all. Just not the way you think."

She went on, "I was about to give up. I was set to leave this place and go back home when somebody ran after the FBI SUV and made me pull down my window. It was a deputy, he had my phone in his hand, I had forgotten it. I thanked him, grabbed it and looked at it. On the home screen was a message from you that I hadn't answered yet... I glanced at your name, and then I thought: Judy."

Brian frowned, not getting it.

"Captain Murphy called me yesterday when we were at Granger's and said that Judy, before disappearing into thin air, was looking into you. He didn't understand why... I didn't either. Why the hell was she looking into you? I found it so weird... until today."

She grinned. Judy felt a happy light shining through her body. *Yes, Charlotte, yes.*

"I really didn't want to be right, believe me," she said. "But as soon as I thought about it, everything started falling into place."

Brian chuckled.

Charlotte ignored him and said, "The notes... they could only be given by somebody very close to me, somebody who knew me, who knew my every move. Perhaps a stalker, but a stalker who seemed to really care for me in the most fucked-up way. Someone who wanted me to become a detective as much as I did. Someone who also was very protective at times."

Brian's smile was fading.

"Then there was Sofia Marlow," Charlotte continued. "who mysteriously disappeared, but... She said she had seen somebody with black hair, brown eyes, who was very tall and young, looking like an insane creep going up the stairs to Ethan Gregory's. The insane creep... it was *you*, I see it now. That fucking look she saw. That look! It scared me in the beginning, when we started dating, but then it became attractive... I shouldn't have looked past it, but I did. There was always something wrong with you. I just lied to myself all this time. You're a damn psycho."

Brian didn't speak or chuckle anymore, just stared at the floor.

There was the sound of movement upstairs! Judy looked up and gazed upon the Sheriff, also with a gun in his hand, coming down the stairs.

"Oh, thank God!" Grant said, seeing Judy's face.

She was grateful to see him too. Brian looked at him, still paralyzed by his world coming apart. Grant let Charlotte keep pointing her gun at Brian while he went for Judy. The Sheriff untied her.

Brian looked away as Judy was let free.

"Enough with the cat-and-mouse routine, Brian. It ends today," Judy stated. "The puzzle has been solved."

There was a moment of silence in the room. Charlotte and Judy stared at Brian as he shook his head, looking as though he was going to cry. The retired detective could have sworn she heard a sob. But at the last second, he lifted his head and glanced at Charlotte. Then he grinned.

"Well done, ladies, well done. Great detective work! Congrats, Charlotte! I am so damn proud." Then he went on, "But you won't stop me."

"And why is that?"

"Charlotte, I'm sure you've read up on Reed, you've probably seen the reports too. If not, you know how bad the FBI wanted him... it doesn't add up well. Not a very pleasant man to have out here. You're not gonna let a man like that walk free, are you?"

The redhead didn't reply right away. Judy looked at her, waiting.

"I'll have to," Charlotte said.

Brian's face turned red. This... he was not happy about. He was disappointed.

"Are you serious?"

"One hundred percent," she replied.

His disappointment transformed into shame. After a moment, he said, "Oh well! At least you're not gonna shoot me."

"No?"

"You're a fighter and a good one, Charlotte. You know how to give a beating, I'll give you that. And you're the bravest person I know... but killing someone, hmm..."

"No, we're not going to kill you... Damyan," Charlotte replied. "We're going to arrest you."

"Arrest me?" He belly laughed. "You gotta be kidding!"

But they weren't. Judy looked at Grant. "Sheriff! It's time," she said.

"No," Grant said.

Judy stared at him, confused.

"You do it, detective. This is your case!"

Charlotte said proudly, "We called Murphy on the way over here. He's giving you your job back—temporarily. One last arrest."

Judy gave Charlotte an adoring gaze.

Then Brian started laughing, perhaps thinking this was a joke.

The Sheriff handed Judy the cuffs and the retired detective turned Brian around and brought his hands behind his back.

Charlotte kept pointing her gun at Brian.

"Damyan Kovachev, we're placing you under arrest for the murder of Ethan Gregory!" exclaimed Judy.

Brian glared at Charlotte. "You don't wanna do this, Charlotte," he said.

"Fred Gibbins!" Judy said angrily.

"Please, Charlotte. You don't want to. He's a madman. You know what he did to those women. To those children... let me at least kill him. Charlotte—he killed my father—"

"And you murdered mine, Damyan!" Charlotte cut him off, fed up and raging. "And so many more."

He didn't say another word. Judy could see that he knew Charlotte had no more love for him.

"Melanie Sheldon," Judy continued. "Rick Carson, Zachary Smith, Julian Franco, Sofia Marlow, and Detective Edward White... You have the right to remain silent. Anything you say will be used against you in a court of law. You have the right to have an attorney. If you cannot afford one, one will be appointed to you by the court..."

When the ropes around his wrists were deemed tight enough, Judy and Charlotte pushed Brian up the stairs and into the light of day.

CHAPTER SEVENTY-SEVEN:

RELEASE

What have I done? Charlotte asked herself as she sat on the New York City subway. Her head was filled with clouds of thought that wouldn't stop screaming at her. How could she not have seen it? This whole time she had been sleeping next to a man whose hobby was murdering folks. Her own fiancé was a serial killer. A sociopath. A fucked-up man. What had she done? Choosing him over millions of other normal guys who would probably have given their eyeteeth to be with her? Any other guy would probably have been kinder and would have taken care of her so much better. *No, Charlotte. You had to pick the abs, the hottest body, the one with the rough edges that could make things very interesting. The bad boy that you could potentially fix in the long run. Of course, he was a serial killer. There was always something wrong with him, and you knew it. You just ignored it. You damn fool.*

She went on like this for the whole ride, going back and forth between demolishing herself, punishing herself for it all, and feeling depressed that it was all happening. A part of her knew she had truly loved Brian... Damyan... whoever he was. And that was the worst part of it all. It broke her heart.

She felt as though her entire world was destroyed. Like she had nothing. Like she *was* nothing.

Charlotte finally arrived at her destination: Brooklyn Bridge City Hall station. Minutes later, she walked into a charcoal-gray building on 26 Federal Plaza, announced herself, and went straight for the elevators.

When she arrived at her floor, she was walking down a hallway towards a desk when her eye caught something in a window. It was Judy. It was an interrogation room. In front of the retired detective were Agents Del Torres and Wallace. They were debriefing Judy Hunter on the case.

Charlotte kept going, and finally reached the reception desk and announced herself. She then sat in the waiting room of the Federal Bureau of Investigation and waited for her turn.

She had been waiting about ten minutes when she saw some men walk out of a room. It wasn't the room Judy had been in. It was two FBI agents she didn't recognize. Then a third person emerged. It was Sebastian Reed.

Reed had no handcuffs on. He wasn't wearing his usual tough-guy clothes, either. Instead, he was decked out in a blue prison uniform and a white T-shirt. He was being freed.

But Reed could be arrested again anytime and might easily go to prison. There was still the case of Viktor Kovachev to solve. Even though Damyan had put the bones of his father in Reed's house to frame him, the case was still unsolved. The police now had proof of death, but no killer. An investigation was ongoing to figure out what had really happened thirty years ago. Reed was still the prime suspect. Would he confess? Would they find something else to tie him to Kovachev's death?

As soon as she saw the Skullhead leader, Charlotte stood up and went towards him.

"Gentlemen!" she said to the agents. "Mind if I have a minute?"

The agents looked at each other, then peered at Reed. He nodded at them.

"I'll be all right, thanks," added Charlotte.

Sebastian Reed smiled at her. "Came here for me, Red? Gosh, I'm flattered."

"You wish," Charlotte said.

They looked at each other for a moment. Sebastian Reed seemed perplexed, but he kept grinning.

"How does it feel to be a free man?" Charlotte went on.

"Well, you know... it's all right," Reed joked.

But Charlotte wasn't exactly smiling.

"Your boy did a number on me!" Reed added.

There was another silence.

"Did you know?" he asked. "At all?"

Charlotte shook her head.

"I'm sorry," Reed said. "This must be... very shocking... disturbing."

Charlotte nodded. *Yeah, like you understand.*

"I don't think I can thank you enough for everything," he said.

Charlotte smiled wryly at this. "No, you really can't." She took a breath before stepping forward and coming very close to Reed. "You've been very lucky, Sebastian," she whispered to him.

He tilted his head, puzzled.

"You know I could have just let you rot in there, let him kill you, even... God knows I could have!"

Reed's face went sour.

"If I ever find out that any of these reports and allegations on you have even a tiny bit truth to them, I'll be the worst thing you have ever encountered in your life. I won't let you go until you burn to ash!"

Reed stared at her, frowning, with newfound respect. Charlotte thought he seemed a bit frightened.

"You're a good one, Red," Reed finally said. "I like you." He patted her on the shoulder and nodded, then walked away.

That went well, Charlotte thought. She could feel herself smiling.

Then the redhead turned around and bumped into Judy, who was staring at her.

"Nice!" the retired woman said.

After giving Judy a long hug, Charlotte and Judy both sighed.

"It might not seem like it right now," Judy began, "but you did the right thing."

Charlotte didn't seem sure of that at all, and she let Judy know it.

"That's what makes a great detective: being able to make difficult decisions in tough times. Sometimes they're decisions we're not fully in agreement with. They might seem irrational, insane, but we know that it's the best decision we can make right now to ensure everyone's safety and well-being."

Charlotte nodded.

"Damyan Kovachev is a dangerous one," Judy added.

Charlotte agreed on that. "Thank you for everything," she said.

"How did you even find me?"

"I didn't know you were there. We just tracked down Brian... to arrest him... I tracked his phone the way he tracked mine this entire time, and of course the Sheriff knew exactly where the house was." Charlotte said. She added shakily, "I thought you were dead."

Charlotte hugged the retired detective one more time.

Then Charlotte noticed Del Torres and Wallace approaching. The redhead greeted them with a less than fervent expression, and the agents showed her to the interrogation room. It took her about half an hour to get debriefed, and then it was all over. She too was free.

PART THREE

-

ONE YEAR LATER

CHAPTER SEVENTY-EIGHT:

THE COP

Judy Hunter felt the fresh spring air blowing on her face as she sat at her seat at the Madison Square Garden. The theater was packed with proud and teary-eyed parents, family members, and loved ones. All of them were looking forward to seeing their children being called onstage so they could become official members of the New York Sheriff's Office.

Judy felt her emotions rising and she could feel Madelaine's too. Charlotte's mother was sitting next to her with her new husband, Patrice Bélanger, a handsome blond man with a thick French accent. They could see Charlotte, her hair tied back in a ponytail, waiting in line with a few other officers-to-be. This was the first time Judy was seeing Charlotte in uniform, and damn, she was wearing it well. The young woman seemed a bit nervous, but she still had that great, unbelievable confidence that the retired detective was used to seeing. Charlotte was talking with a few of her comrades, exchanging laughs and smiles. It was awesome to see her so happy. The redhead had been through a lot.

In his high-pitched voice, Commissioner Lester Crowley was introducing each graduate as they came onstage one by one. His assistant, Penelope Cloud, was right by his side, wearing a less revealing dress than the last time Judy had seen her, at her apartment the night of Judy's retirement.

"Nathan Porter!"

Crowley shook the young man's hand and smiled proudly. He then gave him a diploma and sent him on his way.

"Christian Gordon!"

The new officer hesitated, not registering that it was him they were calling, then he finally looked at the Commissioner, a bit stressed.

The crowd lost control a bit, breaking in laughter, when Gordon finally stood up. But the Commissioner kept a serious face. Crowley shook the young man's hand firmly and nodded.

Then the Commissioner moved on, looking down at his paper. He immediately froze at the name he saw. A heavy silence descended. Penelope Cloud went to him and glanced down at the paper. He mumbled something to her. He was trembling. Lester Crowley appeared to have stage fright.

This was hilarious.

So, Penelope Cloud took the stage and shouted with great excitement, "Charlotte Kennedy Gibbins!"

Now the crowd roared. Judy stood up and heard herself scream. Madelaine got a hold of Judy's hand and grabbed it as tight as she could. Both women looked at each other with tears in their eyes.

Charlotte walked with extreme assurance to the stairs and stepped onto the stage. A man in the seats behind the podium, also in uniform, stood up. It was Captain Murphy. He grinned at Charlotte and gave her a hearty handshake.

Charlotte finally walked offstage, very proud, diploma in hand and a badge on her chest.

Tears kept rolling down Judy's cheeks. This was all Charlotte had wanted! And now she had it. She was a cop! Judy was filled with joy.

The ceremony was over, and all the guests and new officers were invited to a small tent for drinks and some food. Judy stood at the buffet speaking with Captain Murphy and a few of her old colleagues. Then she suddenly saw vibrant red hair coming into the tent. Charlotte held her head high. With a grateful and happy nod, she thanked everyone who congratulated her and went through the crowd. After a few seconds, she finally saw Judy and her mother from far away and started to run as fast as she could towards them, laughing hysterically. Judy was laughing as well, but the tears were coming back as well.

"God, Charlotte," Judy said. "You did it! You did it!"

"Thanks, Judy," Charlotte replied, hugging her tightly.

"My daughter," Madelaine said, hugging her next. "The best! Fabulous!" She gave Charlotte a kiss.

"*Félicitations*!" said Patrice, giving the redhead a kiss on the cheek.

Then Judy and Charlotte just gazed into each other's eyes, beaming. Madelaine saw this and quickly said, "We'll grab some food and be right back!"

Charlotte's mother and her husband walked away, leaving the two women alone.

Judy kept on smiling before finally stating, "I know someone else who would be very, very proud of you, my dear!"

Charlotte was teary-eyed.

"You're really going to make a great cop," the retired detective continued. "You know that, right?"

"You sure you don't want to come back?" Charlotte replied.

Judy found that sweet and stuck her tongue out.

"How's North Carolina?" Charlotte asked.

Judy had sold her place in New York and finally moved to North Carolina in the past year, back to her old family home, the place her father had left her.

"Oh, don't even go there! I thought I was done with the action part of my life. Now water's come in and flooded my entire basement."

"Are you kidding me? That fucking sucks!" Charlotte uttered.

"I was going to renovate anyway," Judy said, not wanting to sound too alarmed, but she shook her head. This was a struggle.

"Does that mean you're coming back to New York?"

Judy chuckled.

"I don't know if I can do this without you, Judy," the redhead clarified. "Seriously. We make a fantastic team. What you taught me last year, what we went through... I don't think I could've solved this case without you!"

Judy looked at her and nodded. "You're not wrong." She grimaced, and then patted the young woman on the shoulder. "But you're still learning. Someday you might be even better than me!"

They both giggled.

After a few minutes, a man walked over to them. Judy recognized him instantly. It was Vincent Price, the CSI.

"There you are!" he said to Charlotte. "I wanted to congratulate you, missy! Welcome to the team."

"Do we know each other?" she said.

"Name's Vincent Price! We met briefly at Judy's party."

Judy then reintroduced them and said Price had been a big help in proving that her father hadn't really committed suicide.

"Well, thank you so much!" Charlotte said. "For everything!"

"I love Judy Hunter!" Price answered. "The modern Sherlock Holmes. I would do anything to be part of one of her cases. So, my pleasure!"

Judy shook her head. "Oh, Price!"

"Yes, 'Oh Price' is right," said a woman who joined them. She wore a gorgeous green dress and had long blond hair. She was in her late thirties.

"Brandy!" Judy exclaimed.

Brandy Thomas was Head CSI of the NYPD, and superb at her job. She was also Judy's good friend. Price had replaced her for a while she was on maternity leave. Her eyes sparkled when she saw the retired detective and then went in for a big hug.

Brandy spoke with a lovely Australian accent. "I hope this one didn't cause too much damage when I was gone. Not fully trained, you might say." She looked mischievously at Price with her big blue eyes.

"Oh, no, no," Judy replied. "He did a lot, actually."

"Good, good. I'm Brandy, by the way," the Head CSI said, looking at Charlotte. "Congratulations."

Charlotte thanked her.

"How's the baby?" Judy asked.

"Just turned one. She's so great!" exclaimed Brandy.

As Judy and she kept talking, Price joined Charlotte, touching her shoulder. "I really look forward to working with you at the precinct," he said.

Brandy started to walk away, saying she had to get back to her family. She gave Charlotte a little wave and then grabbed Price by the ear, taking him with her.

Charlotte went to grab some more champagne from the bar and refilled Judy's glass.

The two detectives soon received a visit from Captain Murphy, who talked to Charlotte and Judy for a long twenty minutes, giving his thanks to both women for their service the previous year, congratulating Charlotte on becoming a new member of the NYPD family, and talking about society and the role of law enforcement in it.

Surprisingly, or perhaps not, Commissioner Crowley hadn't decided to make a special appearance for the women this time around.

After Murphy finally departed, Charlotte heaved a sigh and proposed to Judy, "Do you want to go out and grab a drink?"

"Why? We're having a drink," said Judy.

"I mean a *real* drink..." Charlotte clarified.

"Oh, I see..." Judy nodded. "You don't want to socialize, make fruitful connections? Being a cop isn't all about the action, Charlotte. It's about making friends, too."

"I know..." the redhead said, frowning. "I just really want to celebrate with the person who got me here today... my mentor."

Judy shook her head. "That's too much, Charlotte! Way too much!"

"Okay, fine—I hate parties... and people. Big crowds scare me..."

Judy chuckled. "Okay, then, let's go!"

But before they could go anywhere, someone put his hands on both Charlotte's and Judy's arms, grabbing them. It was the bartender.

"Excuse me, ladies! Are you guys Detectives Judy Hunter and Charlotte Gibbins?"

"Well—" Charlotte began. She wasn't a detective yet.

"A delivery guy just came in and gave me this!" the bartender exclaimed.

He handed them an envelope. Judy and Charlotte looked at each other, bewildered.

CHAPTER SEVENTY-NINE:

THE LAST NOTE

Charlotte's heart was beating fast. She thought this must be a dream.

Way before she had decided to pick up the envelope, she knew what it was, what it contained. She opened it, and both she and Judy read the contents.

CONGRATULATIONS CHARLOTTE!

I TRIED TO CALL BUT IT SAID YOUR NUMBER WAS OUT OF SERVICE, I GUESS THAT'S UNDERSTANDABLE!

HELLO, JUDY...

LISTEN, I WOULD LOVE TO PARTY WITH YOU GUYS AGAIN. I HEARD THERE IS A GREAT FAIR IN ROCKLAND THIS TIME OF YEAR.

There it ended, and there it was: Brian Haze, or Damyan Kovachev, was still in the picture. Or at least trying to be. What was he trying to accomplish? He was locked away in a prison cell at Rikers Island.

Unless...

Judy and Charlotte debated for a moment, and then Judy tried to find Captain Murphy or someone else who could help. But she couldn't find anyone, so she jumped on the phone and made a call instead.

It was too late. At 7:02 p.m., Judy received a call back from the penitentiary and they told her that Damyan Kovachev was nowhere to be found. He had miraculously escaped from his cell and was again out in the world of the living.

Charlotte's red hair seemed to stand on end as she heard the news. Why was this happening? How could this be happening?

"What do we do?" she asked Judy.

"We call Grant and we tell our people what's going on!" the retired detective replied.

"What do you think he's doing?"

Judy shrugged.

Charlotte thought about it for a while as Judy began dialing. It suddenly came to her.

"You think he's finishing this?"

Judy looked at her questioningly.

"Rockland!" Charlotte explained. "He's going after Reed, to finish this... He wanted to kill him, remember?"

"Reed is in a jail cell somewhere. How is he going to do that?"

Sebastian Reed had finally confessed to the murder of Viktor Kovachev. His lawyer had cut a deal for a reduced sentence because he had been so poorly treated by the authorities throughout the whole ordeal. In the end, he had been sentenced to eight years in prison. He was now doing his time in a New York State prison just like Damyan Kovachev, but not in the same prison.

Judy made another call, then turned to Charlotte. "Apparently Reed is transferring to another prison today. Closer to Rockland. He's going to be in a bus."

"You don't believe in coincidences, do you?"

Judy didn't answer.

This was it, Charlotte knew it, and she knew Judy could see it too.

"We have to go, Judy!"

"You can't do this. You're too close to this. Let the proper authorities handle it."

"*I'm* the proper authority!" exclaimed Charlotte. "They're never going to get there in time!"

"Please! Don't play his games."

"I'm going, and you know there is no discussion to be had. We'll still call them, but this is our case."

Judy tried to stop her, but Charlotte just walked away, determined as always.

CHAPTER EIGHTY:

THE FAIR

Judy knew this was a very bad idea. Brian... Damyan. *Let us call him Damyan now,* she thought. *Brian Haze never existed.* He still wanted to play with Charlotte. He still wanted to have some type of relationship with her. An unhealthy one, perhaps, but it was still a relationship. He had most likely remained in love with her. No, not in love—he was obsessed with her, to the point of blaming love for it. Would he be involved with her all her life? Would she have to live with him at the back of her mind throughout her career? Would he ever leave her be? Judy found this all so repulsive.

The retired detective knew she couldn't do anything to prevent Charlotte from going, but she didn't feel right about it. What was the villain up to? What were his true plans? Why involve them again?

They embarked in a Lyft and were soon on their way to the familiar town of Rockland. Charlotte tipped the driver so he would drive faster than normal. Judy read on her phone that the fair Damyan had mentioned was starting today and running for a week. So, who knew if today was even the day? But Judy didn't think Damyan would waste any time. Why would he? He would soon have the whole country looking for him. He would be one of America's most wanted.

The retired detective made a couple of calls on the way, one to Grant and the other to Captain Murphy. Both asked how Judy was in possession of that information, not suspecting that she was going to do anything with it. She made it clear that she was letting them know so they could hurry before somebody got hurt. Charlotte frowned at that but still approved. This needed to be settled very fast.

Murphy said he would make a call to the bus and to the police to ensure Reed's safety during his transfer.

A half-hour later, Judy and Charlotte were on the freeway, some time before arriving in Rockland, when they saw a mountain of flames and smoke rising in front of them. Police cars and firefighters were on the scene. Suddenly, Judy recognized that the vehicle in flames was a bus. It was flipped upside down in the grass beside the road. Judy could see people being rescued from it by men in orange uniforms.

Judy and Charlotte looked at each other, disturbed and shocked.

The Lyft passed the scene of the emergency and kept going. Charlotte tipped the driver once more so he would go faster, but he just grunted. The young woman and the retired detective continued to pressure him all the way.

The car finally stopped after an hour. They were in Rockland but didn't see any signs of the fair. They were about to turn onto Main Street when they discovered the street was closed to traffic. So this was the fair!

Judy and Charlotte jumped out of the car and ran through the barriers into Rockland's annual party, looking frantically for Damyan Kovachev.

There were massive numbers of fairgoers. Circus performers were rolling onto the grounds, performing magic tricks, spinning and twirling around, contortionists twisting their bodies every which way. Most of the audience were children holding their parents' hands and dancing around, having a great time. This was not the place for a murder.

The two women kept walking, on their guard. Charlotte reminded Judy that she hated crowds. Judy kept glancing around, analyzing the scene. She could see some deputies watching everything, but those people were always going to be part of the fair anyway, for security purposes. As predicted, the big guns hadn't arrived.

Was Damyan here yet?

After five minutes of looking for the man, they heard a noise blasting through the crowd. It sounded like a gunshot. Then another was heard. And another. People started screaming, while deputies ran towards the danger. The shots were coming from the center of the fair. Judy and Charlotte started following the deputies. Then the women saw four men appear, dressed in orange. They were hitting people and brandishing their guns. None of them looked like Damyan Kovachev.

The men in orange started shooting, aiming for the deputies, battling with them through the crowd. Judy suddenly saw an opening and went for one of the men in orange and hit him in the back. The man dropped his gun but quickly got back to his feet and started fighting with Judy. Charlotte joined in, going after another prisoner.

They both tumbled around, fighting their way through the men.

The prisoner she was fighting finally brought Judy to the ground with his foot. She couldn't breathe. She was growing red. He was smiling, but she finally got a grip and gave him a good elbow punch to the knee, and he followed her to the ground. Judy jumped on him before he could do anything. She pinned him to the ground and then stood and picked up the gun. Judy pointed it at the prisoner.

Loud shots were fired again. A scream was heard, coming from the speakers.

The prisoners froze and stopped messing around.

"Enough!" a voice commanded through the speaker.

The retired detective looked around. Deputies lay on the ground, apparently dead. One prisoner was dead too. Another had his guns aimed on a set of hostages, and Judy panicked when she saw that one of the them was Charlotte.

Then the voice spoke again through the microphone:

"Judy Hunter and Charlotte Gibbins!"

Both women brought their eyes to the front. There was a stage in the middle of the street, and there they saw him: Damyan, center stage, holding a gun. His head had been shaved, and he was dressed in a prison suit. The gun he pointed was not directed at either Judy or Charlotte. Instead, he had his gun pointed at three individuals onstage, all on their knees, all tied up in tape with black bags over their heads. More hostages!

Then Damyan Kovachev started to move, removing the bags from the heads of his hostages. The first was Sebastian Reed, of course, also in an orange uniform. The removal of the second bag revealed, shockingly, the figure of Sheriff Grant.

And then came the last one, which set Charlotte screaming...

It was Stew.

CHAPTER EIGHTY-ONE:

THE CLOSING STAGE

All three of the men had tape over their mouths, but Charlotte could still hear them screaming miserably. She looked into Stew's blue eyes. He was gazing back at her. His expression was almost apologetic, but he had nothing to be sorry for.

The redhead felt the gun pointed at her head. She turned away from Stew and looked at Damyan. The latter caught her eye and gave her a wicked smile.

He then spoke into the microphone, "Welcome! Welcome! Today, as you may have guessed, is a very special day!"

He started to walk around, with a bounce in his step. The crowd below the stage were looking at him, terrified. All either had their arms up in the air or were on their knees, shaking.

"Let me introduce our honorable guests!" he continued. "Numero Uno: Sebastian Reed. The man who murdered my father in cold blood and made his body disappear for close to thirty years! This man is also infamous in your community. His hobbies include biking. He also loves kicking and violating women without regret. He is a man you probably really hate out here, and I can't blame you."

Damyan moved to Grant. "Numero Dos: Newman Grant, Rockland's own brave sheriff. A man who was supposed to investigate my father's murder, had *thirty years* to find his killer, but just... didn't nearly come close to accomplishing his task. He, just like many of you, forgot about my father.

"Another filthy scum," Kovachev added. "Not really any better than the criminals in this city."

Finally, Damyan moved to Stew. "And then there was this one. The frosting on the cake, as my ex-fiancée would say... Numero Tres: Stewart Allen. This man made me lose everything. Everything I loved, everything I cherished most in this world. My dear Charlotte hooked up with him, thought she was in love with him, and left me to rot like a rat in the sewer."

"Damyan!" Judy shouted. "Stop this now!"

"Or you'll do what, Judy? Kill my man?" Damyan proclaimed. "Do whatever you want!"

Charlotte looked at the prisoner holding the gun on her. He was frowning.

"These men," continued Kovachev, "are all, today, found guilty. The Executioner is here. No need to arrest them, no need to put them in cells, everything will be settled today! For your safety!"

"Please!" Charlotte shouted. "Damyan... Please, listen to me. Reed is already in jail, isn't that enough? He's in there paying for what he did to your father."

"No, Charlotte, it's not enough," Kovachev replied. "It was enough when I was doing it for you, but that's not the case anymore. Look at you—you're a cop now." Kovachev now had tears rolling down his face. After a pause he came back to himself, wiped his face and said, "No, this time, I'm doing it for myself. Pure, hard-core revenge."

He moved his gaze away from Charlotte and surveyed the crowd. He spoke to them: "Sure, Sebastian Reed is in prison, doing a little time for my father's death. Sure... But in—what? Four, five years' time?—he will be out. Playing with your women, hurting them, killing your sons and daughters, your wives maybe, husbands... He will be back on the streets doing his old shenanigans. Now, do you really want him to do that?"

Kovachev didn't get a direct response, but he was steering the crowd his way. People were whispering to each other, debating.

“No! We don’t!” he went on. “And neither do we want these two freaks, believe me.” He pointed at Stew and the Sheriff.

He moved away from the hostages and advanced to the front of the stage, crouching to the audience’s level.

“So today, ladies and gents, we are doing things the old-fashioned way and doing something that I thought was amazing back in the day.”

He stood up and snapped his fingers. The only free prisoner brought a bag up to the stage. He opened it and poured its contents onto the ground.

“It is called—stoning!” Damyan said.

His face was glowing again.

“Now, how this is gonna work: each one of the tough members of the crowd, the ones who didn’t run away, thank you, will pick up one by one a stone, some small, some big, and start throwing them at one of the guilty members here onstage.”

“So, throw them all at him!” shouted Charlotte, pointing at Damyan.

Viktor Kovachev’s son laughed. “Please, Charlotte, believe me, you’ll enjoy this!” He waited a second before adding: “Begin!”

Hostages that were off the stage didn’t move, either not knowing what to do or not wanting to do it. After a moment, the free prisoner pointed his gun at them and yelled, “Let’s go!”

“Effective, aren’t they?” said Damyan. “I made a few friends during my time... I mean, I had to, because Reed here was sending a couple of his faggots over to me every other day... to kill me.”

Reed looked at Damyan and the latter smirked at him.

“Come on, don’t be shy!”

A woman advanced to the stage, reached down to pick up a stone. Charlotte could see her hands shaking. She finally got a hold of the stone and brought it up, ready to throw.

“You don’t have to do this!” yelled Judy.

“Sure she does! They all hate Reed!” Damyan said. “Go on, honey!”

The woman looked at Damyan, then lowered her gaze and stared at Sebastian Reed. She took a moment, and finally threw the first stone at him. A grunt of pain was heard.

"See!" said Damyan. "Let's go faster now!"

The killer waved at more members of the audience, hurrying them along. Stones were thrown again, most of them at Sebastian Reed. One hit Stew by mistake, and Charlotte yelled.

"Stop! Please stop!"

But Damyan shouted at them to continue. They did. Five more stones were thrown. Sebastian was getting badly injured now.

This went on until a noise cut through and the audience stopped. Everybody looked behind them.

It was the roar of motorcycles. The Skullheads were coming, screaming in joy and fury, hurrying to save their boss from this madman.

Then another noise came through. Judy and Charlotte kept looking, and finally saw cop cars and SUVs pulling up. This party was getting busted.

CHAPTER EIGHTY-TWO:

THE SHOT

Judy hit her prisoner assailant hard in the head with her gun, and the latter fell unconscious on the pavement. Then the retired detective looked around. She saw a motorcycle passing through, a Skullhead clamping his hand on Charlotte's prisoner's head and throwing him off her. Judy looked at Damyan and saw the serial killer's expression go grim. He ran to the hostages and grabbed Stew by the hair and took him with him. Damyan started running offstage.

Charlotte saw this and started running after Damyan.

"Charlotte!" Judy yelled at the top of her lungs. "No!"

But the young woman didn't listen. She kept running as fast as she could after Damyan and Stew.

The retired detective ran after her. She followed Charlotte around the stage and into the street. She could see Damyan in the distance, holding Stew in his left hand and a gun in his right.

Charlotte kept chasing him, yelling.

Judy sped up, panting for breath. *And here I thought I had retired,* she thought.

She saw the redhead follow Damyan and Stew around a corner. Judy continued running and turned that corner as well. Then she stopped short.

In front of her was the river. Damyan stood on the bank, holding a gun to Stew's head. Charlotte had hers pointed at Damyan.

"Let him go," she yelled at him. "Now!"

But Damyan clenched his jaw, staying cold and sterile. "Do you love him, Charlotte? The way you love me?"

Charlotte didn't respond, just kept advancing towards Damyan, pointing her gun at him aggressively.

"What do you want?" she said. "Just please let him go!"

"Just answer my question, Charlotte!" Damyan demanded. "Do you love him?"

Charlotte stopped moving.

"Just tell me!" Damyan said. "And I'll let him go."

Charlotte looked down, then brought her eyes to Stew and almost smiled. She took a beat before finally sighing, "I do."

Damyan shook his head. His smile was fading. "Do you love me?"

Charlotte didn't answer, keeping her eyes on Stew.

"Do you?" he yelled.

"I loved Brian Haze," Charlotte finally said. "But that man was a fantasy, a dream. He was fantastic... but made up."

"I still am this person, Charlotte!" Damyan said, pleading.

She didn't give him anything. "Put the gun down, Damyan! Just please put it down."

Judy saw Damyan hesitate. He kept shaking his head.

"Disappointing!" he finally said.

"Put it down!" Charlotte repeated forcefully.

He started to lift his gun, aiming at Charlotte. Judy saw this and pointed her gun at Damyan, ready to shoot.

"I'm sorry you feel this way..." he said.

Damyan turned his gun towards Stew. Judy was ready to shoot when:

Bam!

The retired detective couldn't do anything now. It was all over. Damyan fell to the ground, face-first.

Charlotte had shot him.

CHAPTER EIGHTY-THREE:

REUNION

Charlotte was paralyzed for a few seconds. This was her first-ever kill. Even though she was now an officer of the NYPD, killing was not a normal part of the job and never would be. She stared at Damyan's body for a second or two, then looked at Stew. She saw his terrified eyes and immediately ran to him.

"Oh my God!" she screamed.

She began to free him from the tape. She then realized he couldn't speak and could hardly breathe because of the tape over his mouth. Charlotte undid it and she turned to him placing both hands over his chest.

"Stew!"

"Hi," he said. "Why didn't you call?"

Charlotte chuckled. "I'm so sorry, I wanted to! I'm so sorry!"

"It's all right!" he grimaced.

"You're safe!"

"I am!"

Charlotte looked at his lips, took a second and gave him a passionate kiss. "You are," she said.

"I love the uniform!" Stew exclaimed.

Charlotte laughed.

After a moment, the redhead felt a hand on her shoulder. She turned and saw Judy. Charlotte stood up and gave her a hug.

"Jesus Christ, Judy!" Charlotte said. "This was an adventure!"

Judy grimaced. "That's the job!"

They kept hugging and holding each other, so content to be alive and well.

THE END

Judy and Charlotte will be back
for another amazing adventure.

AKNOWLEDGEMENT

Thank you to my mother, Nathalie Viau for supporting me, you know what you did for me, all my life, thank you again.

Thank you so much to John Arthur Sweet for all your terrific feedback, your well-thought-out editing and great encouragement. You've been like a mentor to me throughout this whole process.

Thank you to Lucia Ferrara and Leah LeDrew for copyediting and proofreading this novel.

Thank you to Rosalie Nardi, my best friend, for reading sentences, chapters and drafts of the manuscript multiple times when I'm sure she had better things to do.

To my family, my late grandmother and to my wonderful friends this is for you and I hope you enjoyed this story.

And lastly, to all women: keep being so badass and amazing. This world would not do very well without you in it.

ABOUT THE AUTHOR

GABRIEL VEIGA

Born in Montreal, Quebec, Gabriel Veiga is a graduate from York University in Toronto. He holds a Bachelor of Arts in English with Honors. Aside from being a writer, he is also an actor and a radio personality. *Yesterday Is Not Yet Gone* is his first novel. He is now working on his second.

www.gabrielveiga.com
Follow @veigagabe on Instagram

Manufactured by Amazon.ca
Bolton, ON

12987449R00270